W9-BRS-500

Orchids and Diamonds

BY THE SAME AUTHOR

The Smuggler's Bride
Ride the Blue Riband
Warwyck's Woman
Claudine's Daughter
Warwyck's Choice
Banners of Silk
Gilded Splendour
Jewelled Path
What the Heart Keeps
This Shining Land
Tree of Gold
The Silver Touch
To Dance with Kings
Circle of Pearls
The Golden Tulip
The Venetian Mask
The Sugar Pavilion

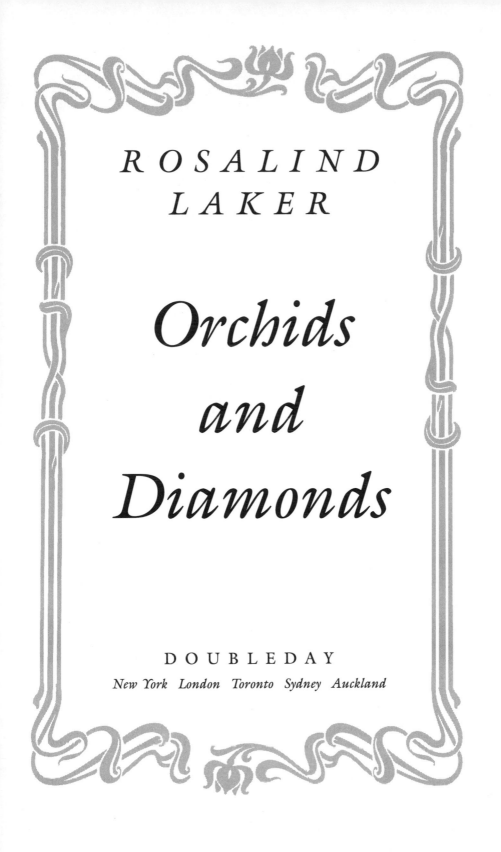

ROSALIND
LAKER

Orchids

and

Diamonds

DOUBLEDAY
New York London Toronto Sydney Auckland

PUBLISHED BY DOUBLEDAY
a division of Bantam Doubleday Dell Publishing Group, Inc.
1540 Broadway, New York, New York 10036

DOUBLEDAY and the portrayal of an anchor with a dolphin
are trademarks of Doubleday, a division of
Bantam Doubleday Dell Publishing Group, Inc.

With the exception of historical figures, all of the characters
in this book are fictitious, and any resemblance to actual persons,
living or dead, is purely coincidental.

Library of Congress Cataloging-in-Publication Data

Laker, Rosalind.
Orchids and diamonds / Rosalind Laker. — 1st ed.
p.   cm.
1. Man-woman relationships—France—Paris—Fiction.   2. Paris
(France)—History—1870–1940—Fiction.   I. Title.
PR6065.E9073   1995
823′.914—dc20   94-19000
CIP

ISBN 0-385-47281-1
Copyright © 1995 by Barbara Ovstedal
All Rights Reserved
Printed in the United States of America
January 1995
First Edition

1   3   5   7   9   10   8   6   4   2

To Muriel and John in friendship always

Orchids and Diamonds

One

I F NIKOLAI KARASVIN had not been stuck in a traffic jam caused by the many horse-drawn carriages on the Rue Pierre Carron, he would not have seen her. Something about her gripped his gaze. With a quick, light step she was walking along the pavement in the soft April sunshine of the Parisian afternoon, carrying a piece of labeled hand luggage that suggested she had just arrived in the city. She was looking eagerly at everything around her, but she failed to notice him, long-legged and relaxed, seated in the back of a chauffeur-driven 1909 Rolls-Royce. He was on his way to the Russian embassy before keeping an engagement of his own, one that had nothing to do with his diplomatic duties.

He smiled to himself. She was a welcome diversion, even in Paris, which always had something new to offer. Appreciatively he noticed that she was tall, with a good figure set off by her well-fitting cream jacket and long skirt, but she also had that gift, inherent in French women, of imbuing whatever she wore with style. Not conventionally pretty, her face was interestingly piquant, with a thin, longish nose, a firmly pointed chin, hazel eyes that were lively and sparkling, and a wide, inviting mouth. As for her hair, it was pale copper and piled up under her hat, with a few escaping tendrils shot through by sunlight to a burnished hue.

Juliette Cladel was glad she had decided to walk from the Gare de Lyon, where she had deposited the rest of her luggage. It was a relief to find that her birthplace had not changed in the eight years she'd been first a pupil at the convent school and then, for the last twelve months, a teacher of embroidery. The city still had its own particular potpourri, blending the aroma of roasting coffee beans with the pungency of garlic, the fragrance of flowers, the bouquet of fine wines, delicate perfumes, and the whiff of expensive cigars. Paris exuded an atmosphere of opulence, pleasure, and enormous wealth. Surely there was no better place in all the world to be when one was eighteen and life was about to begin at last!

Juliette stopped to put down her hand luggage and buy a bunch of violets from a flower-seller. She raised the flowers to her nose and closed her eyes as she inhaled their scent. Turning to face her reflection in the window of a perfumery, she tucked the stems under her hat ribbon, letting the blooms lie along the brim. It was then that she sensed she was being watched. Self-consciously, she put a gloved hand to the back of her hair as she glanced to the left and right before picking up her luggage.

At that moment the traffic began to flow once more. Although Nikolai looked back, she was already disappearing among the other pedestrians as she continued on her way.

Juliette glanced at the numbers above the doorways as she went past, looking for the Maison Landelle. Her sister, Denise, sixteen years older and her only living relative, widow of the late Baron Claude de Landelle, had been careful to choose the right address for her *haute couture* business, one where she could be sure of collecting the best clientele. Juliette knew that Denise would be far from pleased by her unexpected arrival in Paris, especially when she heard the reason!

Yet, in spite of the trouble ahead, it was wonderful to be home. Juliette was determined never to leave Paris again, or at least not for as long as the exile that had just ended. She was determined to know her birthplace again, even though some parts of the city would always evoke poignant memories of her late parents.

She had arrived. Taking a step back, she looked up at the imposing frontage, which seemed to warn of the high prices to be expected within. As Juliette moved toward the entrance, a liveried doorman swung open the door. Inside, she faced a wide marble staircase with swirling wrought-iron banisters. Denise had opted for the style of décor that had become generally known as *Art Nouveau* and the effect was quite splendid. The walls were paneled in copper with embossed decorations of stately irises. Elegantly simple vases shaped like elongated trumpets held the fresh flowers that perfumed the air.

At the top of the stairs, Juliette reached the reception area, which was enhanced by screens of Lalique glass, the designs both clear and opaque, with light glowing through them from silk-fringed lampshades held high by female figures of gleaming silver. She could hear the buzz of conversation in the salons. By one of the screens, two women in large hats stood chatting. Their necks were made gracefully swan-like by the illusion of boned lace, their fashionably S-shaped silhouettes achieved by fullness to the front of their bodices and to the back of their skirts. Juliette could only guess at the restrictive corsets that aided this effect. Thankfully she had never yet resorted to such uncomfortable underpinnings herself!

"Bonjour, mademoiselle." A smiling woman, elegant in black silk, had come forward to greet her.

Juliette guessed this must be Madame Millot, Denise's *directrice* and trusted right hand. In any great couture house, the woman holding this position was the pivot around whom the clientele and staff revolved. She had to be dignified, calm, and gracious at all times, whatever the crisis.

"I'm not expected," Juliette said, after explaining that she had come to see her sister after a long train journey.

"The Baronne de Landelle isn't here at the present time, but I feel sure she would wish me to tell you where to find her. She is calling on an old friend, who is back in Paris today on a visit from Louisiana, in the United States, and is staying at the Hôtel Bristol in the Place Vendôme."

Juliette's face had lit up. "Would that be Madame Garnier?"

"Yes. That's the name."

Juliette hastened back down the stairs. Lucille Garnier was an old friend of her parents, whom she and Denise had looked on almost as an aunt even after she had gone to live abroad. The move from Paris had come about when Lucille's husband had accepted an important business appointment in New Orleans, promoting and protecting French interests. Lucille had made only one trip back since then and that had been for tragic reasons. But this trip, Juliette knew, would be for renewing old friendships and seeing her homeland again. Denise had been a poor correspondent, which had made Lucille's letters even more welcome at the convent, and all the more enjoyable because they were written from a faraway place, where French customs still lingered and yet so much was new and thriving.

Riding the omnibus to the Place Vendôme, Juliette's thoughts turned to her sister's success. She well remembered when Denise had first revealed her intentions of going into the fashion business. It was after Claude de Landelle's funeral, when Juliette herself had already been a year at the convent. Denise was furious that he had bequeathed the bulk of his fortune to the children of a previous marriage, while she had been left only a modest income and the grand house in the Faubourg St. Germain for her lifetime unless she remarried.

"How can I live on a pittance?" she had stormed, to her young sister. "It's Claude's revenge! Oh, he was generous enough at first, but then he began niggling about my so-called extravagance." She paced the floor, biting her lip and fuming. As the visitors' room at the convent was chilly, she had not removed her sable coat, and it swirled about her ankles with a hiss of silk lining. "Thank God I had the sense to stash away as much as I could while he was alive, and that I made sure he gave me Cartier jewelry on every possible occasion."

"Shall you marry again?" Juliette had asked from where she sat. On the table beside her were the samples of embroidery and sewing that the nuns had thought her sister would like to see. It was a craft at which Juliette was beginning to excel, but Denise had not glanced at any of them.

"Marry again?" Denise had come to a halt at the question. "Never! Old men get jealous and possessive. Younger men are never faithful. I know!" Her tone was bitter. "I can tell you there is not a marriage in all Paris to compare with Papa's and Maman's." She glanced at the clock. "I'll have to go, but don't worry that I won't be able to afford to keep you here. Claude made provision for your school fees, and there's a small nest egg for you when you've finished your education."

Juliette had liked Claude. He'd had kind eyes, but perhaps they had saddened in the time since she'd last seen him. "That was very good of him."

"He should have been good to his widow!" Denise tossed her head. "But I don't intend to rot in poverty for the rest of my days."

"So what shall you do?"

"My assets are my business instincts and my flair for fashion. I intend to capitalize on both."

"But how?"

"That's all I can tell you at the present time, but I'll let you know later how my plans work out."

Juliette had known that she would not hear any more for a while. Denise's letters were infrequent, but when one finally came, it was headed Maison Landelle. Denise, totally without sentiment, had sold some valuable paintings that had been birthday gifts from Claude. One had been bought at auction by the Louvre and the others went at exorbitant prices to an American millionaire. The proceeds she had invested in a fashion house. With her social connections, the right people had come to view if not to buy, and had succumbed to day wear that rivaled Maison Worth in cut and style, and to sumptuous evening wear that outshone many of Maison Paquin's wonderful ensembles. Within a week her order books were full and she had taken on twice as many hands as when she started.

"Are you selling cheaper than anyone else?" Juliette had asked naïvely when Denise appeared on one of her flying visits.

"No!" She gave a satisfied laugh, her mood ebullient and entirely changed from her previous visit. "I'm far more expensive. That's what makes my creations so exclusive and sought after. I've begun to make lingerie too. Really lovely items that any woman would give her eyeteeth to wear. That reminds me—" She dived into a pocket and produced a parcel. "I've a present for you."

It was only a small package, which, when opened, revealed a flimsy chemise trimmed with pink ribbon and delicate lace. Juliette gasped with delight and held it up.

"It's gorgeous, but the nuns would never allow me to wear it. Oh!" She was suddenly embarrassed.

"What's the matter?"

"It's so fine," Juliette whispered, wide-eyed. "Are you producing lingerie that can be *seen* through?"

Denise smiled indulgently, took the chemise from her, and folded it up again. "I'll keep this and start a bottom drawer for you. You'll feel differently about such wear one day."

"When shall I come back to Paris?"

"You have to finish your education first."

The omnibus had arrived at the Place Vendôme. Juliette sprang out and crossed to the Hôtel Bristol. It was a grand, aristocratic establishment much patronized by royalty. In the vast lobby with its marble pillars, potted palms, and circular seating, she heard plenty of English voices among the well-dressed people milling about. If Edward VII had been on one of his trips to France, she might well have seen him there. She made her way across to the reception desk and asked that her name be given to Madame Garnier. The clerk rang through and then turned back to her with a bow.

"Madame Garnier's suite is number Fourteen on the second floor. She wishes you to go up."

Juliette was about to take the elevator and then changed her mind. With everything becoming dearly familiar to her again, she wanted to savor every minute. Mounting the stairs, she wondered if Lucille had felt the same when she arrived earlier that day. Her joy at the prospect of seeing this good friend again was tempered by the thought of the hostile reception she could expect from her sister, but there was nothing Denise could say or do that would sway her from her chosen course.

She recalled how the nuns had wished her well in her new life, having accepted some time ago that their best needlework pupil had no vocation to join the Order and would not want to stay on indefinitely as a teacher of embroidery. Unfortunately Denise never saw any viewpoint but her own.

Pausing with her hand on the gilded banister rail, Juliette looked down into the lobby. What a splendid sight it presented! Almost like a flower garden with the women's large hats perched on their hugely padded pompadour coiffures and trimmed with every kind of bloom, massed ribbons, and gauzes. Some had nodding plumes or whole exotic birds with wings spread, tails upmost across the brims, and glass eyes glinting. She glimpsed the iridescent blue of a kingfisher and the gem-like gleam of a cockatoo. As for the men, there were the gleaming top hats of those formally attired, but there were also the bowlers of businessmen, the derbies of newly arrived travelers, and the panamas of those who had been strolling along the boulevards and the Bois.

As Juliette scanned the scene her gaze came to rest by chance on a tall young man standing on his own by one of the potted palms. The wide brim of his slouch hat hid his eyes from her as he read a newspaper folded to a single column, but what she could see of his face was striking—wide cheekbones pleasingly hollowed, a handsome nose, a worldly sensual mouth, and a strong broad chin. Coming to the end of what he was reading, Nikolai Karasvin tucked the newspaper into the pocket of his coat as he raised his head and glanced at the lobby clock with an impatient frown. Now she could see that his brows and lashes were as dark as his curly hair.

There was no doubt in her mind that he was waiting for a woman. His wife? His betrothed? Maybe an actress from the Folies-Dramatiques, or a singer from the Opéra. She hoped whoever it was would arrive within the next few seconds, for her curiosity was aroused. Then, unexpectedly, he looked up swiftly and their eyes met.

She caught her breath. His heavy lids had suggested that any glance from him would be moody and bored, but she had been mistaken. His eyes were sharply alert, a clear steel-gray, and piercing. She felt a tremor up her spine. This was not a man to be crossed in any way! Even as their gaze locked, his deepened with warm recognition, and yet she had never seen him before. Inexplicably she felt wildly drawn to him.

From his viewpoint, she stood in the light of a window, her tawny hair and cream-colored suit set against the dark fleur-de-lys pattern of the wallpaper on the landing behind her. Although there was nothing coquettish about her, he could tell she was as magnetized as he by the powerful attraction between them. If he had been able to touch her she would have trembled.

Then a couple talking loudly on the stairs distracted her. She glanced toward them and then back at him. He grinned at her, his eyes dancing. Unable to resist, she returned a smile of her own before turning to continue up the stairs.

Out of his sight, she flung her head back exuberantly. What a dangerous exchange! She believed that if he had not been waiting for someone, he would never have let her go without speaking. She had been taught, of course, to look away from such predatory glances, but today she had ignored the rule wonderfully, and she was glad of it. Apart from anything else, it showed that at last she was in control of her own life!

Two

JULIETTE FOUND Lucille Garnier's suite at the end of a long corridor, where it would have a prime view of the Place Vendôme. A light tap and the door was opened by a uniformed maid onto a gilt-mirrored hallway.

"Madame Garnier is expecting you, mademoiselle," she said in foreign-accented French. She took Juliette's hand luggage and showed her into a luxurious salon with crystal chandeliers and Louis Quinze furnishings.

Lucille rose immediately from one of the sofas and flung out her plump arms in a rustle of cinnamon silk, her rope of pearls swinging. "Dearest child!" she exclaimed emotionally.

"Tante Lucille!" The pet name of childhood had come spontaneously from Juliette's lips as she rushed forward into Lucille's embrace. They kissed each other's cheeks and hugged again. "How is Oncle Rodolphe? Is he with you?"

Lucille shook her head. "He hasn't retired yet and couldn't spare the time, but in any case he has never liked traveling and is content to stay at home." She held Juliette by the shoulders and studied her fondly at arm's length. "How like your dear mother you've become. I'd have known you anywhere!"

"As I would have known you! You're just the same!"

Lucille smiled a little ruefully at the compliment. "If only my mirror could convince me of that!" Although she was almost sixty, her complexion, aided by cosmetics, appeared remarkably smooth.

The only wrinkles clearly discernible were the laugh lines at the corners of her twinkling blue eyes, for she had always had a lively sense of humor. As for her thickly puffed hair, it had been skillfully tinted to its original golden hue, defying the passage of time, and in spite of being a large woman, she was firmly corseted into the S-shape that fashion demanded.

"Why didn't you mention in any of your letters that you were coming to France?" Juliette demanded happily as she removed her hat and pulled off her gloves.

"I wanted to surprise you with a visit to the convent and then bring you back to Paris to stay with me." Lucille led her across to the yellow silk sofa, where they sat down together. "It's for that reason I booked this suite with an extra bedroom."

Juliette was sitting bolt upright in her delight at this unexpected reunion. "So you have surprised me just as you wished, and I have saved you a journey. I could scarcely believe my ears when I was told at Maison Landelle that Denise was calling on you here." She glanced about quickly. "Where is she?"

"Denise left just before I picked up the receiver to hear that you were in the lobby. I don't know how you missed her."

"She must have taken the elevator while I was coming up the stairs. Oh well, I'll have plenty of time to see Denise later, and I'd like to talk to you on my own first."

Lucille raised an eyebrow. "If you want to spare me the scene that's likely to erupt when she sees you, I'll tell you now that I've heard all about the telegram Denise received from the convent earlier today. So why not enlighten me as to why you made this move so unexpectedly. Denise declared that you had only to ask and she would have made arrangements."

Juliette arched her eyebrows quizzically. "Did she? Yet Denise has never encouraged me to return. At first it suited me very well to stay on as a teacher. I was studying dressmaking with one of the nuns in my free time, and there was a special task I wanted to complete. Dear old Sister Berthe, whose sight was failing, had asked me to help her finish the beautiful altar cloth for Chartres Cathedral she had begun over a decade ago."

"I recall your telling me about it in one of your letters."

"When I put in the final stitches yesterday, I had already packed my trunk." Juliette looked triumphant. "The Mother Superior had arranged for another nun to take over my classes, and so there was nothing to keep me there any longer. What did cause a furor was my traveling without a chaperone! The nuns were quite frantic, but suddenly I was so desperate to get home that I couldn't have waited another hour."

"I can understand that."

"If I may, I'd like to send a telegram from here to let them know I've arrived safely."

"I advise you to take no more upon yourself at the moment. Leave that to Denise. As soon as I judge she's had time to get back to Maison Landelle, I'll telephone to say you're here with me. You can speak to her too. Now tell me about that suitor who had permission from Denise and the Mother Superior to call on you under a nun's chaperonage."

Juliette sighed. "Denise liked him because he is a prosperous man and has a fine house. But he's more her age than mine and nothing would ever have made me marry him. Unfortunately, the more I showed my lack of interest the keener he seemed to become. Finally he accepted that I was determined to remain single and became most annoyed about it."

"Men in love can be very perverse. Denise spoke to me at length about the advantages such a match would have given you and how foolish you were to have thrown the chance away. I believe she's more angry at your refusing the marriage than at your leaving the convent as you did. To be frank, I've never approved of her packing you off as she did after your dear mother died."

Juliette shrugged. "I honestly don't hold it against her. She had a demanding life of her own, and I was happy enough at the convent once I overcame my terrible homesickness. But I'll soon put Denise's fears to rest. I have career plans of my own and I intend to stick by them."

"So you're going to work!" Lucille clapped her hands approvingly. "I'd have done the same thing myself if I were young again. But before we talk anymore, how long is it since you've eaten?"

"I had a snack at midday."

Lucille promptly picked up the telephone and ordered coffee and pastries to be sent up at once. Then she settled back against the cushions. "I'm sure you'll excel at whatever work you intend to do," she continued. "I'm glad to see that your generation has more sense than mine. We thought only of being married and having babies. Every woman should have some freedom first."

"Judging by my fellow pupils, I think I'm the exception."

"Then think of yourself as a pioneer. Through our correspondence I've seen your character develop and your will become strong. I have to admit I was delighted when you wrote of your first mischievous escapade because I knew then that you were no longer the docile, malleable child I remembered."

Juliette's eyes danced. "Thank goodness for that! I certainly had plenty of reprimands from the nuns in my early years, although my pranks were harmless enough. Somehow I knew you would understand."

"Indeed! I don't wonder you became something of a rebel, shut away there in the convent, never allowed home for any of the holidays."

"Denise did what she could for me in other ways," Juliette defended her sister. "I never wanted for new clothes or books or pocket money, and she came to visit me three or four times a year."

Lucille did not look impressed. "So I should think!"

"As I grew older, she seemed to become fonder of me and treated me as a confidante, pouring out her troubles. As for the holidays, I was lucky to have a good friend in Gabrielle Rousset. Her parents invited me to stay quite often and always when they were at their villa at Antibes. I missed Gabrielle so much after she was sent to finishing school in Switzerland."

"Shall you be seeing her again?"

"Yes, as soon as possible. We keep in touch."

Then the coffee came in a silver pot with thin blue china bordered in gilt, and the pastries proved to be as delicious as they looked. Juliette enjoyed every flaky crumb as Lucille chatted on.

"Luckily I've accepted no invitations for this evening, although I'm looking forward to seeing old friends again. I hope you'll stay for all or at least part of the six weeks I'm here, but that must be as you wish. You must also feel free to come and go as you please."

Juliette put down her empty cup and saucer with a contented sigh. "How you are spoiling me and I love it! It will be wonderful to stay here with you."

"Good! That's settled then." A gilded clock struck the hour with a tinkling chime, reminding Lucille of the call she had to make to Denise. The conversation was brief. Denise's voice came clear and terse over the line and was audible to Juliette.

"By all means have Juliette stay with you, Lucille, and I'll let the convent know she's arrived. No, I don't want to speak to her and neither am I in any hurry to see her. In any case, I'm going out of Paris on business for two days. I'll let you know when I'm back. Good-bye."

Lucille replaced the receiver. "So, Juliette, you have forty-eight hours' reprieve before you meet your sister."

Juliette nodded. "That's most opportune. It will give me the chance to find employment before she and I come face to face. It's what I would have liked to do in the first place, but naturally I had to try to see her as soon as I arrived."

"So, tell me now, what line is your career going to follow? Has it anything to do with your embroidery skills?"

Juliette gave a happy nod. "I want to work in a couture house— not Maison Landelle, I assure you. I hope to get into Maison Worth."

"You've chosen well."

"I know from the way my needlework has been displayed in a recent exhibition that I'm too advanced to be an apprentice, but I could be a second-degree seamstress and rise from there. I've examples of my work with me to show what I can do."

Lucille leaned toward Juliette conspiratorially. "So what is your ultimate aim?"

"To have my own dressmaking establishment, but not in competition with Denise. When it proves financially possible I'd set up in one of the bigger cities that is close enough to get to Paris easily."

"Not a couture house then?"

"One would have to be in Paris for that."

"Wherever you are I'll be your first client. It will be a change from being dressed exclusively by Maison Paquin. If I'm not too old and doddery I'll even come myself to be fitted instead of having everything made on a mannequin and sent to Louisiana."

"You'll never be old!" Juliette protested vehemently.

Lucille laughed. "What a tonic you are to me! You make me realize how much I've missed young company. With our two sons in different parts of the world, Rodolphe and I rarely see our grandchildren. But I can't help wondering what Denise will say about your becoming a seamstress. Have you ever visited a couture house, other than calling at Maison Landelle today?"

"No. I was too young to accompany Maman when she went for her fittings at Maison Worth."

"Then come with me to Maison Paquin tomorrow. I'm going to choose a new wardrobe to take home. It will give you a real insight into the atmosphere and allure of high fashion."

This was exactly what Juliette needed. To see everything from a client's viewpoint would give her extra authority when she applied for work, and she thanked Lucille with heartfelt enthusiasm.

"And speaking of clothes," Lucille continued happily, "what do you have with you?"

"Just overnight things in my hand luggage with some spare shoes and so forth. I left my trunk at the Gare de Lyon, thinking that I would retrieve it once I had found permanent accommodation. Also, if I'd had it with me, Denise would have supposed I was landing myself on her."

"Let me have the deposit ticket, then, and I'll arrange to have it collected." She rang the little bell that stood by the telephone. When the maid, Marie, appeared she gave instructions and handed over the ticket. Then Lucille spoke of the evening ahead. "I thought we'd dine at Foyet's. I'm sure we shall find the cuisine and the service as superb as I remember."

"My parents often dined there. It was their favorite restaurant."

"I know. That's why I thought it would appeal to you. Now I think you'd like to see your room and have a bath and a rest after your tiring day. I always lie down for a while before dressing for the evening."

Juliette found her room to be as sumptuous as everything else she had seen in the suite. There were fresh flowers in a vase, a large complimentary box of chocolates from the management, as well as a basket of fruit. Everything was such a contrast to the stark walls and bare floors she had lived with for so long. Although she was not in the least tired, she flung herself backward onto the satin coverlet, flinging her arms wide while she luxuriated in its downy comfort. It was not long before she heard Marie running a bath for her.

By the time Juliette returned to her room from a long, scented soak she found her trunk had been delivered and Marie was on her knees unpacking it. Seeing the package of needlework was still in the upper tray, Juliette asked her to put it in a drawer on its own as she did not want the items crushed. As this was done Juliette turned her attention to her dresses, which had been hung up in the wardrobe. All her clothes had been made at the Maison Landelle and, although simple in style, they had been sewn by some of the best seamstresses in Paris. As a needlewoman herself she had always appreciated the exquisite workmanship.

When she was dressed and the maid had left the room, Juliette crossed to the window and looked out at the twinkling lights of Paris. She wondered who that interesting stranger had been meeting, and where they were spending the evening. She hoped not to see them at Foyet's, for that would distract her. He had looked prosperous enough, judging by his well-groomed appearance and tailored clothes, to patronize anywhere he chose. Maybe he had taken his partner to one of the other top restaurants or, if she was in the theatrical profession or otherwise not quite a true lady, they could be out to enjoy themselves at some more risqué place such as the Moulin Rouge. What fun that would be!

Juliette's parents, Michel and Catherine Cladel, had spent an evening at the Moulin Rouge when they were newly wed. She learned of it as a child when she had asked her mother about a framed sketch on the wall. Although the lines were sparse and the effect rather strange, it was an unmistakable likeness of her parents merrily drinking champagne. Catherine, half-laughing as if the merriment of the occasion was still with her, explained how it came to be there.

"I had to persuade your papa to take me," she said, holding Juliette's hand as they stood looking at the framed sketch, "because it wasn't a place where ladies ever went, but I'd heard so much about the scandalous cancan that I just wanted to see it. I'm told it's still danced, but not so outrageously as it was in those days."

"Who drew the picture, Maman?"

"An artist named Toulouse-Lautrec. We saw him there, but had no idea he might be including us in his sketching. About two years later, your papa came across the drawing in a shop and bought it. I chose the frame and we hung it here on our bedroom wall to remind us of a wonderful evening."

There had been many memorable evenings throughout their marriage. Juliette could remember clearly how her parents had moved in a splendid social whirl, having their own box at the Opéra, always in the best enclosure at Longchamps, giving parties that filled the house with music and laughter, and all the time Catherine dressed only by Worth from head to toe. In all, they had lived a charmed life, never dreaming it would end tragically.

It was not until Juliette began staying with Gabrielle during the summer holidays that she discovered many marriages were different from the loving and no doubt passionate union of her late parents. Monsieur and Madame Rousset moved in a similar social circle, and on her first visit to Antibes, Juliette was astonished to observe how they bickered and seemed to prefer the company of other people. Wide-eyed, she also witnessed discontent among some of the other couples who made up the house party there. On the surface, a bubbling joviality prevailed. All were there to enjoy themselves, but not necessarily with their own partners. Once she saw Gabrielle clap her hands over her ears and run from the villa when her parents' voices were angrily raised yet again behind a closed door. Juliette had found her sitting on one of the rocks by the vivid peacock-hued sea. It became apparent that the rock was Gabrielle's place of refuge.

"I don't know how I'd endure these holidays if you weren't here, Juliette," she said on another occasion. "At least we can get away on our own whenever we like. They don't want me under their feet."

"It's the reason I'm invited," Juliette replied sagely, pulling off her socks and shoes to dip her toes in the water.

Gabrielle, brown-eyed and round-faced, pushed a fall of soft brown hair back from her face. "Thank goodness for that! Letting you come to stay is the best thing they've ever done for me."

The annual happenings at Antibes gave Juliette plenty of food for thought as she matured and spent quiet hours with her stitching. She began to wonder if Denise, who had always demanded to be the center of attention, had resented her parents' devotion to one another. Then, when Denise was sixteen and just emerging socially, her mother had caused her excruciating embarrassment by giving birth, at the age of forty-three, to an unplanned but totally welcome new daughter. Denise saw her sister lavished with the parental love she imagined she'd lacked, and this became another cause of jealousy. Juliette was not very old when she began to be aware of the long-standing discord between Denise and her mother, for her sister's quick temper could make life very difficult for everyone in the Cladel household.

Juliette still thought it strange that Denise, who set a high value on love, should have decided when she was twenty-four to marry solely for money a man nearly three times her age. Juliette was present at the unhappy scene when Denise stood ready in her bridal finery.

"It's not too late to change your mind about this marriage, my dear," their mother had urged, her gentle face distressed at the loveless step being taken.

"I've told you often enough, Maman," Denise had snapped, "Claude is very rich and, as you know, highly respected in the government and other important circles. There is even aristocratic blood in his veins, and if he weren't such a true son of the Republic he would use the title to which he has the right." Her eyes glinted. "In time I intend to see that he does. In any case, I'll be invited everywhere that matters and can have everything I want. That will make a change from Papa, who doesn't seem to like paying for anything these days."

"How can you say that! You know he has business problems at the moment, yet he is giving you the grand wedding you wanted and no expense has been spared."

"Only because he's glad to be getting rid of me!"

"You're so cruel! And on such a day!"

Juliette had watched the whole scene miserably, until somebody came to escort her to the bridesmaids' carriage. She had looked back over her shoulder then, and seen the tears of hurt in her mother's eyes. This was the first inkling Juliette had had that all was not well with the Cladel business empire. Eighteen months later her father suffered a fatal heart attack brought on by the stress of his financial difficulties.

That was when Lucille returned to France in order to comfort the grief-stricken widow. She stayed as long as she could, but eventually she had to return home. Catherine found it impossible to readjust to life without Michel and, weakened by her bereavement, fell an easy victim to influenza.

Immediately Denise took capable and compassionate charge. Juliette had long since concluded that this was when her sister had felt needed for the first time. Denise had nursed her mother tirelessly, and Claude, who under pressure from his wife was using his title again, had engaged the best of medical care. Still, it was all to no avail.

A tap on the bedroom door jolted Juliette from her memories. It was the maid.

"Are you ready, mademoiselle?" asked Marie. "Madame would like to leave now."

"Yes, of course." Juliette picked up her wrap and beaded purse.

Lucille, waiting in the salon and resplendent in crimson brocade and rubies, nodded admiringly at the sight of her young companion.

When they crossed the marble floor of the lobby Juliette glanced about for the stranger, but he was not to be seen. Neither was he at Foyet's. She did not know if she was disappointed or glad.

Three

M AY I ASK why you patronize Madame Paquin, whom Denise sees as her deadliest rival, and not Maison Landelle?"
Juliette asked Lucille the following morning. They were setting
out for the Maison Paquin in the carriage Lucille had hired for the
duration of her stay.

"I shall buy some lingerie from Denise," Lucille replied. "But I
was one of Madame Paquin's first clients and she has looked after
me for many years. I always know her garments will be comfortable
as well as elegant, because she wears every design herself before
offering them for public view."

"But Denise does that too."

"Is that so? I didn't know." Lucille's casual tone showed that
she had no intention of switching her patronage.

Happy for the company, she had asked Juliette to take a free day
before seeking work. It was a warm, sparkling morning. The spring
foliage was fresh and green, not yet made dusty by summer. As
they passed Napoleon's memorial column in the Place Vendôme
the bronze plaques depicting his victories seemed to glow in the
sun. Juliette looked about her as the horses clopped along. Motorcars were for speed and convenience, plenty of them tooting their
horns on all sides, but an elegant carriage was still the best way to
ride when you wished to see and be seen. And there was so much
to see!

The tall old houses were still in need of paint, their weather-

faded shutters flanking lace-curtained windows where flowering
potted plants provided bright splashes of pink and red. Rainbow-
striped awnings spread their wings over café tables where people
sat talking and drinking and watching the world go by. Along the
Champs Élysées, the milliners displayed hats as frothy and appetiz-
ing as the pastries in the pâtisseries; satin-ribboned boxes vied for
space with pastel-colored sugar almonds in every confectionery;
exclusive displays of jewelry glittered, and sumptuous fabrics were
swathed and draped in the windows of expensive shops.

"I'm glad we didn't drive direct to Maison Paquin," Juliette said
when the carriage eventually bowled into the gracious width of the
Rue de la Paix, Lucille having instructed the coachman to take a
circuitous route.

"I wanted to see everything again as much as you, my dear,"
Lucille answered.

Just before they passed through the portals of number 3 into the
courtyard beyond, Juliette glanced toward Maison Worth at number 7. It was there she would present herself and her needlework
the next morning.

Within minutes of their entering Maison Paquin they were wel-
comed by the *directrice* and Lucille's own *vendeuse* led the way
through the luxurious salons. Juliette saw immediately that Maison
Paquin was a favorite rendezvous for smart Parisiennes. Women sat
gossiping, their ornate hats bent close together. Some were being
shown lengths of rich fabric or were studying designs that had
been specially drawn for them. Several had brought tiny lapdogs
trimmed with bows. Inevitably there was the occasional yelp when
somebody inadvertently trod on one. This meant exclamations of
distress, and much petting and cooing to soothe the little victim.
There were also a few bored-looking men, who sat or stood hap-
lessly dangling hats and canes. Several fine-looking girls known as
mannequins, after the dressmaking dummies used in the trade,
paraded gracefully about in Paquin creations.

Lucille and Juliette were eventually seated in one of the smaller
private salons to view the clothes Lucille's *vendeuse* had selected for
her client to see.

"You wrote of wanting a lace gown, madame," she said to Lucille. "There are several in exquisite Venetian lace for your consideration."

At some unobserved signal, the first of the mannequins came

through a draped archway wearing an almond-green morning gown. There followed more dresses for the same hours of the day, as well as all the other changes necessary for any fashionable woman from morning to night. Costumes for walking and calling preceded outfits for the races and motor drives, afternoon and tea gowns, dinner gowns, and finally evening creations. Madame Paquin was renowned for her evening wear, and each garment displayed seemed more sumptuous than the last. In Juliette's opinion, those of Venetian lace were the loveliest of all, although she would have preferred less ornamentation in the pearl and gold and silver trimming, the lace being beautiful enough in itself to her eyes. But in any case, none of the clothes were for her, and although her taste ran along simpler lines, every one of these garments would suit Lucille's Junoesque figure to perfection.

When all the ensembles had been seen, those that most appealed to Lucille were shown again. Since she needed so many to take home with her, not all could be decided upon in one session. In any case, no final decisions could be made before a personal consultation with Madame Paquin, when modifications of style and color would be discussed.

"The joy of *couture* clothes," Lucille said later, when she and Juliette were lunching lightly and deliciously at Voisin, "is that everything one orders is made specifically to one's exact measurements, even to the circumference of one's wrist. It's well worth the tedium of three or more fittings, because the result is always perfect. No dressmaker in all the world can compare with a Parisian seamstress. I only wish I could have asked for some clothes to be shown for you, Juliette. I'd love to buy you some pretty things, but I'm afraid Denise would be outraged if she saw you wearing something by another designer."

Juliette laughed. "I know she would! But in any case I'll be a working girl very shortly and I'll have no need of anything as grand as the clothes we've seen this morning."

The afternoon was spent driving through the Bois. Many other people of leisure were also in their carriages, and in the tree-dappled sunshine the flanks of the high-stepping horses gleamed as if polished, harnesses shone, and all the parasols, looking like pastel-hued mushrooms, were held in white-gloved hands. Old acquaintances of Lucille drew up alongside to exchange greetings, and invitations were forthcoming at once for her and Juliette, whom she proudly introduced. Although she had already accepted several written invitations from close friends, which had been awaiting her arrival, she found, after consulting the small engagement book in her purse, that she could accept each new occasion on behalf of Juliette and herself.

"There!" Juliette exclaimed triumphantly as they drove on again after the third halt, "I told you that you hadn't changed! Everybody knows you at once."

They discussed the invitations, Juliette delighted to have been included. One was to dine that same evening, another to join a party at the Théâtre-Français at the end of the week, and a third was for the Opéra two days later. Juliette felt as if Paris were already taking her back into its heart. Then, suddenly, she saw the young man from the lobby approaching on foot.

He was strolling in deep and serious conversation with an older, equally well-dressed man with a short, neatly trimmed gray beard. Although there was little likelihood of his seeing her, Juliette felt her pulse quicken as he approached.

Then came an unexpected development. The bearded man, happening to glance absently toward the carriage, gave a start of recognition when he saw Lucille and quickly raised his panama hat. The young man turned sharply in the same direction, automatically following suit, and as Lucille bowed in gracious acknowledgment, he saw who was sitting at her side. His intense, passionate eyes held Juliette's with the same magnetism as before. It was all over in seconds, and although she did not look back, all her senses told her he was staring after her.

"That was Prince Vadim of St. Petersburg and his nephew, Count Nikolai Karasvin," Lucille said, who apparently had not noticed the exchange of glances. "They're related to the Romanovs. I knew the prince's late wife, Augustine. She was a fellow Parisienne and we were friends from our school days. Sadly, she died four years ago, and recently the prince married again."

"Would the prince be in Paris on vacation?"

"No, he has a residence here. He usually winters in Monte Carlo and returns to Russia whenever he feels obliged to show himself at court."

"Does Count Karasvin lead the same kind of life?" Juliette almost held her breath in her eagerness to learn as much as possible about him.

"He has some minor diplomatic duties at the embassy these days. When I was last in Paris he was still an assistant/student at Rodin's studio."

"So he is a sculptor too!"

"It was a whim that his father indulged, according to Augustine. When I last saw him he didn't look as if he owned a franc, although, of course, he is quite wealthy, and he kept odd company then."

"Do you mean he led a Bohemian life?"

"He lived wildly with other artists in Montmartre. I know Augustine used to worry about him. But he's older now. At least twenty-five or so." Lucille twisted in her seat to look penetratingly at Juliette. "Why all the interest?"

Juliette assumed a nonchalant air. "I liked the look of him."

Lucille tapped the back of Juliette's hand with a warning finger. "Never let yourself be bewitched by a man's fine looks, my child. Such men can be self-centered and faithless. It's far better to find a good, plain man for yourself. Reliability is what counts in the end. There's enough heartbreak in the world without inviting it." She sighed as she looked ahead again.

The rest of the afternoon passed uneventfully. They had tea and ices and then returned to the hotel, where the concierge handed Lucille a letter in a crested envelope. She opened it as soon as they entered the suite.

"It's from Prince Vadim," she said, after reading it through. "He has apologized for not knowing I was in Paris and invites us both to dine this evening."

"How would he know you were staying here?"

"It's easy enough to make inquiries, and there are only two or three top hotels where a woman of my position might stay. More surprising is how he discovered your name, but no doubt the hotel gave it to him. I'll reply at once that we have a previous engagement and send it by special messenger." Lucille sat down at the secretaire and drew a sheet of paper toward her. "I suppose he wants me to meet his new wife, which I must do eventually, but it will be painful for me, because I shall miss Augustine at his side. The men of that family have always been charming womanizers and poor Augustine had a very difficult time."

Going into her room, Juliette could not help wondering if Nikolai Karasvin had instigated the invitation. Then she dismissed the idea. He would have no such influence with his uncle and most likely would not have been at the dinner party either. Yet she felt curiously in limbo, as if waiting for him to make the next move.

When dressed for the evening in one of her best silks, Juliette passed the time waiting for Lucille by checking again the items of needlework she had put ready to take to Maison Worth in the morning. She had just added one more piece of embroidery when Marie knocked on the door and entered with a beribboned white box.

"This just came for you, mademoiselle." She handed the box over and left again.

Mystified, Juliette sat down on the bed and removed the lid. Then she flushed with pleasure. Inside was a corsage of pearly white orchids with green flecks rising from the deeper green surrounding the golden calyx. She took up the accompanying card and read it:

Mademoiselle Cladel. Since we are not to meet this evening after all, I hope you will still spare me a few minutes of your time in the lobby now. Nikolai Karasvin.

She sprang to her feet at once. According to Lucille's warning words, she should tear up the note and toss the corsage away. What he had suggested was in itself outrageous, for he was flouting convention completely. She checked the time. It would be at least another twenty minutes before Lucille appeared from her room. That gave ten minutes to keep Nikolai Karasvin waiting in suspense, five in his company, and another five to be back in the suite before any awkward questions could be asked. She was only too certain that Lucille would never condone such a meeting, but it was one she did not intend to miss.

After pinning the orchids to her green velvet waistband, Juliette went to the mirror and gave a few unnecessary touches to her hair. She could see the excitement sparkling in her eyes.

She watched the clock until the exact moment came to leave. Not even Marie saw her go from the suite. She thought Nikolai would expect her to take the stairs, so went to the elevator instead, planning an element of surprise in her arrival and wanting to see him before he saw her. As she descended, her heart began to beat a little faster.

When the elevator operator sent the gates rattling back, there was Nikolai, standing once more by the pillar where she had first seen him. As she had anticipated, he was looking toward the stairs. She began to stroll in his direction, taking in every detail of his features, studying him as she had been unable to do before. There was a powerful curve to the nostrils of his straight nose and a tan to his skin, as if he rode a lot in the open air or followed the increasingly popular sport of skiing. His whole frame bore out this possibility, lithe and athletic as if full of controlled energy. Another few steps and she would address him by name.

"Juliette!"

She halted abruptly. It was Denise who had called out to her, advancing with ostrich feathers dancing on her hat, a pale silk scarf floating about her neck, arms outstretched.

"I hadn't expected you to return yet!" Juliette exclaimed in dismay, able to see out of the corner of her eye that Nikolai had heard her sister call and had turned to look quickly in her direction.

Denise embraced her warmly, so full of high spirits that for the time being she seemed to have forgotten her previous fury. "Yes, isn't it splendid! I had such a successful trip that I was able to conclude my business and return to Paris twenty-four hours sooner than I had expected." Standing back, she tilted her head assessingly as she looked Juliette up and down. "Yes, your hair put up in that new style suits you and you're as slim as ever." She began glancing about searchingly. "Where's Tante Lucille?"

"Upstairs."

"Then we'll go up to her straightaway. She'll be glad to see me back."

Just before the elevator gates clanged shut, Juliette saw Nikolai smile at her and shrug.

Denise talked all the way up and along the corridor about her new Mercedes, which had been delivered during her short absence and in which her chauffeur had driven her to the hotel. Juliette scarcely heard her, angry with herself for having delayed going downstairs at once after receiving the corsage, and even angrier with her sister for having returned to Paris so soon. She was further exasperated with herself for placing any importance on what would have been no more than a brief flirtatious encounter that she should never have contemplated to begin with.

In the suite, Lucille was just emerging from her bedroom. Denise's exuberance and her affectionate greeting gave Lucille no chance to consider why Juliette should have been in the lobby to meet her. Then Denise, sitting back with a satisfied sigh, looked indulgently at her sister and unwittingly launched the topic that was destined to disrupt their present harmony.

"I've forgiven you for your hasty and foolish departure from the convent yesterday, Juliette. I knew I had this business trip coming up and intended to send for you afterward. As for Monsieur Pechaire, I had no wish to force you into any marriage that was not to your liking. It was just that he is a dear man and I hoped you'd come to see that he would have made you a good husband. But never mind. There are plenty more fish in the sea, and I shall make sure you meet the best of the eligible bachelors. We had better see about getting you all the clothes you're going to need, so come along to Maison Landelle tomorrow morning."

"I'm sorry, but I can't do that." Juliette spoke composedly from the chair where she sat. "It's very generous of you and I don't want to hurt your feelings, but I've made up my mind to work for my living and to have a small place of my own, even if it's only one room at first."

"Work?" Denise narrowed her eyes incredulously and sat forward. "What could you do?"

"I can use a needle, and in Paris a skillful seamstress and embroiderer will always find employment. I believe I have an eye for fashion too, and I want to gain training for myself so that eventually I can start a dressmaking business of my own in some nearby city. Tomorrow morning I'm taking samples of my work to Maison Worth."

Denise screamed. There was no other way to describe the furious shriek she emitted, springing up from the sofa as if about to throw herself into hysterics. Lucille leapt to her feet in concern. Yet she was not in time to stop Denise darting across to deal Juliette a vicious slap across the cheek that snapped her head back across the cushions.

"You little traitor!" Denise burst out on the same high-pitched note. "After all I've done for you! What ingratitude! What heartlessness!" She would have struck Juliette again if Lucille had not grabbed her by the wrist.

"No, Denise! No! Calm yourself! This is no way to settle anything. Juliette has every right to choose a career for herself."

"But not like this! She's stabbing me in the back!"

By now, Juliette had also risen to face her sister. "I don't understand you," she protested in angry bewilderment. "I only want to follow my own path in life."

"But at my expense!" Denise, seeing her sister's dismay, became calmer, although no less intractable.

"How can that be?" Juliette demanded. "You made it clear enough that you wished to be rid of me through marriage. Well, I've chosen my own way to relieve you of the responsibility for my future. I know you consider Madame Paquin to be your rival, so I'd never sew for her, but surely Maison Worth would be neutral territory?"

"No! There's no such thing as far as I'm concerned." Denise's eyes glittered with sudden savage triumph as she delivered the ultimate blow to her sister's dream. "I'll tell you something else! No matter how good your work, no *haute couture* house would ever employ you."

"Would you have me blackballed?" Juliette's own rage burst forth.

"I wouldn't have to. Every door would be slammed in your face!"

"Why?" Juliette's demand was fierce.

"Use your intelligence! We are both Papa's daughters! He is still spoken of with respect in spite of his financial misfortune, and everyone knows I was a Cladel before my marriage. In no time at all it would become public knowledge that we are siblings."

"Where's the harm in that?"

"All harm! You'd never be trusted. Each couturier's new designs are a closely guarded secret until the day they're shown, and as soon as you revealed your identity you'd be suspected of being a spy. The first question you'd be asked is why you were not giving me your support. The brothers Worth themselves would be held up to you as examples of the family bond."

"You know it's not a question of loyalty!" Juliette exclaimed in distress. She had not thought of herself being viewed in this light, but she could see how it might happen.

Denise drew in a deep breath. She was shaking, but she had regained full control of herself and was now intent on gaining the upper hand. "As it happens, I believe that you intended no treachery toward me, but unfortunately nobody else will. If you wish to test the waters for yourself, by all means go ahead and take your needlework samples wherever you wish, but you will cause me the worst humiliation I have ever suffered. I'll be ostracized by all the other couturiers as the one who tried to plant an informer." Her voice choked deliberately on a note of appeal. "I can't believe that you of all people would do that to me."

Juliette, her eyes wide with disappointment, raised her head a little as she answered almost inaudibly, "You are right. Nothing on this earth would make me betray you in such a way. I'll leave Paris and find work where nobody will connect us as sisters. You need never fear that I'll compete with you."

Denise concealed her satisfaction; she wanted more. Gossip flew swiftly, and even if her sister was working far from Paris, it could still filter back that there was a rift between them, which would be even worse for Denise if Juliette should begin to make her own mark in the fashion world. So far there had never been any threat to the good name of Maison Landelle and Denise was determined that not even the slightest shadow of a family scandal should fall across it. She had always spoken of her convent-based sister in the fondest terms, continually on guard against any criticism for not having the girl with her, at least during vacations.

"If you wish to overcome this obstacle I've put in your path, Juliette, you can always work for me."

"No! That's out of the question! I'm not being ungrateful, but it would never do! I have to progress and rise through my own efforts. It's vital to me!"

"Listen. I'll take you on as if you were any other applicant for work at the Maison Landelle. Your sewing ability is recommendation enough. If you're as capable of advancement through your skills and intelligence as you believe, it will come to you through those who supervise your work. Gradually you'll be fully trained in all aspects of the business. Isn't that what you want?"

"Yes, but—"

"There would be no privileges, and you'd have to adhere to the same strict discipline as everyone else. You'd have to live with me, which society would expect, and scrimp along on your wages as a beginner, because I'd pay you no more and no less than others engaged in the same tasks. Only out of working hours would we ever be as sisters."

Juliette wanted to trust Denise, but to live with her and to work under her jurisdiction would be impossible. Then Lucille, as if reading her thoughts, spoke to Juliette directly.

"Think carefully, my dear. Take your time and weigh all that has been said. I'm sure Denise would be the first to admit that it won't be easy for you in any way, but then you never expected to follow anything but a difficult path."

What Lucille said was true. Abruptly Juliette turned away, struggling with her emotions. Denise watched her, more anxious for her sister's acceptance than she was prepared to reveal. She tried another avenue of persuasion.

"I now know your opinion about early marriage, so don't fear that I'll put pressure on you ever again. I'll allow no man to pester you and the subject of matrimony need never be raised unless you yourself should wish it. We'd be starting afresh. The two Cladel sisters united in harmony."

There was a long pause, and then Juliette faced her sister again. "You never wanted me in your home before. Why should you change now?"

"I've never had any patience with children and you were better off where you were. Now it would embarrass me to have you living elsewhere. People would talk."

"At least you're being honest with me."

"Think a few moments. Have I not confided my personal problems to you on several occasions? Is that not reason to think we are now able to sustain our relationship. Had you not returned to Paris I doubt we would have seen each other very often, but since you are here, we have sibling duties that bind us, however much you might wish it otherwise."

"I've never wanted to break the tie between us!" Juliette declared in a tortured voice. "It's my personal liberty that I must defend."

"Then out of working hours you shall have it," Denise conceded. "All I ask in return is that you conduct yourself respectably. Don't reject my goodwill. Be tolerant and let the arrangement be made."

Juliette drew in a deep breath before making her considered reply.

"So you would keep your vow always to treat me as an ordinary employee at the Maison Landelle."

"You have my promise. Tante Lucille is your witness."

Juliette straightened her shoulders resolutely. "Then I will do my best for you as I would have done for any other employer."

Neither sister noticed Lucille heave a silent sigh of relief. Her great fear during these minutes of conflict was that Juliette would refuse the employment offered and end up sewing in a sweatshop somewhere far from Paris. She would not have received the right experience for a prestigious future, and even her health could have suffered. So many seamstresses died young of tuberculosis from poor working conditions.

"I ask only one favor, Juliette," Denise continued. "I want you to agree to accept the wardrobe of new clothes I mentioned earlier, and I want you to wear my designs whenever you appear at a social occasion." She gestured appraisingly. "Look at you now with those orchids pinned to your waistband, allowing the blooms to hang in just the right way. I noticed that detail as soon as I saw you in the lobby. But even years ago, as soon as your figure began to develop, I could tell you were like me in having inherited Maman's gift of wearing clothes with ease and elegance. Papa was quite a dandy too, and so I suppose we get it from both of them."

Lucille nodded in agreement. "Your sister is right, Juliette. She's not flattering you." A twinkle close to mischief appeared in her eyes. "And I agree that those orchids are perfectly placed."

Juliette could tell that Lucille had by now guessed the corsage was from an admirer and how the meeting with Denise in the lobby had come about. The fact that there was no sign of disapproval in her friend's eyes lightened Juliette's heart considerably. She was sure Lucille had also been romantically adventurous on occasion, and the thought encouraged her as she answered her sister.

"If I can look half as well in Landelle clothes as Maman always did in her Worth ensembles, I'll feel very proud to wear them."

"You will." Denise was prepared to be magnanimous in victory. "Now enjoy whatever you and Lucille are planning for this evening. Tomorrow morning have your things sent to my house and present yourself at the employers' entrance at Maison Landelle. We'll start as we mean to go on."

"Yes. I'll come in the morning, but until Tante Lucille leaves, I'll stay on at the Hôtel Bristol."

Lucille intervened quickly, not wanting to be the cause of any further dissension. "No, Juliette, my dear. Circumstances have

changed since. As you will have much to learn, I think you should
be with Denise in the evenings to talk over the events of each day.
But I shall count on seeing you for those engagements to which we
have already been invited, and whenever you can spare time to be
with me."

"That will be often!"

Denise was ready to leave. "It's all settled then." She made her
farewells, kissing both her sister and Lucille, and then she was
gone.

But Lucille was thoughtful. There had been a smugness in Denise's expression as she departed that stirred a certain mistrust. It
was impossible not to wonder what was in her mind. Then Juliette
was indicating the orchids at her waist. "Do you want to know his
name?" she inquired evenly.

Lucille read the determination in her face, and replied, "I believe I can guess. It explains the urgency of the Russian invitation
that arrived earlier. But be wary. Remember what I said about
handsome men and the Karasvin males in particular."

"Don't worry! I'm in Paris to work, not to lose my heart."

As Denise descended in the elevator she smiled to herself with
satisfaction. It had suddenly come to her during their conversation
that it could be to her immense advantage to have her sister at
Maison Landelle. Her only regret in not having a child of her own
was that she could never boast of having established a family business, and that had caused her to harbor a secret envy of Maison
Worth. But with Juliette trained and then making the right marriage, there would be offspring to draw into the business. There
was no doubt the cloud of her sister's unexpected return had
turned out to have the proverbial silver lining.

Four

AT EIGHT the next morning, when Juliette arrived at the employees' entrance of the Maison Landelle, she was shown
where to hang her hat and jacket and was given a crisp white apron
with a bib at the front and straps over the shoulders to tie at the
back. Then she was taken to Madame Tabard, who was in charge
of the sewing atelier.

"The baronne let me know you were coming, Mademoiselle
Cladel. In future you will arrive at seven o'clock and you will work
until a break at noon for refreshment. Then you will leave your
sewing apron on your chair, because cleanliness is of utmost importance when handling costly fabrics. Let me see your hands
now." She gave a nod when Juliette had displayed them. "Good. I
see you take care of your nails, which is what I would have expected in your case. Some girls have to be taught the first day.
After that, if a beginner, whether apprentice or seamstress, snags or
soils a fabric, it can mean instant dismissal. So clean, neat hands at
all times. Is that understood?"

"Yes, madame."

"Your day will end at six o'clock unless there is a rush of work
for some specific reason. The fact that you are the couturière's
sister will make no difference in how you are treated here, except
that you will be addressed as Mademoiselle Cladel as benefits your
position as a future head of Maison Landelle."

"Is that necessary? I don't want to be marked out from my fellow workers."

"But it is. How do you suppose you'd hold respect and keep a disciplined fashion house later on if the start wasn't made now? Not even a *directrice* gets appointed from her own training ground for that reason. You may face some hostility."

"I hope to prove there's no need for it."

"That will depend on you. I've been told that in addition to excelling in embroidery you were taught dressmaking by a nun who had been an experienced seamstress before taking the veil. But you can consider that just an apprenticeship. Here you will be shown all the finer details of couture. Now show me the samples of your work that I see you've brought with you."

Madame Tabard realized as she examined the work that this new girl had been taught all she needed to know of stitching. Afterward, as was the custom, she took Juliette on a tour of the whole establishment. It was important that each new employee view the various stages involved in the making of a garment, from its drawn design until ready for the client. Juliette was shown some designs, each with fabric samples pinned to it. She knew that the next stage for any *haute couture* garment was to be made up as a *toile,* the name taken from the light fabric used.

Madame Tabard led her on to the cutting room where the male cutters and their assistants were hard at work. Juliette looked through a glass panel set in the wall of the corridor at the embroiderers engaged in their intricate tasks, and was able to peek into several of the sewing ateliers before she followed Madame Tabard into the one where she would work. The seamstresses, each in a white apron like her own, sat at long tables. All of them, even the apprentices who were picking up pins or fetching reels of thread, hushed their quiet chatter as Juliette entered at Madame Tabard's side. She knew already that everyone had been informed, either directly or through the grapevine, that the Baronne de Landelle's sister was joining the workforce.

"This is Mademoiselle Cladel," Madame Tabard announced.

Juliette smiled at everyone there. *"Bonjour."*

They all replied, some mumbling the words. Two or three gave her a cautious smile, and several eyed her with curiosity, but she could see that the majority were uncomfortable in her presence. Madame Tabard spoke to the senior seamstress at one of the tables.

"I'd like Mademoiselle Cladel to sit beside you for a few weeks, Aude."

"Yes. I can move Françoise to the end of the table," the woman replied. Then she gave Juliette an amiable nod. "I'll have some work ready for you when you return."

From there Juliette was shown the pressing room, the storerooms, and also the packing room where sheets of tissue paper billowed and rustled as the costly clothes were placed in the green and white striped boxes of Maison Landelle, ready for delivery.

"As you have seen for yourself," Madame Tabard continued as she led the way from the ateliers up an uncarpeted flight to the showrooms and salons, "everything connected with the making of a garment takes place downstairs in an area the client never sees. Neither do they see the design studio on the floor above the salons. You will see it only when the baronne takes you there. It is her domain and that of her designer, Monsieur Pierre."

Juliette knew that Denise relied heavily on Pierre Clémont, as did other couturiers on their designers when, like Denise, they had no atelier experience themselves. Yet it was Denise who decided the season's line, made preliminary sketches, and introduced the touches that gave Landelle clothes their particular mark of distinction.

The luxury of the salon floor struck Juliette anew after the starkness of the area she had just left. In the mannequins' *cabine* the girls were getting ready for the day, some sitting in front of their mirrors and putting discreet touches of rouge on their lips and cheeks. Fluffy powder puffs left clouds in the air as arms and shoulders were dusted. They were not yet wearing the clothes they would display later, but were dressed in negligees, supplied by Maison Landelle, over beribboned corsets, their stockings black or white. Juliette noticed there were two mannequins with red hair like her own. Both smiled at her, as did most of the others, and wished her well. All were intrigued, but they had no need to be wary of her, even though she was the couturière's sister, since her work would not overlap theirs. Then it was back downstairs again, and she took her place beside Aude, who gave her a pink velvet skirt and told her what had to be done.

"If you have any problems with work you're given," Aude said, "always ask me or Jeanne, who's sitting at your right hand. She's a first-degree seamstress too."

Nobody else spoke, all conversation having stopped with Juliette's return. When she had threaded her needle from the reel an apprentice had placed in front of her, Juliette let her gaze travel around the faces bent over their work. Suspecting that they were all glancing at her from under their lashes, made her decide to speak out.

"I hope you'll all soon get used to me, because I'm here to stay. That is, if I don't snag my material or—worse—soil my first task with a grease spot."

The unexpectedness of her declaration of vulnerability made some of the younger girls giggle in surprise.

"Would you really be thrown out?" one asked. "After all, you're—"

Juliette interrupted firmly. "I'm a new seamstress with much to learn and I'll stand or fall by the standard of my work."

Another spoke to her. "Have you served an apprenticeship?"

Juliette, who had begun to sew, told of the nun's instruction. Gradually those around the table became more relaxed and began chatting together again, although they did not draw her into their conversation.

The room where the women ate their packed lunches had an electric plate on which coffee could be heated. As Juliette opened her own lunch packet she was exasperated to see that the Hôtel Bristol chef had given her pâté de foie gras, hard-boiled plover's eggs, dainty rolls, and a chicken breast garnished with aspic and cradled in a lettuce leaf with asparagus tips. Everybody else had bread and cheese. Tomorrow she would prepare the same for herself.

It was mid-afternoon when a bold-looking seamstress, clearly egged on by her neighbors, asked Juliette a pointed question. "Are you wearing a Landelle dress now? I seem to recognize the cut of the collar."

Juliette looked straight at her. "Yes, it is one of my convent dresses."

"But what happens next? Shall we be sewing grand gowns just for you?"

"I expect you will," Juliette replied evenly. "I won't be sufficiently qualified." As she renewed her sewing, she could feel the chill of the seamstresses' hostility seeping out toward her, but she

would not make any excuses for herself. Then, next to her, Aude
rested her needle and spoke up.

"I think we are very fortunate to have somebody in our midst
who will be wearing the result of our efforts. It will make a refresh-
ing change from sewing for the unknown clients upstairs. Perhaps
Mademoiselle Cladel will let us see her in some of the finished
garments."

There was silence as all watched for Juliette's reaction. She
looked at Aude in surprise, grateful for the tactful intervention.
"I'd be glad to."

There was a murmur of interest and approval around the table
and Aude gave a nod of satisfaction. "Well said, Mademoiselle
Cladel."

There was a diversion then as a fitter came from upstairs with
two gowns that needed additional trimming, and the rest of the
day was uneventful as far as Juliette was concerned. Before going
home, she thanked Aude for helping her through a difficult moment.

"I've no wish to flaunt my benefits," she said. "All I want is to
be an ordinary trainee here, but that doesn't seem to be possible."

Aude looked at her sympathetically. "Don't worry about it, even
though you're not out of the woods yet. Some of these women
have hard and difficult domestic circumstances—drunken husbands, dependent elderly parents, widowhood, a sick child—I've
heard it all."

"They come to you with their troubles?"

"Yes, they do. Sometimes if it's a broken heart, no more than a
few words of comfort are needed, but I've had desperate cases
sometimes when a poor girl is pregnant. So if you encounter jealousy, or what might seem to be unreasonable spite, just spare a
thought for what those seamstresses might be going home to every
evening and try to be tolerant. After a while everything will settle
down. If you're not proud—and I don't think you are or else I
wouldn't have intervened on your behalf—you'll gain their respect. You'll also have their loyalty in the years ahead."

"I hope so, and I do appreciate your kind advice."

That evening Juliette went straight from work to Denise's large
house in the Faubourg St. Germain. Her sister was already at home
and came to meet her in the spacious entry hall.

"So you found your way here all right. How did your first day go?"

"It was very interesting and all my work was approved."

"Good. I'll take you upstairs and show you your room. It's the same one you had after Maman's funeral, before I took you to the convent, but it's been redecorated since then."

Juliette looked around as she accompanied her sister up the gracefully curved stairway. Nothing was as she remembered it. "You've changed everything since I was here."

"Yes, Claude hated the upheaval, so I sent him off to the family villa in Tuscany until it was all done. Incidentally, the villa is mine now too. I managed to get him to sign it over to me when we were on our honeymoon there, but I never seem to have time to take a vacation these days." She opened a bedroom door and entered ahead of Juliette. "You have your own bathroom. I had one installed for every bedroom."

This was the height of luxury, and Denise was proud of it. Even the best hotels had a meager number of bathrooms and few, if any, grand homes in France could offer guests the individual facilities to be found in her house.

"I shall appreciate that," Juliette said. She could tell that her trunk had already been unpacked, for her hairbrush and hand mirror were on the dressing table. The room was light and restful in soft green and white, very different from the dark décor of eight years ago, when she had sobbed herself to sleep every night.

"Remember the chemise I brought to the convent?" Denise said, pulling open one of the drawers in a tall chest. "You'll find it here, along with all the nightwear and lingerie you need. I'd thought these would be part of your trousseau, but now that you're in Paris you'll need them. The housekeeper took away all your convent underwear and after dinner we'll talk about the new clothes you're to have. I brought some designs home with me."

For a few moments Juliette felt as if she could not breathe. She clenched her teeth at the manner in which Denise was so high-handedly sweeping her along, as if she had no will of her own. Then she reminded herself that this was part of the agreement. At least Denise seemed to be acting with good will and she must be glad of that.

Her rising color must have given her away, for Denise suddenly regarded her with rare understanding. "If I seem overbearing at times, it's just my way. You should know better than anyone it's how I've always been and ever will be. But I want you in the business and I'm pleased you're here, even though I didn't expect to be when I first heard you'd left the convent." She moved to the door. "Come down as soon as you're ready."

After taking a bath, Juliette put on a set of the new lingerie, which was of softest lawn trimmed with handmade lace and satin ribbons. After the thick cotton she was used to, there was a sensuous pleasure in feeling these dainty garments against her skin. She continued to be aware of them even when she had put on a dress and redone her hair. Downstairs she found her sister in a salon paneled with flowered Lyonnais brocade. Denise was glancing through the designs she had mentioned, and one of the tables was piled with fabric swatches in various colors.

"Pierre sketched some of these today," Denise said, looking up as Juliette came toward her. "The rest are ideas we had in the pipeline, so nobody else will have anything just like them. I've already made some changes and," she added indulgently, "you may have a few suggestions of your own. But we can discuss all this later."

Over dinner the talk was inevitably of Maison Landelle. Denise had never before had anyone with whom to talk over the day's events and now she was able to chat away, knowing she had her sister's intelligent attention. It had been the same when she poured out her pent-up troubles on visits to the convent. And, above all else, she knew Juliette would keep to herself whatever she was told in confidence.

When the time came to look at the designs, Juliette selected several and then made a final choice. It was difficult to persuade Denise to dispense with the extra frills and loops on some of them, but eventually they reached a compromise on each design. Only on the evening gowns did Denise refuse to budge. She was determined to uphold her reputation for magnificent evening wear and anything too simple would not be to her standard.

"People will always be eager to see what my sister is wearing, and in the evenings I want you to dazzle. But night or day, you'll be the best advertisement I could have because, even though I wear my own creations, you have youth on your side."

It seemed churlish not to accede to Denise's wishes and, since the evening gowns were beautiful, Juliette gave in and agreed to all the designs.

"That's good." Denise was satisfied. "Another advantage you'll have in wearing these clothes is that you hold yourself with a statuesque pride."

"Do I?" Juliette raised her eyebrows with a smile. "It must come from all the times I was punished by having to stand with a book on my head!"

Denise knew it was more than that. "Now, choose the fabrics and the colors you like best."

There was no dithering when Juliette made her choices. Denise was able to see that her sister knew instinctively what would be right both for herself and for each particular design. Juliette looked amused when Denise commented on this with approval.

"I learned about choice from you long ago."

"From me?" Denise was surprised.

"I was too young to notice Maman's clothes, except to know that she always looked pretty and had a sweet fragrance about her. But at the convent, where everything was dark and somber, you would burst on the scene looking like an exotic peacock. From your first visit, I noticed every detail of your attire. The rich patterns of your dresses, the colors of the fabrics, even to the silk linings of your furs and the summer gauzes on your hats. A love of fashion was awakened in me and has been with me ever since."

"You never told me!" Denise said wonderingly, quite overwhelmed to discover she had been such an inspiration.

"My passion for sewing was always for the day when I could enter the world of *haute couture*."

Denise felt triumph burst anew within her. Maison Landelle was indeed destined to be a family business. She wished Juliette were already trained and that it was time to find the right husband for her, a rich man who was malleable enough to allow his wife to continue working between babies and who could be made a director, thus ensuring his support and interest from one generation to the next. And she, Denise Landelle, would become a legend in her own time just like the couturier Worth himself!

Quite overcome, she threw up her hands joyfully and then clasped them together, as if her dream were already realized. "How fortunate it is that you have Titian hair!"

She was thinking of the sensation her new evening gowns would cause when Juliette was seen in them.

Juliette's measurements were taken the next morning before the clients arrived. She observed the meticulous care of the fitter and remembered Lucille's words as her wrists were measured.

When it became apparent that none of the gowns could possibly be ready for her evening at the theater, Juliette chose to wear a topaz chiffon from the current Landelle collection, and it was adjusted to her measurements. She was dressed and ready to go downstairs when Denise came into the bedroom with a jewelry case, which she opened to reveal a necklace and earrings of pearls.

"These were Maman's. I intended to give them to you on your wedding day, but now I think you should have them to wear whenever the occasion arises."

Juliette, deeply moved, embraced her sister. "I had no idea. I thought everything had been sold to meet Papa's debts. Have you anything of Maman's for yourself?"

"Yes, a ruby brooch. That was all she kept."

"I'll treasure these always."

Lucille noticed the pearls as soon as she collected Juliette in her carriage. "You're wearing Catherine's pearls."

"You remember them?"

"Naturally. They were your father's gift to her when you were born. So it's right and proper that you have them."

Juliette touched the pearl necklace lovingly. Denise had not told her that. Perhaps she had forgotten.

At the theater, their host, Monsieur de Bourde, was in the foyer to take them to his box where his wife greeted them warmly and they were introduced to the other guests. Juliette was given a chair where she would have a superb view when the curtain went up. She scanned the boxes opposite and the rest of the auditorium through ivory opera glasses looking for Nikolai, but in vain. Soon she was enjoying the music and spectacle of the operetta and was too absorbed to notice the arrival of a party of latecomers, who took their seats in the third row of the *fauteuils d'orchestre*. The highlight for her came in the last scene before the interval when a group of dancers created a delicate rippling and swirling of gossamer silk veils patterned asymmetrically in wonderful colors. She joined in the thunderous applause. Then, as the curtain descended, she turned enthusiastically to Madame de Bourde. "Those lovely veils! What a spectacle!"

"They're called Knossos scarves by their designer, Fortuny. I first saw them in a ballet performed in the Comtesse de Béarn's private theater here in Paris. I've heard that those veils are being adopted as a fashion accessory by some women."

"I'm not surprised. They'd be very flattering." Juliette was turning the pages of her program. When she found the designer's name, she read it out. "Mariano Fortuny y Madrazo. I see he designed all those splendid lighting effects too. His name sounds Spanish."

"That's what he is. He was born in Granada, the son of a very distinguished artist, not far from where my husband and I have stayed on vacation. That's how I know. Apparently there's a custom in Spain of linking the father's name with the mother's for a child's name, but normally he's known simply as Fortuny."

"Is Fortuny married?" Juliette felt she wanted to know as much as possible about this talented man.

Madame de Bourde raised her fan and whispered behind it. "He associates with a divorced woman! They live together!"

So Mariano Fortuny was not afraid to flout society! The rose-tinted lights of the auditorium were beginning to lower again. Juliette made up her mind to ask Denise more about the designer at breakfast the next morning. To her disappointment the Knossos scarves did not appear again.

The foyer was teeming with people waiting for carriages or cabs when Juliette was addressed by someone close by.

"*Bon soir*, Mademoiselle Cladel. Did you enjoy the performance?" It was a Russian-accented voice, deep and beautiful, that she had never heard before, but which she recognized instantly.

Her lips parted in a quick, indrawn breath. As she turned her head, she saw Nikolai beside her, even more powerfully masculine and attractive at close quarters. He was smiling at her with an intimacy that went far beyond the few times they had glimpsed one another.

"Yes, I did," she replied quickly. "Especially the wonderful scene with the Knossos scarves."

"Ah! Fortuny." He nodded approvingly. "A master in many fields of invention. I've been an admirer of his theatrical lighting effects for some time."

"I knew nothing about him until this evening."

"I'd like the opportunity to tell you more. I'm sure you're keen to know how and why his theatrical lamps and illuminating devices are being adopted all over the world." His eyes were dancing at the obviousness of the ploy, and she was equally amused.

"Not particularly. I'm not technically minded. It was his use of color that appealed to me most. Is his work the reason you came here this evening?"

"No, although he works only with the best, such as Diaghilev's Ballets Russes, La Scala opera, and so forth. Unfortunately I was late going in this evening as the friends I was to meet here were not on time."

She recalled his impatience when he was waiting in the hotel lobby. "I think you are always on time yourself!"

He grinned. "How did you guess that? Yes, I am, except in certain circumstances when time loses all meaning."

She wondered if that was when he was sculpting. "Did you miss much of the performance?"

"Only about ten minutes." Then he gripped her arm to steady her as someone jostled past and the contact brought her close to him. She realized that she had been separated from the rest of her party, but she did not care. Neither she nor Nikolai made any attempt to draw apart again, and he lowered his voice, even though no one could overhear anything either of them said in that babble of noise. "I saw you in the interval. If I had known any of the party you were with I'd have called at your box."

"So that we could be formally introduced?" she questioned quizzically.

He laughed quietly. "I fear I've rather taken that for granted since my uncle and I are acquainted with Madame Garnier."

"She was with me in the box."

"I didn't see her!" He threw up a hand in exasperation. "If I had, I'd have been there. Instead I watched for your leaving."

"You've given me the chance to thank you for the beautiful orchids you sent me at the Hôtel Bristol."

"That attempt at a meeting was a fiasco. Who was the lady who whisked you away?"

"My sister, whom I live with. If she had known I was meeting a stranger without a chaperone . . ." She left the sentence unfinished, rolling up her eyes expressively, and he laughed with her.

"Socially it was unforgivable of me, but I couldn't take the risk that you'd vanish forever. I asked your name at the reception desk."

"You instigated the dinner invitation too, didn't you?" She was amused.

"Yes. One would have been forthcoming in any case, but I wanted no delay."

"You're being very frank."

"And you're being very tolerant. Since both of my previous attempts failed to result in a meeting, would you agree to my making a third try? This time I'll ask your sister's permission first."

"It would make matters easier."

"Then let's—"

But Madame de Bourde, all unwittingly, had come blundering between them. "We thought you were lost in the crowd, Mademoiselle Cladel! Come along quickly! You're keeping everyone waiting. The carriage taking us on to supper has been blocking all the rest for minutes! Oh, how I hate this crush!"

Juliette looked back over her shoulder as she was hustled away. Nikolai called to her. "What's your address?"

She answered, but was not sure he caught what she said. He grinned and shook his head in mock despair. Then he was lost from her sight in a sea of top hats. She was undismayed. She knew he would soon find her again.

At breakfast the next morning, Juliette spoke of Fortuny to her sister. Denise, eating a croissant with strawberry preserves, was unenthusiastic.

"I admit those Knossos scarves are quite pleasing, but not as a fashion accessory. They're so large. Why would any woman want to swathe herself to look like a Greek statue? As for Fortuny's achievements in the theater"—she paused to shrug his achievements away—"that's only because he knows a lot about lamps, being a photographer as well. So you can tell what he is in all, can't you? A jack-of-all-trades. In the end that kind of person comes to nothing."

Juliette could not help wondering if Denise was jealous because she had not designed those scarves. "I can't agree. On the strength of what I've seen on a single occasion I'd say he was greatly talented."

Denise smiled indulgently. "Naturally you were impressed. Everything is new to you, Juliette, but there is really nothing unusual about whisking scarves about on the stage. Isadora Duncan does it all the time. She's to dance again in Paris next week. We'll go to see her and take Tante Lucille, too."

When the evening came, Juliette thought the barefoot dancer in her loose, flowing robes was marvelously fluid and vibrant, and her grace with a long trailing scarf was a delight. But it was not a Knossos veil and the dream-like effect was missing. Juliette's curiosity about Fortuny remained unsatisfied.

Five

TWO LETTERS bearing the Karasvin crest were delivered to Lucille within half an hour of each other. The first was from Prince Vadim with another dinner invitation two weeks hence for herself and Juliette, which, of course, she would accept. The second was from Nikolai and caused her deep concern. She read it through several times and then paced the salon of her suite holding the letter he had enclosed and asked her to forward to Juliette as he did not know her present address.

She sat down in a chair and rested her forehead in her hand. What was she to do? Nikolai's letter to her had been brief, but to her eyes very revealing, showing that his selfishness was limitless. She had to consider Juliette before all else. When she had first warned the girl about the Karasvin men she had never supposed for an instant that Nikolai might loom as a shadow across the girl's life.

The orchids had not seemed important, for the gesture was typical of Karasvin men with their wealth and eye for beautiful women. It had given Juliette pleasure and that had been all that mattered. Before that there had been the sighting in the Bois, making excitement throb in the girl's voice, even though she had been unaware of it, and then had come that telltale radiance in Juliette's face when she told of meeting Nikolai in the theater. In all it added up to very little, but Lucille could not dismiss from her mind Victor

Hugo's observance that a single glance could plant a flower in another's heart.

If only it had been any other man who had sent a glance at Juliette! Lucille remembered Augustine writing in one of her last letters how ruthless he was with women. Too handsome, too rich, and too spoiled had been her summing up of her nephew by marriage.

Slowly Lucille rose to her feet, unsure how long she had agonized before finally reaching her decision. In her bedroom, she unlocked her jewel case and put the letter at the bottom, then turned the key again. Her conscience would plague her, but Juliette's well-being came first. Had not she herself, after many innocent, romantic encounters, finally fallen in love with a similar handsome womanizer, who had left her so broken-hearted that she had married kind, sensible, and dull Rodolphe mainly because he was going abroad to work. It had given her the chance to get away from Paris and all its memories. She did not deny that time healed, but it never filled the emptiness left in the heart.

Juliette was delighted that the first of her new dinner gowns was delivered in time for the evening at Prince Vadim's. It was of heavy cream satin with a pattern of roses in a deeper shade, with folds at the back ending in a slight train and a décolletage that skillfully avoided showing the cleavage.

"This modest whim of fashion gives all women a kind of mono-bosom," Juliette joked at one of the fittings. "I can only hope that mine won't look like a pumped-up cushion!"

"Yours," said the fitter as she adjusted the hem, "could never look like that, although I've thought differently about the photographs I've seen of the Gibson Girl. But then she has never been dressed by Maison Landelle. You will always look as nature intended."

Juliette could see for herself that her figure was not disguised when she stood before her bedroom cheval glass as Denise's maid fastened the last of the tiny hooks and eyes at the back of the gown. She understood now what it was truly like to wear couture clothes. Her simple convent garments and those she had worn on vacation had been beautifully made to her exact measurements, but as she was never in Paris there had been no fittings. This gown was in a different category altogether. Her narrow waist, held in the gown's underbodice, was smooth as a stem, not the minutest pucker anywhere. She might have been sculpted in this gown by Michelangelo—or by Nikolai. The thought made her eyes sparkle. In less than an hour she would be seeing him again!

Yet when she and Lucille arrived at the prince's house and entered the gilt and green salon she knew instinctively, even without looking around, that Nikolai was not there. She had pictured his coming forward at once to greet her and her disappointment was acute. He was late! How could he not have arrived on time! It must be the traffic. She smiled as she was presented to the other guests and made light conversation while constantly anticipating his appearance in the doorway. Then the prince happened to mention casually that his nephew had returned to St. Petersburg on important family business. Instantly, all the luster faded from Juliette's evening.

"When will he be back?" she heard herself ask bleakly.

"Who can ever say what the young will do?" the Prince replied jovially, greatly taken by her. He considered himself a connoisseur of the arts and of women, and this fine-looking girl, with her seductive figure and innocent yet passionate mouth, delighted his eye.

Juliette wanted to cry out that Nikolai had most surely left a message for her, but at the same time she realized what a foolish notion that was. Clearly she had read far more into the way he had looked at her than had ever been meant. She swallowed hard.

"What of his interest in sculpture? Would that not bring him back to Paris?"

"It can only be a hobby for him despite the fact that he is exceptionally talented. He has responsibilities and commitments in Russia that he can never relinquish. His duties stand before all else."

"Is any of his work on public view?"

"Not at the present time, although he has exhibited on half a dozen occasions at the invitation of the Société Nationale des Beaux-Arts in the Salon at the Grand Palais, which is a considerable honor."

"Yes, indeed!"

"As you're interested in sculpture, I have a bust of myself that my nephew did about two years ago if you care to see it." Taking her answer for granted, he took her white-gloved hand into his, smiling into her eyes through his black ribboned pince-nez. "It would be a pleasure to show it to you later."

But he had no chance. His second wife, eagle-eyed and twenty years younger, had no intention of being another betrayed Augustine, and it was she who showed the ladies the bust of her husband after dinner. Juliette went forward to study it closely, although, with the exception of Lucille, the others showed only polite interest. Cast in bronze, it was strongly and vigorously sculpted into a penetrating likeness that had brought searingly to the surface the weaknesses as well as the strengths of the aristocratic man whose likeness it was.

"This bust should be in a better light!" Juliette exclaimed involuntarily. It was set back in an alcove where even by day it would be in gloom.

Her hostess made a deprecating little gesture. "The prince doesn't really like it, but he accepts it is an exceptional work of art."

Juliette could see how it would offend the prince's conceit, for although it showed laughter at the corners of the eyes, courage in the line of his jaw, and resolution in the chin, it did not flatter in any way. The fleshy mouth was sensual and there was a sag to the handsome jowls. She saw that Nikolai had signed his name on the base and had to restrain herself from running her fingertips along it. On the drive home, she and Lucille discussed the sculpture.

"Nikolai Karasvin has his own individual style," Lucille said after consideration, "but the influence of Rodin is there. With the exception of certain great masters, there's probably never been a sculptor more committed than Rodin to depicting the truth of what he sees in men and women. The prince's nephew is following the same decisive lines."

When Juliette had alighted at her home, Lucille, alone again in her carriage, breathed a sigh of relief. She had seen for herself how the news of Nikolai's departure to Russia had taken all the light from the girl's face. It was as if a bright candle had been snuffed. But Juliette would learn a lesson from this disappointment. By the time Nikolai returned, if ever he did, she would be far more sophisticated and used to the irresponsible ways of men. She would not be so easily snared again.

At home, Juliette, having been helped out of her gown by Denise's maid, sat in front of her dressing table mirror to brush her hair. As soon as the maid had gone from the room, her offer of further help declined, Juliette stopped the strokes and let her head drop disconsolately. It was over with Nikolai before it had begun. She would never allow herself to be so vulnerable to any man again.

It was very hard for Lucille to leave Paris when her vacation came to an end. Her conscience continued to trouble her over the letter she still had in her jewel case, but there it would stay. She and Juliette both wept on the platform of the Gare du Nord as they kissed each other's cheeks and embraced in farewell. Denise, who had already said *adieu,* glanced surreptitiously at her watch as she waited by the open door of the carriage.

"Don't stay away so long again, Tante Lucille," Juliette implored as she and her friend drew apart.

"Not if it lies in my power," Lucille promised in a choked voice. "Be sure to keep writing."

"I will."

Lucille paused on the step of the carriage and, regardless of Denise's presence, spoke earnestly to Juliette. "Remember, if ever things don't go well and you want to leave Paris, you'll always have a home with Rodolphe and me."

Juliette felt some surprise. Had Lucille guessed how deeply disappointed she had been that Nikolai had gone without leaving her a message? She shook her head gently. "You told me I hadn't looked for an easy path and nothing has changed."

"I should think not. Nothing worth having comes easily, as I know to my cost!" Denise snapped.

Through the open window, Lucille exchanged a smile of understanding with Juliette. Denise had not the least idea what either of them meant.

As soon as Juliette's new wardrobe was finished, Denise launched her into society with a series of dinner parties and musical evenings. From the first, Juliette was included in all the return invitations and many others as well, for people of her own age, mostly the sons and daughters of Denise's acquaintances, drew her into their circle. Everyone knew she was being specially trained at Maison Landelle, and some of the girls, who yearned for a chance to do something with their lives beyond preparing for marriage, declared themselves envious of her chance. But Juliette knew that none of them had any conception of how hard she worked.

She was popular with the young men, her dance program always full, but while she liked two or three of them more than the rest, even permitting a kiss now and then, she remained uninvolved. And since neither she nor any of the other girls was ever without a chaperone nearby, no complications ever arose.

With Lucille gone, there were no more invitations from Prince Vadim. Occasionally Juliette saw him with his wife at the Opéra, or in a restaurant. If they passed her, she was graciously acknowledged with a slight bow, but they never stopped to speak and she knew nobody else who could give her news of Nikolai. As time went by, she was sure he had not returned, and it was a wonder to her why she could not erase his image from her mind. It was even painful to accept that he might have forgotten her by now. Once she pricked her finger while thinking of this as she sewed, but a little drop of spittle luckily erased the tiny spot of blood from the fabric.

When writing to Lucille, Juliette often covered several pages entertainingly about her work as well as her social activities. Once she wrote that nothing had surprised her more about Maison Landelle than to discover it was anything but a peaceful place, and she had been told it was typical of all the other *couture* houses. Whenever a new client came, there was competition for who would become her personal *vendeuse*. The *directrice* had to cope with temperamental clients, who screamed and cried with disappointment when they decided a finished gown did not suit them after all, or if something else had seemingly gone wrong. There were arguments at the sewing tables and squabbles in the pressing room; fitters displayed their fury when some alteration was not done to their specification, and sometimes hair-pulling matches erupted in the mannequins' *cabine*. Occasionally Denise herself stormed through the workrooms.

Juliette viewed it all like a spectator at a circus, intrigued by everything. At first her work was simple and mundane, however rich the fabric, but she was never bored and took pride in the seams and hems and tucks that flowed from under her needle with barely visible stitches. Then she advanced to setting in panels of silk, velvet, and net, as well as those of silver-gilt threaded with diamenté imported from Turkey. Fastening intricate trimmings from lace to bobbin fringes was another of her tasks.

It pleased her that she was no longer given the easier work, and the more difficult her tasks became the more she felt she was passing another milestone. Sometimes she found she was sewing a garment for herself. Denise was increasingly promoting Landelle designs through new outfits for her sister.

"You turn heads wherever we go," Denise exclaimed on one occasion when several orders came in for the design her sister had been wearing the evening before. She often regretted that Juliette could be seen only on weekends or in the evenings after work, but that could not be changed, for the whole future of Maison Landelle depended on her sister's full training. "I think you should have a soft green silk for the Longchamps races."

"Won't I match the track?" Juliette joked. "I could be lost against it."

"You're right," Denise answered, failing to see she was being teased, for she had almost no sense of humor. "Let's make it apricot. All the citrus colors are so dramatic with your hair."

Later Juliette paraded in her apricot ensemble for her fellow seamstresses as she did with all her Landelle clothes. It was when she was wearing a newly finished blue chiffon *robe de dîner* and was waiting for the fitter's assistant to accompany her down to the atelier, that Yvonne Rouband, one of the two red-haired mannequins, came along. They had always exchanged silent smiles, but this time the young woman paused to compliment Juliette.

"That blue suits you very well, Mademoiselle Cladel!" Yvonne was looking very fine herself in a striped gown she had been displaying. They began chatting about the colors they liked to wear.

"Are you ever allowed to wear pink or red?" Juliette asked.

"Not here," Yvonne replied with a laugh, "but I'd love to appear in scarlet, and I have a crimson blouse at home."

"I feel the same yearning for scarlet," Juliette agreed, "and I should think you look splendid in crimson."

"Thank you!"

In her own mind, Juliette thought Yvonne looked marvelous in everything she wore, even the simple clothes in which she came to work, for apart from her good looks she had a beautiful figure, with full breasts and tapering hips.

"As you can see," Juliette continued, "I'm on my way downstairs to display my new gown. Could you give me any tips as to how to do it professionally? I think it would amuse everyone."

"I'd be glad to," Yvonne said willingly, "even though you really need no instruction. So much of being a good mannequin is in the walk. But if you insist, then go slowly along this corridor for a few paces and turn to look back over your shoulder. After another three or four paces, do a half turn and look the other way. I'm talking about display in the limited space between the tables of the ateliers. When coming through the salons there is much more space for a mannequin to move around."

"Is this right?" Juliette asked as she looked back the second time while following instructions.

"Excellent! Do the same again and this time try making the ruffles on the half train dance a little by kicking out slightly as you turn."

Later Juliette gained more tips from Yvonne, who showed her how to swirl a cape, toss a scarf carelessly over the shoulder, the most graceful way to dip one's head in order to display a hat specially created for an ensemble, and even how to hold a parasol to show sleeves to advantage. After that, they chatted whenever they met.

It was when Juliette was sewing in the atelier that she happened to hear Yvonne being discussed by two of the most sharp-tongued seamstresses at another part of the sewing table.

"It's true," one was saying, "she's been an artist's model for some time. I always thought she was vain as a peacock about her figure. It's not enough for her to flaunt herself with clothes on; she has to reveal herself with them off!" They both sniggered.

"How did you find out?" asked another seamstress on the opposite side of the table.

"My sister's new beau knows Yvonne. He works in the Montmartre gallery where the artists hang their work, hoping for a sale. He's seen several nudes of her displayed and sold."

"How could she pose with no clothes on! I'd die of embarrassment!"

"So would I!" There was another explosion of malicious giggles.

Juliette, busy with her sewing, thought to herself that their assumed shock was probably rooted in jealousy. Aude, snipping threads with her scissors, spoke for Juliette's ears alone.

"If these particular seamstresses didn't live at home, they might be thankful to earn a few extra francs in honest work. Yvonne has to find rent for her room and I know she's been saving to bring her sister to Paris."

"But she's Maison Landelle's best mannequin. Isn't she paid accordingly?"

"She may get a little extra, but mannequins are not well paid."

Juliette spoke to Denise about the mannequins' wages that same evening. "Why aren't they paid more?"

Denise raised her eyebrows incredulously. "What a notion! Why should they be? All they have to do is walk about in the most beautiful clothes in Paris. *Mon Dieu!* I wish my daily routine were as easy as theirs!"

"But it can be very hard work too. Just think what they have to put up with when a difficult client explodes with temper."

"I admit that some clients can be cantankerous, but most of the girls would be mannequins for no pay at all, if the truth were known."

"Whatever do you mean?"

Denise regarded her cynically. "I'd have thought that by now you'd have heard enough tittle-tattle in the ateliers to know that by being a mannequin a working girl has a better chance of meeting a rich man than anywhere else. No other kind comes to the salons of a couture house, and three of my mannequins have the most favorable addresses through being mistresses of such men."

Juliette gasped. "I hope you don't take that chance into account when you fix the girls' wages."

"Of course I don't! What a foolish question to ask! I pay the same rates as most of the large couture houses; the others pay far less. So if you're angling for a raise in your own wages, it's too soon yet." Denise quickly held up a placating hand. "All right. I see by your expression that you weren't. Now let's end this discussion before we have a falling-out. Things haven't been going too badly up till now."

Juliette flushed, remembering the many times she had bitten back retaliatory remarks, reminding herself that she and Denise had struck a bargain. No good could come of constant disputes.

Six

THE FIRST TIME Juliette was followed, she was not aware of it at first. She had been given time off from the atelier while a cut finger healed and had decided to go to Rodin's studio on the rue de l'Université in the hope of seeing some of Nikolai's sculptures. It was as she was waiting to cross the street that out of the corner of her eye she caught a woman sketching her from the pavement nearby. Since Paris was full of artists, she would have thought no more about it if the woman had not darted across the street ahead of her to continue drawing as she approached.

It was then that Juliette realized the woman was one of the notorious dress spies who, knowing her identity, had seen she was wearing one of Denise's new autumn designs, perhaps even knew she was the first to wear it. These spies rushed their information to manufacturers, who in turn competed with one another to bring cheap copies into the shops in record time.

Hoping for Denise's sake that the spy had not managed to get all the finer details of the buttons and braiding on the jacket and skirt, Juliette broke into a run and glimpsed the surprised fury on the woman's face as she darted past. Passersby also turned their heads. She ran the rest of the way, and when she reached the studio she darted through the open double doors.

Astonishment as well as breathlessness brought her to a standstill. It was a vast place and the scene was bustling with noisy activity. She had always supposed that sculpting took place in silent concentration, as it would in a private studio. But here several sculptor-assistants were at work clad in linen overalls, and the only sculptress among them wore the traditional triangular cap that kept her hair free of the tiny chippings that flew from the marble she was chiseling. All were engaged in individual tasks. As far as Juliette could see, only two were working from life. One model was an old man and the other a mother cradling a baby in her arms. It was a wonder the child did not wake, for all around was the hammering of scaffolding being erected and sculptures being crated for transport, the rumbling of trollies pushed by work-boys over flagstones, shouting, whistling, and a whole cacophony of sounds echoing and re-echoing among the high rafters. Dominating everything were the great high "Gates of Hell" sculpted by Rodin himself, about which she had read so much. The work had been commissioned by the state and was still unfinished after many years.

Juliette took a few steps forward, feeling singularly out of place in her bright corn-yellow costume amid the muted grays, terra-cottas, whites, and browns of the cavernous studio. One of the sculptors, spotting her, thought she looked like a living flame in her vivid attire with her tawny hair topped by a plumed hat. He was in the process of rearranging a series of wheeled screens that would shield his nude model from general view. Leaving this task, he strolled across to greet her.

"Mademoiselle?" he said inquiringly, certain she was not a model and wondering if she was one of Rodin's latest conquests. In spite of the *maître*'s age and gray beard, women still found him immensely attractive. "I'm Anton Casile. May I be of any assistance? If you want to see the *maître* he's at one of his other studios."

"Oh, no. I've no wish to trouble him. I came hoping to look at some sculptures."

"You've come to the right place, then," he remarked dryly.

She caught his amused glance and smiled. "It's not Monsieur Rodin's masterpieces that I wish to see, but the work by another sculptor, a Russian whom I met a little while ago."

"To my knowledge there's only one Russian who's ever been here. Is it Nikolai Karasvin?"

"Yes. So you know him." It gave her pleasure just to hear his name spoken.

"We've often enjoyed a few bottles of wine while discussing and arguing about art with our fellow artists." So, he thought to himself, she is one of Karasvin's conquests and not the *maître*'s as he'd first supposed. "But he has gone away. Did you know that?"

She nodded, feeling again the painful tug of disappointment. "It's his work I'm interested in," she said deliberately.

"Of course."

She heard the mocking tone in Anton Casile's voice and knew she had failed to convince him. "So, have I made this visit in vain?" she persisted.

"I'm not sure." Anton turned to speak to one of the work-boys going past with a bucket of wet clay. "Marcel, are any of Karasvin's pieces still here?"

"There's the 'Athlete' and a couple of others."

"Put that bucket down then, and show them to our visitor." Anton smiled at her again. "Mind you don't slip on the wet clay, mademoiselle. It gets dropped around when we're working and isn't always cleared away as quickly as it should be."

"Thank you. I'll take care."

Marcel led the way and Juliette followed, looking about her at this strange world of marble, bronze, and plaster.

"There you are!" Marcel said finally, with a sweep of his hand. "That's the 'Athlete' and next to it is 'Sea-Bather.' The third one is covered with cloths because it's unfinished."

"But the cloths are damp. When is he expected back?" Hope had made her voice tremulous.

"Don't ask me, mademoiselle. It's my job to keep unfinished works damp so the clay doesn't crumble away. I'll go on doing it until the *maître* or somebody else tells me to stop. I'll leave you now. You'll find the way out, won't you?"

Left on her own, Juliette lost all sense of time, even the din of the studio seeming to fade away. Both the finished works were cast in bronze, the athlete caught in a last strenuous effort to pass the finish line, his face tortured and every straining muscle of his nude body taut with this final burst of energy and power. Stark and dramatic, the figure looked as if at any moment it might speed from its base into the distance.

The sea-bather was a woman, lusty and seductive and beautifully shaped, sitting nude with one leg tucked under her, her back arched and her elbows high as she combed back her wet hair with her fingers. This figure was as tranquil and at ease as the other was alive with furious movement, but in no way was it overshadowed. Each piece commanded attention in its own right. Juliette studied each one for a long time. Finally, with a soft sigh of appreciation, she moved away, glancing again at the covered sculpture as she wondered what was concealed and if it would ever be finished. Then she made her way back through the great studio, stopping only to study the anguish and torment and beauty of the figures that gave Rodin's gates such splendor.

She did not see Anton Casile again and guessed he was at work behind the screens. When she emerged into the sunshine, there was no sign of the spy, and she walked home slowly, her mind full of the magnificent work she had just seen.

A few days later Juliette needed some fabric for binding and, seeing that the apprentices were all busy, went to fetch it herself. No usable scrap of fabric was ever thrown away, and pieces left over by the cutters went into large lidded chests. She knew that the fabric she was working on had been popular of late and she expected to find what she wanted very easily.

It was as she was sorting through one of the chests that she happened to find a narrowly pleated length of silk in what at first looked coppery in color. When she pulled it out, it swirled about her hands like a soft snake, its sheen creating a shimmer of gold and coral. Fabrics were often pleated in various widths, but this was entirely unusual, the pleats so narrow as to give the illusion of a deep rippling of the silk. She knew she had never seen the original garment, for she would not have forgotten it. Almost without thinking, she held the soft fabric to her cheek, where it seemed to cling in a caress.

Fascinated, she began to search in the chest to see if there were any more pieces. Three more lengths came to light, and she realized she was holding the sections of a kind of gown that might have been worn by a woman of ancient Greece. She could only suppose it was one of Monsieur Pierre's designs that had been made up and discarded, although it was not his usual style at all.

Taking the pieces with her, Juliette went to the cutting room. "Do any of you know anything about these cast-out remnants?" she asked the cutters and their apprentices.

All shook their heads. She was more successful with one of the seamstresses who specialized in pleating.

"Yes, I remember it," the woman said. "About a year ago Madame la Baronne called me to her office. She and Monsieur Pierre were trying to discover how the pleating in that fabric was done after it had been unpicked. In all my years I've never seen narrow pleats quite like those. Whoever made it must have some trick unknown to the rest of us."

"There are some eyelet holes. What was it laced with?"

"Thin cords rolled of the same silk."

Juliette returned to the chest where she had found the pieces but could not find the original lacings. She could only suppose they had been thrown away.

"What are you doing, Juliette?" It was Madame Tabard.

Juliette straightened up. "I came originally to find a scrap of fabric for binding, but I became interested in this pleated silk."

"You haven't time to waste. Put it back and take whatever it is you're looking for. Next time send an apprentice."

Juliette was highly reluctant to relinquish the silk, lest somebody decide to cut it up before she could retrieve it again. Swiftly she rolled the pieces together and thrust them deep down at the side of the chest.

She could hardly wait to get home and ask Denise about the pleated garment that had been so ruthlessly taken apart. When she had changed for dinner she went to the garden room where her sister sat in a cushioned basket chair reading a newspaper. The doors were open to the green lawn, the flower beds, and the evening air. She paused to greet her sister.

Denise answered without taking her eyes from the newspaper. "What a lot of depressing news there is to read these days. A runaway horse killed an old woman on the Rue Royale; there's been an earthquake in Japan; the Kaiser is enlarging his army; and some peasants have created more trouble in Russia."

Juliette sat down in a neighboring basket chair. She always read any snippet of news about Russia in case the Karasvins should be mentioned, but that had not happened yet. Instead she had learned a great deal about a vast country that had barely piqued her interest in past geography lessons. *Le Figaro* had reported brutal arrests there and the merciless prison sentences imposed on the pathetic-sounding troublemakers. It made grim reading. The Tsar could take a lesson from what had happened to Louis XVI of

France, although such a tempest of revolution was unlikely to flare up anywhere ever again.

"Today I found some most unusual pleated silk in one of the chests," Juliette began.

"Did you?" Denise answered absently, turning to the social column. She liked to keep abreast of any news concerning her clients.

"I was told the manner in which it was pleated remains a mystery."

Denise lowered the newspaper to look at her. "You must mean Fortuny's Delphos robe. I managed to get one from his Venice workshop. Not under my own name, of course. I didn't want the word spreading that I was at all interested in what he was making, but I had heard remarks here and there about his garments and wanted to examine one for myself."

"I didn't know he designed clothes for women other than for the stage."

"He doesn't. They're just shapeless nonsense. They're supposed to be inspired by some ancient Delphic statue, but anyone in *haute couture* can see that they are in no way related to fashion. In any case, what can he hope to achieve stuck so far away in Venice? Nobody would go all that way for an inferior garment when Paris offers only the best. In my opinion the Venetian air has addled Fortuny's brain."

"I'd like to buy that silk for myself," Juliette said. It was the custom at Maison Landelle to let the seamstresses purchase surplus remnants at a reasonable price when the fabric was at least two years out of season or rejected for some other reason. "I realize it's only been in the chest for probably less than a year."

"That doesn't count in this case. It was not my fabric originally and it should have been burnt. I don't know why it wasn't. So let Madame Tabard set the price, and remember I never want to see it again. That means not using it to make one of your pretty little evening purses as you have with some of the other scraps you've bought. Make shoe bags or cover some coat hangers. Anything that is normally out of my sight."

Juliette smiled. "I promise!"

She knew Denise hated to be beaten by anybody or anything, and the sight of the pleated silk would be anathema to her, reminding her of a mystery she had failed to solve.

For weeks the silk lay untouched in its tissue paper in one of

Juliette's drawers. She had not forgotten it, for it was linked haunt-ingly in her mind with the ethereal beauty of the Knossos veils and, far more important, with the last time she had seen Nikolai Karas-vin.

Afterward, Juliette would never be entirely sure when she had reached the decision to join the pieces of silk together. She hap-pened to be alone at home on an evening when Denise was invited out and she went upstairs after her solitary dinner to take the silk from the drawer. Carefully she spread the pieces out on her bed and was able to see exactly how the sewing should be done.

It could not have been simpler. She re-sewed the original seams, and the result was a cylindrical robe that would hang straight from the shoulders when laced through the tiny, exquisitely bound eye-lets, leaving the neckline bateau-shaped and giving the effect of bat-like sleeves. On another evening she laced the shoulders with rolled silk ribbons. Then she took off her own dress, but hesitated before putting on the new garment. Surely her petticoat would spoil the line of the gown. She took it off and on impulse removed everything else too.

She slipped on the gown. Even as she crossed the room to the full-length cheval glass she gasped at her own reflection. She saw that the tiny pleats of the Delphos robe clung shimmeringly to the contours of her figure without any violation of modesty, revealing and yet skillfully concealing while emphasizing her femininity and the freedom of her body beneath.

What Fortuny had begun with the veils, he had brought to fru-ition in creating this glorious, deceptively simple, yet sensual gown, which was fine enough to pull through the proverbial wedding ring, yet was first and foremost a celebration of the female figure. Even the rich copper-gold of the silk glowed and deepened with the slightest movement, the hem gently rippling. Whenever she stood completely still the pleats of the skirt curved slightly inward from calf to ankle, almost like a mermaid's tail, while the hem spread out on the floor and concealed her feet. She marveled again at the genius of the designer. This exquisite gown made all her other evening gowns, with their boned bodices and extravagant decoration, seem archaic.

Yet she would never be able to wear it. Not only would Denise be offended, but she herself had promised to keep the silk forever out of her sister's sight. After twirling once more before the mirror, she took off the Delphos robe to lay it back in the drawer. To her surprise, now that the pieces had become a garment again, the pleats coiled like a skein and she could see this was the perfect way to keep it uncrushed.

In the morning Juliette went early to work and searched again in the chest. She thought that perhaps the designer's label might have been thrown in with the pieces. Unfortunately she did not find it.

Seven

THROUGHOUT HER TIME in Paris, Juliette had corresponded with Gabrielle Rousset. Their exchange of letters was infrequent, each being busy in her own activities. Then Gabrielle wrote of Derek Townsend, a thirty-year-old English merchant banker whom she had met in Monte Carlo. She said they had fallen deeply in love.

Juliette was pleased for her, but the courtship was not running smoothly, hampered by Derek's business commitments, which kept him in England for weeks at a time, and the determined opposition of Gabrielle's mother. Her father, always at loggerheads with his wife, apparently approved. It was an impasse that would prove difficult to overcome.

When Juliette had been at Maison Landelle exactly a year, she was upgraded to first-degree seamstress. She had been doing advanced work for some time, and the main difference now was that she received instructions as to what adjustments were needed after fittings from the fitters themselves. She and the other seniors then delegated work within the capability of lower-grade seamstresses, keeping the most complicated work for themselves.

"Madame Tabard has always had every confidence in your ability," Denise said one evening at dinner in a rare moment of praise. "She would have upgraded you earlier if she could have been sure it would not cause dissention among two or three other seamstresses waiting to step up."

"It was the right decision." Juliette was thankful she had not been given priority sooner. Her relationship with most of her fellow workers remained good, but it was a delicate balance.

A triumphant letter from Gabrielle the following day gave the good news that finally she and Derek were to marry, thanks to her father, who had threatened her mother that he would give them permission to elope if she persisted in opposing the match. Madame Rousset's objections had crumbled in the face of the scandal that would have resulted.

So we are to meet again at last, dear friend, Gabrielle continued in her neat hand. *Mother and I are coming to Paris for my bridal gown and trousseau. She is making the best of the situation and now intends to outshine all her friends with her daughter's wedding! My only regret is that we are to get everything from Maison Worth. I had hoped that you would sew my bridal gown, but she is insistent and my father says we must try to avoid any more terrible scenes.*

Although Juliette explained the situation, Denise took offense immediately, seeing the Roussets' decision as a slight to herself.

"I would have thought," she said sarcastically, "that since you and Gabrielle were supposed to be such friends the order should have come to Maison Landelle. When I think how I allowed you to visit the Roussets when you were at the convent, I'm even more surprised!"

Nothing Juliette could say would pacify her.

The reunion between Juliette and Gabrielle took place at four o'clock on a warm June Saturday afternoon. They met at the English Tea Rooms near the Opéra and Juliette was already seated at a table when her friend arrived in a primrose muslin gown and pretty hat. Juliette sprang to her feet and Gabrielle's brown eyes lit up joyfully in recognition. She hastened to Juliette and they embraced exuberantly, laughing and talking at the same time.

"It's been so long, Juliette!"

"How wonderful to see you again!"

"It seems like yesterday and yet so much has happened!"

When they sat down, Juliette would have ordered tea with lemon and pastries, but Gabrielle shook her head. "I wanted to meet you here so we could have an English tea together." To the waitress she said, "A pot of tea for two with milk not lemon, scones and jam, and also fruitcake." Almost shyly she faced Juliette again. "I'm trying to become as English as possible in readiness for living in London, although Derek says he wouldn't want me to change in any way, because he loves my French accent when I speak English. Oh, how I wish I'd studied harder during English classes at the convent."

"I'm sure he loves your accent. And my English is a little rusty too."

"No, you always had a gift for languages—not only English but Italian and Spanish."

"You exaggerate!" Juliette laughed. "We only had Spanish for half a term when those two Spanish nuns came to study Sister Berthe's special embroidery. The other two languages I did enjoy learning. Have you met any of your future in-laws?"

"Not yet. Derek's mother and his brothers and their wives are all coming to the wedding. I wanted you to be my bridesmaid, but"—here Gabrielle shook her head, exhibiting some of her old sadness—"I'm to have six of my cousins and nobody else. You see, I've had to compromise on several issues."

"I understand," Juliette reassured her sympathetically. "Yet the worst is over. You can look to the future now."

Gabrielle smiled again. "What of you, Juliette? Never have you written of any man being important in your life."

"There isn't anyone. I thought there might be once, but nothing came of it." Juliette shrugged regretfully.

"Did you fall in love?"

Juliette shook her head quickly. "I didn't mention anything about love. It was just someone I found attractive."

Gabrielle listened attentively to her friend's account of the brief episode with the Russian. "At least you've found out that one man can overshadow everything, even though you thought yourself dedicated to a career."

"I am still! That didn't change!"

With a wave of her hand, Gabrielle dismissed the protest. "After Derek and I are married, I want you to come and stay with us in London. He knows so many people and I'll watch out for a charming bachelor and make sure you meet him straightaway."

Juliette laughed. "Are you turning into a matchmaker already? I thought one had to be a plump, mature matron to fill that role. But," she added humorously, eyeing the tea being set before them by the waitress, "I think you've every chance of becoming the right size very quickly if you indulge in a spread like this every day you're in England!''

They saw each other again several times before Gabrielle and her mother left Paris. Denise, still harboring her pique, had her petty moment of revenge when the wedding invitations arrived. She declined hers and forestalled Juliette's expressing a wish to attend.

"It will be at the height of the rush, when clients want everything ready for the autumn season. No other first-degree seamstress would be granted time off just then, and when we first arranged your training you yourself insisted that you were never to be granted any special privileges."

Juliette accepted the situation, but it was a bitter disappointment for her and the bride.

September was as busy as Denise had foretold. Juliette was putting the final stitches to an evening gown when she happened to glance toward the interior windows of the atelier, which looked out into a hallway and the cutting rooms beyond. Yvonne's sister, who had come to Paris some time ago, was going past. Although Juliette knew her by sight, she had never met her. She wondered if the girl had come to apply for work and then thought no more about it as her sewing absorbed her again. Later, over dinner, when Denise's careful tone showed she had something on her mind, Juliette still did not make any immediate connection with Yvonne or her sister.

"There's something I'd like you to do for me," Denise said, toying with her wineglass as if uncertain how her request would be received.

Juliette was interested. "What is it?" she asked.

"I've an important Russian client coming to Maison Landelle tomorrow. She has light auburn hair very similar to yours and she'll only view clothes displayed by mannequins with the same coloring."

"You've Yvonne and Isabelle."

"That's just it. Unfortunately Yvonne is away sick and, as you once told me she'd taught you how to display clothes, I'd like you to fill the gap temporarily."

"So that's why Yvonne's sister was in the building today! Did she say what was the matter?"

"At first she said it was a bad cold, but the *directrice* had her suspicions already, and a few astute questions brought out the truth. Yvonne has had an abortion.''

''Poor Yvonne!'' Juliette exclaimed compassionately.

Denise frowned impatiently. ''Don't be sentimental! There's no excuse. Whatever trouble Yvonne is in, she brought it on herself. Any woman can say no.''

''You're not going to sack her?''

''I think so. I don't want her coming back tearful and too weak to stand for hours and all the rest of it. It's happened with other mannequins over the years, and usually I find it best to get rid of them. It would never do, either, for clients to suspect what has happened.''

''There's no reason they should if Yvonne takes enough time to recover. I'll stand in for her as long as you like on condition you don't sack her.''

Denise glowered. ''One can't be softhearted in business. I could get red wigs for some of the other mannequins.''

''I don't think that would please your client.''

''Very well.'' Denise gave in ungraciously. ''Yvonne did teach you the tricks of a mannequin's trade, and that in itself is helping in this crisis. There'll be no need for you to display clothes to anyone other than my Russian client. Her uncle is Prince Vadim. Although you went to his house once you won't have met Countess Anna Dolohova, because it's over two years since she was last in Paris.''

Juliette drew in her breath. No doubt the prince had any number of nieces, but could this woman be Nikolai's sister? Although it was foolish to still be interested in him, he continued to haunt her. Sometimes, lost in realms of fantasy, she thought it might be because he still thought of her; but in the cold light of day, that possibility had to be dismissed.

''Tell me about the countess,'' she requested.

''She was widowed soon after her last visit and is enormously rich. The Russian aristocracy never heed the cost of anything, and she has always spent a fortune with me, which is why I want nothing to go wrong. This time I'm expecting an even larger order, because she'll be replenishing her entire wardrobe after two years in black. It means she must only be shown clothes in subdued colors, because Russians still observe a third year of mourning, but there need be no restrictions on the actual designs and the evening gowns will be décolleté.''

"I'll do my best for you," Juliette promised.

"I know you will."

In the morning Juliette had to try on some of the clothes that would have been shown by Yvonne and was viewed in them by the *directrice* as well as the countess's *vendeuse* and her fitter, all wanting to be sure that everything fit well. Fortunately, Juliette's measurements were virtually identical to Yvonne's and all was satisfactory.

"What's the countess like to deal with, Hélène?" Juliette asked the *vendeuse* who was helping her out of the last gown. Hélène was always pleasant, unlike some of the other *vendeuses* and also the fitters, who seemed to take upon themselves the status of their clients. Although Hélène was *vendeuse* to two British princesses and three duchesses, who were considered equal to Russian royalty, she gave herself no airs. Members of minor European royal families came next in importance, but French women whose titles went far back into history, gave special status to those in *couture* houses who attended them.

Hélène put the discarded gown on a padded hanger. "The countess is very charming and dignified, but if she's displeased she's a terror. So watch out!"

"Thanks for the warning!"

By now clients had begun to arrive. When Juliette went into the mannequins' *cabine,* the girls were all in various stages of dress and undress. Dressers' nimble fingers fastened hooks and eyes, smoothed down the folds of skirts, and dealt with the tiny loops of sleeve buttons. Their assistants darted about, fetching clothes from racks, shoes of the right color, and whatever accessories were needed. Yet it was organized chaos, except when a mannequin's squeal told of a glove momentarily misplaced or a hat pin that had been driven in too hard. The senior dresser sighted Juliette.

"Over here! The hairdresser is waiting for you."

Juliette's hair was brushed until she thought it must surely pop from its roots and then to her dismay was dressed over padding to achieve the exaggerated pompadour that fashionable women favored. When the rest of her long tresses had been pinned into a coil like a rose on the top of her head she was claimed by a dresser named Sophie.

"It's day gowns and calling costumes first for you and Isabelle."

When the two of them were dressed, they had to wait for Countess Dolohova to arrive. Isabelle, in gray velvet, buffed her nails, while Juliette, in cinnamon silk, observed the little dramas that occurred when shoes pinched, a corset lace broke, or a mannequin gave vent to wrath after parading for over an hour in the same gown for a client who still could not make up her dithering mind. Then there came the signal from Hélène that she had brought the countess into the best of the individual viewing salons. Juliette, who was to go in first, stepped forward.

"Good luck!" Isabelle said.

Juliette gave her a grateful smile, but as she entered through the draped archway to the private viewing salon a spasm of joy hurtled through her. Nikolai, his back half-turned toward her, hat and cane in hand, stood talking to the countess, who sat gracefully against the tasseled cushions of a sofa, her sable coat thrown back from her shoulders. Clad in black, Anna Dolohova's rich tawny hair set off a triangular, finely boned face, a thin, arrogant nose, curved brows, and darkened lashes that gave drama to her violet-blue eyes.

"We'll meet later then, Anna," Nikolai was saying. "It will be good to see Boris back in Paris again." He grinned at her impudently. "I'll leave you now to your orgy of new clothes."

"Don't tease!" she replied good-humoredly, making a little pretense of kicking out her foot at him. "You never change."

"You may count on that," he gave back in the same vein. "*Adieu* until this evening."

He drew away, intending to go out the door to the reception area, but he took no more than a single step. He had caught sight of Juliette just as her hands jerked up involuntarily to make her presence known to him. But his reaction was not at all what she had expected. For no more than a second or two there was dazzled disbelief in his eyes, but this was immediately swept away as a glacial fury engulfed him. "You didn't write!"

His outburst was equally astonishing to the countess. "Nikolai!" she murmured in protest. "What are you saying?"

He did not seem to hear her, but took a step toward Juliette. "At least you could have given me the address of this place if you wished to keep me at a distance when I returned! I didn't have to know where you lived!"

She was too bewildered to be angry. "I don't know what you're talking about! How could I write? I had no address and in any case when you left Paris I'd no idea if you'd ever be back. Not even your uncle knew."

"But I sent you a letter telling you why I'd been called away. I asked Madame Garnier to—" He broke off as realization dawned on both of them. "So she didn't forward it to you as I requested?"

"No," Juliette replied quietly. She felt shattered at such a betrayal of trust by Lucille, even though she knew that her friend would have had her best interests at heart.

He was as devastated as she. "I must ask you something, Juliette," he said, forgetting he had never addressed her by her Christian name before. "Would you have written to me if you had received my letter?"

"Oh, yes!" she replied without hesitation, realizing that throughout the past eighteen months neither of them had forgotten the other.

On the sofa, the countess gave a discreet little cough to remind them of her presence. Nikolai became animated at once and took Juliette by the arm to draw her forward. "I'm delighted to introduce you to my sister Anna, Countess Dolohova."

As the introductions took place, Juliette could see Anna's astonishment beneath the surface politeness. For her, being introduced to a mannequin was akin to being expected to exchange social pleasantries with a servant. Nikolai, oblivious to his sister's reaction, went on to tell her that he and Juliette had last spoken in a theater foyer.

"We discussed Fortuny. Isn't that so, Juliette?" He wanted her to know he remembered everything.

Juliette nodded. "I've seen nothing of his on the stage since then."

"Neither have I. But that can be put right very quickly. He has created several lighting innovations at the Opéra in the new production opening next week. He also had some influence on the costumes, which should please you. Anna shall be chaperone. Won't you, Anna?" He had tossed the question over his shoulder, taking an affirmative answer for granted as he continued talking to Juliette. "So tell me your sister's name and where I can call on her to ask permission to escort you as we arranged at our last meeting. Would she be at home if I went there as soon as I leave here?"

Juliette, her eyes sparkling, could guess the further consternation of the countess at being expected to chaperone a mannequin. "No, my sister isn't to be found at home at this time of day, but she's not far away. Denise happens to be the *couturière* of Maison Landelle and is in her office now."

Anna spoke up in surprise. "Do you mean the Baronne de Landelle? I'm well acquainted with her! But I didn't know she had a sister." From the tone of her voice, Juliette could tell the countess was relieved to find she might just be socially acceptable after all.

"I was away at a convent school for a long time. In fact, I saw Nikolai for the first time on the day I came home to Paris." Briefly, Juliette explained that she was standing in for a mannequin who was indisposed and that normally she was sewing garments and not displaying them.

"But why are you a seamstress?" Anna inquired incredulously. "I should have thought the baronne would have found—well—a pastime more suited to you."

"But it isn't a pastime. It's my career."

"I suppose you come into the category of the New Woman!"

Nikolai interrupted, knowing how his sister resented her own lack of freedom during her marriage and subsequent mourning. "I admire you for it, Juliette! It's time women gained recognition of their rights."

Anna had become impatient with this interlude. "You must go now, Nikolai. You are holding up everything with your presence. Go and see the baronne. Mademoiselle Cladel has been delayed long enough."

He turned to Juliette. "Say you're not otherwise engaged this evening and will join Anna and myself when we go out to dine. An old friend will be coming too if he gets back to Paris in time."

"Yes, I'm able to come." Nothing could have prevented her from accepting.

He wrote down her telephone number and address in his diary and she told him where to find Denise's office. Then he left the salon, pausing at the door to look back at her. His satisfaction at the outcome of their reunion was as transparent in his expression as it was in hers.

"Now," Anna said as the door closed after him, "there should be no more delays. So let me see what you're wearing, Mademoiselle Cladel."

But as Juliette paraded to and fro, Anna's mind was on more than the gown. She had been astonished by her brother's behavior. He had been like a man in love. But why? He'd had other women far more alluring and never shown his heart so transparently. Maybe he found Juliette more of a challenge than the rest, sensing a difficult chase to get what he wanted from her. He had even spoken of her, although not by name, one snowy afternoon in Russia when he was particularly cast down by the circumstances controlling his life. Nikolai had been in the studio of his apartment within their father's palace. She herself had come home for a while after selling the house near St. Petersburg where she had known only unhappiness with her late husband. Nikolai was working in clay, sculpting a young woman's head. He saw she had brought him some mail, which she had taken from a servant on her way upstairs.

"Is there anything from Paris?" he asked at once, his hands becoming still.

She glanced through the letters and shook her head. "No. Were you expecting something important?"

He resumed his task and did not heed her question. "I'm impatient to get back to France. There's work at the studio I left unfinished. So often the momentum goes if a project is left too long."

"As soon as Father is confident there'll be no more disturbing uprisings in the district, you'll be free to return."

"Free!" he echoed bitterly. "I'm as tied as any peasant to the land."

She sympathized with his predicament, but in her opinion it was infinitely better than hers had been at any time until widowhood mercifully released her and left her a rich woman. At least when he was away from home Nikolai enjoyed the liberty that was a man's privilege, was even allowed to study sculpture as he wished. She knew their father had believed it was a passing whim, a mere excuse to sow wild oats in the most exciting of all cities before settling down to marriage at home and a more ordered way of life.

Instead, Nikolai had proved himself dedicated from the start, and she had understood better than anyone how torn he was between the creative work he loved and the duties imposed on him by their uncle Vadim, which involved an entirely different, intensely social existence. His being attached to the embassy was a compromise settled by the Tsar himself when their father, fearing that Nikolai might break away forever, had anxiously sought the advice of his son's imperial godfather.

Anna wanted to cheer up her brother. "Come now," she urged consolingly, "things aren't as bad as all that. Remember it's in your own interest as much as Father's that matters are kept under control here. After all, it is you who'll inherit everything one day."

He shrugged impatiently, pausing to wipe his hands on a damp rag, as if the blackness of his mood had come between him and his work. "If Father had used his influence to lessen the peasants' unbearable suffering, these crises might not occur."

Politics bored Anna. She thought he was about to elaborate on his theme and was quick to divert him. "Things change here, there, and everywhere. Be patient. Life is full of unexpected happenings." Somewhat smugly she had smoothed the black taffeta ruffles of her sleeve. "Who would ever have anticipated that Leonid would die as conveniently as he did?"

Nikolai, who had been her confidant since childhood, regarded her with a flash of macabre humor. "I've never asked you, but did you poison him?"

Surprise made her burst out laughing. "No, of course not!" Then more soberly she added, "But often I was sorely tempted. If I'd known how to keep suspicion from myself, I'd have done it."

"He would have deserved it. It sickens me to see you in mourning for that brute."

She shrugged resignedly. "It does me too, but I have to bow to convention for Father's sake, as well as the rest of the family. But as soon as I'm out of mourning, I shall emerge like a butterfly from a chrysalis." She had been circling the clay bust as she spoke, but came to a standstill as she studied it more closely, and there was curiosity in her voice as she commented on it. "This is going to be very fine. You've had an interesting model for this work."

"But not a professional model. She's a girl I met only briefly in Paris and I'm relying on my memory." He had begun working on the head again as if mention of the girl had drawn him back.

Now as Anna studied Juliette's face, she knew that this was the girl he had been sculpting from memory. Then she jerked her thoughts back to the present as Juliette left and another mannequin entered the room. How dull these garments looked!

It soon became apparent to Juliette and Isabelle as they alternately displayed one ensemble after another that the countess was becoming increasingly disappointed. Nothing was pleasing her. Once Hélène caught Juliette's eye expressively. This was followed by a telling grimace from Isabelle as she passed Juliette under the archway. They all knew how furious Denise would be if the countess should leave without ordering anything.

Suddenly, while being hooked up at the back in the first of the evening gowns, Juliette realized what was wrong. Anna Dolohova was bored with mourning clothes and somber shades. Maybe she felt she had shown respect for the late Count Dolohova long enough! It did not matter that any garment she viewed might be in the color she had requested, because in her present mood she saw only bleakness.

There was no time for Juliette to change out of what she had on, but she looked about quickly and saw a mannequin in a scarlet and gold spangled cape coming from another of the salons.

"Quick!" she said to her dresser. "Find something vivid for Isabelle to wear next! And for me after that, or else there won't be a single sale!"

As she swept forward in a rustle of olive green satin to parade again, she whisked the scarlet cape from the mannequin, ignored her shrieks of protest, and whirled it about her shoulders with a dazzling sparkle of spangles. Hélène looked at her in horror as she appeared, but Anna's whole attitude changed.

"That's delicious! Why has everything else been so dreary? That scarlet looks wonderful with your hair, as it will with mine." It was the first time she had addressed Juliette throughout the showing and her face had suddenly become animated.

"Reds are fine for us if they have an orangy tint and are carefully coordinated." Juliette swirled the cape away from her shoulders, letting it spread out like a vivid petal as she displayed the gown, and even that met with Anna's approval as it was viewed in a new light. "One of the day gowns I showed you is also available in russet red. Would you like to see it? There's another in emerald, and many of the ensembles are in bright topaz, apricot, coral, and a lovely pumpkin shade."

"I'll see them all."

Juliette thought to herself that the countess was like a woman desperate for the sight of a flower garden. Hélène was still bewildered by this turn of events, but satisfied that everything was going to be well after all.

Afterward, Denise was similarly pleased, although she did not like having to admit that her original judgment had been wrong. She sent for Juliette to come to her office.

"You used your wits in the nick of time, Juliette. The countess is returning tomorrow to discuss with me the clothes she liked best, and it looks as though her order will be three times larger than last time. But there is something else. Count Karasvin came to see me as you know he intended." Denise hesitated, getting up from her desk to come round and face Juliette. "I'd prefer you didn't go out with these people this evening. He's not the right company for you. Surely you have enough beaux in our own circle to please you?"

"What is your objection?"

"The Karasvins are selfish, extravagant people used to having their own way in everything, powerful as a result of the feudal laws in their own country and equally so through their vast fortunes everywhere else. I don't want your head turned."

"I can't think of anything more unlikely," Juliette said confidently.

"I could still exert my authority and forbid you to go."

Juliette knew it was an idle threat. Denise's sisterly concern, although genuine, could not outweigh the importance to her of not offending the countess on the brink of a huge order.

"You mustn't worry about me, Denise. To reassure you, I'll tell you where we went and everything else when I come home. Well, almost everything," she added teasingly.

Denise did not smile. "I'll be home later than you, because I'm attending a civic banquet with Monsieur Noiret and there's dancing afterward followed by a champagne breakfast. You can tell me all about it later tomorrow."

When Denise left the house at seven o'clock with Monsieur Noiret, a distinguished banker in his fifties, Juliette went upstairs to get ready. As arranged, Denise's lady's maid had laid out the gown she had chosen for the evening, complete with shoes and accessories, but Juliette had everything put away again.

"I've decided not to wear that gown," she said. "No, you needn't wait. Whatever I choose will have fastenings I can manage myself."

The lady's maid was puzzled, but in the wardrobe there were at least four evening gowns with tiny buttons at the front.

"So don't wait up for me," Juliette added. "Just set an alarm clock for the baronne's return."

"Yes, mademoiselle."

As soon as the door had closed, Juliette crossed the room and turned the key. From the first moment of Nikolai's invitation she had known what she would wear and at the same time keep the promise she had made to Denise. Her sister being out of the house had made the whole operation easier than she had expected. Swiftly she pulled open a bottom drawer and lifted the Delphos robe from its tissue paper. Briefly she held it close to her, almost in an embrace of reunion, and then put it on. It seemed to her more beautiful than ever, the tiny pleats shimmering about her in changing hues of coral-red, copper, and gold as the light played on them. The neckline when tied was not low, but left the base of her neck scooped free. Her only jewelry was a pair of gold earrings Lucille had given her one birthday.

She had a variety of Landelle evening jackets and capes, but she did not want to wear anything that would be out of harmony with the gown. Instead she took a wrap of creamy diaphanous chiffon, which she had bought herself that day because it was as much like a Knossos scarf as she could find. Full of anticipation, she went downstairs to await Nikolai's arrival. The doorbell rang even as she reached the hall.

Eight

NIKOLAI SAW HER as soon as he was admitted. She stood poised at the foot of the staircase, the lights of the chandelier flaming her hair, her silken gown agleam over the contours of her figure. He went toward her, his admiration apparent in his eyes.

"You look wonderful!"

"This is my Delphos robe by Fortuny!" Happily and unself-consciously, she twirled around for him, the tiny pleats swirling out in their gleaming fire colors.

He stood regarding her with deep pleasure. "Have you been all the way to Venice to buy it since I saw you this afternoon?"

"Only in spirit," she declared merrily, her mood matching his.

"I want to hear all about it." He handed her a boxed corsage and watched her take out a spray of the same ivory orchids he had given her before. Her whole face revealed her delight as she pinned them on.

"These are my favorite orchids, Nikolai!" She wondered if he would guess that her preference dated from the first corsage he had sent her.

"I have to tell you there's been a change of plan. My sister can't come with us after all."

"Is that so?" She met his eyes. Denise had been most strict about her chaperonage that evening, but she saw he had no doubt that she would go with him. Instantly, she made up her mind. "In that case, there is no need for us to delay any longer."

He swept her out of the house to the waiting taxicab, and within minutes they were being driven away, the light of the street lamps flickering across their faces.

"I've booked a table at Larue's in the Rue Royale," he said as they talked.

"I've never been there."

"I'm not surprised. Until very recently it was just another restaurant, but it's been bought by Monsieur Nignon, who was formerly a renowned chef himself, and now it offers the best food in all Paris. Russian dishes are a specialty."

"Are we to dine *à la russe?*" she asked eagerly.

"If you would like that."

"Yes, indeed!"

When they arrived at Larue's it was Monsieur Nignon himself, black hair smooth as paint and a red carnation in his silk lapel, who came forward to welcome them.

"Bon soir, Count Karasvin! Mademoiselle!" There followed two deep bows. "What an honor! My best table awaits you."

An orchestra was playing light music, and the restaurant with its white and gold décor, an abundance of mirrors, and seating upholstered in rose velvet was well patronized. As they were led to their table, Juliette did not notice at first what an effect her appearance was having on those around her. She was used to admiring glances, but it began to dawn on her that this was something different. People were staring, knives and forks stilled, glasses remaining poised in mid-air, and the sound of hushed voices filled the room. It was her Delphos robe! She had let the chiffon wrap waft away from her shoulders when entering the restaurant and could imagine how the light was playing across the pleats to create their unique effect.

A group of young army officers, dining alone, sighted her as she approached and when she drew level they sprang to their feet with flirtatious grins, raising their glasses in tribute. Nikolai saw her acknowledge their homage with one of her generous smiles. He was not in the least surprised that she was dazzling everyone—and certainly shocking some—in this revolutionary gown, which proclaimed her to be free of the whalebone corsets, padding, and layers of petticoats no other woman in the room was without.

When they were seated at their table, which was set in a recessed alcove amid a bower of flowers, Nikolai ordered apéritifs. Juliette had not expected to attract so much attention. There was every likelihood that someone present had recognized her and that, sooner or later, Denise might hear about it, but that was unimportant now. Nothing should cast a shadow over the happiness of this evening.

The apéritifs had been served, and Monsieur Nignon returned after a suitable interval to discuss the menu with them. There was to be caviar served with tiny glasses of ice-cold vodka and also borscht, since Juliette had never tasted it, but made according to his own recipe into a soup supreme. When each of the remaining dishes had been rhapsodically described, Juliette turned her attention back to Nikolai.

"I know it was the study of sculpture that brought you to Paris originally, but don't you miss your homeland as well?"

"At times," he admitted with a frown, "but I resented having to leave Paris as abruptly as I did so soon after meeting you. Unfortunately I had no choice." He went on to explain what had happened and how it had taken time before he was able to return.

"You did right to stay, but how do you reconcile your creative work with the demands made on your time by your embassy duties?"

His jaw set grimly. "It's a compromise I made with the Tsar himself when I was considerably younger. Now I'm honor-bound to uphold it."

She was sympathetic. "I was also compelled into a compromise at my sister's insistence, but it's possible to live through these restrictions. They can't last forever."

For a moment he hesitated, as if about to disagree with her, but then his brow cleared as he smiled again. "Enough serious talk for this evening. We're here to enjoy ourselves. What was it you were going to tell me about your Fortuny gown? The designer himself would have been a proud man if he could see you in it."

Juliette made Nikolai laugh as she described how she had discovered it in pieces and sewn it together again. "So," she concluded merrily, "this is the first time I've worn it!"

"A perfect choice for our celebration!"

She raised her eyebrows quizzically. "Is this a celebration?"

He leaned forward. "You know it is. Today we found each other again!"

Although he spoke lightly, there was a depth of feeling behind his words. He would have said more, but two waiters arrived to serve the caviar, and the vodka was poured into thimble-sized glasses.

Every course proved to be as delicious as promised. If other diners left and more came, they were too absorbed in each other to notice. Juliette told him about her visit to the studio.

"I didn't know you'd been there," he exclaimed, surprised.

"Do you mind?"

"No, quite the reverse. You saw my two figures, did you?"

She knew Nikolai wasn't waiting for praise and guessed that he was like Rodin in never being fully satisfied with his own work.

"I like them both," she said firmly, "for being so physically alive and sensual. The woman looked to me as if she had been caressed by Poseidon himself, or maybe just by the sea."

If he was surprised by her outspokenness he did not show it, although his lids drooped slightly over his lazily handsome eyes as if he were reassessing her. "And the 'Athlete'?"

"To me it seemed as if winning the race would be a kind of rebirth for him."

He released a slow breath in satisfaction. Juliette had shown a deeper insight into his work than he would have deemed possible. He realized then that she would never disappoint him, and, more than ever, he wanted to make love to her.

"What about the clay figure still under cloths in the studio?" she asked. "Shall you finish it now that you've returned to Paris?"

"The 'Bacchante'? It is finished."

She was taken aback. Somehow she had assumed that since Anna had only arrived from St. Petersburg a few days ago that he had traveled with her.

"You were in Paris and we didn't meet!" she exclaimed involuntarily.

His brows drew together fiercely and he leaned forward. "There's a good reason for that! I'd have turned the city upside down to find you if I thought you wanted to see me. As it was, I threw myself into my work, scarcely surfacing for food, drink, or rest, to try to get you out of my mind."

She guessed that her supposed rejection had hurt his pride. It was probably the first time in all his pampered life that he had ever suffered a supposed slight. "In future you must learn not to jump to conclusions," she advised. "Consider the possibilities first."

He relaxed, grinning. "You're right. Would you like to see the 'Bacchante' before it goes on exhibition with the other two figures?"

"I would very much." She smiled in return, knowing that a difficult moment had passed.

Their conversation flowed easily from then on, with Juliette describing her convent days and especially her fondly remembered holidays with Gabrielle. "She's living in England now," Juliette explained, "and has invited me to visit her whenever I can, but that will have to wait until my training is finished. Have you ever been to London?"

"Yes, a couple of times. I was there two weeks ago to buy myself a British sporting car, but I settled on a Grand Prix Benz instead."

"Does it go very fast?"

He laughed. "Not fast enough for me. Would you like me to teach you to drive?"

Her eyes widened. She did not know personally any women who drove, although she had seen those of her own sex behind the wheel of a staid motorcar now and again. "Yes!" she exclaimed eagerly. "When shall I have the first lesson?"

"As soon as you like."

It was arranged and they finished their meal in perfect harmony.

"So, what would you like to do now?" Nikolai asked over the coffee. "Shall we go dancing?"

Juliette had already mentioned that her sister would not be home until dawn and that nobody would be waiting up for her. She clapped her hands together eagerly. "Take me to the Moulin Rouge. I've always wanted to go there!"

Nikolai's eyebrows shot up in surprise and he threw back his head with a laugh. "My dear Juliette! If that's what you wish, of course we'll go."

It appeared at first that there was not a spare place to be had, but Nikolai was known to the *maître d'hôtel* and they were given a table for two in an advantageous position. Once again, Juliette attracted attention, and several men, merry with wine, threw her kisses from their fingertips. Nikolai ordered champagne. She was exhilarated by the vibrant atmosphere. It was all so colorful, noisy with laughter, and hazy with the curling smoke of good cigars. Here, as at Larue's, all were in evening dress, although some of the men had not removed their jauntily angled top hats, which showed they were with women of a low class. Busy waiters in long white aprons darted between the tables, carrying loaded trays. Champagne corks popped spasmodically in various directions. The music and general air of good humor were contagious.

Juliette was certain that little had changed since her mother sipped champagne here. It was still not a place a gentleman would expect to bring a lady, but Nikolai had indulged her, and she wondered impishly if he would be able to refuse her anything.

"Well?" Nikolai asked with a smile, having heard how she had longed to follow her parents' footsteps to this famous place. "Has the Moulin Rouge come up to your expectations?"

"Oh, yes! I love it. No wonder my mother did too! I think we're at the very same table where she and my father sat." She spoke less in jest than she made it appear.

"Perhaps we are." Reaching across the table, he covered her hand with his. "I'm as glad as you that we came."

"Thank you."

"Would you like to dance now?"

The floor was full of couples rotating to a Strauss waltz, the men white-gloved with coattails flying. Nikolai put his arm around Juliette's waist as he led her into the throng, but the dance ended even as they reached the floor. Almost at once the orchestra struck up a tango. He swept her into its steps and her gown rippled out in waves with every sweeping movement. Several couples drew back to watch them, and more followed suit, until they were tangoing on their own in the middle of a wide circle of spectators.

Juliette had danced the tango before, but never this slow version, which was considered by Denise and the older people in her circle to be too outré and erotic. But how glorious it was! How sensuous! And Nikolai was such an excellent dancer! They swayed and dipped together as if attuned exactly to each other's bodies, almost as if they were one. His smiling eyes probed hers as if he could read her thoughts, and it seemed to Juliette that there was a passionate intensity to their perfectly matched movements.

Thunderous applause greeted the end of their tango, and as Nikolai hastened Juliette through the crowd back to their table, one bright-haired blonde addressed him by name and kissed his cheek exuberantly, leaving a pink imprint, which he wiped away with a napkin as soon as they were seated.

"Do you always create such a stir when you leave a dance floor?" Juliette teased mischievously.

"Mon Dieu, no!" He shook his head humorously. "You're casting a spell everywhere we go tonight!"

"It must be my Delphos robe! Perhaps it has magical powers," she joked.

He shook his head again more seriously. "You've magic enough of your own."

They did not dance again, but sat talking through the polka that followed, and then it was time for the nightly cabaret. It was a splendid show, featuring comedians, acrobats, jugglers, singers, and dancers, with the cancan as a grand finale. Black-stockinged legs kicked high, providing a gleam of thigh in a mass of lacy frills. When the girls streamed down the steps from the stage into the hall itself, the audience rose to its feet, singing and shouting and clapping, for the cancan had lost none of its power to excite and inflame. As the dancers threw themselves down one by one into the splits at the end there was such a roar of appreciation that it seemed as if the roof would blow off.

When Nikolai and Juliette left in the early hours of the morning, Paris was still vibrantly alive with passing motorcars and carriages. Flower-sellers thrust nosegays at passersby, and restaurants remained brightly lit.

"Let's walk," Juliette suggested.

Nikolai had been about to hail a taxicab but took her hand instead as they strolled along, describing the tiny studio and cramped living quarters he'd had in Montmartre when he first came to Paris. He and his friends had patronized the Lapin Agile café, a favorite gathering place for the Bohemian element. Picasso, Utrillo, Van Dongen, and a dozen other struggling artists and sculptors, some of whom were beginning to make a name for themselves, had been among his drinking companions.

"Have you ever been back to your first studio?" she asked.

"Not for a long time."

"I'd like to see it one day."

They began to plan where else they would go together. There were no passersby just then and he drew her to a standstill under a tree. They stood facing each other, dappled by the lamplight through the branches.

"You're so lovely, Juliette," he said huskily. "God knows what lies ahead, but if it means anything to you, I want to see you again and again.''

She was very still, deeply moved by the tenderness with which he was gazing at her. "I want that too," she answered softly.

She moved into his arms then, as he caught her close. His mouth was warm on hers, his kiss slow and subtle at first, but soon his embrace tightened and his surge of passion ignited her into an abandoned response such as she had never experienced before. When he took his lips away from hers and drew back his head, her eyes were still closed. She felt him stroke her hair, then the side of her face, and a delicious tremor went through her, as if a current of love had passed between them. Only then did she open her eyes, as if awakening from a dream.

They smiled at each other and kissed again. Then they strolled on once more, having no further need of words, until dawn began to lighten the sky. His arm was about her, her head resting against his shoulder. At the house she gave him her key, and when he had unlocked the door for her, she paused on the threshold.

"It was a wonderful, unforgettable evening," she said.

"You made it so for me."

"*Bonne nuit*, Nikolai."

As Juliette went upstairs she recalled what he had said about the uncertainty of the future. Perhaps he had been remembering how they had almost lost each other once already, or how the demands of duty might snatch him away from her at any time. Her own plans for the future had certainly not included falling out of her depth in love with anybody, which was now a possibility she would have to face. Perhaps she and Nikolai would find a way to take every moment as it came, with no regrets afterward.

Nine

DENISE SLEPT LATE the next morning, and Juliette went to work as usual, so she did not see her sister until summoned to the office at mid-morning. Although Denise was looking out the window, Juliette could see by her posture that she was in a towering rage.

"You wanted to see me, Denise?"

Denise turned immediately, thin-lipped, eyes flashing. "What in heaven's name did you wear yesterday evening? A friend rang to tell me she'd heard you'd been immodestly dressed in the company of Count Karasvin."

"It's not true!" Juliette was indignant.

Denise's tirade went on unabated. "And if that were not enough, the *directrice* is trying to placate two clients who saw you at Larue's and are clamoring for gowns in the same pleated silk that I know did not come from here! How dare you go anywhere in anything but a Landelle design! I assume you made the dress yourself?"

"It's a Delphos robe by Fortuny."

Denise was aghast. "Where did you get it?"

"I told you a while ago that I had found it. The pieces were in the remnant box and you said I could have them. It wasn't my original intention to sew them together, but the idea became irresistible."

"How could you!" Denise clutched the back of her chair as if to keep from physically attacking her sister. "You've created a scandal and shamed me! Don't you know that in a Delphos robe you're *en déshabillé*? Respectable women would never wear such a thing in public!"

"Surely you are exaggerating? There's nothing new about loose-fitting gowns being worn in public."

"And by whom?" Denise countered savagely. "Only fast women leading a Bohemian life with no morals whatever!"

"That's a sweeping judgment of women who simply want free-dom of movement in their clothes!"

"Don't argue with me!" Denise hissed, her lips drawn back over her teeth. "I'll remind you that I'm not only your sister and guard-ian, but your employer as well. Did you go anywhere else last night?"

"Yes. To the Moulin Rouge. Anna Dolohova had another en-gagement, otherwise I don't know if Nikolai would have taken me there as I requested."

Denise, momentarily beyond speech, let her hands rise and fall expressively. "I've heard enough. You'll not see Count Karasvin again and you'll destroy that Fortuny rag."

Juliette spoke determinedly. "I'll do neither."

"You'll do as I say if you want to stay on here!"

"Then I must leave."

"No!" Denise struggled to control herself, suddenly seeing how close she had come to destroying all her plans. "I'll not let you go to another couturier! I haven't trained you to be of use to someone else! I'll move you from the sewing rooms. I know you've been looking forward to studying design with Monsieur Pierre. I'll let you start there today."

Juliette raised her eyebrows incredulously. "What are you say-ing, Denise? I don't have to be bribed to stay. If you want me to continue working for you, I will and gladly, but I can't agree to your demands about either Nikolai or the gown."

"I realize that." Denise sank down in the chair at her desk. "You always were stubborn, but at least promise me you'll not wear the Fortuny gown in public anymore."

"All I can vow is that I'll not cause you distress about it ever again."

Before Denise could reply, there came a tap on the door and the *directrice* entered looking anxious. "Madame! The clients are insistent! Nothing I've said—"

Again Denise turned furiously on Juliette. "There! See what you've done! I'm likely to lose two valuable accounts and more when word of this gets about."

"Why not just tell them the truth?" Juliette exclaimed in exasperation. "Find something else to please them. There are some beautiful tawny silks in the storeroom that haven't been used in the present collection. They're not the same as Fortuny silks, but they would look elegant if pleated in the Landelle way."

Denise sprang to her feet again, her face hard and maliciously triumphant. "All right then, you can fetch that silk and try to placate those women. I'm giving you your first chance to handle clients diplomatically!"

The *directrice* was dismayed. "Madame! Is that wise? It's you whom they wish to see."

But Juliette was out the door, and when the *directrice* would have rushed after her, Denise called her back. "No! Let my sister try. It will be a hard lesson for her whether she wins or fails."

Juliette did not fail. The two women were pleased to see the girl who had worn the gown and were soon plying her with questions and demands. She explained that the gown had been made by Fortuny and then displayed a selection of the silks she had fetched, suggesting alternative designs from ideas of her own. They left quite satisfied.

"I've promised the designs will be ready for them to see tomorrow," Juliette reported back to Denise.

Her sister's cold expression did not change. "Very well. Take your ideas to Monsieur Pierre and tell him what you have promised. As I said before, you'll work in his studio until further notice."

If the designer had not been an even-tempered man, he could not have worked well with Denise. She had told him some time ago that her sister would take her place eventually, so it came as no surprise to hear that Juliette was being transferred to his studio.

When she entered, sample lengths of the silks chosen by the clients over her arm, she found Pierre adjusting the sleeve of a *toile* on a wooden mannequin. Pierre was a short dapper man whose fair hair and neatly pointed beard were streaked with gray. He looked over the top of his gold-rimmed spectacles at Juliette and waved her forward.

"Toss the silk over the back of a chair and tell me what's been going on downstairs. I gather there was quite a crisis." When he had heard everything, he nodded toward a drawingboard. "Put down your ideas in rough sketches for these two pleated gowns and we'll work together on them afterward."

The outcome was that he and Juliette worked late into the night. Before going home, Denise came to check on their progress. Only Pierre knew how unusual it was that she made no suggestions of her own upon seeing the finished sketches.

When Juliette arrived home, a maid informed her that Denise had gone to bed and that Count Karasvin had telephoned twice. She tried to get through to him at his apartment in the Rue de Lille, but a manservant told her he was not yet home.

She was undressing when there came a rattling of gravel against her window. Opening it cautiously, she looked down. Nikolai stood on the lawn, grinning up at her.

Amused, she whispered, "Are you mad? What are you doing here at this hour?"

"I came to say good night," he answered, rewarded by her fascinating, throaty little laugh, which he liked so much.

"How many vodkas have you had?" she asked mock-censoriously.

He shrugged merrily. "I lost count."

"I thought so. Go home now."

But he was more sober than she realized, having become so possessed by the need to see her that he had left a party early. The light in the room behind her made a red-gold aura of her hair and, although she had thrown on a wrap, he could see the tops of her breasts. "Come down," he requested seriously.

She hesitated as if torn by indecision, but then she shook her head. "Go home," she repeated and closed the window. The curtain flicked back into place.

Almost at once, she turned out the light, wanting him to think she had gone to bed, and finished undressing in the dark. When she did lay her head on the pillows, she sensed that it was only then he went away. A few moments later she heard a faint clang as one of the double gates closed after him.

·   ·   ·   ·

The furor created by the Fortuny gown continued the following day and the salons were busier than usual. The *directrice* found herself inundated with demands to see this new gown, which had not been shown in the collection. The more adventurous women wanted to try it on, although with no intention of wearing it in public. As before, Juliette was sent for. She took five of the *vendeuses* to the storeroom and made the storekeeper bring out every silk that was in a vivid autumn tint, no matter how long it had been on the shelves. She tumbled the shimmering lengths into the *vendeuses'* arms. When they walked behind her into the salon, the heaped and flowing silks were as glorious as the most splendid Venetian painting.

"Any of these silks," she said, as the luscious fabrics were draped, twirled, and spread out for each group of seated clients, "will pleat and hang perfectly, although not as Fortuny does it. Yet," she added, lowering her voice to a confidential whisper, "there's a secret of the Delphos robe that I discovered by chance."

"What is it? Do tell," they whispered in return.

"No corsets! In fact, nothing at all!"

There were gasps and giggles. Gloved hands were clapped over mouths to smother surprised—and sometimes shocked—laughter. But nobody walked out, for all were intrigued that a respectable young woman, sister of the baronne herself, had dared to wear it in the name of fashion, even if they would not do so themselves. They assumed she had done it to attract notice for Maison Landelle, and in that she had succeeded.

On Sunday, as arranged, Juliette went for her first driving lesson with Nikolai. She was ready and waiting when he drew up outside the house and ran down the steps to meet him.

"What a splendid machine!" she declared, gazing admiringly at the deep yellow two-seater elongated raceabout with its handsome brass radiator and headlamps. Denise watched dubiously from the window as they drove away.

Word of the scandal caused by the Fortuny gown had reached Nikolai through Anna, and he and Juliette laughed about it together as Nikolai drove some way out of Paris into a quiet village. There he drew up and began to instruct Juliette in the rudiments of driving.

"Let's see you start," he said, finally, jumping into the seat beside her after cranking the engine.

"Here we go!" Juliette depressed the clutch, engaged the gears, and they were away. She found it easy enough to control the thick mahogany wheel and caught on quickly after a few false starts and erratic jolts.

They had taken a picnic basket, for it was a mild September day, and settled on a plaid rug by a river, eating the food Juliette had brought and drinking the wine provided by Nikolai. Her obvious happiness was matched by his own, and before they set out again he kissed her as he had done in the lamplight of Paris.

The salons at Maison Landelle continued to be crowded with clients clamoring for the new pleated designs, which were not only lovely but also totally respectable. Their popularity put vivid autumnal colors and an abundance of pleats at the height of fashion.

Apart from the extra work, complications arose when clients wanted to change the color of clothes already ordered, but eventually everything was sorted out. Denise could scarcely believe the good fortune that had come her way as a result of her sister's indiscretion. Not only had she gained new clients, but all the other fashion houses had to follow the trend set by Maison Landelle for the most stylish winter colors.

She discussed Juliette's initiative with Pierre, who advised her to let her sister have a voice whenever the two of them discussed new ideas.

"Juliette has an instinctive flair for fashion and color," he said, "as well as the nose to scent change in the air."

Denise possessed it as he did—that indefinable sixth sense that so often led couturiers simultaneously onto the same trail. "You're sure Juliette has it?"

He nodded. "Only yesterday she showed me some sketches she'd done, all with the softer lines you and I discussed only the other day. She pointed out that the S shape had been in too long and is no longer in keeping with the new freedom that women are winning for themselves."

"Very well, Pierre. We'll include her in future, and if all goes smoothly I'll start teaching her the business side as well."

By now Nikolai considered Juliette to be a capable driver, and it was a great day for her when she drove through the Paris traffic for the first time. After that she took it in stride, hooting back at taxicabs when they cut in on her, the sporting car's horn loud and magnificent.

Nikolai's embassy duties and Juliette's late working hours prevented their seeing each other exactly when they wished, but it made their times together all the more valued. They went to an opera that had been costumed by Fortuny and were able to see Nijinsky dance. They attended the preview of an exhibition where Nikolai's "Bacchante" held pride of place. Already it had been bought by an American collector and was about to be shipped to the United States.

There were many Sunday afternoons when they went to the Louvre and other galleries. They liked to wander through the gardens of the Palais Royale, depleted now by winter, but still showing unexpected touches of color here and there. At other times they were to be found amid the statues of the park at the Luxembourg Palace or strolling, always hand in hand, by the Seine.

If rain forced them inside, they took refreshment at the marble-topped tables of tiny cafés. Later in the evening, unless they dined grandly at Larue's, they would have supper at one or another of the many little restaurants scattered throughout the city. Juliette's favorite was one with balalaika music and men in Cossack costumes dancing wildly. Once Nikolai joined in, more than a match for the other dancers, his yells mingling with theirs, and Juliette sprang excitedly to her feet to clap to the reckless rhythm. When the dance ended, the dancers, the orchestra, and the other diners applauded him, as he did in return, according to the Russian custom.

Laughing and exhilarated, Juliette flung her arms about his neck exuberantly. "Nikolai! That was fantastic! I didn't know you could dance like that!"

He held her tight about the waist, his eyes bright. "There's so much you don't know about me yet, Juliette!" Then, with a raised hand, he acknowledged a cheer before he and Juliette sat down again to resume their meal.

She thought at times like this that she was happier with him than at any other time in her life.

Juliette had never mentioned the undelivered letter to Lucille. Instead, she wrote of meeting Nikolai again and of how she had enjoyed his company. As she had expected, Lucille returned the sealed letter when next she wrote, but did not make any reference to it. Their correspondence continued as if nothing untoward had ever occurred. It was a misjudged action that was forgotten by mutual understanding. If Lucille continued to have misgivings about the relationship, they were never expressed.

In contrast, Denise still voiced her disapproval openly to Juliette. "You couldn't see Count Karasvin more often if you were engaged to him," she pointed out sharply.

"He's not in Paris forever," Juliette replied with a casual shrug, "and there's no question of an engagement. And we like each other's company."

"He'd never marry you anyway, so it's as well you're being sensible."

Juliette flushed. "I know that Nikolai will be expected to take a wife of aristocratic birth, and I haven't a drop of blue blood in my veins. Our ancestors probably cheered every time the blade fell at the guillotine."

"Don't say that!" Denise grimaced, clapping her hands over her ears.

Juliette smiled ruefully and took her sister's wrists to pull them gently down. "I was only trying to emphasize the gulf that lies between Nikolai and me. The rules of class aren't easily broken, especially by someone tied so rigidly to his own society. Certainly I've seen those rules at work often enough at Maison Landelle."

Juliette gave no indication of how difficult it was to keep herself anchored to reality and not give way to foolish hopes and dreams. And Denise was fully reassured by her practical attitude. The older woman realized that, not for the first time, she had underestimated her sister. It meant she need not harbor any fears that her plans for the future of Maison Landelle might be ruined. Juliette, no doubt, had been alerted to the true state of affairs from the very beginning, when Anna Dolohova made some excuse not to accompany her and Nikolai on their first evening together. It had been Denise's own conclusion that the countess would do nothing to help a romance between her brother and her couturière's sister. Although always charming when the occasion demanded, the countess had never invited Juliette to any of her parties. Denise would have had to admit that, so far as she knew, Nikolai was never there either, but she thought that was probably because he refused to attend without Juliette.

Then Denise took added comfort from the thought that Anna

Dolohova would never allow her brother to make a fool of himself by suddenly declaring honorable intentions toward Juliette. The countess would have strings to pull and could bring imperial pressure to bear if need be. Yet Denise's concern was not centered entirely on the possible threat to what she wanted for herself from her sister. She had come to care for Juliette, as much as she was able to care for anyone, and was proud of the united sibling strength that was blossoming at Maison Landelle.

So, reassured about Juliette's relationship with Nikolai, and with work finally under control in the ateliers, she decided to make a trip to England before Christmas. Her purpose was to visit silk mills in Macclesfield, which was the heart of the British silk industry, and also another mill in London, the owner of which had had the initiative to send her some very attractive samples.

"You must send me a cable if anything goes wrong," Denise insisted as she departed.

"Nothing will," Juliette answered cheerily. "Go and look at those silks and enjoy yourself in London too."

"And send me the design for your ball gown. I have to approve it. Remember that!"

She and Juliette had both been invited to the New Year's Ball at the Russian embassy and, in a benevolent mood, Denise had said that her sister might design a new gown for herself under the Landelle label, so long as it did not resemble a Fortuny robe!

Juliette knew, as Denise did, that the couturier, Poiret, was stocking a few Fortuny gowns in his boutique, but whether they were being bought was impossible to tell, for none had as yet been seen in public.

After her talk with Denise, Juliette had realized just how much her life had become centered on Nikolai and how much time they spent together. She knew it was unwise. Her work had not suffered, but the fact remained that she was totally in love with him. More than once, recently, she had found herself glancing at the clock when she was at the designing table, thinking more than was sensible about the hour when they would be meeting.

That would have to stop. Her will was strong, and somehow she would manage it. In the meantime she was going to a moving-picture theater with him that evening and then to supper afterward. On Sunday afternoon they were going to see where his old studio was in Montmartre.

It was a long time since Juliette had been in Montmartre by daylight. She remembered going with her father to a gallery where unknown artists displayed their work, hoping a buyer would pay enough for an absinthe and a solid meal. She had become hot and tired and her father had bought her a lemonade. On that occasion he'd bought a painting of ballet dancers tying their shoes. She'd loved it, but it must have gone in the sale of his effects at the time of the bankruptcy, because it was not in Denise's house.

When Sunday came, Juliette and Nikolai left the sporting car parked and walked hand in hand up the steep, narrow streets of the Butte, which was crowned at the top by a windmill. When the nightspots and brothels had been left behind, Montmartre retained its old rustic charm. With its old houses and cobbles, even with the trees bare of leaves, it was easy to see why so many artists had chosen to paint what was on their doorstep instead of seeking more exotic views.

Nikolai drew her to a halt as he pointed to the sprawling, untidy buildings clustered on the hillside. These were the artists' studios known as the Batoir-Lavoir.

"That lopsided window on the second floor of the third studio was where I worked, lived, and slept when I came to Paris after a year at the St. Petersburg Art School. It's where I sculpted the two heads and a figure that resulted in my becoming one of Rodin's pupils." He was also remembering that it was where he'd kept his first mistress, discovered how to drink companions under the table, and learned a great deal about art, women, and how to exist on a few francs like everybody else.

Juliette glanced sideways at him. There was a faraway look in his eyes as he gazed at the ill-formed buildings. It was a chilly day and as he stood there in his warm tweed coat, scarf, and wide-brimmed slouch hat, she found it easy to picture him coming up this hill as a youth, eager to immerse himself in the Bohemian life of Paris. After a few moments she plucked at his sleeve.

"You're looking nostalgic and you're too young for that."

He laughed, turning to her, and tucked her arm into his. "You're right! It wasn't really all that long ago, and I was here barely six months, but so much has happened since then, especially meeting you. We'll go now to the Lapin Agile and have a glass of wine."

On the way there, they met a street photographer, his tripod over his shoulder, camera box in hand, who was returning from taking winter scenes of Montmartre that would be sold for post-cards. He promptly offered to take a photograph of them together. Afterwards, Nikolai wanted one of Juliette on her own. She pro-tested, laughing, but the photographer captured her holding her hat, her scarf and skirt billowing out in a sudden gust of wind, and congratulated himself on a perfect picture. He gave Nikolai his card and said the photographs would be ready at his shop within a few days.

The warmth of the green-shuttered Lapin Agile was welcome after the chill outside. The room was full of people smoking and talking over glasses of wine, and the walls were decorated with a conglomeration of art, including plaster figures, a striking oil painting of a harlequin left behind by Picasso, and various others, some quite darkened by time and tobacco smoke.

They were soon hailed by two artist friends of Nikolai, who joined them, along with their young female companions. When she heard the young women were models, Juliette asked if they knew Yvonne. They did, and one of them added gravely, "She had a hard time with that wretch who put her in the family way and then deserted her. Yet when he died of booze in a pauper's bed she sat nursing him to the end."

"I didn't know," Juliette said sadly. "Poor Yvonne. She always looks so lovely and yet she's had such trouble."

"He used to get all her money out of her, but she's all right now that she's only herself to keep, because her sister has married a butcher. She has a nice little place of her own now."

Juliette knew Yvonne had moved since she returned to Maison Landelle. She also knew it was in all probability due in no small part to her own insistence that top mannequins be paid more. Denise had not been easy to persuade, but two exceptionally good mannequins had joined Maison Landelle as a result.

As the conversation continued and it grew dark outside, more people came in and were drawn to their table. The lively talk neces-sitated the ordering of more bottles, the air grew thick with to-bacco smoke, and the talk came hard and fast. Eventually, Nikolai ordered bread and cheese for everyone, and then he and Juliette joined those who streamed off to the Moulin de la Galette dance hall. Nobody wore evening dress, and all the men, as well as the women, kept on their hats. Plumes and ribbons bobbed around the dance floor with high bowlers, derbies, and caps.

"Are you enjoying yourself?" Nikolai asked Juliette as he whirled her in a riotous gallop.

She threw back her head joyously. "I'm having a wonderful time!"

It was late when they left, arms about each other, and she asked why he had not returned more often. He frowned as he answered, his jaw set.

"It's not easy to be a part-time artist among those whose lives are dedicated solely to art. I'll not come back again."

She brought him to a halt, gripping his lapels and giving him an impatient little shake. "But you are an artist in your heart! That's all that matters."

He folded his arms gently around her and looked at her tenderly. "Darling Juliette. No wonder I love you."

She caught her breath. "I think you said you loved me."

"I have from the start."

"Then why haven't you told me before?"

"I've been hoping that the complications in my life would disappear through some kind turn of fate, but unfortunately that hasn't happened yet."

She touched his face tenderly with her fingertips. "I love you no matter what happens."

His embrace tightened. "I never want to lose you!" Then he kissed her as passionately and hungrily as if at that moment they were on the brink of being torn apart.

When Nikolai collected the photographs taken in Montmartre he gave Juliette the one of them together, which she put in a silver frame on her dressing table. He kept the one of her in his wallet.

Ten

THE NEW YEAR'S EVE BALL at the Russian embassy was one of the great occasions of the social season. Denise used it as a chance to wear one of her own magnificent evening gowns, thick with pearls, with a view to advertising Maison Landelle in a new sphere. It was the first time she had attended the ball, and many of the foreign women present would normally patronize only Maison Worth.

Her visit to England had gone well. She had begun to have misgivings about allowing Juliette to design her own gown, but she need not have worried. The girl looked remarkably lovely in softly shaded cream and peach silk chiné as she and Nikolai danced the last waltz of the old year.

The orchestra suddenly stopped, bringing all the dancers to a halt, and struck up a triumphant chord to herald in 1911. Bells began to ring throughout the city. The horns of motorcars hooted and fireworks began soaring into the sky above the Eiffel Tower. At the ball, rainbow-colored streamers cascaded over those greeting one another. Denise, looking for Juliette to give her good wishes, saw that she had both her hands in Nikolai's as they stood smiling at each other, creating an oasis of intimacy in the midst of the celebration. Then he lowered his head and they kissed.

Denise felt a sickening sense of dread. She knew the look of love when she saw it. All her anxieties about her sister returned a thou sandfold. Something would have to be done to break up this relationship before it was too late. At the moment she was too confused to think of anything, but she would watch out for the first opportunity to do whatever was possible.

Nothing presented itself for three weeks, and then Pierre unwittingly gave Denise the chance she had been wanting. He spoke of Juliette's affinity for silk in all its forms and said that he thought she would benefit from knowing more about its origin and the art of its weaving.

"You're right," Denise declared. "I want her to have the best grounding possible in all areas of the fashion business."

When Pierre had left her office, Denise rang for her secretary and dictated a letter to a business acquaintance in Lyon.

Nikolai, managing to get some leave from his embassy duties, rented a studio of his own and moved in with his tools, materials, and several small blocks of Pitacci and Soissons marble he had bought at various times for future projects. He was like Rodin in preferring to work in clay and have the result cast in bronze, but marble was still at times his medium of choice.

When he was settled in his studio, the *maître* himself came to view his premises and see what work he had in hand. Rodin, always well dressed since success had finally put an end to his years of poverty, made an impressive figure in his silk top hat, immaculate clothes, and cream chamois gloves. He was broadly built with a craggy brow and a thick gray beard still tinted in places by its original red, his black-ribboned pince-nez glinting on his aquiline nose.

"Don't stop work," he said when Nikolai had shaken his hand in welcome. Then Rodin waved aside the chair that Nikolai's assistant would have placed for him and went forward instead to view the sculpture of a young man that was in progress. The model knelt on the stand, looking up over his shoulder in a pose that brought out the muscles of the neck, shoulders, and thighs. Rodin nodded approvingly at the vibrant, pulsating life already captured in the marble.

"When are you going to rid yourself of those pettifogging duties at the embassy, Karasvin?" Rodin was violently opposed to this talented sculptor being thus tethered. "You know as well as I that you're throwing away valuable time there. Any fool could dance attendance on visiting dignitaries and write a few letters, but, as

I've told you many times before, the ability to sculpt is a God-given gift and you've no moral right to relegate it to second place."

Nikolai stiffened. "Do you think I don't still wish to be free? Nothing has changed regarding those conditions laid down when I was seventeen and so desperate to become your pupil that I would have promised anything."

Rodin inclined his head understandingly. He was only concerned that too much time away from sculpting would eventually kill Nikolai's initiative and drain the gift from his talented fingers. So far that had not happened, but nobody knew better than he the anguish that could result when domestic and other problems came between an artist and his work. It was easy to see that his onetime student was sculpting like a man long starved of food. Rodin felt a word of warning would not go amiss.

"Do me one favor, Karasvin. Promise me that when those wretched duties continue to drag you away from this studio, you won't seek consolation in the bottle as you did once before. Not only did you make yourself the most notorious young man in Paris, but, worst of all, your work suffered."

Nikolai stopped what he was doing and shrugged ruefully. "Never again, *maître*. I was younger then, and it did me no good in more ways than one. You almost threw me out. I've always been grateful that you didn't."

"It would have been a waste. Did you do anything worthwhile while you were at home? I know we've talked since then, but I don't think I asked you."

"A few pieces that I had cast into bronze."

"Good. At least you're still keeping your hand in, and you'll have a studio waiting when eventually you go home to live. Russia has given us great literature, music, and glorious ballet, even a number of artists, but the world has yet to applaud a sculptor from your vast land. Remember that."

Nikolai grinned. "I will."

Nikolai continued working that day long after his tired model had dressed and gone home. Juliette had yet to see his new studio, because her sister had sent her to stay in Lyon.

"I'm to learn all about the weaving and dyeing of silks." Juliette had been excited by the prospect. "Such knowledge will be invaluable to me."

"How long shall you be away?"

"A month. Two months at the most."

"So long!" he had exclaimed in dismay.

She had flung her arms about his neck. "I wish you could be with me, but I'll write. You'll be sculpting in your new studio and you won't miss me at all!"

He knew she was hiding her own pain, and he went along with the deception. "Then you won't expect me to come and see you."

She melted and clung to him. "I'll die if you don't!"

So he had spent three cold March days in Lyon. Juliette had been as overjoyed to see him as he was to see her, but the couple with whom she was staying, Monsieur and Madame Degrange, were conscientious about her chaperonage and at no time were they ever alone. The Degranges were hospitable and Nikolai gladly accepted their invitation to dine at their home every evening, there being no other way he could see Juliette at the end of the day.

She was not the only guest staying in the house. The Degranges' Italian son-in-law, Marco Romanelli, was there too. A dealer in fine fabrics, he had met the Degranges' eldest daughter, Françoise, on business at the silk mills of Lyon. And even though she had died four years before, in childbirth, his business still brought him back from Venice at irregular intervals. Juliette introduced him to Nikolai on the first evening.

"Here's somebody you'll be interested to meet, Nikolai," she declared as Marco Romanelli entered the salon where they were talking together. "Signor Romanelli knows Fortuny very well and is buying undyed silk velvets for him among other fabrics for his own business."

Nikolai had shaken hands with the Italian, who was as tall as he but larger and broader in the chest, like a La Scala baritone. A good-looking fellow in his thirties, his face almost square and olive-skinned, his chin deeply cleft, Marco was at ease with himself and everybody else. He spoke French fluently, which was a relief to Nikolai, who knew no Italian.

"Why undyed silk velvets?" Nikolai asked with interest. "Why not silks as well?"

"Fortuny likes to use his own dyes and print his own patterns," the Italian explained. "I import a great deal of Lyonnaise silk in my business, but not for Fortuny. I get undyed silk from Japan for

him. He'll use no other. Mademoiselle Cladel told me that you and
she have been interested in Fortuny's work for some time."

"I've long admired his innovative effects in the theater and,
more recently, his designing skill in another sphere." Nikolai
grinned as he glanced deliberately at Juliette, who was wearing her
Delphos robe under a full-length silk-chiffon dévoré evening coat
to avoid shocking her host and hostess. She had worn the gown for
Nikolai and he knew it.

Her face flushed with pleasure at his compliment. "I've told
Signor Romanelli how I came across my Fortuny creation in pieces
and sewed it together again."

Nikolai guessed she would have avoided revealing her sister's
somewhat dubious attempt to discover its secrets. "It was a lucky
find."

"I agree." Marco Romanelli's quick, almost boyish, grin was
accompanied by a crinkling at the corners of his brown eyes. "I
haven't asked yet if I'm permitted to tell Fortuny the story."

"Of course you may," Juliette replied lightheartedly. "If you're
sure it will please him."

"I know it will. He'll want to hear what I thought of the result."
He stepped back and threw his hands wide. "I shall tell him it's
bellissimo!"

Nikolai nodded in agreement. Merrily Juliette twirled around
once, as if she were a mannequin, and then they all laughed together.

Then it was time to go in to dinner. There were other guests
present, and to Nikolai's disappointment Juliette was seated some
distance from him with Marco Romanelli at her side. The conversation was generally depressing. A retired French general held
forth on the threat he foresaw from the German Kaiser. Nikolai
held the same view, but it was difficult to be attentive when he
could not stop looking in Juliette's direction. To his joy, she frequently caught his eye and rewarded him with a twinkling smile.
The lovely sight of her kept flooding his heart. Her pearly skin
seemed to glow against the coppery silk of the gown, its tiny pleats
shimmering across the alluring rise of her breasts.

To Nikolai's increasing annoyance he found he was being
watched in his turn by the Degranges' twin daughters, who at
sixteen seemed even sillier than most girls of their age, batting their

lashes at him and trying to draw his attention with fatuous remarks.

After what was to Nikolai a long and tedious meal, in spite of the
excellence of the food and wine, he and Juliette and the Italian
came together again in the salon where coffee was served. They
had some animated discussions, Nikolai and Juliette arguing quite
fiercely on one point to their mutual enjoyment, and before the
evening was out they were on first-name terms with Marco and he
with them.

The next day Marco took Nikolai to visit the Degrange silk mill.
Juliette had already been there since early morning. She was learning to weave and seemed not to hear the deafening clackety-clack
of her own loom and the rows of others all around her. She flashed
Nikolai a radiant smile.

"If the result is any good you shall have a new necktie out of it."

The rest of the day would have been long for Nikolai if, after a
tour of the mill, he and Marco had not lunched together and then
hired a carriage to drive through the historic quarters of the old
city and also to the heights to take in the view from Fourvière. He
learned, as Juliette had already, that Marco was the youngest son of
a prosperous Milanese financier, and that he had four brothers and
one sister. Three of his brothers had emigrated to the United
States, where they had started successful businesses, while the
fourth had become a captain in the army, only to be killed in a
tragic accident.

"As for my sister," Marco concluded, as they drank wine together in a hotel bar after the drive, "she is a nun nursing at a
mission hospital in Africa."

"How did you get into the silk business?"

"It was not by my choice. I'd had hopes of becoming a doctor,
but that was to no avail. My uncle had no sons, although he has
since rectified that through a second marriage. In Italy blood-ties
are strong and my father felt obliged to let his brother take me in
and teach me his silk business. Fortunately I became interested in
the work and by twenty-five I was managing the mill. It was then
that my widowed uncle married a woman many years younger than
himself." Marco shrugged expressively. "I found her too attractive
for her good or mine."

"So what happened?"

"I left when matters began to get out of hand between us. Be-

fore all this happened, I had met Fortuny several times and supplied him with silks for his theatrical costumes before he began to
favor Japanese silk. After my departure from the mill I had a spell
in the retail silk trade and happened to visit Venice on business. I
went to see Fortuny again and during the course of conversation
he told me about a local wholesale business for sale. It dealt with
the import and export of luxury fabrics. On his advice I investi-
gated and found it would be a venture I could build up and ex-
pand. That was six years ago and I'm pleased to say all has gone as
I'd hoped." He sat back in his chair. "So there you have it. My
career so far."

"You've no regrets?" Nikolai took a mouthful of wine.

"None now. I met my late wife through the silk trade and I'll
always be thankful for that, even though our marriage was tragically short."

"I'm sorry," Nikolai said with genuine feeling, for he liked this
man and sympathized with his loss.

"There's not a day when I don't still miss her." Marco shook his
head and then briskly looked at his watch. "Drink up! We promised Juliette we'd be at the mill gates to meet her and it's almost
time."

The next day, after Marco had finalized his orders, he and Nikolai went with Juliette to a silk farm. Nikolai found it all interesting,
but it was a less pleasant visit when on his last day the three of them
went to a dyeing plant in a nearby village. The stench of the place
was nauseating and they were all glad to leave.

"How quickly your time here has flown, Nikolai," Juliette said
sadly during the final dinner party. They had already arranged for
Marco to contact them when he was next in Paris, for he had also
come to the end of his stay in Lyon.

"How long do you think it will be before you return home?"
Nikolai asked her.

She was uncertain. "I can't say exactly when that will be. I'm to
start learning all about screen and block printing next, and some of
my designs are to be woven. I have to see that through."

When the time came for them to part Nikolai kissed her as long
as he could with Madame Degrange glowering at him and her
giggling daughters peeping round the door.

"I'll miss you every day, Juliette." He resented being overheard.

Her eyes were loving. "I think of you all the time. And I'll keep writing as often as possible."

She kept her word, but another month went by.

Eventually he received the good news that she would be returning the following week. But at the same time there was a message from the embassy curtailing his six months' release. Important diplomatic developments required his presence. Since his role at the embassy was a minor one, he swore in exasperation at this needless interruption of his work.

When Juliette's train arrived back in Paris, Nikolai was waiting on the platform. They rushed into each other's arms, and he swept her off her feet as they kissed, heedless of the stares of strangers.

On the drive home, she was full of questions, wanting to know if he had finished the "Crouching Man," as he had called his present work, and was sympathetic when she heard of his having been called back to the embassy.

"Is there much left to do to it?" she asked.

"A little. Whenever I have a spare hour I go to the studio."

"I want to see it as soon as possible. Now I'll give you your present from Lyon."

He opened the small package she handed him and saw it was the silk tie he had been promised. "This is splendid! But I thought you were weaving emerald silk."

"So I was! And I saw you recoil at the color! I'd already planned to make you a tie in the kind of gray you like."

"This is perfect!" He pulled off the one he was wearing and replaced it with hers. Proudly she adjusted it for him, and he caught her hands and kissed them.

Denise came home early and found her sister talking on the telephone, catching up with friends she had not seen for so long. Juliette rang off as soon as she could, and they kissed each other's cheeks. Denise was more glad to see her than she would ever have imagined.

"I want to hear everything," Denise declared eagerly. "Your letters were wonderfully informative but there's still much I want to ask."

She was impressed by all that Juliette had learned and even more so by the lengths of silk imprinted with her own designs. There were feather and fern prints in silver on a luscious blue, ivory on black, and cinnamon on cream; stylized blossoms in pale pinks and blues creating a lilac tint, and other delicate patterns in amber, ripe corn, and pumpkin yellow.

"Monsieur Degrange will be writing to you," Juliette said, relieved to see how pleased Denise was with the designs. "He would like to use my patterns and color combinations, but I thought we ought to have exclusive rights to them for eighteen months, or even for two years before the release of the fabrics on the open market."

Denise's eyes sharpened speculatively. "Just as manufacturers serving the crowned heads of Europe withhold the materials that royal ladies have selected for themselves."

"That's right. More important, it would give added prestige to Landelle clothes if the fabrics were exclusive to our label."

"I'll think about it," Denise promised, seeing the possibilities of the idea, "but I'm not sure I wouldn't let the designs be made up at the little silk mill I visited near London. The price would be cheaper and the quality is comparable to what we stock already."

The matter was left for further discussion and Denise congratulated herself once again on her own foresight in taking her sister into the business. She had forgotten the circumstances that compelled her in the first place. Her jubilant mood faded, however, when she heard that Nikolai had met Juliette's train and that they were continuing to see each other. If separation could not cool their ardor, she would have to find some other means. But what? Whatever her anxieties, she must not turn Juliette against her. She was left in a quandary, hoping to find some solution.

When Juliette visited Nikolai's studio for the first time, it was late afternoon and he was working by the last of the daylight, his assistant having just left and the model no longer needed. He opened the door to her with a dark blue bandanna knotted at the back of his head, white dust clinging to his lashes and linen smock. She had a basket on her arm covered with a cloth, a bottle of wine sticking out of it.

"I've brought supper for us," she said after they had greeted each other. "I thought it would be fun to eat here. That way you can work as long as you like and I'll be happy to sit and watch you."

He praised her thoughtfulness as he took the basket from her

and put it on a table. She glanced about her as she removed her
gloves and slid the pearl-headed pin from her hat, which he hung
with her jacket on a peg. She went at once to gaze in admiration at
the "Crouching Man."

"What can I say?" Her voice was almost breathless. "You've
looked into the soul of the model and seen all that was tormenting
him."

He took her by the shoulders and turned her toward him.
"Maybe he acted as a mirror to my own."

Compassion for his predicament showed in her eyes. No artist
should be torn apart as he was by demands that ought never to
have interfered with his true vocation. She touched his face with
her fingertips. "I'm not here to interrupt your work. I want to be a
quiet, undisturbing presence."

Privately it amused him that she should suppose he could ever be
other than totally aware of her presence. "Talk as much as you
like," he said as he picked up a pumice stone to resume the polishing he had been doing when she arrived. A bucket of clean water
stood ready for washing away the dust that the pumice stone created as it smoothed the marble.

"Is that a long task?" she asked.

"Yes, it has been and always is when using pumice. Henri, my
assistant, worked on it earlier today and looked tired enough for
his arms to drop off, which is why I sent him home. In any case, I
want to finish it off myself, because there comes a delicate point
when the marble can pass from being perfected to being refined to
a fault."

She was intrigued by the process as she was by everything about
his work. Looking around the studio, she saw mallets, differently
shaped chisels, hammers, scrapers, gouges, rasps, and far too many
other tools for her to ask the purpose of each one. There were also
rolls of wire, which she knew would be used to make the armatures
on which to build up work in clay or terra-cotta. Pigeonholed
shelves were filled with the same kind of clutter she had seen in
Rodin's vast studio. And behind a curtain was a tiny kitchen with
an old cooking stove and a yellow stone sink with one tap. There
was a kettle, a much-used coffeepot, and a cupboard that held
some cheap crockery from a street market. A door led to an outdoor privy in a tiny courtyard.

She wandered on around the room and came to a deep recess in which there was a table that had seen better days and benches fixed to the wall. "I'll lay our supper there later," she said. "Was the furniture here when you took over the place?"

"Yes, it's just as it was, except that Anna insisted I brighten the place up with that Russian shawl and the cushions you see covering the leather couch."

These items did make a brilliant splash of crimson, purple, and scarlet, but nothing else gave any touch of comfort. Juliette smiled to herself. Nikolai had avoided bringing any of the luxurious trappings of his other life into this retreat.

Having explored the whole studio, she seated herself on the shawl-spread couch. Daylight was fading and he had switched on an electric light, which shone directly down on him. She was half-shadowed by the saucer-shaped lampshade, but her hair still caught red-gold highlights, her white blouse and dark skirt set off by the brightly woven covering and cushions behind her. He glanced at her with a smile and continued his polishing.

He liked having her near him as he worked. It was a new experience for them both. As they talked, she asked him to tell her more about his childhood. She really knew very little about his life except that he had no brothers and his only sister was Anna. His mother had died some while ago.

"My parents' marriage was arranged, as such matches always are, for reasons of inheritance, property, and land. My father was fifteen when the betrothal took place and my mother was fourteen. They married eight years later when, I suppose, he'd had time to sow his wild oats."

"Surely such an archaic custom has died out by now?"

"Not altogether. Young people are still subject to extreme pressure if they refuse to marry according to their parents' wishes."

"Were your parents content in their marriage?"

"Against all odds, I believe they were. I know our home always seemed a happy place and was the center of constant family gatherings, with aunts and uncles and cousins coming for house parties in celebration of anything my mother could think of, from birthdays to national feast days. Those were wonderful times in my childhood."

"Please tell me about them."

As he talked, she formed a mental picture of the wide green lawns and flower gardens where he and his cousins had played shuttlecock and hide-and-seek, pirates and Cossacks and explorers, the boys in sailor suits, the little girls in frilly dresses, and, much to their annoyance, sunhats covered with dancing layers of white embroidery anglais. As they grew older there were archery, tennis, dances, balls, and parties, as well as hunting and shooting for the older boys. Nikolai himself had been wild for riding and more than once had taken fast horses from the stables even though he was forbidden to ride them. He had suffered a fall or two, but nothing had deterred him.

"So, in the midst of all this," Juliette questioned with keen interest, "how did you discover your wish to sculpt?"

"The classic answer would be to say that it was from the time of making mud pies, but it wasn't like that. I had an uncle who liked to paint and sculpt in his leisure hours. When I was about ten, he gave me a lump of clay to model whatever I wished. I remember I chose to do one of the hounds, and when I'd finished, in about an hour, he stared at it so long and hard that I thought I'd made a terrible mess and he didn't know what to say for fear of hurting my feelings. Instead, he grabbed me by the arm and pushed me to another stand, stuck some handfuls of clay on it, and told me to make something else. Even if he hadn't liked that first effort, it would have been too late. The seed had been sown. Everything grew from there. It was that same uncle who persuaded my widowed father to let me have a year at St. Petersburg Art School to assess my potential, and then brought me to Paris when I was seventeen."

"Does he still paint and sculpt himself?"

"Unfortunately not. He has developed arthritis in his hands, but his interest in art is as lively as ever. I visit him as much as possible whenever I'm at home."

"Does he have any of your work?"

"Yes. He has a bust of himself in bronze and another of his late wife. When he last wrote, he offered to buy "The Wolf," one of my early works, which he saw when once in Paris. I'm going to ship it to him as a birthday gift next week."

"I've never seen it."

"It's in that cupboard." He nodded in its direction. "I'll show you later."

When he had done all the polishing he could that evening, Juliette pulled the curtains across the windows and put a kettle on to boil for fresh coffee. He hung up his linen smock and hooked the bandanna over it before he washed his face, arms, and hands at the yellow stone sink. Meanwhile, she spread the red and white check cloth on the table and arranged the food from her basket on plates she had found in the kitchen. There was pâté, cold meats and cheese, salad, a long loaf of bread, and some fruit. Having found a candle in the kitchen, she stuck it in a saucer and set it in the center of the table.

Nikolai poured the red wine and they sat for a long time over their meal, sometimes holding hands across the table. Afterward she washed the dishes while he dried. Then he took the bronze wolf from the cupboard and set it on a stand within the light. As with all his work, it was dramatic, the animal fearsome and alert, its hackles risen. It was when he was replacing the wolf on a shelf that a stack of drawings caught Juliette's eye. The top one was of herself.

Wordlessly, she took it up and saw there was another underneath, and yet more below that. The whole of the little stack consisted of sketches of her. He watched her in silence as she took them across to the table and spread them out in the candlelight. They showed her seated and standing, even glancing down as she knew she did when she was trying to keep her feelings in check.

"When did you do all these?" she asked in surprise.

He came and stood behind her. "While you were away. Remember, I mentioned once that I always make preliminary sketches for my next project."

"So I'm to be your next model!"

"Not for the first time. I did a bust of you from memory when I was at home."

She looked over her shoulder at him. "Do you still have it there?"

"Yes, cast in bronze. It has a place of honor in my apartment."

She returned her gaze to the sketches and smiled. "So I'm to pose for you. It will be difficult to fit in the sittings, but we'll just have to take whatever time we can. I'll enjoy being here with you away from other people." A little laugh escaped her. "La! This will be different from your other sculptures, as I can see from these drawings. I'll be fully clothed!"

He nuzzled the nape of her neck. "Not by my choice," he said softly.

She drew in a sharp silent breath at the suddenly charged atmosphere his words had created. Slowly she leaned back against his chest, closing her eyes in pleasure as his hands moved from her waist to cup her breasts caressingly and his lips traveled to her ear and into her hair. His tender fondling made her nipples rise through the satin of her chemise and the soft chiffon of her blouse. Her body began to throb with long-suppressed yearnings. He had caressed her many times before, but then they had never been sure of remaining alone as they were now.

Slowly yet willingly, she turned to him, tilting her head back to meet his lips with her own. Immediately his arms were tight about her while she flung hers round his neck and they kissed wildly, his mouth fierce, her own response exultant and abandoned. They were possessed by passion, all restraint flown. Nothing existed for her but him and the force of her own desire. She did not know when he switched off the light, leaving them in the candleglow, but it might have been in the last second before he gathered her effortlessly up in his arms and carried her across to the couch.

He uncovered her breasts swiftly, her chiffon blouse flying apart with a gleam of tiny pearly buttons, and with his stroking fingers and his tongue he explored the lovely shape of her, creating such delicious sensations that her spine arched and involuntarily she dug her fingers into his shoulders. With his every touch making her tremble ecstatically, he removed all her clothes, kissing every part of her body as it was revealed to him. When he moved away from her briefly to undress, she raised her arms and held them out to him. He loomed over her then like one of his own powerful sculptures, before gathering her close, a warm and living and loving man, and locking his passionate mouth on hers.

His adoring exploration of her body banished her last vestige of modesty and awakened her to new realms of pleasure that were at times almost too exquisite to bear. He waited no longer and entered her with a deep groan of joy, sweeping her with him through all the rhythms of passion to a mutual and colossal explosion of total ecstasy.

In the quiet contentment that followed, they lay close, limbs entwined, murmuring the talk of lovers. He pressed his lips to her palm when she rested her hand against his cheek, and she smiled when he stroked back a long tendril of her hair, which had long since tumbled from its pins. Then, after a while, he began to touch her again with such intimate tenderness that she melted once more into his ardent lovemaking.

The candle was close to drowning in its own wax when Juliette awoke and sat up with a start. She had been lying within the circle of Nikolai's arm, but he was still sound asleep and her movements had not disturbed him. He lay magnificently sprawled, one leg against hers, the other flung outward, his foot over the side of the couch.

She left the couch and found her gold fob-watch amid the tumble of her clothes. It was three o'clock. Hastily she dressed, hesitating as to whether she would waken him and then deciding against it. But as she moved to the door in the near-darkness, she knocked into a chair and the resulting clatter awakened him instantly.

"You're leaving!" He pushed back his hair with one hand and swung himself from the couch.

"I have to go."

He took hold of her shoulders and drew her toward him. "I want to keep you with me forever."

"And I would love nothing more, but I must leave now," she protested, fighting her own wish to stay.

Seeing that she would not be persuaded, he released her reluctantly. "I'll get dressed, then. Please wait. You'll not stop me from seeing you safely home."

When they went outside he hailed a passing cab, and before long he was leading her up the steps to her door. He kissed her adoringly once more and this time she clung to him, the intimate hours they had spent together uniting them as never before.

"Until tomorrow, my darling," he said softly.

"Tomorrow," she echoed in a whisper.

Eleven

POSING FOR NIKOLAI was not the easy task Juliette had expected it to be. She had thought he would make allowances for her not being a professional model, and she would sit comfortably in a chair, but it was not to be like that at all. He had asked her if she would wear the Delphos robe, but, remembering her renewed promise to Denise, she had said she could not, in case the sculpture should go on exhibition. But she agreed to make something similar, slightly Grecian in feel.

So she created a simple, sleeveless tunic in cream silk with a round neckline and took it with her to the studio in a plain cardboard box.

She went behind the models' screen to change, and when she emerged, Nikolai grinned his approval.

"Wonderful! Couldn't be better!"

He took her face between his hands, then kissed her before he led her to the modeling stand.

"Let me tidy my hair," she insisted, for his fingers had loosened a few strands.

"I like it as it is. Don't touch it."

On the stand he arranged her pose, taking her wrists to draw her hands down just a little behind her, and tilting her chin to the angle he wanted. She thought that if he asked her to be on tiptoe she might look as if she were about to take wing, but he did not mention that. Apparently satisfied, he crossed to the large window and pulled a curtain half across it, creating just the right amounts of shadow. He proceeded then to twist the stand this way and that on its castors, which rattled on the stone floor. She raised her eyebrows half-mockingly.

"Are you trying to make me lose my balance?" she asked.

Drawn from his concentration, his gaze cleared. "Not at all," he said with a smile. "I just wanted to view you from every angle."

He took up a sketchpad and began to draw her from various viewpoints. She was surprised how difficult it was to remain absolutely still. Twice her chin sank and he raised it again with his fingertips. But his pencil moved swiftly and the drawings were soon done.

"That's all for now." He put the sketchpad down. "By the time you come again I'll have made a small clay model or two. Then we really can get to work, because the finished sculpture will be life-size."

"May I see the sketches?" she asked as she stepped from the stand.

She had expected them to appear static, but it was quite the reverse. If he had drawn her with every breath she'd taken, he could not have captured her more as a woman poised on the brink of some new venture. But what could that be? She almost asked him and was indirectly reminded of what needed to be said.

"Naturally I'll model for you as much as I can, but you have to remember that Denise wants me to go to England soon!"

Her sister had finally decided that two British silk mills were offering the best prices and delivery times for Juliette's own designs. Denise wanted her to make the final choice.

Nikolai sighed resignedly as he embraced her. "How could I forget? But you shouldn't be away as long this time as you were in Lyon."

She laced her fingers at the back of his neck. "Of course not. Only long enough to see the first patterns come off the looms."

"I think I'll go home for a short visit while you're away. There are a number of matters that are impossible to handle from here."

"What a wonderful idea. That way we won't miss any time together."

"That's what I thought too. Anna is going home for a few months at the end of the week, so I'll be able to travel with her. Have you heard from Gabrielle yet?"

"Yes. She and her husband are waiting to welcome me whenever I arrive."

But he no longer wanted to discuss her going away, and began to cover her face and neck with kisses. Never had he expected to want to cherish any woman as he did her for the rest of his life.

Denise was surprised to hear that Countess Dolohova wished to speak privately with her in her office. The many outfits she was taking back to Russia with her had already been delivered and, not expecting to see the countess again until next spring, Denise's immediate thought was that she had some complaint about the bill. She was used to her rich clients trying to beat her down when it came to pay. It was a hazard more common in *haute couture* than those outside the business ever realized, but she and the *directrice* always stuck to their guns in a smiling, tactful way.

Yet, as Denise waited for the countess to be shown in, she dismissed this as a possible reason for the visit. The idea of such a woman even deigning to talk about money, especially as she never even asked the price of any garment, was ludicrous. Anna Dolohova never lost her inherent haughtiness, even when at her most charming. Puzzled, Denise rose from the desk to greet her as she entered. When seated, Anna came straight to the point.

"As you know," she commenced briskly, "I'm leaving for St. Petersburg at the end of the week, but before I go I want to speak most seriously to you about the relationship between your sister and my brother."

Denise was alarmed. "I don't understand."

"Don't you, Madame la Baronne?" Anna spoke with an edge to her voice. "Nikolai has told me he is in love with Juliette and intends to marry her. I see you are shocked, as was I. Believe me, I have nothing against Juliette, but the match is impossible. Nikolai has obligations at home that he cannot surrender under any circumstances."

"I can't see Juliette ever wanting to leave Paris. Maybe they plan to live here, and he'll make visits home as I understand he does now from time to time." Denise was clutching at straws.

"My father is in poor health. He's a proud man and would not admit it, but the call for Nikolai to return home permanently could come at any time. There are too many problems that cannot be delegated. My brother is a talented sculptor, but he can sculpt as easily in Russia as he can here. Paris is a dream for any young artist, but there comes a time when reality has to take over."

"Have you said all this to him?" In despair, Denise was seeing every one of her wonderful plans for the future draining away like sand.

Anna sighed to herself. Out of her immense concern and sibling affection for Nikolai, she had spoken bluntly to him, only to arouse his displeasure. "Everything I said to my brother fell on deaf ears. He is unshakable in his decision to return home with me for a short stay in order to make arrangements for his marriage to Juliette. I felt compelled to discuss this crisis with you since it is of equal concern to both of us. If Juliette were a divorcée or an experienced woman of the world, as so many of Nikolai's previous fancies, I'd know it was no more than a passing *affaire,* but this time it is different."

"In what way?"

"Because Juliette is young and beautiful and no doubt believes and encourages whatever he's promised her. He's convinced himself that it's possible, but I foresee only disaster for them both if they aren't stopped before it's too late."

Denise was confused. "How can you be so sure?"

"He is the Tsar's godson, madame! My father will turn to his old friend to intervene as he did once before when Nikolai's youthful ambition to sculpt in Paris for the rest of his life created an impasse that nobody else was able to overcome."

"Young men in love can be very determined. Perhaps he will not listen to anyone."

Anna shrugged and sat back in her chair. "Then his life will be made wretched by ostracism both at home and abroad. Juliette will be unhappy on his behalf as well as her own, because, when the first flush of desire wanes, he will come to see her as a burden as well as a barrier to the society he enjoyed previously. As his wife, Juliette would never be received by the Russian nobility. Forgive me for speaking bluntly, but I have to emphasize that she is at present a humble seamstress. Doubtless you are training her for a more important position in your business, but she will still be a working girl. I have made inquiries about your parents and find that although reported to be most respectable persons, they were nevertheless engaged in trade. My brother has acquired ridiculously liberal and modern ideas while in Paris, ideas that are quite unacceptable in Russia. The situation is impossible."

Denise had never hated a client before. Their money and their patronage had always enabled her to overlook their faults, but the countess's words had caused the blood to rise in her cheeks as she forgot her own snobbery in light of the vicious snub she now heard directed against her and her sister. Cold fury erupted within her.

"What you are saying, Countess," she exploded harshly, "is that if Juliette had been Russian instead of French she might well have been in the crowd of poor starving people—working girls among them—who, a few years ago, were shot down by guards at the Tsar's own gates when they came unarmed to kneel in the snow and implore his aid!"

Anna sprang to her feet, her eyes blazing. "How dare you! I shall never enter this building again! I reject everything you've just made for me, and do not ever dare to request payment!"

She pulled open the door and stalked out, leaving it wide behind her. Pale and tight-lipped, she swept on down the stairs and out to her waiting carriage.

As the wheels rolled forward she sat glowering and drummed the ferrule of her folded parasol on the floor with every thought that pounded in her brain. There had been something else she'd been on the point of telling that upstart dressmaker, but now the moment was lost. Not even on the telephone would she speak to that creature again.

More than ever she was determined that Nikolai should finish with Juliette. If he had chosen a well-born girl, even as she herself had once loved a titled man whom she had not been allowed to marry, she would have fought tooth and nail to see that they wed, but she could not condone this betrayal of their class. All the troubles in Russia were being caused by peasants demanding the right to vote, to lower taxes, education, and everything else that belonged solely to their betters.

Her thoughts turned to the beautiful clothes she would be sending back to Maison Landelle. Her only hope was that Madame Paquin would work her employees day and night to supply her with what she needed to take back to St. Petersburg immediately. Surely, faced with such a stupendous order, Madame Paquin would be eager to oblige.

Anna stopped drumming her parasol's ferrule. Her frown cleared. She adored choosing new clothes.

When Denise had closed the door after the departing countess she sank down in the vacated chair. She was shaking. What a terrible scene! Heaven alone knew how many Russian clients she would lose when they heard about her outburst.

Gradually her anger turned against Juliette. Of all the young men who had danced attendance on the girl during the nearly two and a half years since her homecoming from the convent, she'd had to fall in love with a foreigner. In retrospect, Denise supposed the countess had come to her in the hope that together they could stop Nikolai and Juliette from making the false step that would lead only to misery. But what was to be done? Denise recalled her own vehement rejection of her parents' advice to wait before rushing into marriage with Claude de Landelle. The more they had wanted her to reconsider, the more determined she had become. Juliette would react the same way. The young always did.

Restlessly Denise moved back to her desk and sat abstractedly tapping a pencil at one end and then the other. The girl's trip to London should be brought forward. Separation had made no difference before, but in Russia Anna Dolohova would take sterner measures to make her brother see sense. It was a faint chance, but there was nothing else to do at present.

Denise's tumbled thoughts turned to another problem. How to explain the countess's rejection of the clothes she had been so pleased with before? Juliette would want to know the reason, as would Pierre and the *directrice*. There seemed to be only one solution. She would instruct the doorman to bring the boxes directly to her. After working hours, when she was on her own, she would go through them, remove the Landelle labels and all valuable trimmings, then package them herself to send to a woman she knew in the provinces, who dealt in good cast-offs and paid well for any *haute couture* garments that came her way.

With this decision made, Denise checked her anxiety-ridden face in the mirror. She composed herself as best she could as she rang for her secretary. The full account for all that Anna Dolohova owed was to be dispatched immediately. Denise was determined that the countess should at least pay her dues. But the account was returned that very evening with an accompanying lawyer's letter stating that none of the clothes had been to the countess's satisfaction and if there were any further communication, the matter would be taken to court. Denise almost tore out her hair. No couture house could risk the scandal of pressing for payment, especially when such a fashionable woman as Anna Dolohova declared the garments to be below par.

Yet Denise's humiliation was not yet complete. The countess did not send back the clothes in their original beribboned boxes, but bundled together in a canvas sack. It was the ultimate snub. Denise wept with helpless fury behind the locked door of her office.

Juliette was not surprised when the date of her trip was brought forward. She knew how keen Denise was for the matter to be settled. A cable sent to Gabrielle brought an immediate reply: the new dates were as convenient as those previously arranged. Juliette told Nikolai over the telephone. It meant she would be able to model for him only once more before she left.

When she arrived at the studio late the following Saturday afternoon, Nikolai's assistant, Henri, opened the door. Nikolai had already built up the clay on the supporting armature and it was taking its first shape. He paused to have a few words of smiling conversation with her before resuming his task. Behind the model's screen, she changed and carefully arranged her hair as it had been—slightly disarranged by Nikolai's hands—on her previous visit.

"That's exactly right," he said as she took up her pose on the stand. "Perhaps the chin a fraction higher. Good."

As the time passed, she was fascinated to see how the clay took shape under his strong, long-fingered hands. When Juliette took a rest, Henri made her and Nikolai fresh coffee, but Nikolai's became cold and remained barely tasted as he worked on. It was quite late when finally he called a halt to the session. Henri, eager to get away, gave the floor a final cleaning and set everything to rights very quickly. As soon as he was gone Nikolai locked the door after him.

Turning back into the room, he saw that Juliette had already removed her silk tunic and stood ravishingly beautiful in her nakedness, her glorious hair hanging free of its pins. He went to kneel before her, enfolding her thighs in his arms as he pressed his kiss against her with all the devoted homage of a truly loving man.

.   .   .   .

On the eve of their leaving Paris, Nikolai took Juliette to dine at Larue's, where she had first worn the Delphos robe and where they had dined many times since. As a wrap she wore the Knossos scarf that he had given her on her birthday, its green silk soft and diaphanous as a sea mist, its geometric motifs, reputed to be inspired by Cycladic art, in deeper shades with touches of gold.

At their favorite table, he took a Fabergé ring box of white holly wood from his pocket. When she did not accept it from him, he placed it in front of her.

"Please open it," he urged.

Slowly she pressed the catch and the lid flew up to reveal a dazzle of magnificent diamonds. Immediately her expression became anguished, her lips trembling. "Oh, Nikolai! You know I wanted us to wait. We have so much to work out, so many difficulties to solve."

"That needn't stop me from giving you a gift of love. If I choose to see it as having a more special significance, then that is my privilege." He took the ring from its velvet bed and explained that the three kinds of gold used in the setting were a Russian tradition for such rings.

"Rings of betrothal?" she challenged.

"Rings of love," he countered, with a smiling shrug that neither denied nor endorsed what she had asked. "Let me put this on your finger."

She could see how much it would mean to him, but instinctively she clenched her hands in her lap. They had discussed and argued their marrying ever since they had first made love. She had emphasized everything that common sense told her would be against their union, but he would not be dissuaded. No one was more aware than she of the intense snobbery and rigid lines drawn by high society, for she came in contact with them almost daily at Maison Landelle. Not even the fact that she was a baronne's sister would ever gain her entré to the old aristocracy of France, and still less to that of Russia. She knew that her one and only visit to Prince Vadim's house had been tolerated solely because of his old friendship with her tante Lucille. Love had not blinded her to reality.

Yet she did not want to spoil this last evening with Nikolai before they went their separate ways, however temporary the parting was to be. "Let us wait until you've been home and talked everything over with your father. I don't want to be the cause of a family rift."

He was determined. "You won't be. My father has become more tolerant in his old age."

She thought it a vain hope. Nikolai planned that after he inherited they would spend three or four months of every year in Paris. This, he believed, would make tolerable any social problems they'd have to face the rest of the time. He had a cousin, who shared his own liberated ideals, whom he could trust to take control of the great estate in his absence. But just the thought of living in Russia dismayed Juliette. She had avoided offending Nikolai's loyalty to his own country by reminding him that more enlightened nations thought of the Tsar as a tyrant. Yet he knew she abhorred, as he did, the terrible conditions of the Russian peasants, which were being fully reported in the French newspapers. It made no difference to her that Nikolai was resolved to make changes when the Karasvin estate was his. His efforts would be no more than a drop in the ocean of the troubles in that vast land, and she wanted no part of such an oppressive system, even as the wife of the man she loved so much. It was an impasse that seemed insurmountable.

He had found her clenched hands in her lap and was gently but firmly releasing her fingers. "I love you, Juliette. Surely that is enough reason for you to accept my ring as a constant reminder of what you will always mean to me."

She let him draw up her hand, and he slid the beautiful ring onto her finger. For a moment she could not be sure if it was the sparkle of the marvelous diamonds or the tears suddenly glittering on her lashes that made him appear to be already far away from her.

Later, when she had closed her bedroom door behind her, she stood gazing at the ring before eventually sliding it from her finger and returning it to its box, which she placed in her jewelry casket. There it would remain, except when she wore it to please Nikolai. Perhaps one day there might be another reason as well, but in no way was it yet possible to see how that might come about.

Twelve

THE CHANNEL CROSSING was not unpleasantly choppy. When the white cliffs of Dover appeared on the horizon, Juliette pushed aside the plaid traveling rug over her knees and went to the rail, holding her hat in the stiff breeze.

Her thoughts drifted to Nikolai, who had been traveling on a train with his sister for some hours already. His was a far longer journey, and his purpose entirely different from hers. He had said it would be a tedious ride to St. Petersburg since he and Anna were not on particularly good terms. He did not give the reason, but she saw the strained relationship as the first sign of what he could expect to face at home. He could not be forbidden to marry whomever he chose, no matter what displeasure it caused his family, but that was not the issue.

"Informing my father of my intention to marry you," Nikolai had said before his departure, "is a filial duty I'm pleased to perform. He and I haven't always seen eye to eye, and many differences still remain, but if he was strict when I was a child, he was also just, and I'm counting on that sense of justice now to spare any estrangement between us in his old age."

It was as if he had not heard or heeded anything she had said to him. And now he was on his way, traveling in the luxurious family railway coach that Anna had ordered attached to the rest of the train. Despite herself, Juliette found it impossible to quell a tiny flicker of hope that in some unforeseeable way all their problems might be solved. It was as though his decisive action had ign.. ~d an optimistic spark without her being aware of it. But now, physically detached from France and in a kind of limbo, she was able to reflect on the situation with a curious clarity.

Might it be said that she was even able to review matters in the faint tint of a rosy light? If Nikolai's father should live to be very old—and by all accounts the Karasvin men were long-lived if not struck down by the hazards of war or other disasters—it might be years before any thought need be given to residing in Russia. Perhaps by then the young Tsarevitch would have inherited the throne, and who knew what reforms he might introduce for the benefit of his poor downtrodden subjects. Everything in this new century was moving so quickly—men even taking to the air and women breaking into realms that were formerly masculine strong-holds—that surely a time would come when the love of a couple from different classes would be greeted with tolerance instead of social ostracism.

During Juliette's reverie the white cliffs had come nearer. She moved away from the rail to prepare for going ashore. After disembarkation there was almost no delay in showing her passport or going through customs. The London train was waiting. Soon she was looking out at the lush green countryside of Kent, the pale golden sunshine playing softly over thatched farmhouses, orchards, hopfields, and the warm red, russet, and brown brickwork of conical oasthouses. After a glimpse of Chatham dockyard, it was not long before she and Gabrielle were greeting each other affectionately at Victoria Station.

"You're here at last, Juliette! It seems aeons since we last met in Paris!"

"Why haven't you been back?"

"Impossible! Since Derek became a director of the bank he's too busy to get away for any length of time, and I won't go anywhere without him. It's my pet excuse for keeping a safe distance from my mother."

"Have your parents been to see you instead?"

"They've been twice." Gabrielle rolled her eyes expressively. By now she and Juliette were seated in the gleaming Daimler, a liveried chauffeur at the wheel. "I'm always glad to see my father, but my mother creates trouble as soon as she crosses the threshold." She chatted on as the London traffic closed in around them. Sud-

denly she pointed through the window. "Look! There's Bucking-
ham Palace! Derek and I have been invited to several functions
when the King and Queen were present. I must say that royalty
does give a wonderful sense of occasion to any event."

After gazing out at the palace with its scarlet-coated guardsmen
at the gates, Juliette sat back in her seat. The Daimler was sweeping
down the tree-lined Mall. She regarded her friend humorously.
"What talk is this from a staunch French Republican? Are you
becoming a royalist in your new land?"

Gabrielle burst out laughing. "Perhaps I am! Maybe it won't be
long before you see me marching along the Champs Élysées with a
banner saying, 'Bring back the Bourbons! All is forgiven!'"

Juliette was pleased to see Gabrielle so carefree. "You're so different. It's as if a burden had been lifted from you. I'm delighted
to see you so happy," she exclaimed.

"Yes, I am," Gabrielle declared eagerly. "Being married to
Derek still seems like a miracle to me. He came into my life like a
knight on a white charger and took me away from all that had
made my life wretched."

"Nobody could be more glad for you than I."

"I know." Gabrielle's voice softened. "That's why it means so
much for me to have you staying a while. It's not easy for a foreigner to make English women friends here. The only new friends
I've made have been among the French community; the rest are
just acquaintances." Suddenly her eyes twinkled mischievously.
"You won't find Englishmen unfriendly. A pretty face and a
French accent are magnets to them. You're going to enjoy yourself
in London! I'm giving a party for you, and I've accepted lots of
invitations on your behalf as well as for Derek and myself. He's also
booked seats for all the best shows and for the opening night of
Tristan und Isolde at the Royal Opera House at Covent Garden!"

Juliette felt quite overwhelmed. "Have you forgotten that I'm
here to work?"

"Of course not." Gabrielle gestured dismissively. "That can be
fitted in somewhere."

The Townsends' residence was in an elegant terrace of houses in
Berkeley Square. When Derek came home, he and Juliette met for
the first time. With his prematurely gray hair, she thought he
looked older than his years, but then he held a highly important
position and youthful looks would only have worked against him.

Nevertheless, his skin was clear, his jawline crisp, and he was lean and trim in build.

"It gives me great pleasure to welcome you to our home, Juliette," he said.

Gabrielle slipped her hand into the crook of his elbow, smiling up at him. "Aren't we lucky to have her here! We'll lock Juliette up if she even thinks of going back to France before weeks and weeks have gone by."

He caught Juliette's eye with a look of understanding and then glanced down into his wife's upturned face. "I'm sure Juliette will stay as long as she is able, but she is in business as I am and isn't free to do exactly as she might wish. You and I know what that means, don't we, my dear? We'll have to let her go when she feels compelled to depart."

Gabrielle reached out a hand to Juliette in appeal. "But you will stay as long as you possibly can?"

"You know I will," Juliette promised. "But it can only be for a few extra days. Another time I'll come just for a holiday."

Later, Derek spoke to Juliette on her own. "My wife still suffers a great deal from homesickness. She has looked forward to your coming so much, not only because you've always been her best friend, but also because you represent all the better times of her childhood in France. Love of one's country becomes more acute during the first few years away from all that was familiar."

He did not know how much meaning his words held for Juliette. Once again she thought how impossible it would be for her to tear up her roots and go to live in Russia. "You're very understanding."

"As you were to Gabrielle in her convent days. She has told me many times that you were the only person she could trust in her unstable, unhappy youth."

Juliette tilted her head. "I think her memory has enhanced the role I played. I know now that Gabrielle needed an anchor, even though I'm sure I didn't realize it at the time, and she will always need one. That's why I can see she has found the right husband in you."

"I'll never fail her."

Juliette could tell he was a man who would keep his word.

That night when Derek was in bed with Gabrielle, he discovered tears on her cheek. Immediately he reached over to switch on the bedside light. "Whatever is the matter, my darling?" he asked in concern, leaning over her again.

"I'm so afraid for Juliette!" She clung to him. "I've a terrible feeling that when she leaves here it will be to go so far away that there's no telling what will happen to her."

"Why ever should that be? She's only going back to Paris." He spoke soothingly, supposing the premonition to be no more than his wife's own dread of being cut off forever from her beloved France. He made up his mind to find some way to take her to Paris soon, but as yet he could not promise anything. "Go to sleep. There's nothing to worry about. Imagination can play such tricks sometimes."

"Are you sure?" She looked at him appealingly, anxious for her fears to be banished.

"Yes, I am. Now close your eyes." He kissed her lids and she snuggled closer to him, seeking still further the security of his arms.

The lamp was switched off again. He was a sound sleeper, and if it took longer than usual for Gabrielle to doze off he did not know it. This was the first time she had not been wholly reassured by him. Though she tried to take comfort from the knowledge that Juliette had always faced tribulation courageously, she could not overcome her immense concern for her friend's future.

Before leaving Paris, Juliette had arranged to telephone the silk-mill owners in both London and Macclesfield after her arrival. As it was, she had been in London a week before she was able to escape the entanglements of Gabrielle's social arrangements in order to get down to business.

The London silk mill lay north of the Thames. Juliette had a very satisfactory discussion with the owner and approved the samples of finished work she was shown. Some of the raw silk had come from English silkworm farms, but most was imported from China and India. She would have been prepared to allot the order to this silk mill, but Denise had wanted her to visit Macclesfield as well. She decided to leave for Macclesfield in the morning.

"You can't possibly go tomorrow!" Gabrielle protested. "We have a box for the Wagner gala performance in the evening! In any case, I want to go to Macclesfield with you. I'll not let you travel alone in a foreign land."

So the Macclesfield trip had to be postponed. Juliette wore the Delphos robe to the opera. Such a magnificent event demanded her best gown, although for the sake of her host and hostess, she wore her silk chiffon dévoré coat with it to avoid creating a scandal.

The Royal Opera House, with its gilt and crimson, was a rich setting for a glorious performance. The auditorium sparkled with jewels and the gleam of stiff white shirt fronts. In the royal box, a princess and her party added to the grandeur of the evening. During the interval Juliette left the box to stroll with Derek and Gabrielle. Suddenly she was addressed unexpectedly by someone who had come unnoticed to her side.

"What a wonderful surprise to find you here, Juliette!"

She knew his voice instantly. Her companions, engaged in conversation, did not see her turn toward the man who had spoken. "Marco Romanelli! Of all people!" she exclaimed delightedly. "How are you? Why are you in London? We were to have met some time in Paris."

He laughed with her in their mutual astonishment. "I'm well and I've come to London on business," he began, craning his neck. "Where's Nikolai?"

"He's far away, in St. Petersburg on a visit. How he would have liked to be here to make our trio complete! I'm in England on business too, but combining it with a visit to a dear friend and her husband. I'll introduce you." She would have attracted her host and hostess's attention, but he stayed her.

"One moment first. There's somebody who is waiting to meet you. As soon as I sighted you I pointed you out to him."

Then she saw that a tall man of immense presence and striking good looks had come forward and stood smiling expectantly at her. Every instinct told her who he was, even as Marco made the introduction.

"Juliette, allow me to present Don Mariano Fortuny."

She scarcely heard anything else he said, so thrilled was she to be meeting the designer whose work she had so admired. It flashed through her mind that Marco had told her in Lyon of Fortuny's passion for Wagner, which would explain why he had come to this particular gala. He was strongly built, with a splendid nose, luminous blue eyes, thick, dark hair, and a neat mustache and beard.

Immaculate in his evening clothes, he had a dashing air about him, as if he belonged to a more romantic era.

He bowed deeply to her. If he had added a flourish it would have seemed entirely natural.

"I'm honored to meet you, Mademoiselle Cladel. Marco has told me the tale of how you found the Delphos robe discarded somewhere and sewed it together again. I would like to thank you for enhancing the gown with your elegance."

From anyone else the compliment would have been effusive, but from him it was simply a sincere tribute and Juliette accepted it as such.

"I'll never own a gown that will mean more to me."

He nodded in satisfaction, pleased with her reply. "You design clothes yourself, I believe."

"I've some experience in that work, but my interests also include textile design, which is what has brought me to England."

"I'm leaving for Venice tomorrow. If ever you visit there, I hope you will call on me. I'd like to hear about your work and show you my own designs."

"I'll remember your kind invitation."

"Now I must rejoin my party. This has been a pleasure. Pray excuse me. *Adieu,* mademoiselle."

Juliette turned back to Marco as Fortuny left them. "What luck! Two splendid surprises in as many minutes! Now I want you to meet Derek and Gabrielle."

For the rest of the interval Marco conversed with all three of them. When he heard that Juliette and Gabrielle would be leaving for Macclesfield in the morning, he said that he would be visiting the silk mills too.

"It would be a pleasure to travel there with you both."

It was agreed, and Gabrielle was relieved. She did not like traveling without a male escort. When the bell rang for the end of the interval, Derek invited Marco to the party he and Gabrielle were giving for Juliette when the Macclesfield trip was over. He accepted at once.

It proved to be a very pleasant expedition to Macclesfield. Juliette and Marco conducted their business during the day and they all spent the evenings together. Eventually she decided to give her order to the London silk mill, which offered the best delivery time, and on the third day they traveled back to London together.

"I think," Gabrielle remarked, when she and Juliette had parted from Marco at Euston Station, "that Signor Romanelli is very attracted to you."

Juliette shook her head laughingly. "You've said that about practically every man I've spoken to since I arrived."

Gabrielle smiled but said no more.

A letter was waiting for Juliette in a handwriting she did not recognize. As she opened it, a silk label slipped out of the envelope onto the floor. She picked it up, realized what it was, and read the letter eagerly. It was from Fortuny:

I was told that when you found the Delphos robe in pieces, its lacings and label were missing. You have replaced the lacings. I enclose the final touch with my compliments.

Juliette rushed to show Gabrielle what she had received. "He would never have sent this label to me if he had been able to see any fault in my remaking of the gown!" she exclaimed. "I wish I could thank him personally, but I know that he will be on his way back to Italy by now."

When Juliette had sewn the label into the back of the gown's neckline, she wrote to Nikolai of her good luck. She did not see Marco again until the Townsends' party, which was on the eve of his departure. He already knew about the label, and his eyes twinkled at her enthusiasm for the gift.

"I've written my thanks to him at his Venetian home," she said. "The Palazzo Pesaro degli Orfei! Is it as glorious as it sounds?"

"Yes, indeed. It's one of the largest palaces in Venice and was built in the thirteenth century by the great Pesaro family. These days it's known as the Palazzo Orfei."

"Is it on the Grand Canal?"

"No, a short distance away. Fortuny—or Don Mariano, as he likes to be addressed—has lived there since he moved out of his mother's palace, the Palazzo Martinengo, which is on the Grand Canal, some years ago."

Juliette was much in demand and was not able to dance with Marco as often as she would have wished, but he was a very sociable man and at ease with people. Whenever she glanced across at him, he was clearly enjoying himself, and the women were finding his Italian good looks very attractive.

She had saved the supper dance for him. "Shall you be seeing

Nikolai in Paris on your way home?" she asked when the waltz ended and they joined those moving toward the buffet.

"Not this time. I've a busy season ahead of me."

"Have you ever visited the silk mills in Japan?"

"I was there three years ago. Were you thinking of my orders of silk for Fortuny?"

She nodded. "I wish his Delphos robe would get the recognition it deserves."

"You need never worry about Fortuny. He's such an individualist that public acclaim means little to him. He's a man in love with the past, its riches and its magnificent textiles, its works of art and its architecture. It's her ancient links with the East that make Venice the ideal city for him. If he could robe himself like Marco Polo I believe he would be in his element."

"Everything you say about him makes me more fascinated by his achievements."

When the party was over Juliette bade Marco farewell. "Until we meet in Paris one day, Marco."

"Until then," he replied. "Remember to give my regards to Nikolai."

Juliette was now more than ready to return to Paris herself. Her business was settled. She had seen the first of her designs come from the looms, and there was no reason for her to stay in London any longer, except that Gabrielle had so many more sights and events for her to see and attend. Nikolai had been unable to say exactly when he would return to France, but she was sure it wouldn't be long now. She had received one letter from him. Except in his expressions of love, he had been restrained and concerned, talking of how conditions had deteriorated since his last visit and of further outbreaks of unrest. His father had installed armed guards at the gates, but he himself viewed this as a sorry state when he remembered the freedom and lack of fear that had prevailed in his formative years. Reading between the lines, she could also tell that the announcement of his intention to marry her had been no better received than she had anticipated. More than ever she wanted to be back in Paris when he returned.

"I really must leave on Friday," Juliette said firmly at breakfast, the morning after the party. "I've looked up the times of the boat train to Dover, and I can be in Paris by early evening."

Both Gabrielle and Derek went to see her off at Victoria Station. Gabrielle wept uncontrollably, imploring her to take care and to return to them in England if ever she felt herself to be in any danger. Puzzled, Juliette looked at Derek for an explanation.

"Gabrielle has some strange fancy that unless you are here with us to look after you all might not go well, but I think you are more than capable of managing your own life," he said, reassuring them both.

"Indeed I am." Juliette smiled into Gabrielle's anxious face. "Don't worry about me. The world of fashion may be a jungle, but there's nothing about it that is life-threatening."

Her encouraging cheerfulness had some effect. Gabrielle managed a watery smile at the final parting.

Although Paris was aglitter with early evening lights when Juliette arrived home, Denise was still at Maison Landelle. A hand-delivered note from Nikolai was waiting on the hall salver. Juliette tore it open and saw it had been written three days before. He had returned to Paris only to receive orders from his uncle to go to Brussels on diplomatic business, but he was delaying as long as he could in the hope of seeing her again before he left.

She rang his apartment immediately and was informed by his servant that the count would be leaving Paris at noon the next day and was presently at his studio. Not even stopping to change out of her traveling clothes, Juliette darted from the house and hailed a taxi. Breathless with excitement, she saw the studio lights shining through the curtains when she arrived.

He was standing by the finished statue of her and spun round at her entry, his whole face lighting with joy and relief. "Thank God you're back!" he exclaimed hoarsely.

She threw herself into his arms and their kisses were violent and wild with a desperate need to assuage some of the lonely yearning that had tormented them both. Their clothes were scattered and within moments they were lying on the couch together, exulting in their reunion. Such passion possessed them that she cried out in almost unbearable ecstasy when they both climaxed as soon as he drove into her.

In the delicious languor that followed they smiled at each other, touching and stroking and kissing again, each loving the other's body, each made whole in being together once more.

"You are my life," he murmured, leaning over her, "my only love and my darling."

She raised her head and pressed her mouth to his, not wanting any talk yet of what he expected their future might hold. These present hours were theirs, with nothing of the outside world able to assail them. He made love to her again, but with no haste this time, his kisses and caresses pleasuring her in ways that stirred her to renewed heights of desire. The night hours passed in dozing and lovemaking. Not until dawn did they sleep soundly, arms around each other, her hair lying like a coppery wave half over her face and across his shoulder.

In the morning Juliette did not know he had gone from the couch until he returned from the kitchen with two cups of steaming coffee in his hands. He had thrown on the robe that the male models wore.

"Good morning, *chérie.*"

She sat up to see it was broad daylight and shook back her hair as she returned his smiling greeting. "What time is it?" she asked, plumping up the cushions to lean back against them.

He handed her a cup. "It's nine o'clock. Too early to wake you, but I have to go back to my apartment and to the embassy before I leave." His face had grown serious. "Maybe we should have talked last night, but now we must."

She nodded reluctantly, knowing the time had come and dreading what she might hear. "Yes, I agree."

His opening words chilled her through.

"I have to return home as soon as my mission in Belgium is done at the end of next week. My days in Paris are over."

She was staring at him, her pupils dilated with shock. "What happened?"

"I came to my senses," he stated grimly. "I've been living in a fool's paradise here in France, with no thought for how greatly I'm needed at home."

"Is your father ill?"

He shook his head, frowning. "No. He's in failing health, but then he is an old man. The doctor assures me that by taking care he will have many more years yet."

"Then what caused you to make such a decision?" She was frightened. He looked so resolved, with such a set to his jaw and such a determined light in his eyes.

"It is the present state of Russia." He passed his fingers across his brow, seeing again the starved and terrified faces of the crowd being dispersed by the Cossacks on horseback. The screams of the women, the crying of the children, and the groans of the dying rang again in his ears as he had stood, a helpless witness to the carnage. "It was the second day I was home. I was on my way to see the Tsar when the road was suddenly blocked by a group of panic-stricken people running from a band of blood-lusting, saber-wielding madmen. I leapt out of the automobile, but there was nothing I could do. A poor woman died at my feet."

There was horror in her eyes. "How is it all to end?"

"I don't know. Changes must be made and quickly. That's why I have to go back. I can't stay on here when there's so much to be done. I know many senior ministers in the government, some since my childhood. In many ways I have influence, but only if I'm at home and able to make my voice heard. Without being disloyal, I have to say that the Tsar is a weak man, too much influenced by his wife, who in her turn is dominated by that villainous monk, Rasputin, whom she thinks has more than once saved the life of the poor young hemophilic prince." He took her free hand and pressed it within his own, his face wretched with appeal. "Say you'll come with me. I can't go without you."

"This is all happening far sooner than I ever supposed," she replied, agitated and utterly confused. "What was the reaction of your father and the family when you told them of your wish to marry me?"

"Not good," he answered honestly, "but that need not concern us. Ahead lies a time of change and untold difficulties, but when everything begins to improve we can think of making long visits to France." Gently he held her by the arms. "In the meantime, as I've said, it's not going to be easy. I can't offer you the life I once thought we would have, and yet I want you with me always."

She turned her face away, feeling as if she were being torn apart. "What chance would you have of doing any good if you were ostracized by our being married?"

For a moment he hesitated as his conscience took control, but he was too determined to keep her to let anything stand in his way. He dismissed the question immediately. "I've many good friends in Russia and there's too great a need for men like me for that to happen. I can be a bridge, serving both the government and the people as I have done in minor ways whenever I've been home on previous visits. The workers trust me." He leaned toward her, forcing her to meet his searching gaze. "So what do you say, my darling? I love you. You're everything to me. I'll not leave Paris until you agree to meet me in Brussels next week. We'll travel to St. Petersburg together."

Her eyes were tortured, and her heart seemed to be crying out that she could not refuse him. He meant too much to her. She could see how witnessing that terrible scene of slaughter had jerked him out of his complacency. In a way she was glad that this metamorphosis had taken place, revealing the deeper qualities she had long known were there. He had spoken of his country's need of him, but there was also his need of her. How could she turn away from this loving man for the sake of her own selfish ambition. Not even the bond of her birthplace could be allowed to stand in her way. She pictured the isolation she would have to face in his homeland, perhaps even the open scorn of people like his sister, but that was nothing compared with the thought of parting from him, perhaps forever. With time, when she had learned the language, she might even help in his crusade.

Slowly she cupped his desperate face between her hands. She would allow nothing to daunt her. Love was sharing the hard times as well as the good. "I'll meet you in Brussels," she said.

Exultantly he embraced her, although his kisses were tender, for he understood the sacrifice she was making. "You'll never regret it, my darling! I swear it!"

There were some practicalities to discuss. She would need all the available days to see Denise through the transition of her departure. He spoke of where they would live in St. Petersburg. There was no question of their occupying the apartment he had always had in his father's mansion, but he also owned a town house where they would reside. There were plenty of rooms from which she could choose a studio to continue her textile designing. He had already arranged for his tools and sculpture to be shipped to that address.

When they were both dressed and ready to leave they stood together quietly, their arms wrapped around each other, her head on his shoulder, as they savored these last sweet moments. She knew she would always love this place, which had been a retreat for them both.

"In time to come," she said softly, "a plaque will be placed on the wall of this building, stating that it was the studio where the Russian sculptor Nikolai Karasvin created some of his greatest works."

He laughed quietly at her fantasy. "I think that's unlikely."

She raised her head to look at him. "But it is! Because whatever else you do with your life, you must always keep on with sculpting."

"Well, if such a plaque should ever appear, none will ever know how much this studio meant to me for other reasons."

"That will always be our secret."

"Yes, it will." He kissed her lips lovingly. Then they went out and he locked the door behind them.

Thirteen

JULIETTE INTERRUPTED Denise's tirade over her night's disappearance by breaking the news that she was going to St. Petersburg with Nikolai. It was as well that there was an outer office to block off the sound, for Denise screamed, cried, and shouted her outrage. Finally she collapsed in tears and temper into her chair. Juliette, deeply distressed, tried to put a comforting arm about her bowed shoulders, but it was shaken off.

"I had such plans," Denise wept self-pityingly. "I foresaw Maison Landelle established through you and your children and grandchildren throughout the century and beyond."

"But that could never be taken for granted. Children grow up to decide their own path in life."

"Not yours! I'd have seen to that," Denise shouted wildly.

"Listen to me! Please!" Juliette urged, deeply concerned at the tempestuous outflow. "My leaving Paris must inevitably cut me off from Maison Landelle, no matter that I might wish it otherwise. I'll no longer be at the pulse of fashion, and whatever textile work I get will have to be for the Russian market. All I can promise is that I will always send you any ideas that I believe would be right for Landelle clothes."

Denise looked up with wet and swollen eyes, glaring furiously. "Where would you ever find inspiration in that godforsaken land?"

"From the icons with their gold and rich colors. From the great paintings there. Why not a Russian line for a future winter collection, with Cossack coats and fur hats and swirling cloaks? You mustn't think I'm cutting myself off from France forever. I could never do that. Nikolai has even promised that at some time in the future we might return for long periods of time. Meanwhile, there are just ten days before I leave for Brussels. Let's not waste time being angry. There's work I want to finish and we've the London deal to discuss."

Denise knew that if Juliette had wished, she could simply have walked out, yet she felt no gratitude. She was wallowing too much in her own disappointment to make any allowance for Juliette's wishes. Only one thought had managed to penetrate. A Cossack collection. In the depth of her misery the idea had caught her imagination.

With that ray of hope, Denise began to realize what it would mean to have Juliette and Nikolai in Paris for weeks, even months on end. Their children would be with them. She herself would introduce her nephews and nieces to the world of fashion and pick out the one most susceptible to its fascination and spectacle. She could see herself playing the role of a devoted aunt, even persuading Juliette to let the young person stay on with her when the rest of the family returned home.

Sitting up in her chair, Denise forced herself to become more agreeable, even though she still burned with red-hot resentment. "As you say, we must make the most of the time you have left. We'll keep in constant touch. I'd like you to work on that Cossack theme in St. Petersburg and send everything to me. Now tell me about London."

In relief Juliette pulled up a chair.

During the following days Juliette was busy from morning to night. Extra trunks were purchased, for Denise was insistent that she take all her clothes, wanting her to be a walking advertisement for Maison Landelle. Nikolai sent her a first-class train ticket to Brussels, his accompanying letter full of love.

It was the morning before Juliette was to leave that Denise sent for her to come to the office. Juliette had finished all her work and was tidying her drawing table for the last time. She supposed Denise had thought of another last-minute task. Happily she went downstairs to her sister. Now that only a few hours separated her from seeing Nikolai again, she was filled with excited anticipation.

To her surprise Denise stood in front of the desk with a strange expression on her face. Juliette experienced a sudden rush of fore-boding.

"What is it?" she asked falteringly.

Denise hesitated, but was still unable to conceal entirely the note of jubilation in her voice. "Prepare yourself, Juliette. You'll not be leaving for Belgium or Russia or anywhere else. Nikolai Karasvin's fiancée is here from St. Petersburg with her stepmother to choose her wedding gown and her trousseau."

Juliette made no sound. She stood as if frozen, all color draining from her face. Denise, thinking she was about to faint, guided her to a chair where she sat upright, staring blindly. Only her hands, clenched together in her lap, gave any outward sign of her reaction to the knife-like thrust that had been delivered. Going to the door, Denise told her secretary to bring some hot coffee. When it arrived, Juliette still had not moved.

"Drink this," Denise urged, genuinely concerned, holding out a cup.

For a moment Juliette stared as if unable to comprehend what it might be. Then she took it and sipped twice before speaking in a clear, low voice. "What's her name?"

"Natasha Berberova."

"Have they been here long?"

"About twenty minutes. The *directrice* informed me as she always does when new and distinguished clients come for the first time."

"Have you seen Natasha Berberova?"

"Yes. I was told that Countess Dolohova had recommended that they come here." She did not add that it was the last recommendation she had ever expected in view of what had happened previously. "The young woman spoke of her forthcoming marriage to Count Karasvin, who is presently in Belgium before going home."

"When is the marriage to take place?"

"She did not say, only asking if delivery would be possible in six weeks. She and her stepmother are staying that length of time with Prince Vadim and his wife."

Juliette put down her cup and stood. "Where are they now?"

"In the Blue Salon, looking at designs for wedding gowns. The girl has her own ideas of how she wants her ensemble to look." Quickly Denise darted across to stand with her back to the door as

Juliette moved toward it. "You're not thinking of going to see her?" she asked in alarm.

Juliette, her face still expressionless with shock, regarded her with disturbing calmness. "What else would you expect me to do?"

"Promise me you'll not make a scene! Think of the other clients within earshot."

"A scene? Why ever should I do that? It's never been my way in any case, and it may be that Natasha Berberova is as ignorant of my existence as I was of hers until a few minutes ago."

"If she is?"

"I'll not disillusion her. I'll simply say that delivery can't be made within six weeks and send her elsewhere. What I have learned is a matter between Nikolai and me."

"You're not behaving rationally. You don't know what you're saying or doing!"

Juliette closed her eyes briefly before she could speak again. "I know only too well. Stand aside, please."

Reluctantly Denise did as she was asked. Then she followed Juliette to the door of the outer office and stayed to watch her sister disappear in the direction of the salon.

Natasha Berberova, looking through a number of designs, sat beside her stepmother, an austere and haughty-looking woman, who was studying them with her through a lorgnette. The *vendeuse* in attendance drew back as Juliette approached. Intent on the designs, Natasha did not notice her at first, enabling Juliette to study her for a few moments. She was about Juliette's own age, with a provocative bosom and a tiny waist, her hair pale gold and worn in a coil at the back of her head. The wide brim of her hat shadowed a pretty face with flyaway brows over long-lashed eyes that were presently cast downwards, a turned-up little nose, and an unmistakably stubborn chin.

"*Bonjour.* I'm Juliette Cladel."

Had her name not been known to the two women, there would have been no untoward reaction, but Natasha became tense immediately, although she did not glance up from the designs she was holding. The older woman had looked up automatically and then, as the significance of what she had heard dawned on her, crimson flooded her high cheekbones. She was about to rise in her outrage, but even as she shifted in her chair, opening her mouth to speak,

Natasha shot out a hand to clamp down warningly on hers in a signal that this development should be left entirely to her.

"But—"

"Please, Stepmother!" Her grasp on the older woman's fingers tightened still more. Then Natasha lowered the designs she held in her other hand onto her lap and raised her head slowly to turn azure eyes, glacial with hostility, on Juliette. "Is there anywhere you and I can talk privately?"

"Yes. Follow me."

Almost contemptuously, Natasha brushed the designs from her lap to the floor as she stood up, her pleasure in them gone. The older woman shook her head anxiously, but made no move to rise from her chair.

In one of the small private viewing rooms, Natasha took a few paces up and down as if it were impossible for her to sit yet as Juliette had done. Then she spoke.

"Had I known this was the fashion house where you worked, I would never have come here. I've always admired Countess Dolohova's clothes and when I said I wanted my wedding gown made by the same designer, she gave me no warning."

"No doubt the harm she intended was directed toward me, never supposing I would speak to you. How long have you and Nikolai been engaged?"

"It is a long time since it was agreed between his father and mine that he and I should marry." Natasha sat down. "I have loved Nikolai for as long as I can remember. We were officially betrothed with the Tsar's blessing five years ago."

Juliette's heart contracted in agony. "But since you know of me, he must have asked you to release him."

"He did. I refused."

"Yet it is I whom he loves."

"At the present time he does, but that will pass. I'm not a fool, mademoiselle. I've never expected him to live like a monk, in Paris of all places, but I was not alone in supposing that he would conduct his *amitiés amoureuses* in a sensible manner. Naturally I was upset to hear that something more serious had arisen, but as my father and stepmother pointed out, it is not the first time, and neither will it be the last, that a man loses all common sense over a lovely face in a foreign land." Her voice took on a note of sympathy. "He will soon forget you, mademoiselle."

"I happen to believe otherwise."

Natasha leaned forward slightly in her chair, as if to emphasize her words. "But you'll be far away in Paris and I, as his wife, will be with him. He has always found me intensely attractive and his memories of you will fade quickly in the pleasures of marriage and the birth of his children and mine." She saw by the look in Juliette's eyes that she had struck the final blow and found it was possible to feel pity even in her moment of triumph. "Your love for Nikolai was doomed from the start. Even if I had been willing to release him, my father would never have permitted it. It would have been too great a scandal."

Natasha went from the room then, and Juliette sat on, her hands loosely clasped in her lap, her head bowed under the crushing weight of her despair. She was remembering everything Nikolai had said during their last hour spent together. It came to her now that he had no longer spoken of marriage. There was his regret that he could no longer offer her the life he had hoped for originally and that nothing would be easy. She saw now that he had been too afraid of losing her to confess that he was not free to marry her as he had planned. Instead, he had meant to get her to St. Petersburg, perhaps telling her the truth on the way, and counting on all they felt for each other to keep her there. He, who had always had everything he wanted, had been unable to let her go.

It was a *vendeuse,* supposing the room to be empty, who interrupted her reverie. Juliette left at once, smiling automatically, and returned to Denise's office. "Would it be possible for me to go away for a little while before I start work again?" she asked.

"Yes, of course. Where do you want to go? Back to stay with Gabrielle?"

Juliette shook her head. "No, I need to be quiet. I must have time to take in all that has happened. I'll go back to the convent and stay with the nuns. It will be peaceful there."

"That's a good idea." Denise nodded approval. Her sister would soon recuperate in those environs and return with fresh ideas and renewed vigor. Love was a transient emotion. "When shall you leave?"

"Tomorrow morning."

"No need to bother with trains. After I get to work, I'll send the Mercedes back for you. The chauffeur will drive."

It was a generous gesture that Denise regretted as soon as it was made. It would mean the inconvenience of taxis for her, but it was too late to withdraw the offer.

On the way home, Juliette went into a post office and sent two telegrams. One went to the convent. The other was to Nikolai to let him know that she would not be joining him in Brussels and that she had met Natasha. The words were few, but the very brevity of the message said it all.

In the morning, just as she was securing her hat with a pearl-headed pin, a maid tapped on her door.

"Count Karasvin is here to see you, mademoiselle."

For a second or two Juliette felt quite panic-stricken, but she forced herself to be calm. He must have set out for Paris as soon as he received her telegram and traveled all night.

"Tell the count I'm unable to talk to him as I'm going away."

While the maid returned to deliver the message, Juliette fastened the buttons of her coat with shaking hands, drew on her gloves, and took up her purse.

"Juliette!" Nikolai's voice boomed loudly up the stairs. "I'll not leave until I've seen you!"

Taking a deep breath, she went out onto the carpeted landing and came to a standstill at the head of the curving stairs. He was wild-eyed and unshaven, standing with one foot on the lowest tread and a hand on the newel post, as if about to rush up in search of her. Behind him the street door stood open in readiness for her departure. Before she could speak he shouted angrily again.

"Where the hell do you think you're going?"

Until this moment, she had been beyond tears, the lack of release adding to her torment, but now, seeing him so wretched and with her love for him unquelled, she had to fight to keep from weeping. "It's over, Nikolai."

"It can never be over between us. We are life-bound."

"That's not so!"

"I'll never let you leave me!"

The butler, alarmed by this passionate fury, had sent the maid to fetch the other menservants, but Juliette raised a hand slightly, shaking her head and indicating he should leave the hall.

Then, alone with Nikolai, she took a few of the steps down toward him. "How could you have expected me to share you with someone else?" she asked brokenly.

"You wouldn't have to! The marriage will be in name only. I'll make sure of that. You'll always be first with me. As long as I live."

"You must have loved Natasha once to have become engaged to her."

"Good God! It was all arranged when I was a schoolboy and she was in plaits! Yes, I liked her. Yes, I became engaged to her when the time was considered appropriate. I was nineteen and she was sixteen. Love doesn't usually count in such matches. Couples think themselves fortunate if they can simply get along. Natasha and I were always friends. I thought we still were, which is why I was so sure she would release me when I went to see her."

"But she is in love with you. Naturally she wouldn't agree."

"I didn't know how seriously, any more than I knew she'd take it into her head to come to Paris! I loved you too much to accept any obstacle in our path. Her refusal was the last thing I expected. I even went to the Tsar himself to get permission to put my case to Natasha!"

"Did he give it?"

"No! But I went anyway. The ultimate decision was hers."

"You should have told me the truth long ago!" It was a cry from the heart.

"I never lied! And I truly believed that I would return to Paris able to make you my wife. Then I would have told you everything. Instead there was only one way for us to be together."

"If you were free I'd have gone anywhere with you, whether we ever married or not, but that can never be." She was continuing down the stairs as she spoke. Then she stopped abruptly as he blocked her way, his face torn by desperation.

"I'll come back to Paris whenever I can. My time here will continue to be ours alone. It will be as if nothing had ever happened!"

"Stop dreaming, Nikolai!" She was frantic, fearful her knees would buckle, and then he would sweep her into his arms as he had done so many times before. "Go back to the woman who's waited five years for you. I never want us to meet again!"

"You can't mean that!" He reached for her, his voice so full of love and yearning that the panic she had subdued earlier flared again as her strength of will was snapped by the force of her feelings for him. Tears she could no longer hold back burst from her eyes. Blindly she hit out at him with her hands and her purse, striking the side of his face and his arms. As he stepped back in disbelief, she threw herself past him, ran out of the house and down the steps to the waiting motorcar.

"Quick!" she cried to the chauffeur. "I have to get away. Drive as fast as you can!"

He slammed the door shut after her and threw himself behind the wheel. She was sobbing helplessly, but somehow she managed to look back through the rear window as the vehicle gained speed. Nikolai was running behind, his arms wide, his coattails flying, but as the motorcar accelerated, he was gradually left behind. She saw him stop finally, his arms falling to his sides. It was the moment when she understood fully the meaning of heartbreak.

Fourteen

JULIETTE STAYED SIX WEEKS at the convent, wanting to be sure that when she returned to Paris neither Nikolai nor Natasha would still be there.

It was less peaceful than she had anticipated, for all the nuns were excited to see her and wanted to chat at every opportunity. Kindly old Sister Berthe was overjoyed at her visit and showed her photographs of the altar cloth they had embroidered together, in its place in Chartres Cathedral. At the Mother Superior's request Juliette gave several lessons in textile design and, in all, the days went by quickly. It was the nights that were long and sad, when sleep refused to come and memories of Nikolai were so vivid that she wondered why she did not die of anguish.

Toward the end of her visit she had a twinge of uncertainty about herself, but dismissed it as a result of all the emotional up-heaval she had been through. When she set off for home again, it was with the determination to work harder than ever and to over-come the emptiness of Paris without the man she loved.

Denise, who had been impatient for her return, loaded her with work. The first silks, satins, and velvets had arrived from London and decisions would have to be made about how they would be used.

Juliette had been back in Paris for a week, steeped once more in routine, when a wave of nausea attacked her as she left her bed one morning. In her bathroom she vomited copiously before returning to her bedroom, where she sank down on the dressing table stool. There was no longer any doubt about her condition. She was pregnant! What was more, she knew exactly when it had happened. In her ecstatic reunion with Nikolai after her return from London, they had been so caught up in passion that for the first time he had failed to protect her from pregnancy, both in that immediate and glorious coming together and later when they had made love again and yet again.

A tremor of shock rippled through her as she realized that sooner or later the possibility of her being pregnant would occur to Nikolai as well. He would see it as a way to retain his hold on her. He would come back again and again into her life, making any kind of future impossible for her and ruining all chances for himself. She thumped her fists on the dressing table. That must not happen!

Wearily she finished dressing. There was so much to think about. Denise would never tolerate a child in her immaculate household and neither would Juliette want to be there. She remembered with fresh gratitude the small legacy she had received from Denise's late husband and which she had kept untapped. She had never thought how helpful it would prove at what was surely the most difficult time of her life.

She pressed her fingers to her temples. How was it possible for the mind to race on, sanely making plans so soon after a traumatic event had been comprehended? Maybe just the certainty of being pregnant had instantly sparked a desire to protect her unborn child in every way. At least it would be a few weeks before anyone became suspicious of her condition. She would have to find the right moment to tell her sister, who was certain to react with revulsion and rage.

Throughout the day, whether Juliette was at her drawing board or talking to clients, her thoughts would leap unbidden to her dilemma. Still in an agonized state of mind, she could not yet conceive what it would mean to have Nikolai's child. There were still too many layers of pain and sorrow and despair to know if the baby were to be a comfort to her or a constant torturing reminder.

The morning sickness continued for its allotted spell, but Juliette's secret still remained her own.

·   ·   ·   ·

It was when Juliette was being fitted for a new gown that she realized the time had come to break the news to Denise. In the mirror, she saw the fitter frown at the tape measure after putting it around her waist and then check again. Fortunately the boned corset Juliette had started wearing to disguise her condition made the difference too slight for suspicion.

Juliette chose her moment when she and her sister were at home alone one evening. For the first time ever Denise did not react as Juliette expected. Instead, she nodded her head resignedly and went on stirring her coffee.

"I thought so."

Juliette looked at her in surprise. "How did you guess?"

"You had a spell of looking very pale at breakfast and lately you've been avoiding the chef's richest sauces at dinner. But apart from that, I'm probably quicker than anybody in Paris at seeing slight changes in the face and figure. The fashion business has given me a sharp eye."

"I thought you'd be furious."

"I'm far from pleased!" Denise snapped back dangerously with a rapier flash of her eyes. Then she took a deep breath to bring herself under control and continued in normal tones. "How could I be surprised at what has happened? Count Karasvin is a handsome and virile man of considerable reputation. I never supposed he would be content to hold your hand, and you were obviously head over heels in love with him. I foresaw trouble from the start. It's why I disapproved so strongly of your association with him, but you wouldn't listen."

"I've no regrets."

"Hmm. Not yet perhaps, but you must realize what it means to be a single woman with a child."

"I do."

"He will have to pay you a lavish allowance and provide generously for his offspring."

"No!" Juliette's protest was fierce. "Nikolai is not a man to give up easily and I fear he will come back to Paris before long just to discover if I'm pregnant." Her voice broke. "I can't rebuild my life if I'm never to be free of him."

"Are you considering adoption?"

"No! I'll never part with my baby."

"Fostering?"

"No!" Juliette exclaimed again. "I'm going to raise my own child away from Paris where Nikolai won't find us. Claude's legacy will enable me to have my own apartment and I'll hire a competent nursemaid to take charge when I'm at work."

"What work would that be?"

"I shall teach design. I enjoyed the teaching I did at the convent recently. I can also offer English and Italian lessons."

"Very commendable," Denise remarked dryly, "but quite impractical."

"What do you mean?"

"Claude's legacy won't be enough to keep you indefinitely, and you'll never get work that will pay an adequate wage."

"Why not?"

"No respectable school would ever employ you. With no wedding ring and a baby you'd be seen as a bad example to the pupils. You'll both be outcasts. Is that what you want for your child? The world's cruelty descends on those who bear the stigma of illegitimacy."

"I'll buy a ring to wear if need be!" Juliette gave back with spirit. "My baby will not suffer for anything I have done."

Denise sighed. "Brave words. So what role will you play? The deserted wife? The young widow? The sailor's spouse awaiting the return of her husband, which never comes about? Employers in any sphere know all those tales. I've heard them often enough myself."

Juliette twisted her hands in her lap. "All I know is that I can't stay in Paris," she cried determinedly.

Denise paused for a few moments before speaking again. "Why are you so certain that Count Karasvin will give up pursuing you if he doesn't find out about the baby?"

"Because then he'll have no hold on me."

"You seem very sure."

Juliette nodded, looking down sadly at her bare hands. She had carefully wrapped Nikolai's beautiful ring and taken it to the Russian embassy, where she had asked that it be delivered personally to Count Karasvin in St. Petersburg. She had been assured most courteously that this would be done speedily. She guessed that Nikolai had gone there after their parting and left instructions for any mail to be forwarded without delay in the hope that she would change her mind and write to him.

Denise broke into her troubled thoughts. "Fortunately the plans you've made run almost parallel to those I've been making on my own. There's no need for you to leave Maison Landelle."

Juliette raised her head in astonishment. "But you have such a fear of scandal. I thought my employment would be terminated from the second you knew of my pregnancy."

Denise carried on as if her sister had not spoken. "I suppose you've been thinking of having your baby in some place where no one will know you, but I don't want you to have a clumsy delivery from some ham-fisted midwife. This baby is too important for the future of Maison Landelle, and I have the perfect solution. You shall go to my villa in Tuscany."

"I thought you had a tenant at the Casa San Giorgio."

"He left some time ago. My caretaker and his wife, Antonio and Candida Bonini, would look after you. Once when Claude was taken ill a young local doctor named Morosini saved his life. I know from Candida's letters that he is still in practice in the nearby town of Lucca, and he shall attend at the birth."

Juliette was taken aback that Denise had already worked things out so carefully. The clarity of thought with which she had made her own plans seemed to have deserted her, and she felt quite overwhelmed. "I suppose it would be sensible to go there."

"Of course it would!" Denise could see she had gained an advantage and continued to press on. "You can soon leave for Italy. In the meantime, I'll explain your absence by telling everyone that because you did so well in London I'm sending you on an exploratory tour to various countries with a view to my opening a series of shops abroad. Many people know that I have mentioned this from time to time."

"So much horrible subterfuge!" Juliette declared unhappily.

"It's for your baby's sake, not yours!" Denise said sharply and saw with satisfaction that she had silenced any more opposition for the time being. "For the same reason, your child must be given a surname other than your own."

Juliette felt she was being hammered mentally and physically, and yet everything was being arranged in the baby's best interests. She had to remember that, no matter how humiliating it was for her to submit to these deceits.

"Although you don't want to be involved in fostering," Denise continued firmly, "it would be a wise move for you to leave the baby with Antonio and Candida for a little while. It would give you the chance to take up the threads in Paris again." Secretly, she wanted the baby kept out of the way for much longer, but she needed to lead Juliette gently. "Italians love babies and children. Heaven knows why! It's a national trait."

Juliette sprang to her feet, needing to take some control. "I'll never leave my baby with strangers!"

"Of course not! But the Boninis won't be strangers after you've spent the next few months with them and discovered for yourself what good people they are." Denise stood to put a reassuring arm about her sister's waist, realizing that she must be careful lest Juliette balk and ruin everything. "After all, the journey between Paris and anywhere in Italy isn't so long these days. There are fast trains and good connections. I'd let you take time off whenever you wished to visit your infant." It was a promise she had no intention of keeping, for the less Juliette saw of the child the better. "Remember, this is the only way you can ensure a safe and secure future for your offspring. Surely that is worth any sacrifice?"

"But would it be the right one?" Juliette asked with resignation.

"Of course it would be! First, there could be a convent school— one can surely be found in Lucca—where little ones of either sex can receive first schooling. Afterward, a top boarding establishment in France, and then training at Maison Landelle for a brilliant career and eventual ownership. What could be better?"

Denise could scarcely control her greed for the baby's future. Whether boy or girl, it made no difference. Either sex could hold equal power in the fashion world. And there might never be another child.

Juliette was full of uncertainties, yet grateful that Denise seemed to be doing everything in her power to help. "Forgive me, but I don't feel able to make any promises or decisions at the present time."

"I wouldn't want you to," Denise lied blithely. "Naturally you're under a great strain and that could distort your judgment. Take your time. Just trust me. All I ask is that you hold on to the knowledge that you and I are the same flesh and blood, able to stand together at this time of crisis. Let your mind dwell constantly on that certainty when you're relaxing quietly in the Italian sun." Then she added the final inducement that would be guaranteed to penetrate Juliette's indecision. "Count Karasvin would never find your baby at the villa, even if he should come back to Paris as you fear. You can be certain of that."

Within a week everyone had heard either from Denise or indirectly about Juliette's important assignment on behalf of Maison Landelle. Juliette herself said nothing. At the Casa San Giorgio, the caretaker and his wife had been informed of the reason for her forthcoming visit.

Juliette stayed several days in Florence before going on to the villa, needing some time to adjust to the changing pattern of her life. She found cheap accommodations near the Ponte Vecchio and was able to eat inexpensively since she had developed a craving for fruit and pasta. It was early spring and, amid the Renaissance splendor of the city, flowers blossomed profusely. There were quite a number of foreign visitors, and she was alert to the danger of running into someone she knew. She wore a veiled hat and carried a parasol to protect her anonymity, and visited places of interest early in the morning and at other times less popular with visitors on vacation.

She would have liked to send a picture postcard to Gabrielle and Derek, who had spent part of their honeymoon in Florence, but she had written before leaving Paris to say she was going away for a while and assuring them that there was no need for concern. She could not risk revealing her whereabouts to anyone and, for the same reason, had promised Denise she would post all correspondence to her at a Paris post office for personal collection.

Having let the Boninis know by letter that her arrival at the villa would be delayed, Juliette set out every day to view yet another museum or gallery. She gazed in silent wonder at the many glorious sculptures, from Michelangelo's "David" to Donatello's harrowing "Mary Magdalen," which moved her to tears. There were several paintings in the Uffizi gallery that had a similar effect, for her emotions were painfully near the surface at all times. She concentrated on improving her Italian, realizing how good a grounding she'd been given at the convent.

Juliette might have been tempted to stay a little longer in Florence if she had not thought she sighted Nikolai. She was coming down the steps of the Duomo when she saw a man ahead of her with the same fine height, broad shoulders, and thick black hair curling under the brim of a panama. Her heart seemed to stop and she pressed a white gloved hand to her throat. Then he turned his head and she saw a stranger's face in profile. Almost blindly she stumbled back into the cathedral and sat on the nearest seat to recover from the upsetting mistake she had made. What alarmed her most of all was that if it had been Nikolai she would have run to him, unable to stop herself. When she emerged again into the sunshine, it was to go straight back to her hotel to pack. She would leave for the villa later that same morning.

Juliette took the train to Lucca and hired a horse-drawn carriage to take her the rest of the way. It was a leisurely drive along a winding, dusty road amid delightful, undulating countryside. Now and again she glimpsed the entrance to a villa or an occasional window sparkling in the sun, but most of the houses were tucked away behind high walls.

She had never seen a photograph of Denise's villa, but since her sister had always appeared more interested in getting good rents from its tenants than visiting it herself, Juliette had supposed it to be of moderate comfort and size. Once Denise had remarked that the flower gardens were extensive, and now, as her carriage passed through the gates, she saw that her sister had not exaggerated. There were many fine trees, a stretch of formal gardens, and an abundance of flower beds with a profusion of multicolored blooms sloping gently out of sight. Then the villa itself came into view.

Contrary to Juliette's expectations, it was not the modest place she had expected, but a small palace, its façade sumptuous with balconies, loggias, and statues in niches. Then Juliette realized she should have guessed how it would be, for the late Claude de Landelle had been a rich man and would have wanted the best. Gazing at it, she was enchanted. She felt drawn already to the beautiful, age-mellowed house in which her baby would draw its first breath.

Having sighted Juliette's carriage while it was still a distance away, the Boninis were waiting to greet her on the steps of the arched entrance as the coachman drew his horse to a halt. Both came forward, he to bow and she to bob.

"*Buon giorno,* signorina," they both said at once. He was a genial-looking man, squarely built with merry eyes, and his wife was plump and maternal in appearance, her face round and smiling, her black hair drawn back from a middle parting into a coil. Behind them were two girls, not yet twenty, wearing crisp white aprons, who smiled and bobbed when presented as the Boninis' daughters,

Lucietta and Katarina. Juliette, lingering on the steps, asked Antonio if he was the gardener.

"Yes, signorina, but an old man from the village, who's been tending the flowers since he was a gardener's boy and who trained me in my turn, comes every day to give a hand and make sure I'm keeping up to his standard!"

She smiled at his little joke. Candida was waiting in the pink-marbled entry hall to show her into the villa. Even inside there was a sense of light and air. Diaphanous white curtains billowed at the windows, which were also fitted with shades to draw against the sun. Her bedroom had a painted ceiling, and gilded cherubs held garlands above the ornate bedhead. Later Candida showed her another bedroom that was much plainer, with a narrower bed, which was to be prepared for her confinement.

During her first weeks at the villa, Juliette finished several textile and dress designs, which were sent off to Denise. Until the grip of summer took hold, she made a few trips into Lucca. The first time she went to see Dr. Morosini, who was to deliver her baby. He wore gold-rimmed spectacles and his attitude was reassuringly considerate and responsible.

"It's not so unusual," he said, sitting back in his chair, "for a young woman of good upbringing, as you undoubtedly are, to be sent away from her family to give birth discreetly, but you've been left so entirely alone. Usually a trusted nurse or a relative would have come too. Was there nobody the Baronne de Landelle could send?"

"Nobody."

"The father?"

"He's marrying someone else." Her voice was curiously toneless. There was no indication of her heartache, the agony of which seemed to be getting worse every day, if that were possible.

"So what is to happen to the baby?"

"I'm keeping my child!" She was unaware that she had cried out defiantly, as if already forces were trying to wrest them apart.

"Very well." He made no further comment. "Take plenty of exercise. Walk daily in the cool of the morning and in the early evening if you're not tired. Rest through the daily siesta hours. Eat sensibly and forget that old wives' tale about eating for two."

She heeded his advice. Lucca, with its wealth of treasures, open squares, and magnificent churches, was a place she could have explored indefinitely, but as summer progressed the heat kept her away. She was perfectly content at the villa and when her morning walk was done she would work on her designs, continuing to dispatch them at regular intervals. There were also garments to make for the baby and clothes for herself, which she needed as her figure expanded. She had bought the fabrics in Lucca; those for herself were of cheap soft cottons and muslins, which she made up in loose styles that were comfortable to wear. At other times she read, played for her own amusement on the grand piano that Claude had installed, and learned several new ways to play patience from Candida, who was fond of cards. The two daughters had a gramophone, and at their request Juliette taught them all the latest ballroom dances from Paris.

Once she could no longer go to Lucca, Dr. Morosini called on her. Her legacy from Claude not only enabled her to pay for her keep, but also meant that her medical bills presented no problem, although Dr. Morosini's fees were moderate compared to what she would have paid in Paris.

"How are you today?" he would ask, usually finding her in the garden.

Invariably she was well, and sometimes they would stroll together through the groves of cyprus trees. Afterward he would accept refreshment before leaving. She guessed his purpose was to alleviate her isolation. Although he had no knowledge of the heartache she felt, she was glad of his company. He was an interesting man, well-read and with a wide knowledge of world affairs. More than once he expressed the wish that he were as fluent in her language as she had become in his, but, as she pointed out, she had spoken nothing but Italian since arriving in Italy, which had given her plenty of practice.

In contrast to her schooldays, Juliette now received a regular stream of letters from Denise, who was determined to keep her involved in the business of Maison Landelle. Personal news was always minimal. Instead, there were sales figures and details of staff changes as well as a listing of any new and important clients. The fabrics from London had been made up in the latest floating and layered styles, with chemise-like bodices and semi-tunics over underskirts. Soon Denise wrote exultantly with the news that these same gowns were causing a sensation and orders were flowing in. By now Juliette had been at the villa for over four months and was just coming into her seventh month. She was still sending Denise new designs and had another two started when her sister wrote again.

Juliette left her work and took the letter out onto the loggia, which gave a splendid view of the mountains. Sitting down in one of the cushioned wicker chairs, she opened the letter, which was shorter than usual. Realizing that it was one of her sister's rare personal letters, she began to read at once.

Although Juliette had always half-expected to hear such news, she was entirely unprepared to receive it. Without preamble Denise announced that Nikolai had been back in Paris.

I heard that Count Karasvin was combing the city for you, even though he is now a married man. When he called on me I was well prepared. In your best interests I told him a falsehood that I knew would settle everything. I said you had had an abortion and I had sent you away for several months to recover, which was why nobody else knew your whereabouts. It was easy to see by the effect the words had on Count Karasvin that I had set you free of him forever. I have heard since that he left Paris that same evening. I know you will wish to thank me . . .

Juliette had stopped reading, a cry of desolation bursting from her. She dropped her face into her hands and wept silently and despairingly as wave after wave of love and compassion for Nikolai swept over her.

Half an hour later, Dr. Morosini found her in the same distressed state. The very silence of her tears concerned him. He put down his medical bag and drew up a chair to sit close to her.

"Let me help. Tell me what's upsetting you."

At first she did not move, but after a few moments she lowered her hands and, still without looking up, held the letter out to him. He took it and saw her turn her face away as if she could not bear to let him view the depth of her private unhappiness. When he had read the letter through he picked up the envelope, which had fallen to the ground, and folded it away.

"Don't read this letter again," he advised.

Her voice came hesitantly, laden with sadness. "I feel Nikolai's suffering as my own."

Dr. Morosini sighed at the force of love that possessed her. Few women would be as charitable to a man who had deceived them. Most would rant and rave and exult in his downfall.

As if Juliette had read his thoughts, she turned at last to look at him. "Nikolai and I wanted to be together for the rest of our lives. Nothing can change that for either of us."

"Then the time has come for you to concentrate solely on what will be best for his child. Any faint hope you were secretly cherishing of some miracle has been finally banished."

She shook her head uncertainly, brushing away the tears that still ran from her eyes. "Was that thought really lingering at the back of my mind in spite of everything? I can't be sure. I'll never know." She stood up slowly and went to the loggia's balustrade, where she stood gazing abstractedly at the vista before her.

Dr. Morosini stayed where he was for a while, giving her time to come to terms both with what her sister had written and with the self-knowledge he had caused her to experience. Then, seeing her silent tears had still not ceased, he left his chair and went across to hand her the clean handkerchief he had taken from his breast pocket. She wiped her eyes, and he saw his timing had been right. She had reached some decision. Perching his weight on the edge of the stone balustrade, he waited with folded arms for her to speak.

"I am free now," she said quietly, turning toward him. "Not from Nikolai as my sister supposes, because, as he said once, he and I are bonded for life. No, my freedom is from any obligation I might have felt until now about returning to Paris." She gave an apologetic little shrug. "I must seem to be talking in riddles since you know so little of my life before I came here."

"I can get the gist of it, even though the details are yours." He had avoided putting her under the slightest obligation to give them, but he hoped that sooner or later she would enlighten him. From the start, she had been something of a mystery and he was interested in her.

"I know now that I can't go back to Paris," she declared purposefully. "That would involve several partings from my baby. All along I've declared I'd never do that, and it's been the right decision from the start."

"What had put you in a quandary over it?"

"The chance that Nikolai might make claims I couldn't counter." She saw the doctor's puzzled expression. "Maybe I should tell you a little of the circumstances that changed his life and mine. I'd like you to understand. You've been so kind."

"You're my patient. I want the best for you."

When she had told him the facts quite briefly, he agreed with her that returning to Paris would be a mistake. Some of the reasons were his own. He had not liked the baronne with her arrogant and discontented ways and had pitied her unfortunate husband, whose convalescence had been hindered by her impatience to get back to Paris. The peace of the countryside had not suited her at all. Juliette had been under her control long enough. It was easy to foresee that the woman would want to control the baby's life. No matter what dreams and ambitions the child might have, the baronne would use every weapon in her power to destroy them.

"So now that you've set Paris behind you, where do you plan to make a new start?" he asked.

Juliette looked again toward the mountains. "That depends on several matters I have to sort out. "But, Doctor," she added, giving him a serious little smile, "I promise you shall be the first to know."

When he had gone, Juliette wrote two letters. The first was to Denise, confirming what she had said originally about never parting from her child and seeking a livelihood away from Paris. She also implored her sister not to sever the ties of kinship, which had come to mean so much during their time together. As Juliette closed the letter, she thought there was every likelihood that Denise would turn up at the Casa San Giorgio in a rage. But whatever the storm her anger created, it would be weathered with nothing changed.

The second letter she wrote was to Fortuny, telling him of her circumstances and asking if he had a vacancy in his workshop for a seamstress. She hoped that he, having already approved one example of her skills, might be prepared to employ her.

That afternoon when Antonio drove his wagonette into Lucca to fetch some purchases, he posted the two letters.

Fifteen

JULIETTE BEGAN WATCHING daily for replies to her letters. Denise's ignored entirely all that she had written and dealt solely with business matters, except for the last line. There Denise stated that she had heard pregnant women often developed strange fancies and after the baby was born Juliette would surely come to her senses. A postscript asked for speedy delivery of the latest designs.

Juliette sighed, weary in the final month of her pregnancy, and felt unable to write any more about the matter for the time being. How could Denise believe so implicitly in her own iron will that she would brush aside what was to Juliette the most important letter she had ever written? While she continued to work on the designs Denise wanted, she kept hoping to hear from Fortuny, but nothing came.

Realizing that time was running out, she reverted to the plan she had made tentatively in her mind while she was still in Florence. There were some elegant gown shops in the city, and as soon as she was able after the birth, she would take a day's outing to seek employment. She would need to show some examples of her own work, but she had brought some of the good clothes she had made herself in Paris. This train of thought reminded her of the Delphos robe, which she had been unable to leave behind in spite of the poignant memories it aroused. It would have been ideally comfortable at the present time, but she could not foresee wearing it ever again.

Although flowers still gave a lovely variety of color to the terraced gardens, autumn had begun to show itself across the grand landscape. The days were cooler and often wet, with rain unceasing from morning until night. Nearly a week of wet weather had just lifted, and some sunshine was showing through in the late afternoon when Juliette came slowly down the steps of the Casa San Giorgio, holding on to the stone balustrade. She was eager to get out in the air after being virtually a prisoner indoors since she had finished the last of the designs for Denise and posted them off to Paris. Now she had only to await the baby's arrival.

She was only halfway down the flight when she saw a taxi coming from the direction of the gates. Her heart sank. Denise must have had second thoughts and come after all. As the taxi drew up, Juliette steeled herself for what was to come. Then, to her dismay, she saw it was Marco stepping out of the taxi.

She leaned against the parapet in consternation and alarm. Her letter to Fortuny had been personal. The designer had had no right to disclose her whereabouts to anyone else. All she could hope was that Marco had not chanced to write the news to Nikolai.

"So we meet again, Juliette." Marco had come toward her as the taxi drove away, his face full of pleasure, as if her distorted figure had escaped his notice. "It never seems to be in Paris, does it?"

"Now it never will," she answered emotionally. "But you shouldn't be here. And I pray you haven't told Nikolai anything about me. It's his baby I'm expecting and I don't want him ever to know!"

His expression became serious. "I haven't heard from Nikolai for months, and neither have I written." He did not add that he had heard indirectly, through Russians in Venice, of the magnificent wedding in St. Petersburg.

She was overcome by relief. "Have you come far today?"

"I left Venice early this morning. Fortuny and Henriette have been away and he didn't open his personal mail until late yesterday evening. It was Henriette who took matters into her own hands after he had discussed your letter with her in confidence. She insisted that he agree to her telling me. After all, I had spoken of you to her several times. And, as she had expected, I said I would come to you without delay."

"You'll stay overnight at least, won't you?"

"Would that be convenient? I've already booked into a hotel in Lucca."

"But I want you to be my guest. I'll send Antonio to collect your luggage." She half-turned, intending to go back to the villa, but Candida appeared, having sighted the taxi as it left. Immediately she took charge, summoning her husband. Juliette turned back to Marco. "Do you mind if we stroll a little before you see your room?"

"Of course not. Take my arm."

She took it, glad of the support, and they followed a path through the garden. "As you can guess," she said, "I'm longing to hear if Fortuny is able to offer me any work."

"Yes, there is a place for you in the studios of the Palazzo Orfei."

Again relief swept over her and she paused, leaning her forehead against his shoulder, scarcely able to speak. "How kind of him! And how good of you to come all this way to tell me."

"I wanted to see you again."

"Even like this?" she remarked defensively, conscious of her bulk.

"Yes, except that I would have wished to see you married to your baby's father for the sake of your happiness. I never thought it would end between you and Nikolai."

"Neither did I ever suppose we should be parted as we were."

He knew she would tell him the circumstances in her own time, and he kept the conversation light, asking her how she had passed the days at the villa and talking of his own travels.

That evening it rained again, and as they sat in the flickering glow of a fire she told him what had happened and why she had hidden herself away. His kindness and understanding were particularly comforting to her, because—unlike Dr. Morosini—he had known Nikolai.

It seemed natural that Marco should stay on from one day to the next. There was so much she wanted to ask him about the work she would be doing for Fortuny. She was to start as a seamstress, but once she had fully recovered her strength, the designer was prepared to take her into the textile workshop where the physical tasks involved hours of standing.

"The Palazzo Orfei is a gigantic workshop with the Fortuny

shop on the ground floor and a showroom, studios, and ateliers on the upper levels. Mariano and Henriette have living quarters adjoining."

"What is she like?"

"A charming, friendly woman. She assists Fortuny in all aspects of his work. I'm sorry you didn't meet her that evening in London, but she and some of the other ladies had already returned to their seats. I know she was disappointed to miss you, because she had been delighted by my account of your salvaging the Delphos robe."

Juliette smiled in acknowledgment. "I look forward to meeting her, but I shall have to stay in an inexpensive hotel in Venice until I find accommodations for myself and my baby. Could you recommend one to me?"

"I could, but there is an alternative." Marco paused. They were in the gardens again, seated by an orderly row of cypress trees. The day was mild and sunny, as if the rain had never happened. "I came to see you not only to offer employment."

Instantly Juliette knew what he was about to say, and her hand tightened on the arm of her seat. She had known since their first meeting in Lyon that Marco was attracted to her. Maybe he had never realized how often his gaze lingered on her, how quick he had been to assist her in any way, or how special his smile had been when directed at her. He was looking ardently at her now as he took her hand into both of his.

"I love you, Juliette. In Lyon you made me realize that the time had come for me to look to the future, even though tender memories of Françoise would always remain. Then Nikolai arrived, and as soon as I saw the two of you together, I could tell how much in love you were. I knew I didn't have a chance, but you were never out of my thoughts."

"Marco," she began, but he pressed her hand in appeal.

"Please hear me out," he urged. "When we met again in London I was lucky enough to spend more time with you. I know you think of me only as a friend, but friendship is a good and solid foundation for any marriage. I'm asking you to be my wife, to let me give my name to your child, whom I shall always think of as my own. You will always be my beloved."

She was deeply moved. He was an exceptional man and she liked him. She even felt affection for him, but never as anything but a friend. It was impossible to consider marriage. "I can't accept, dear Marco," she said at last. "Nikolai will always be too much with me."

"I'm willing to take the chance that with time you'll become fond enough of me to let go of the past even as I have done, because it is the only way to go on with life. You and I have both experienced the awful sadness of losing someone who meant everything in the world to us. Surely that should give us a kind of unity and understanding as husband and wife that other couples lack."

"You would be counting on too much," she insisted, shaking her head, "and I can see now that it would be a mistake for me to accept Fortuny's offer of work. You and I would be seeing each other all too often. It would not be fair to you."

"But I want you to be there! Most Italian men would want you to remain a wife and mother, but I know you're an artist who needs to create. I like that, and I would be glad to marry a woman whose interests were similar to mine. Apart from that, think of the baby, Juliette! Consider what it would mean to the child to have a father, a name to be proud of, and a stable home and background that nothing could destroy."

He saw that at last he had broken through to her. He saw the resolute look in her expressive eyes fade as she understood that through marriage to him she would ensure parental love and security for her child. She could not in good conscience deny her baby that right. Slowly she nodded in acquiescence.

"You're a good man," she said very quietly. "I could tell that when I first met you. You deserve a better wife than I can ever be."

"I want no other!"

She smiled wanly. "At least I can promise that I'll always appreciate your love and be grateful for what you're doing for my baby and me."

"I would die for you!" he declared fervently. He bowed his head then and pressed her hand to his lips, swept away by emotion. She leant forward and gently kissed his brow.

They were married before the week was out. The ceremony was held in the fourteenth-century church of Santa Maria della Rosa. Juliette wore a deep blue velvet gown in a loose tunic style under a cape, both of which she had made during her sojourn at the villa, and a wide-brimmed hat she had brought from Paris. She carried a bouquet of flowers that had been picked from the villa garden by

Lucietta and Katarina. The two girls were at the church with their mother, all three in their prettiest hats and Sunday clothes. Antonio, straight-backed in his best suit, his mustache waxed to fine points, acted as witness with Dr. Morosini. At the close of the ceremony, Marco kissed Juliette on the lips for the first time.

Afterward they all went back to the Casa San Giorgio where Candida had left two women in charge of the wedding luncheon, most of which she had prepared herself. Juliette had wanted her to sit down as a guest, but she put on an apron and took over her customary role waiting on others.

It was a quiet celebration. As soon as the meal was over, Juliette went to take her usual siesta while Marco walked Dr. Morosini to his car.

That evening when Juliette and Marco sat again in the firelight, he told her about the house he had bought recently in Venice.

"I moved in three months ago, but as yet it's still sparsely furnished. You'll be able to add anything you want. I'd like you to take time with the baby until you feel ready to start work at the Palazzo Orfei."

"I'd originally intended to begin work without delay, but I would like a few weeks first," she admitted. "What made you move from the apartment where you lived before?" She had learned from him in Lyon that he had sold his first home soon after his wife's death, finding it too difficult to stay on there without her.

"It was never convenient, but when I bought it I was in no mood to spend much time looking. The windows looked out on the Rialto bridge, and I suppose that appealed to me, although I really don't remember. The new house, which is yours and mine now, hasn't any splendid views of the Grand Canal, but it's situated in a peaceful courtyard close to the Palazzo Orfei. When you feel able to leave the baby with a nursemaid, it will take you less than two minutes to go home from the workshop and check that all is well."

They talked for a while longer, until she felt too tired to stay up any longer. Marco came with her to her door, where he took her face tenderly between his hands and gazed into her eyes.

"You'll be happy in the new life you're starting with me," he promised. "It may take a while, but the time will come."

She was unable to imagine ever knowing true happiness again, but she acknowledged his heartfelt words with a serious smile. He kissed her lovingly, then, but without passion, for which she was thankful. She bade him good night and entered her room.

Fortuny was informed by telegram, while Juliette wrote her sister to break the news of her marriage. In the same letter, she promised to continue sending designs, and she closed with the sincere hope that Denise would visit them in Venice, where she would always be welcome.

It was raining again the morning Juliette awoke to an awareness of new and unfamiliar twinges in her body. When Angelina arrived with her breakfast tray, Juliette asked her to send for Candida.

The woman came hurrying, her face abeam. "Is it beginning?" she asked joyfully, clasping her big hands together.

"I think there's no doubt about it," Juliette replied with a wry grin.

Her labor was not easy, but she gave birth just before dawn the following day. Marco, who had paced the floor for most of the night, rushed to the foot of the stairs when he heard the infant's wail. It seemed an interminable time to wait until Candida appeared briefly to announce jubilantly over the landing balustrade, "It's a boy!"

"How is Juliette now?" he asked anxiously, when Dr. Morosini came downstairs.

"All is well! She has asked to see you."

A spasm of joy went through him, and he mounted the stairs two at a time.

A cable was sent to Denise announcing the birth, and Marco returned briefly to Venice to inform his housekeeper that he would soon be bringing home his wife and son.

The baby was to be named Michel after Juliette's father. The day before the christening a bulky envelope arrived by post. When Juliette opened it she cried out in distress as the torn-up pieces of the last designs she had sent to Denise fell to the floor. Although no letter was enclosed, Denise had made it clear that their kinship was ended in her mind.

Sixteen

JULIETTE'S FIRST SIGHT of Venice was by night. She stood on board a *vaporetto*, with Michel tightly bundled in her arms, and became instantly enchanted. Street lamps, probably radiating no more light than the candle lanterns of previous centuries, illuminated ancient doorways, streets so narrow no carriage could pass through them, and even narrower passageways known as *calli*. Chandeliers sparkled in the exotic windows of great Renaissance palaces, and once there came the sound of a woman singing to the accompaniment of a lute, as if time had stood still since the days when Venice was ruled by powerful doges.

"You should be seeing this city for the first time in sunshine," Marco said apologetically, knowing she must be tired after the long journey.

"No," she answered at once. "This is wonderful, and unlike anything I've ever seen before."

"I'm glad then, but aren't you getting cold? The next stop will be ours. I promised Henriette that I'd take you to the Palazzo Orfei tomorrow morning," he continued, "and afterward we'll go along to see my business premises."

"I'm looking forward to seeing everything."

As Marco had telephoned ahead, there was a porter waiting with a hand truck when they alighted by the fitful light of one of the lamps. Their luggage was piled onto the truck, Juliette's trunk to be collected from the railway station in the morning. She found it strange that the only way to get to Marco's house was on foot, but there was compensation in the lack of hooting horns and in the quiet that prevailed. Marco led the way along the same kind of *calle* she had seen from the *vaporetto,* the porter trundling his hand cart behind them. From time to time they passed a little wall shrine with a candle flickering at the foot of the Virgin and the Christ Child. Finally they came to a small paved square, the Campo San Beneto.

"That's the Palazzo Orfei," Marco said, indicating the large and ornate palace that soared up against the stars and occupied the whole of one side of the square. Its handsome Gothic windows sent golden rectangles of light down into the square where she stood.

"What a grand building!" she exclaimed.

Marco smiled. "You'll like what's inside it as well. But come now. Our house is only a few steps away," he said, leading her into a small courtyard.

"There's your new home, Juliette." Marco indicated the tall house facing them. Before she could reply the door was flung open, releasing a flood of light and warmth.

"Buona sera, Signor and Signora Romanelli!" cried the house-keeper, Lena Reato, as she stood aside for them to enter. She was a short, full-breasted woman in her mid-fifties with graying hair and capable hands. "Ah! The baby! Let me take him from you, si-gnora." As he was placed in her arms, Michel opened his eyes and blinked, to her delight. "What a fine baby he is!" she exclaimed. "I can see the Romanelli likeness! He'll be the image of his father when he grows!"

Juliette glanced at Marco, not knowing how hurt he might be by these well-meant comments, but he seemed unaffected by them. Perhaps he had already banished Nikolai from their lives. She guessed that it was the only way possible for him to look to the future.

She was relieved to find they were to have separate bedrooms. Lena apparently assumed it was for Marco's benefit, so that he would not be disturbed by the baby's crying at night.

"I thought you'd like to have Michel's cot right against your bed," she said, as she showed Juliette into the room that would be hers. "Then you can pick him up quickly, before his crying gets too loud. I expect you'll want to choose a nursemaid, but I have a niece, reliable and conscientious, whom I could recommend."

Juliette thanked her and stood looking about as she took off her hat and coat. Marco had warned her that the house was sparsely furnished. Admittedly there were only outside shutters across the windows and no rugs on the tessellated floor, but she liked what little she had seen. She thought her magnificent bed must surely date from the eighteenth century. Its pale green paint was decorated with flowers and bordered in faded gilt. There was a matching chest of drawers as well as a dainty chair set at a delicately-shaped table with a swing mirror on a gilded stand. The house itself, its carved doors darkened with age, was surely much older and well suited to the other antique pieces she had seen when coming up the stairs. Lena had noticed her appreciative survey.

"Signor Romanelli inherited all this furniture from his grandmother last year. It was still in storage when he returned to Venice recently and told me you were coming."

"Did you know his grandmother?" Juliette asked, unbuttoning her blouse, for Michel had begun to wail hungrily and it was time she put him to her breast.

"I worked for her many years. After she died I had a post I didn't like and it was my lucky day when Signor Romanelli asked me if I'd like to housekeep for him in his new home. I knew how much he traveled for his business, but it was quite a surprise to discover he had a wife whom he would be bringing to Venice with his newborn son."

"I'm sure it was." Juliette had seated herself, and when the woman handed Michel to her, she cradled him in the crook of her arm. "Does it put your employment here in a different light?"

"Not at all, signora. I'm glad to see him with a family, and I'll do my best for you."

"I'm sure you will. I've heard that you are very capable and an excellent cook."

The woman looked pleased. "I have a good supper waiting for you when you've finished feeding little Michel. While you're downstairs I'll unpack for you."

She went out of the door, then, closing it quietly behind her. Juliette gazed down at the suckling infant and stroked the black down on his head with gentle fingertips. She had not realized until he was born that in him she would find a new kind of love to ease the emptiness Nikolai had left in his wake.

When Michel was tucked into his cot, she went downstairs to find Marco waiting for her in a large salon with cushioned high-backed sofas of Venetian design. The only other furniture was a carved cupboard and side tables.

"I never knew I should find such beautiful furniture here," she said wonderingly. "You spoke of the house being so empty and yet these pieces demand space to set them off. So they're family heirlooms that your grandmother bequeathed to you?"

"Yes, every one of them. I suppose the furnishings seemed sparse to me, because there are boxes of clocks and paintings and other things in a room at the top of the house that haven't even been opened yet." He poured them each a glass of white wine.

"May I unpack them one day?" she requested eagerly, wondering what other lovely things lay waiting to be rediscovered.

"Yes, indeed. That's what I've been counting on." He handed her a glass. "Let's see if you like this *ombra*. It's quite a dry wine."

Juliette raised her eyebrows. "Why do you call it a 'shadow'?"

"It's always known as that in Venice. In the past, when wine was sold on stalls in St. Mark's Square, people would move out of the summer heat into the shade to drink it." His eyes dwelt on her as he raised his glass. "May no shadows ever fall across us in this house."

She sipped from her glass, echoing the toast in her mind. All her shadows belonged to the past. For Marco's sake and her own, they must remain there.

They had their supper at one end of a long table, seated in two ornate, high-backed chairs, the rest of the dozen set back against the walls. She felt that to do her chair justice she should have been robed in velvet with jewels in her hair like a Venetian woman of the Renaissance. When she said this to Marco he laughed and replied that once she had been in Venice for a while, she would be surprised only by anything that was new. This amused her and eased the strain of being in such strange surroundings. As always, he kissed her good night at her door. She wondered how long it would be before that changed.

In the morning Juliette looked out of her bedroom window and had her first sight of Venice by daylight. Although the wintery sun was bright and the sky a clear pale blue, there was nothing much to see, for the courtyard below was shut in by the walls of other buildings and the only outlet was the narrow passageway through which she and Marco had come the night before. She looked down into the garden where the trees spread branches over a patio and statuary set amid ornamental bushes. She remembered Marco telling her that Venice was full of lush hidden gardens like this one. It would be a cool and shady spot when the summer sun scorched the city.

When Juliette went down to breakfast only one place was laid, but Lena, coming to pour her coffee, had a message.

"The signore has gone to work and said he would come back for you in the late morning. He thought you would wish to rest after your journey."

"I had more than enough rest during the last weeks of my pregnancy," Juliette replied, unfolding the linen napkin and spreading it on her lap. "Now I want to make the most of the time Michel allows me."

Later, when she had bathed and fed Michel before putting him in his cot to sleep again, she explored the whole house. In a top room she found the boxes Marco had mentioned, but opening them would have to wait for another day. It was still not ten o'clock when, dressed for outdoors, she went to ask Lena to tell Marco when he returned that she had made her own way to the Palazzo Orfei.

In the square, she stood by the mushroom-shaped well that had long since been covered over, while she looked long and steadily at the Palazzo Orfei, letting her gaze wander over the balconies, which were supported by maned lions, and the ornamental stonework. Over the grand entrance was the coat of arms of the powerful Pesaro family, who had built the palazzo centuries ago. In one of the houses behind her, someone was playing a piano and the music danced lightly in the air. In the morning light she could see, as she'd been unable to by night, that the palazzo's great windows were made up of tiny leaded panes of what was surely medieval glass that shone blue, silver, and gold in reflected sunlight. With a sigh of satisfaction she watched two fashionably-dressed women ring at the door for admittance.

It was opened by a fine-looking woman with patrician features, magnificent dark eyes, and a mane of soft brown hair worn in the

Greek style, piled softly up and bound with ribbons. She was wearing a green velvet skirt and a hip-length tunic printed with an Oriental pattern, its sleeves floating like soft wings and unmistakably Fortuny-designed. She greeted the two arrivals by name, but formally, which made it apparent to Juliette that they were clients.

It was as the woman was about to close the door again that she caught sight of Juliette and hesitated. Then she moved forward onto the step and spoke with a smile.

"I'm sure you must be Marco's wife. I'm Henriette Negrin."

Juliette came across to her, full of smiles herself. "Yes, I am. How did you guess? I suppose Marco described me as a redhead."

"Titian was the word he used. Please come in. Where is Marco?"

"He was going to bring me a little later this morning, but I couldn't wait to see the palazzo by daylight," Juliette replied as she was ushered inside.

"Then you'll give me a chance to show you around before he comes. It's such a pleasure for me to have a fellow Parisienne as so near a neighbor. I know we'll have much in common. Marco has talked so much about you. This is the shop where we are standing now, although I doubt you'll ever see another one like it anywhere."

Enthralled by her surroundings, Juliette had realized that already. Exoticly patterned fabrics in Fortuny designs presented a vista of rich Renaissance colors such as sapphire, ruby, and emerald, many of them subtly aglitter with gold, silver, copper, or bronze. Every inch of the walls under the enormously high ceiling was covered by multihued fabrics either mounted under glass or hanging in abundant lengths. As Juliette moved forward, she saw that the great curtains, hanging from rods across the width of the room, were there both for display and to create partitions.

"I've never seen so many glorious silks and velvets in all my life!" Juliette exclaimed.

"Ah! Of course you haven't. They are all unique. Mariano has researched the processes used by Venetian weavers centuries ago, and now he uses the same vegetable dyes they did to re-create similar glories."

"How well he has succeeded!" Juliette fingered a fabric of scarlet and gold that might have clothed an early doge.

"Marco has told us of your exceptional designing skills," Henriette said, "so I can guess how much all these fabrics interest you.

In fact," she added with a twinkling glance, "when he came back from Lyon, he talked of little except meeting you." She had begun leading Juliette toward an opening at the side of the first dividing curtain, its motif of Persian origin. Beyond it the delights continued, with the additional enhancement of Delphos robes and other Fortuny gowns displayed on mannequins. In Paris no *haute couture* house ever displayed its clothes publicly in such a way, and these garments were no less exclusive. Other items for sale included cushions in Fortuny designs, his silk shawls, Knossos scarves, and evening jackets of dazzling splendor.

"As you said, this is not like any shop I've ever seen," Juliette remarked with pleasure as she continued to look around.

Amid the sumptuous drapery, long antique tables served as counters, the young male assistants in black velvet suits with flowing cravats, the girls with wide collars of Burano lace spread out over their shoulders, their dresses also of black velvet.

"Buon giorno," Juliette replied to their greetings. As yet there were only three customers in the shop, and Henriette explained that the busy hours were about to start as visitors to the city found their way there.

"There's always a demand for Fortuny textiles and the items on sale here. Women of discernment have also fallen in love with the gowns, but they mostly wear them as tea gowns. Several actresses have worn them on stage. Apart from you in Paris and myself here, the American women have been the first to wear them at social functions in public venues. Yet so far they have remained cautious enough to wear an evening jacket or mantle at the same time!"

"I'm proud that I was the first in Paris to wear the robe unadorned, although it was only once without my chiffon dévoré coat. My sister accused me of appearing *en déshabillé* in public!"

Henriette laughed. "Thankfully those views show signs of changing. Don Mariano has created a timeless style that's beyond the dictates of fashion. I'm sure you've thought that about yours."

"Right from the start," Juliette admitted quietly, "I knew for more than one reason that I'd never discard it."

"Don Mariano replaced the missing label for you, I believe. But I suppose you still don't have one of the small round boxes we give each of our customers to keep the pleats stored properly."

"No, I haven't," Juliette admitted.

"Well then, I shall have to see that you get one." Henriette went to speak with one of the male assistants and then returned to Juliette's side. "It will be waiting for you when you leave."

"Thank you." Juliette had paused to touch one of the Delphos robes. She could see the silk must have been dyed more than once to create a silvery, blue-gray effect. "This is extraordinarily beautiful. I've seen that several other silks have been given the same treatment in different colors."

"That is another process Don Mariano has perfected himself. Often a fabric is dyed and treated many times before he gets exactly the delicate combination of shades and the effect that he wants."

Juliette became aware that in spite of all the time she had been looking at everything, they still had not reached the end of the shop. She had lost count of how many partitions they had passed through. "This is an enormous place."

"It's one of the largest areas under a roof in Venice." Henriette talked then about the Palazzo Orfei's centuries-old history, explaining that the powerful Pesaro family had lived in it for over two hundred years before moving to another palace, after which it had continued to be used as the setting for splendid occasions, such as great banquets, balls, concerts, and plays. Eventually Fortuny was able to buy it and maintain its grandeur with his own displays.

While talking, Henriette had brought Juliette within sight of a pair of draped doors flanked by huge flowering plants in Oriental pots. Even as she explained it was the rear entrance from a side canal, a bell rang and a male assistant hurried forward to open one of the doors. He held it wide for a woman and her escort, who were alighting from a gondola.

"What a romantic way to go shopping," Juliette remarked as she and Henriette turned to retrace their steps.

"I remember thinking the same thing when I first came to Venice, but it won't be long before you'll be taking every kind of water transport with no more thought than if you were riding in a taxi or catching an omnibus in Paris. I'll show you over the rest of the palazzo now. We'll start with the salon-studio. We call it that because Don Mariano likes to paint at one end, and we entertain and hold parties in the salon area. Our quarters adjoining the palazzo are quite small." Henriette began leading Juliette toward the stairs. "You'll see some of Don Mariano's own paintings, etchings, and sculptures in the salon-studio. Photography is another of his interests, and he has his own darkroom."

"What does he like to photograph?"

"Everything from family portraits to city views. He has files of them in his library. I need hardly say there are scores of Venice in all its wonderful changes of light and many of me in Fortuny gowns."

They went up the stairs, looking in at a showroom where more gowns were displayed, then coming to a room as vast as the shop area, with side rooms leading off it and glass doors that opened to a loggia. It was similarly partitioned, but here the great curtains were of antique velvet in exotic designs and colors. Not all these had been drawn together, so it was possible to see the whole length of this palatial room to the studio area at the far end. There was an easel with a canvas on it, bathed in the light of the tall Gothic windows that perfectly balanced those behind Juliette, who stood gazing in fascination.

All the way along, suspended from the ceiling, were lamps of Fortuny's design. They reminded her of the planet Saturn in its encompassing rings, and each one had an ornate luster hanging from it. The furniture, all dark with age, was set off by the silk-covered walls. Velvet-upholstered couches piled high with an abundance of cushions positively invited good conversation and laughter among friends.

"I feel as if I've entered the palace of some great Eastern potentate," Juliette remarked with pleasure. The illusion was heightened by the magnificence of heavily embroidered and begemmed, centuries-old cloaks and vestments displayed on mannequins that had been softly swathed in silk to conceal their mahogany tops.

Henriette explained that many of the treasures on display, including the draperies, the armor, the equally old Venetian glass, and the Persian rugs, had been inherited by Fortuny from his late father and that he had continued to add to the rare collection.

Here Fortuny's own paintings and sculptures were further enriched by their surroundings. Juliette, studying everything, suddenly found herself face to face with a large framed painting on an individual stand. She felt almost choked by her startled reaction to it. "What is the title of this one?"

Henriette, seated on a nearby couch, saw how spellbound Juliette seemed by it. "It's one of Don Mariano's Wagnerian scenes and is called "The Embrace of Siegmund and Sieglinde." I'm sure you'll recall that it happens in the first act of *Die Walküre*."

Juliette continued to stare at the couple locked together in an embrace that seemed as wild as the wind that was streaming through Sieglinde's hair and whipping Siegmund's tunic. He had crushed her to him so powerfully that he had ripped her garment, making her half-naked. Juliette felt a tremor pass through her. It was exactly as Nikolai clasped her to him the evening she had come home from London and run frantically to his studio. She seemed to feel again his strength, his muscled body, and his hungry mouth devouring hers.

"Is anything the matter?" Henriette's question jerked her out of her trance.

"No!" Juliette's denial came quickly in her need to dispel any curiosity. "It's just that I've never seen a passionate reunion so perfectly portrayed before."

"Yes, it's a fine painting. You can tell Don Mariano later how it impressed you. I think he still has someone with him at the moment. They're discussing a Titian he's been asked to restore. He often does restoration work on paintings for both the Church and the City. His mother and sister will be coming in later. It will be a good opportunity for you to meet them all at the same time." Henriette made a comical little grimace. "Their visits are rare, because Doña Cecilia Fortuny doesn't approve of me either as a divorcée or because I choose to live openly with Don Mariano."

Although she made light of the disapproval, Juliette guessed that there had been many unpleasant confrontations with Fortuny's mother. "I wish I could have avoided all subterfuge concerning Michel," she said frankly.

Henriette frowned deeply and rose from the couch to take Juliette by the arms. "Your case is entirely different. The choices you've made are for your baby's sake, not for your own. The world is full of cruel tongues and an illegitimate child is marked by society from the moment of birth. It was because I have suffered myself that I wanted you to have a chance to make a new life here. That was before I knew that Marco would have a far better plan himself."

Juliette inclined her head thoughtfully. "I'll always be grateful to him for the action he took."

Henriette gave her an impatient little shake. "He's worth more than your gratitude. A man like Marco deserves to be loved."

Juliette jerked herself free and turned away. "I know you mean well," she said tremulously, pressing her hands together, "but I must ask you to say no more."

Henriette spoke apologetically. "I went too far. I had no right. Believe me, I spoke as a friend. A new friend indeed, but no less sincere for that."

"I'm not offended. Truly." Still Juliette kept her face averted.

"But you're upset." Henriette put an arm around Juliette's waist. "When you get to know me better you'll find I'm inclined to be outspoken at times. Let's go up to the next floor. You'll see the seamstresses at work and people packing and so forth, all of which will be familiar to you. On the top floor we do the screen and hand-block printing of fabrics just as it is done in Lyon. Are you ready?"

"Yes, of course." Juliette straightened her shoulders determinedly.

On the upper floor they went through a maze of workrooms. Only one door bore the sign *No Admittance*. "That's where the process of pleating takes place," Henriette explained. "The secret is known only to Don Mariano's most trusted workers, who are sworn to secrecy."

"Did you know that no couturier in Paris has been able to discover how such minute pleats can be made to stay in place as they do?"

Henriette gave a triumphant little laugh. "Neither shall anyone ever discover it! There are plenty of would-be imitators, but only one exclusive Fortuny method." She glanced at the diamond watch pinned to her tunic. "I expect Marco has come by now. We'll look for him."

But Marco had already heard that Juliette was in the building and was on his way to find her when they met him on the stairs. "What do you think of the Palazzo Orfei, Juliette?" he asked. "Is it all you expected?"

"Much more!" she replied enthusiastically.

Henriette nodded. "Your wife has seen everything possible. Has Doña Cecilia arrived?"

"Yes, that's why I came looking for you. She and Maria Luisa are with Don Mariano, and they're all waiting for us to join them."

Henriette pursed her lips in a silent whistle of resignation. "Here we go!"

Juliette thought Marco seemed a little disappointed that he had not been the one to show her around, and she regretted her own impatience. On impulse, to console him, she put her hand into his and saw by his responding glance how pleased he was by her spontaneous gesture. She experienced a twinge of guilt that it had meant nothing to her.

The three of them went through a door leading off the salon-studio into a large room that was a surprise in itself to Juliette. The room was covered from the floor to its high ceiling with a colorful trompe l'oeil of an Italian garden, even to the marble statues standing amid the blossoms and foliage. As she was to learn later, it had been painted by Fortuny himself. He greeted her immediately, immaculate from head to foot in what she knew from Marco to be his daily attire, for whatever the weather or the season he always dressed as if it were summer in a well-cut dark blue suit of finest serge with a white silk cravat. Today his shoes were black patent leather, but he was equally likely to wear red sandals of his own design. In everything he seemed to be a law unto himself, which, Juliette supposed, was the hallmark of every genius.

"How are you, Signora Romanelli?" he asked in his pleasant, jovial manner. "Or may I call you Juliette?"

"Please do, Don Mariano."

"Did you have a full tour of the establishment? Good. Now I'd like you to meet my mother and my only sister."

Doña Cecilia was an austere, good-looking woman, elegant in a black silk, waisted gown that was not of her son's design. Her eyes were as dark as his and set in an oval face with classic cheekbones narrowing to a small chin. Her nose was long, thin, and aristocratic.

"I hope you will soon settle down in Venice," she said to Juliette, "and not miss Paris too much. Signor Romanelli has kept you a secret far too long."

"There were private reasons," Juliette countered firmly. "As for Paris, I suppose those of us who are born there never forget our city, but from what I've seen of Venice so far, I'm sure it holds all I could possibly need."

"Well said!" Fortuny exclaimed approvingly, taking Juliette by the elbow and guiding her to where his sister sat a few feet away. "I think Christian names are in order here. Maria Luisa, I hope you and Juliette will be friends."

Maria Luisa was as plain as her brother was handsome. It was as if all the beauty to be shared between the two siblings had concentrated itself in him and his creation. Her attitude, however, seemed politely amiable as she invited Juliette to take a seat beside her.

"Are you musical?" she inquired.

"I appreciate music and I enjoy playing the piano," Juliette answered, "but not in any exceptional way."

"How unfortunate! My ear is not accustomed to anything less than the superb. My singing and playing used to be much acclaimed, but I stopped as soon as it dawned on me that there would come a day when I could no longer maintain perfection. Now I channel my energies into a campaign against the killing of any living creature, even a mosquito or a wasp." She launched into what was obviously an obsession, her eyes lighting up with the fervor of the reformer.

Only the arrival of refreshments interrupted her flow, and the conversation became more general. Eventually Marco and Juliette left, she being handed the small round box for her Delphos robe. He carried it for her when they set off on foot for his business premises. As they walked, she mentioned how strangely Maria Luisa had talked on certain subjects.

"She told me the only way to get a rewarding night's rest was to sleep in a chair as she does."

Marco shrugged. "She's become quite eccentric ever since a love affair came to nothing some years ago, but at least there's no malice in her."

"I noticed Doña Cecilia's edged remark about our marriage."

"I hope it didn't trouble you."

"Not at all. Henriette had already given me some indication that she would not be easy to get along with."

"I think she liked you more than you realize. Your patience with Maria Luisa impressed her. She asked me to take you to one of the *salons* she holds occasionally in the French manner. Fortuny has told me that in the past their home was always a center of intellectual gatherings. Some of the most well-known painters, poets, and writers in Paris attended her *salons*. Then, after her husband's death, Paris lost its charm for her. Nothing was the same in her eyes without him. Eventually she moved to Venice, taking Maria Luisa with her. Although Fortuny had begun to make a name for himself in Paris, he accompanied her. Then he rented and finally bought the Palazzo Orfei."

"I can see she has problems with Maria Luisa."

"It also distresses her—and I'm using her words—that Fortuny and Henriette are living in sin."

"She blames Henriette?"

Marco raised an amused eyebrow. "Naturally. Mothers rarely blame their own sons."

Juliette shared his amusement. "I must remember that. I don't want to spoil Michel."

Had the situation been different between them, Marco would have pointed out there would be no chance to spoil the boy when there were other children. But it could not be said. Not yet. Not even soon, when he would have every right to go to her bed. He would have to wait for the moment when she came of her own accord to his arms. His great fear was that by doing otherwise, he might lose whatever mild affection she had for him. He could not endure to have a wife who took him on sufferance.

Juliette, chatting amiably as they walked along, had no inkling of his thoughts. It was not far to his premises, which were close to the Grand Canal and housed, like many other businesses in Venice, in a building dating back three centuries. The painted ceilings and wall murals in the outer office and in Marco's own were evidence of the building's more illustrious past, but everything there, and in the vast storerooms that filled the upper floors, was run with up-to-date efficiency.

Marco showed Juliette some of the exotic fabrics he imported from the Far East and elsewhere, as well as the delicate Burano lace he exported from Venice.

When she arrived home again her trunk had been delivered. She unpacked it herself and transferred her Delphos robe to its new box, where the pleats curled around and settled into place. She put on the beribboned lid and stood holding the box to her for several minutes before finally putting it away on a shelf and closing the door of the closet. It was like parting from Nikolai all over again, the remorseless pain unabated.

Seventeen

BEFORE THE WEEK WAS OUT, Juliette had hired Lena'a niece, Arianna, as nursemaid. She was a chaste, fresh-faced girl of twenty who, on her third morning, came hurrying to Juliette as she stood discussing a menu with Lena in the kitchen.

"There's a delivery man at the door with two large trunks for you, signora."

"But mine arrived the day after I came here," Juliette said in surprise. "There must be some mistake."

She went at once to tell the delivery man, but when he showed her that he had the right address, she saw the trunks had been sent from Paris by Denise. When she opened them it was to find that they contained all her Landelle clothes carefully packed between layers of tissue paper. She was grateful to have them and wished she were not so sure why they had been sent. But she knew that to her sister the chance of still making her a walking advertisement for Maison Landelle was not to be lost, no matter the circumstances. Although she sat down at once to write a letter of thanks to Denise, holding out an olive branch once more by promising to wear the clothes, she knew sadly as she sealed the envelope that it was unlikely she would ever receive a reply.

Juliette passed the weeks remaining before Christmas opening the boxes on the top floor and visiting the Basilica, the Ducal Palace, and the other grand sights of Venice. Warmly wrapped against the cold, she wandered the quiet passageways and squares, lost count of the little arched bridges that she crossed, and found small churches rarely seen by visitors where she would study the unexpected treasures within.

In the Church of the Scalzi, which people hurried past on their way to and from the railway station, she found ceiling frescoes by Tiepolo of immense spiritual beauty that covered the entire vaulting in the most sumptuous colors. Afterward, whenever she was near the church, she would go in to sit quietly, particularly when she had something on her mind.

Marco was in his office all day, but when he came home he was always eager to know what she had done. In the evenings they went quite frequently to a concert or a play. On special occasions, they would be among those arriving by gondola at the grand water entrance of La Fenice to take their seats in one of the tiered boxes and enjoy a superb opera. Two theaters had been converted into moving-picture houses, which they also patronized. Afterward they had supper, often at the Danieli, which had a view of the Lagoon twinkling with the lights of ships and other water traffic. Or else they would stop at Florian's to drink delicious hot chocolate topped by mounds of cream. It was the pattern of a courtship and they both knew it.

The wives of Marco's friends, curious to meet Juliette, invited them to parties and to dine. As a result, Juliette made new women friends, some of whom had babies and young children themselves.

On New Year's Eve, Doña Cecilia held her *salon*. It was Juliette's wish to accept the invitation, although she and Marco had received others to parties he would have preferred. She did not explain the reason for her choice, but in her own mind she did not want the kind of evening she had spent with Nikolai on previous New Year's Eves. She wore one of her Parisian gowns and, smoothing the pearl-sewn cream satin down over her hips, she was relieved to see that she had almost regained her figure.

Marco, already in his cloak, was waiting in the hall for her.

"You look very beautiful," he said, regarding her admiringly as she descended the stairs. "You haven't worn that gown before. I expected to see you in the Delphos robe."

He had taken her velvet mantle from her arm, and she was glad to turn away from him as he put it around her shoulders. She could never be sure how much he guessed of her feelings at any one time. "I have several other Landelle gowns that you haven't seen," she answered lightly. "As for the Delphos robe, I've had it a long time and put it away." Her shrug was casual as she faced him again, her confidence and composure regained. "Let's go," she said, taking his arm. "We don't want to be late."

At the Palazzo Martinengo where Doña Cecilia lived on the Grand Canal, they found an international gathering of people in the three great rooms that had been opened out into one another. The walls were hung with priceless antique draperies in time-faded hues that still glinted with gold and silver threads. Although Fortuny was at his mother's house, Henriette was not present. He would be staying only a short while before returning home for a party with their own friends. Before leaving, however, he took Juliette on a tour of the rooms, explaining the origins of the most interesting fabrics and showing her some of the paintings by his father, which hung on the walls.

Marco knew a number of the people present, and he and Fortuny between them introduced Juliette to all the guests. Some were connected with the arts, others with politics, and many were foreign nationals rich enough to live anywhere in the world who had chosen to reside in Venice. Juliette made sure that Maria Luisa was drawn into conversation, gently discouraging her favorite, well-worn topics of discussion. This thoughtfulness did not escape Doña Cecilia's notice, who saw again some of the sparkle and charm that had once made her daughter so popular and sought after by suitors, before her eccentricity drove them away.

"I like Marco's wife," Doña Cecilia remarked in Spanish to her son when they could not be overheard, "but I've drawn my own conclusions about their marriage."

"Oh? And what are they?"

"They were indiscreet, and when Marco learned that a baby was coming, he made an honest woman of her. I shall invite her here again."

"But you're such an upholder of morality, Mamá," Fortuny jibed wryly.

"She is a respectable wife and mother now, my son," she said with emphasis, never missing a chance to show her disapproval of his liaison. "I shall take an interest in her and the baby. Remember, I'm one of those unfortunate women who have neither a daughter-in-law nor grandchildren."

With a sharp flick of her Spanish lace fan, she swept back to her guests. He made his departure with a resigned sigh.

When it drew near midnight, champagne glasses were refilled and Marco looked for Juliette. She came to him, bringing Maria Luisa with her. The clock struck and the bells of Venice began to chime throughout the city. Glasses were raised amid cheers and laughter. The year 1913 had dawned.

Juliette wanted to walk home. There was so much celebrating along the Grand Canal. Boats were lit up, passengers on board the *vaporetti,* many dressed in colorful costumes, blew whistles and waved to every passing gondola. Fireworks filled the sky, competing with the snowflakes that came wafting down as a hint of more to come. In the square people were dancing, and Juliette and Marco joined them for a while before continuing on their way.

They entered the house quietly, not wanting to wake Michel, who slept now in a nursery adjoining Arianna's room. Marco switched on a lamp in the hall and Juliette removed her mantle, the melting snowflakes sparkling on it as she began to climb the stairs.

"Wait, Juliette! Let's drink a glass of champagne on our own before we say good night."

She looked back at him. He had tossed his cloak and hat onto a chair and was holding out a hand to her. She hesitated. "I've really had more than enough champagne. I felt quite dizzy during that last dance."

He let his hand drop to his side. "Then do something else for me instead," he said in the same even tone. "Throw that Delphos robe away. Now. Tonight. I want us to start this New Year unencumbered by trappings from the past. I'll buy you other Fortuny gowns. Have them in every color and style if you wish. At least I'll know that none of them hold the same significance for you."

She had stiffened, her head jerked back. He had not spoken out of jealousy and neither was he angry. But nothing in this house had any connection with his late wife, and he expected her to dispense with the past as he had done. She had given herself away at the beginning of the evening by admitting she still had the robe.

Wordlessly Juliette let her mantle fall into a soft heap on the stairs. She turned and descended to the salon. There she came to a standstill, her back to him. In the light from the hall she could see a champagne bottle in ice and two glasses, which he must have asked Lena to leave ready for them. He followed and switched on a couple of lamps. Only then did she speak.

"My sister once told me to get rid of that robe. I wouldn't do it then and I can't do it now."

"Then give it into my charge."

"No!" Wild-eyed, she spun around to face him. "You'd destroy it!"

"You have my word that I'd never do that."

"Then why?"

"I want it removed from our lives until such time as you can look upon it simply as a gown associated with memories that have faded in light of all the good times since."

"What you suggest is pointless. The robe is already stored away in its box, but Michel is a living, breathing reminder in his cot upstairs!"

Marco's face tightened, a nerve throbbing in his temple. "He is my son! He has been since the moment of his birth, and I love him. You must never say anything like that to me again!" He drew in a deep breath. "Now drink that glass of champagne with me."

Grimly he uncorked the bottle and poured the champagne into the two glasses. She took the one he handed to her. If he had intended originally to make a toast, he must have thought better of it. He took only a sip from his glass and watched her with narrowed, furious eyes as she gulped hers down as if it were water. She believed she had spilled some, but did not stop to look. Then she banged down the emptied glass, flashed him a glance as enraged as his, and rushed out of the room.

She almost ran up the stairs, snatching up her mantle as she went. For the first time that night she turned the key in her door before preparing for bed. As she lay against her pillows in the darkness she found herself listening for him to come upstairs, fearful that he would try the door.

When at last she heard him, she sat up, breathing rapidly, but his footsteps went past and straight into his own room.

Neither Juliette nor Marco ever referred to the incident, but each knew it was uppermost in the other's mind, for it had created a gulf between them that was seemingly unbridgeable. Although Marco resumed his fond attitude as if nothing had ever happened, his embraces were now even more restrained than they had been previously.

His intense desire for her had never been in doubt. She had known from the time of their arrival in Venice that he was waiting for some indication that she was ready to be his wife in every way. But she had been unable to give him what he wanted. It would have been easy to blame her maternal absorption in the baby, for she had heard that after giving birth many women lost all interest in lovemaking, often for months on end. But it was more than that. The fault was not in Marco but in herself, for as long ago as in Lyon she had been aware of him as a very attractive man.

On the surface, Juliette and Marco continued to maintain the illusion that all was well. They talked as before, exchanged news, and laughed freely. Most important to them both were the times shared with Michel. Marco took an Italian father's immense pride in the baby boy, failing to see any resemblance to Nikolai in the black curls and the fading of his blue eyes to a clear gray that would never match the Romanelli brown.

They dined with Fortuny and Henriette, attended soirées at the Palazzo Martinengo, and entertained frequently. Doña Cecilia became very fond of Michel and liked Juliette to bring him to see her whenever it was not too cold. When he developed a fever she sent a servant every day to inquire after his health.

The doctor was attentive, but the medicine he prescribed seemed to have no effect. Suddenly Michel was desperately ill and rushed to hospital by water ambulance. Juliette and Marco kept constant vigil by his cot, and although they told each other not to worry, their harrowed faces revealed their deepest fears. Finally, one morning, the doctor in charge nodded approval.

"Michel is a fighter. He's still very weak, but his temperature has dropped and the signs are promising."

Although he made steady progress from then onward, Juliette continued to be at the hospital more than at home. Marco went to work, but came straight to the baby's cot afterward.

When they were at last able to take Michel home, Arianna implored Juliette to leave him in her charge that first night.

"You've had so little rest, signora. You need to sleep. I'll watch over Michel."

Although Juliette agreed, going early to bed and thinking she would sleep like the proverbial log, she dozed only fitfully. At midnight she slipped on a robe and went to the nursery. There she found Arianna asleep in an upholstered chair at the side of the cot. Yet the faint creak of the door woke her at once, and she looked quickly toward the cot before she realized that Juliette had entered the room. When Juliette saw that Michel was sleeping peacefully, she tiptoed out again.

It was on her way back to her own room that she heard the faint sound of muffled sobs. She stopped and listened, thinking she must be mistaken, but as she moved on she heard it once more. She went to Marco's door, listened for a few moments, and knew she was not mistaken. She pressed down the handle and went in.

He sat fully dressed except for his jacket, with his elbows on his knees, his head in his hands. Another terrible sob racked through him. Juliette went forward, her robe whispering about her.

"It's all right," she whispered, putting her hands on his shoulders. "Michel is well again and there is nothing more to worry about."

"I know," he answered between sobs, "but those nightmare days have suddenly caught up with me. I thought I was going to lose him as I've lost you."

Compassion, and something close to love, moved her deeply. "You haven't lost me! You never will!" she protested. "I've needed time. Maybe more time than either of us first realized. But I'm here and I always will be."

His groan broke from his heart and he clasped her about the waist and pressed his face against her. She looked down at him and folded his head in her arms, continuing to murmur soothing, reassuring words. Finally she whispered his name, and when he looked up at her she took his face between her hands.

"Marco," she urged gently, "take me to bed."

Her one thought was to give him greater reassurance by becoming a wife to him at last; for herself she expected nothing. All her sexual feelings had been drained away by heartache and maternal devotion. There was no longer any need or wish in her for a return to such yearnings.

When Marco came to the bed, strong, naked, and powerful, she took him into her waiting embrace out of pity. She was prepared to submit to whatever he wanted of her, but nothing happened as she had supposed. There was no pent-up hungry searching, no fierce possession by a man tormented by long waiting, just an exquisite tenderness that made all her tension disappear.

She began to tremble under his stroking touch. With sensitivity and understanding, he was slowly and surely using all his skill as a lover to reawaken her long dormant sensuality and draw her back into a sphere she had never expected to enter again. She was surprised when, after a short time, all her natural desires stirred unexpectedly and then suddenly flared. Her young and healthy body, long deprived, seemed to escape all control, borne along as if of its own volition by his increasing passion. He crushed her close as she almost fought against him even as she succumbed to the sharing of his physical ecstasy.

Afterward she lay with her face turned away from him and he held her quietly in his arms. Finally she turned to look into his loving eyes.

"You've been so tolerant, Marco." Her voice faltered. "All these months . . ." She left her sentence unfinished, looking away from him again.

He turned her face back to him with his fingertips. "There are more ways than one of showing one's love, my darling wife."

Yet again she thought what a good man he was, and this time she understood that he deserved some part of her heart.

They did not sleep apart again. And she knew it was no fault of his that she never reached the heights to which Nikolai had taken her.

On reflection, as the days went by, Juliette could pinpoint exactly when she stopped looking back and turned her mind to the future. It was when she had opened Marco's door and seen him in that state of utter despair.

Gradually she adjusted to living in Venice, the letters she received from Lucille and Gabrielle making up a little for Denise's silence. If there were a cloud on her horizon it was the tension in Europe, the talk of war, and the mad arming by various nations. At social gatherings, the conversation always turned at some point to this growing unrest, but, especially among the fashion-conscious Venetian women lighter topics also prevailed. The hobble skirt had just been introduced by Paris. It gave an elegant line, but also made it difficult to walk. Any mention of *haute couture* made Juliette increasingly restless to get back to work. Finally, she raised the issue with Marco.

"Originally, before we married," she said, "I'd never expected to be at home as long as I have. Michel is over six months old now."

"The choice is still yours," Marco replied. He would have preferred her to stay at home, regretting the promise he'd made when offering marriage, but he would not go back on his word.

She leaned back against her seat, her arms folded and her fingers dancing. "I admit it's been wonderful being with Michel all this time, and I like the freedom of attending daytime events with no obligation to be elsewhere, but somehow I feel compelled to be in touch again with fashion in one form or another."

"I guessed that would happen sooner or later," he said resignedly.

Her eyes queried his. "Do you mind?"

"To be honest, I've come to feel differently about it since we married, but I'll not stand in your way."

"You've no need to worry. I'll only work for a few hours a day if Fortuny agrees. Working full-time is out of the question. I'd never neglect you or Michel. Both of you will always be first with me."

"I'm sure of that."

At the Palazzo Orfei, Fortuny listened to her request. Both he and Juliette knew there was no longer any question of her starting as a seamstress.

"Henriette needs an assistant in the work of coloring the engraved blocks, but I feel it would be unfair of me to engage you only to carry out my designs. You need an outlet for your own creative activity, and what I can offer would not be suited to your talents."

"This wouldn't be the first time I've redirected my interests. I've moved from sewing by way of being a mannequin to designing clothes and then textiles. Just to be linked with fashion again is enough for me at the present time."

"Very well, then. As you've most surely heard, this is the time of year when Venice fills up with visitors of wealth and distinction, and their custom alone makes a seasonal demand on my gowns and fabrics. Would you be prepared to sell gowns for me?"

Juliette was surprised but agreeable. "I was never a *vendeuse* at

Maison Landelle, but I learned a great deal when I was there. I'd be glad to do it."

"Good. Think of yourself as being more the equivalent of a *directrice* in some ways, because you'll be in charge of the show-room, with assistants to fetch and carry for you."

"You're putting an enormous amount of trust in my ability."

"You've had plenty of working experience at one of the best *haute couture* houses in Paris, and Henriette took more note than you realize of what you told her about your time there."

"Such as—?" Juliette questioned smilingly.

He grinned. "For example, how you showed your initiative when you dealt with those women who came clamoring for a Fortuny gown at Maison Landelle."

Juliette shared his amusement. "At least here I'll be able to sell them as many as they want!"

"Yes, indeed. But there's one more thing I'd like to ask of you. Tomorrow morning I'll be taking a series of photographs of Henriette in some of the new gowns. It was her suggestion that you pose in the rest. Would you agree?"

She hesitated. It would be the first time she had worn a Fortuny gown since the last time she had dined with Nikolai. It would not be easy, but it was a hurdle she should try to overcome. She gave a quick nod before her spirit failed her. "Yes, I'll do that."

"Thank you. Could you come along about ten tomorrow morning then, and would you mind bringing your own Delphos robe with you? I'd like very much to have a photographic record of it for my files." He smiled broadly. "It's the only one of my garments—so far as I know—that has ever been remade." He took her answer for granted. "I'm sure you'd like some photographs of yourself in it, and of course you shall have them."

Juliette felt dazed that he, all unwittingly, should have made such a devastating request. She couldn't do it! It was too much! But as she drew breath to refuse, there was an interruption by Henriette.

"Mariano! Could you come quickly?" Then she saw Juliette and apologized for bursting in. "I'm sorry. I didn't know you were here. There's a minor crisis that's not in my department."

"We'll settle your hours of work tomorrow," Fortuny said over his shoulder as he followed Henriette from the room.

After leaving the Palazzo Orfei, Juliette went on foot to Marco's office and told him she was to start work the next day.

"That's what you wanted," he acknowledged, "and I agreed."

"Thank you, Marco." She was sitting in front of his desk and hesitated before she spoke again, looking steadily at him. "There is something more I have to tell you. First of all, tomorrow Henriette and I are to model some of the new gowns for a photographic session. Don Mariano also wants me to wear my Delphos robe."

He raised his eyebrows slightly and sat back in his swivel chair. "What did you say?"

"I didn't answer him, but I'll not do it."

Marco rose to his feet and came around the desk to put his hands on her shoulders. "I'd like you to do as he asked. Why not? Nothing stands between us now. Least of all anything that happened in Paris."

She was still uncertain. Yet, if it were true that Nikolai no longer stood between Marco and her, maybe she should make a decisive move toward diminishing the importance of her Delphos robe.

"I'd like to choose one of the new Fortuny ensembles for myself —a gown, a cape, and a matching purse."

He regarded her calmly. "Why not choose two? It would make a change for you not to wear something you've designed and had made up locally. I'll be pleased to foot the bill."

"That's very generous, Marco! Thank you."

He raised her up and she looped her arms about his neck as he kissed her. She had come to care for him more than she once had believed possible. When she had first disclosed this to him, she had been startled by the triumphant force of his lovemaking. It had been as if he were exulting in her total submission instead of understanding that she had given her love freely to complete their marriage. Until then she had sometimes wondered whether, if she had never known Nikolai, she might have found a comparably rewarding if different kind of love with Marco. But the pattern of his passion that night had shown her that she was mistaken. Perhaps he had not realized himself that his wish was not to share but to dominate.

Yet, as today, in spite of his having admitted his change of attitude toward her working, he continued to show unselfishness where her happiness was concerned. She was grateful, if a little unsure how long that might last. Overall, however, she was far too aware of her own shortcomings ever to care less for him because of his.

Eighteen

WHEN JULIETTE ARRIVED for the photographic session, bringing her Delphos robe in its round box, Henriette had just finished posing and was in her own clothes again. She showed Juliette the selection of gowns hanging on a rail behind a changing screen.

"As you'll see, these are all slight variations of the same design, which in turn follows the basic shape of the Delphos robe, because Don Mariano will never stray from that. These new ones also adjust with silken cords and are similarly ornamented with beads of Venetian glass."

Left on her own to change, Juliette took the first gown from its hanger. It appeared quite shapeless until she put it on and tied the dainty cords. It was in black silk velvet, soft as the bloom on a peach, with a panel of gold silk imprinted with a delicate design, tiny beads aglitter, set into the bodice.

"Are you ready?" Henriette called, having returned.

"Yes." Juliette emerged from behind the screen. "Am I all right for the camera?"

Henriette smiled to herself. This young woman, fussing with the cords and looking critically in the full-length cheval glass once again, never failed to imbue anything she wore with extra style. "I think you'll pass inspection," she commented dryly.

"Oh, good. Marco wants me to choose two of the gowns I like best. He knows how I love Fortuny designs."

"The one you have on is my favorite. It's inspired by a gown worn on a famous occasion here at the Palazzo Orfei in the sixteenth century by the wife of one of the dignitaries. The gown was of gold tissue and black lace. It was said to be the most magnificent ever seen in Venice."

"Perhaps until now!" Juliette declared, stroking the soft velvet with her fingertips.

"Don Mariano would appreciate that compliment. But we'd better not linger. He is waiting for you. Go ahead to the photography studio. I'll come later. Good luck!"

With the hem rippling like little wavelets about her feet, Juliette went along to the studio. Fortuny was under the camera's black cloth when she entered, but reappeared at the first tap of her heels.

"There you are, Juliette. Oh, yes." He nodded his approval of her appearance. "Very good indeed. Just as I'd expected. Stand in front of that curtain and raise your elbows as you clasp your hands gracefully in front of you. That will show the batwing sleeves."

After taking a number of photographs, he asked her to put on the evening jacket designed to go with the gown. It was in the same black velvet with a lining of gold silk. As the day wore on, Juliette lost count of the times he disappeared under the camera cloth to photograph her and of how many times she changed, there being a sumptuous Renaissance-inspired cape, cloak, or jacket to complement many of the gowns.

Finally it was time for her to be photographed in her own Delphos robe. Wearing it was like being caressed by the past, the nestling of the silk against her skin a poignant reminder of hands that had stroked, revered, and loved. Curiously, all her dread of putting it on again was lost from the moment she saw herself in the mirror. Somehow it seemed to evoke only memories of the good times she had shared with Nikolai. She hoped this meant that she had finally conquered all regrets and could concentrate on her marriage and the future.

When the Delphos robe was back in its little round box and Juliette was dressed again, she chose the outfits she would have for herself. Inevitably she picked the black and gold one. The second was a green silk tunic with a pleated silk underskirt. Both had sumptuous cape-like jackets to match. Marco, arriving to see Fortuny on business, found her with Henriette, leaning on their arms as they gazed down into the larger of the palazzo's two courtyards.

"What's the attraction?" he asked, unable to see anything un-usual below.

"I'm showing Juliette where the inspiration for one of her new gowns created a sensation," Henriette answered.

"Oh, yes. At the grand performance of *Miles Gloriosus.*" He was equally familiar with the history of the palazzo. "My guess is that the courtyard looked much like the salon-studio when all the walls were covered with rich hangings for such events."

Juliette straightened up with a sigh. "I was thinking the same. One is never more than a breath away from past centuries with anything under Fortuny's influence."

"You like that, don't you?" Marco commented.

She nodded. "Although I'm far too contemporary in my out-look to draw inspiration from a bygone time, I can see why it suits him so well to live here in Venice. I don't think he'd be content anywhere else in the world."

Marco looked questioningly at Henriette. "Would you agree with that?"

"Completely. There's nothing on earth that could uproot him."

None of them saw anything prophetic in her statement at the time, but Juliette was to remember it much later.

Fortuny had been right when he foretold a busy time ahead for Venice. Foreign visitors of every nationality patronized the best hotels, filled the theaters, the concert halls, and the moving-picture houses. It was often difficult for local people to get seats, but Marco always made sure he secured tickets early for anything Juli-ette would enjoy, even the moving-picture costume dramas in which Italy had begun to excel, although he preferred a contempo-rary plot and setting himself.

Many rich women came to the Palazzo Orfei. Some of them were difficult and demanding, but no different from those who had come to Maison Landelle. Juliette let nothing upset her com-posure, and she found selling to these women a challenge she en-joyed.

Some of her customers admitted that they would gladly discard their boned undergarments if their breasts were more perfectly formed. But what they failed to realize was that the Fortuny gowns could flatter as well as reveal. A young American woman men-tioned hearing of a support for the breasts alone that a New York debutante named Mary Phelps Jacobs had made for herself out of two handkerchieves, but there was nothing like that on the market, and so the boned support had to suffice.

Chaperoned parties of young American girls frequently wanted to buy the gowns that Juliette showed them, but invariably their chaperones considered the designs far too sophisticated.

The first time this happened and the party of young women had departed, the assistant who was helping Juliette made a casual remark.

"There'll be sales yet from those young ladies, signora. You'll see."

"What do you mean?" Juliette asked.

"Didn't you notice that two or three of the girls neither expressed frustration nor argued? They'll be back on their own as soon as they can give their chaperones the slip."

Juliette uttered a surprised laugh. "I'd do the same myself if I were in their shoes," she admitted.

She heard the next morning that three of the girls had indeed been back, and also one of the matrons to purchase for herself. Fortunately they did not all come at the same time. After that Juliette was able to spot those who would return, and put aside their choices in readiness.

She had just carried out this task one morning when Henriette handed her a large envelope. "Here are the photographs of you in your Delphos robe. Don Mariano also put in some of those that have gone to the press, which he thought you might like to have."

"Yes, I would. Thank you!"

That evening Juliette showed the photographs to Marco. He selected one of her in the new green Fortuny gown, which she had already worn twice with great success. When the photograph was set in a silver frame, Marco stood it on his desk next to the one he already had of her with Michel.

Juliette had been working at Fortuny's for two months when she and Marco went to a moving-picture house to see Mary Pickford in *The New York Hat*. Included in the program was a newsreel that showed the King of Italy reviewing his troops, a begoggled driver winning a race in a Bugatti, the Pope in Rome, and finally the Tsar and Tsarina of Russia with their son and daughters processing to their seats at an open-air celebration of three hundred years of Romanov rule. In their wake came a number of top-hatted dignitaries and their wives. One of the men turned his head sharply, as if on the alert for trouble, and Juliette recognized him at once.

She had stiffened and jerked forward involuntarily, gripping the arms of her seat. Marco had seen Nikolai too, and he drew her nearest hand into his and held it tightly, able to feel its trembling.

"Are you all right?" he whispered in the dark. The newsreel had ended to the last lingering notes of Russian music played appropriately by a female pianist and male violinist in the orchestra pit below the screen.

"Yes," she whispered hastily, sitting back in her seat. "I was surprised, that's all. One never expects to recognize anyone on a picture-house screen."

"Do you want to leave?"

She shook her head and drew her hand away from his as the main feature appeared on the screen. Juliette watched, but saw nothing of it. She was trying to cope with the rush of love that had caught her so unexpectedly. It forced her to face the stark reality that the passing of time had done nothing to lessen her love for Nikolai, no matter what she had deceived herself into believing. Before her, Mary Pickford received a new hat from the young minister, but Juliette saw only Nikolai's face, handsome as ever, a slight frown between his eyes. She had a vague impression of a woman on his arm. It must have been Natasha, sharing the imperial occasion with him as she shared his life. This more sobering thought enabled her to get a grip on herself by the time the performance ended.

As she and Marco walked home, she was able to say quite casually that she thought Nikolai had looked well and it was surely a sign of his imperial godfather's favor that he had been given such a prominent position among so many high-ranking officials. Marco agreed with her, but remembered her violent reaction. Neither of them mentioned the incident again, but he did not forget.

It was soon afterward that Lucille arrived on a visit to Venice. Juliette was waiting to greet her, and they embraced in happy reunion, but, at the first opportunity, Lucille looked anxiously into Juliette's face.

"Have you ever forgiven me for withholding Count Karasvin's letter?"

"Of course I have! Has it been preying on your mind?" Juliette had been taken aback to hear Nikolai's name spoken so unexpectedly, but she could not resist hoping for news of him. "Did you see Prince Vadim when you were last in Paris?"

"No. He has closed his residence there and he and his wife have returned to St. Petersburg to give their support to the Tsar in these unsettled times. Several other distinguished Russians have gone home for the same reason. Oh, but my dear, how good it is to see you again!"

Michel had just been tucked into his cot when Marco came home from his office that evening and met Lucille for the first time. They were to go out to dine, and when Lucille came downstairs after changing, she was wearing around her shoulders a filmy wrap in a pattern that Juliette recognized instantly.

"May I ask where you purchased that wrap?"

"Denise gave it to me. These wraps are a new sideline for Maison Landelle." Lucille handed her a tissue-wrapped package. "She has sent this one for you."

Juliette sat down to open it on her lap. The wrap was in another color with a different pattern, but the design was her own.

"But these designs are among the last I sent to Denise," she said flatly. "After hearing I was to marry Marco, she sent the drawings back to me torn into pieces."

Lucille sat down beside her with a sigh. "You should have known that Denise wouldn't throw away some perfectly good designs without taking copies first, even though she wanted you to think she had destroyed them at the time."

"I've not received a word from her since then."

"So she told me. I've come as a peacemaker, apart from my wish to see you again and also to meet your husband and baby."

Juliette's expression hardened. "You'll think I'm cynical, but I can only believe that Denise must want something of me."

"Only for matters to be mended between you. She regrets her anger and her actions. I know you have every right to toss her request back at her, but she has had her own troubles recently. Monsieur Pierre has had a heart attack and may never work again. The man who took his place is not proving satisfactory, and through his errors she has lost several valued clients."

Juliette made a weary gesture. "You don't need to say any more. Denise wants me to design for her again, but instead of being straightforward about it she is trying to soften me up first by pretending that she misses me."

Lucille sighed again. "I'm not trying to make excuses for Denise, but I truly believe she would have written to you before all these catastrophes happened if her pride hadn't stood in the way. My visit gave her the chance she has been waiting for. She had begun to rely on you more than she realized at the time. You were her hope for the future."

"Surely she realized that I'd never go back to Maison Landelle? My life is here now."

"I pointed all that out to her. She understands that the situation can never be as it was. All she asks is that you design for her again —clothes and textiles."

"All she asks!" Juliette repeated hotly, springing to her feet and taking a few paces across the room. "I work for Fortuny now. Didn't you tell her that?"

"Yes. I said your letters were full of your enthusiasm and pleasure at being back in the world of fashion. And don't think Fortuny hasn't won her respect. She has seen several important women of high rank wearing his creations, some of her own clients among them."

"But how can I design for Maison Landelle? When I thought once I was going to Russia, I told Denise I'd be too far from the pulse of fashion to keep up with it. Italian women are very fashion-conscious, but the same yardstick applies to me here."

"She thinks your ideas will be all the fresher for it."

"But I spend every morning at the Palazzo Orfei. It wouldn't be ethical to design for one fashion house while working for another."

"Your sister knows all that, but she's in trouble. I've never seen her so cast down. I think all her zest for work left her after the accident."

Juliette spun around anxiously to face Lucille. "What accident? You never mentioned an accident."

"Her motorcar skidded on a wet road and crashed into a wall. She broke both legs and is still on crutches."

"Why didn't you let me know at once?" Juliette demanded.

"It happened just after I'd set sail for France. I went to see Denise in the hospital, and since she came home I've been staying with her instead of at the Bristol. That's why it's taken me such a long time to get to Venice and also why I've postponed my departure for home. I'll go back to her in Paris when I leave here."

Juliette sat silently, looking down abstractedly at the rings she was twisting on her fingers. Finally she spoke. "What exactly does Denise want me to do?"

"She wants a whole new collection for next spring. You're to provide the sketches and ideas for it."

"I can't decide anything before I've spoken to Fortuny, because it would mean leaving his employ."

"What of Marco? Would he agree to your returning with me to see Denise?"

Juliette raised an eyebrow. "I do everything I can for Marco, but I'm not his chattel. I would have to visit Paris if I took on this new work." Then she smiled. "In the meantime, I'm going to show you Venice, but you'd have to be here for many years to see even a quarter of its treasures."

As Juliette had expected, Marco was not pleased about her going to Paris and she saw what a struggle it was for him not to forbid it. Yet he gave a nod and wished her well.

Afterward Juliette told Fortuny what she had been asked by her sister, he heard her out before saying anything. He was at his easel and had put aside his palette and brushes to listen to her.

"Since I don't consider myself to be part of the Parisian fashion world," he said amiably, "I see no hint of rivalry in your taking up this obligation that has been placed on you. If it's what you wish, then it's right for you to do it. I would never stand between two sisters."

"You're being very understanding."

"Have you any special ideas in mind yet for this Maison Landelle collection?"

"Yes, I have." Juliette's face lit up. "Naturally my designs won't be in any way related to your creations, but inevitably you will have influenced me."

"I consider that a generous compliment."

She knew she could confide in him and he would keep it to himself. "I've been across to the lace-making island of Burano several times, and I'll take Lucille with me for the day when I go again. I can picture an all-lace collection for both day and evening clothes. After that, Venetian glass will give me the most marvelous colors for winter woolens and velvets. Think of that strong blue and rich red!"

Fortuny smiled. "Whether you realize it or not, you are returning to your rightful path in life. An artistic mind like yours should never be allowed to stagnate."

"That wouldn't have happened all the time I was working here!"

"But it must have frustrated you at times that the gowns you handled were not of your design."

"No, because I was so glad to be dealing again with lovely clothes that make women feel better and more beautiful for wearing them."

"You'll always be welcome at the Palazzo Orfei, Juliette. I hope Henriette and I will continue to see you and Marco as often as before. And remember, if ever you need advice, I'll be ready to help."

"You're a good friend indeed, Don Mariano."

Lucille enjoyed her visit to Burano, making her own purchases while Juliette discussed prices and delivery with vendors.

"I'm glad all has turned out so well in life for you," she said when they sat side by side on a slatted seat as they sailed back to Venice. "Marco's a fine man and you have a beautiful son. You're soon to be reconciled with Denise and that pleases me so much." She put a maternal hand on Juliette. "Count Karasvin would never have made you happy, you know." Then she drew her hand away sharply as Juliette turned and looked at her with tragic eyes.

"Do you suppose I've found happiness without him?"

"But you have so much!" Lucille pointed out falteringly.

"I count my blessings every day, but the kind of happiness I knew with Nikolai is something that comes only once and never again." Juliette's voice softened and she managed a half smile. "Forgive me. I didn't want to make you look so sad after the splendid day we've had together. I shouldn't have spoken."

There was a pause before Lucille answered. "I'm pleased you did. I almost told you when we were in Paris that I'd once loved someone who devastated my life. I realized afterward that even if we had married I could never have kept him faithful to me."

"Have you ever seen him on your return visits to Paris?"

"No, he died when you were a little girl."

There was a moment of stunned silence. "Were you in love with my father?" Juliette exclaimed incredulously.

Lucille gave a weary nod. "He was quite a philanderer in his young days, and I was demented with love for him. We had a very passionate liaison and then one fateful day I introduced him to my best friend." She shook her head quickly in reassurance. "Your mother never suspected what had been or how I felt. He and she took one look at each other and from that moment onward all other women ceased to exist for him."

"But you were a bridesmaid at their wedding."

"Yes, and that was the hardest day of my life. Rodolphe proposed again that same evening and I accepted him."

"Did you ever stop loving my father?"

"No, but that doesn't mean I haven't done my best for Rodolphe. If it's any comfort to you, I can promise that such love mellows and time heals the anguish and the pain."

Juliette was deeply moved. "I always felt we were kindred spirits, no matter the age difference between us, but I had no idea until now why you were so concerned that I might fall in love with Nikolai."

"I think this has been a good day for both of us. It's also the right time to tell you to stop calling me 'tante.' It makes me feel centuries old! In future Lucille will suffice."

Together they laughed and their mood lifted. A blast of the *vaporetto*'s siren announced their return to the Venetian quayside.

Juliette had made up her mind to take Michel with her when she and Lucille set off for Paris. Marco would be leaving on a business trip at the same time, and she did not want to leave the child without one or the other of them at home. Marco strongly opposed her plan.

"Travel and strange surroundings would disrupt Michel's routine," he argued. "It wouldn't be fair to him and you'll be busy."

"I've explained why I don't want to leave him behind. Arianna can come with us. It's a sensible arrangement."

Marco finally acquiesced, but only after he had tried to change the dates of his business trip, which would have enabled him to be at home with Michel.

The journey to Paris went smoothly. Michel at ten months was a good-tempered child and undisturbed by the traveling. As soon as they arrived, Juliette would telegraph Marco to let him know all was well. When they reached the house in the Faubourg St. Germain, Denise came to meet them in the hall with the aid of a cane. She had dispensed with her crutches, but explained that she still had to rest. Otherwise she was on the mend. Reassured by Juliette's letter agreeing that amends could be made, and buoyed up as usual by getting her own way, Denise embraced her sister exuberantly.

"This is a new beginning! No more misunderstandings!" After she had greeted Lucille, she turned to look at Michel, who was in Arianna's arms. Her immediate thought was that the Karasvin likeness was unmistakable. "He's going to be handsome when he grows up," she conceded speculatively.

"There'll be no trouble with him, signora," Arianna said in Italian. She had not understood what was said, but she had seen no warmth for her charge in the baronne's eyes, only a curious calculating study.

Denise turned to Juliette. "I don't know what your nursemaid said, but I've allotted two rooms on the top floor for her and the child." She became full of smiles again. "As soon as you and Lucille have tidied up we'll have some refreshments and talk. Be sure to bring down whatever sketches and the list of ideas you've brought with you. There's no time to lose."

As Juliette and Lucille went up the stairs, they exchanged a tolerant glance. Denise had not changed and never would.

It was a busy time that followed. Juliette visited Monsieur Pierre and found him almost fully recovered and eager to return to work. He had heard that Juliette was to contribute to the Landelle designs again and became as enthusiastic as Denise had been over the all-lace idea. At Maison Landelle, Juliette soon discovered the reason for his replacement's lack of interest and cooperation. Denise had failed to tell the new designer at the start that he was only there on a temporary basis. She understood the man's feelings. After all, Denise had also deceived her and Lucille to gain her own ends. The situation was not as drastic as she had made out, and neither had Denise used a cane since the day of their arrival.

"I should have known that Denise would be up to her old tricks, aiming to manipulate everybody and everything to her own satisfaction," Juliette remarked resignedly to Lucille. "I just wish she could come straight out with what she wants and not always turn to subterfuge.''

"You would be within your rights to withdraw if you wished.''

Juliette smiled, shaking her head. "It's too late. Denise knew that even if I hadn't given a promise to work for her again, I'd be hooked by the exhilaration of Parisian fashion as soon as I was back here.''

It was while talking over the new designs with Denise that Juliette told her about the American woman's idea of making a separate support for the breasts. "You produce such lovely lingerie. Instead of metal strips rising up from the corseted hips and stomach to a stiffened brassiere, why not let the two sections be separate. It would allow women's breasts to retain a natural shape in keeping with the softer fashions being worn. I've drawn several of these separate brassieres and made some for myself. The support comes only from the cut and the stitching.''

Denise was intrigued. "Tell me more.''

Juliette unbuttoned her blouse and drew it down over her shoulders with the straps of her lacy chemise to display what she had made. She had not used the handkerchief basis, but her own design in silk. Denise, who prided herself on the seductive lingerie she sold, was sure it would be well received by the young and the well-formed.

"I'll consider it,'' she said, fully aware that her sister had given her another highly marketable idea, which she intended to follow up.

Within twenty-four hours of Juliette's return to Paris, she began to hear from friends and acquaintances wanting to see her again. She had little free time but did manage to see some of them; the rest she talked to on the telephone. Everyone wanted to know how she liked living in Venice and what she missed most of Paris. On a more serious note, wherever she went she heard talk of the threat to France from Germany's increasing military might. Every young man declared his intention to enlist at once should hostilities break out.

"We'll fight to the death!'' was their fervent vow.

She hoped desperately that such a terrible catastrophe would never arise. The city had been full of memories for her, and on her last day in Paris, Juliette walked alone to Nikolai's studio. When she arrived, however, it was padlocked, and its shutters closed. She set the palms of both hands against the door and closed her eyes, as if willing the clock to turn back. She could almost hear Nikolai approaching the door to fling it wide and scoop her into his arms.

Several people stared at her as they went past, but she did not notice. When finally she turned away, she knew she would never go there again.

When Juliette arrived back in Venice, Marco was on the platform to meet her. She saw him before he saw her, and alighted from the train with Michel in her arms, ready to see him turn with a smile of greeting. But he was hurrying along the platform away from her, looking almost desperately from one person to the next. Even though she had arranged to return on this day before leaving Venice, he must have been afraid she had changed her mind at the last minute. Quickly she handed Michel to Arianna and began to walk swiftly in his direction. When she was near enough to see his anxious face again, a wave of pity swept through her. She understood now that his reluctance to let her take Michel to Paris had been caused by his secret dread that she might never return. Was he still so uncertain of her? Maybe her distressed reaction to seeing Nikolai again on the newsreel had unnerved him more than he had shown.

"Marco!" she called, breaking into a run and waving to attract his attention. Still he did not see her, as he peered into carriages and became more frantic in his search. She increased her pace, bumping into people in her eagerness to put an end to his torment.

It was not until Marco reached the end of the train and turned in despair that he saw her, relief and joy flooding his face.

"Thank God you're home!" he cried, rushing to embrace her.

She could feel his hands shaking as he cupped her face and kissed her mouth.

That night she dispensed with the simple method of birth control taught her by Dr. Morosini before she left the Tuscan villa. She had not intended to have another baby yet, but the time had come to give Marco the ultimate assurance that nothing could take her from him.

Nineteen

IN THE SPRING of 1914 Denise launched her all-lace collection in a natural figure line that was complemented by flower-hued silk coats and plain hats with wonderfully curved brims. It was an instant success and women flocked to buy. Marco had supplied Denise with all the Burano lace as well as the silks selected by Juliette for the coats. Denise still had Juliette's textile designs woven in England, including a recent set of new ones, but otherwise she took her fabrics from Marco, who dealt fairly with her and whose prices she found favorable.

Juliette had been unable to attend the launch of the collection, for she was in an advanced state of pregnancy. Denise sent her copies of *Le Figaro* and other Parisian newspapers with reports of the collection, but there were more serious matters reported as well. The European arms race was gathering momentum. In Russia ten thousand workers had gone on strike, and there were rumors of war between the United States and Mexico.

Marco came into the room just as Juliette was folding one of the French newspapers she had been reading.

"There is nothing like reading one's own national newspapers," she remarked. "The main news items are the same in every country, but one discovers snippets only reported at home. Although I suppose King George V's state visit to France shouldn't be classed as a snippet and I did find a few lines about it in a Venetian newspaper. But *Le Figaro* had a much fuller description of the way all Paris turned out to greet the royal couple." Her face was serious. "It demonstrated just how closely France and Great Britain are allied against the threat of Germany's might."

"I'd like to read through those newspapers too before they are thrown out. Were you pleased with the reports of the Maison Landelle spring collection?"

She rose to her feet. "Yes, but it seemed a very frivolous topic in the midst of so much depressing news. Then again, maybe that's one of the reasons for the collection's success. Women want to reassure themselves that by looking beautiful and elegant they can retain a note of sanity in the present mad state of the world that men have created."

"Let's hope that sanity spreads out like oil on troubled waters."

"You're not very hopeful, are you?" she questioned gravely.

"My dear, I don't know what's going to happen any more than the next man." He cupped her elbows, drawing her as close as was possible, and looked down into her upturned face. "But all the time no fool fires a hasty shot there's still a chance of everything settling down again."

"You mean that the slightest skirmish on any border could act like a spark to tinder?" She did not need a reply. "It's what I've thought myself for some time." Her eyes were troubled. "I worry about you. If there's a war would Italy be drawn into it?"

"That's highly unlikely. The general mood throughout the country is that Italy should not get involved. You've nothing to worry about as far as this nation is concerned."

"France might not be so fortunate," she said soberly.

"We must hope for the best." He chose to change the subject. "The reason I came looking for you is that I've brought home those samples you wanted from the new consignment of Oriental silks that arrived yesterday."

"Oh, good!" With effort she returned her thoughts to the new winter designs she had been working on for Maison Landelle.

"I think you'll like those with the embroidery."

"Where are they?" she asked.

"I took them up to the studio, expecting to find you there."

"I was taking a break." She smiled as she linked her fingers behind her head and stretched her back. "I'm getting lazy."

"No. I think you work too hard in your studio." He never lost a chance these days to persuade her to give up her designing.

"I'm sitting down and no physical effort is involved." She regretted her lighthearted remark. "I'll go and look at those patterns."

Although on the surface Marco did all he could to help her, she knew that he would have preferred her to concentrate entirely on domestic matters. He had changed during their marriage. The most likely cause was a reversion to his roots. She had seen how difficult it was for him not to forbid her to work for Fortuny, but he was not a man to go back on a promise, and she had truly believed he would come around to accepting it. But rather than dissipating, his resentment had grown. He had probably never realized how much he had shown it in various ways. It was that, as much as anything, that had made her agree to design for Denise again. At least she did not have to go outside her own home anymore to retain her contact with fashion. Yet she could tell that Marco was becoming uneasy about that too. He had wished her well when she went to Paris with Lucille, but even though her being pregnant had made him happier, she did not think he would ever want her to go there again without him.

The fabric samples were lying on the studio table. Some were in the jewel colors she required, but the rest were too pale. She ran the fabrics through her fingers. The winter collection would be her best work to date. At least if war came her designs would keep the flag of fashion flying, and that in itself would indicate Parisian defiance of any would-be aggressor.

In May of 1914, Juliette gave birth quickly and easily to a daughter. The baby became the apple of Marco's eye from the moment he first saw her, but did not in any way lessen his love for Michel. He wanted the baby named after his late mother, and so she was to be christened Sylvana as soon as she was a month old.

Marco was contented at last. After a long period of unease, he had Juliette firmly ensconced in their home with family commitments that would make it impossible for her to entertain any future whim to work beyond its walls. When more babies came along, there would be even less time for her designing, and eventually that would come to an end. Loving Juliette as he did made him wonder how he could have made those rash promises at the villa, but then, in his desperation to make her his wife, he had not realized how possessive he would become as time went by. It had been an unspoken bone of contention between them, but from now on all would go well. He even felt amiable toward Denise, who had at least secured a wedge between his wife and her work at the Palazzo Orfei. It made him feel even more benevolent to consider how disappointed she would be when eventually no more designs were forthcoming from Juliette.

"Let's ask Denise if she would like to be godmother to Sylvana," he suggested to Juliette on her first morning down to breakfast after her confinement. "That should put an end to any last vestiges of estrangement between you two."

Juliette was pleased. "I'm so very glad you suggested it. I'll write to her today."

When Denise received the invitation, she saw it as an opportunity to play the bountiful aunt after all. Perhaps in time to come, one or other of the Romanelli children might still be encouraged to take up a career with Maison Landelle. The first step had been coaxing Juliette back into the business, and with that accomplished, even from a distance, it was only another small step to involving the children later on.

She had no idea what to take as a christening gift for her niece. Engraved napkin rings had served on such occasions in the past, but she wanted something special for Juliette's child. Suddenly she knew what to do. Maison Landelle would become a private company. She would allot shares to both Sylvana and Michel as well as to Juliette. Marco could buy his way in, just as she had always planned a brother-in-law would do. She would make it a condition that his shares could only be sold back into the family. Her lawyers would arrange everything. She was jubilant. Her net was cast!

When Denise arrived in Venice, it did not take her long to see that Juliette's marriage appeared to be satisfactory. Had it not, she would have tried to persuade her to return to Paris, but clearly that would not be possible now. She had a further setback when Marco opposed her offer of the shares.

"It is most kind and generous of you," he said, "but I should prefer you to withhold them until the children are twenty-one. If Juliette wishes to accept her shares, I'll not stand in her way, but I myself wouldn't consider any foreign investments at this time."

"But that's absurd!" Denise exploded. "My *haute couture* house is one of the most successful in Paris and has been ever since I started."

Juliette intervened. "Don't be upset, Denise, I beg you. Let's not fall out again. Marco doesn't want to hurt your feelings any more than I do. I'll take the shares if that will please you and thank you for them, but I agree with Marco that the children shouldn't receive such a gift as yet and also that he must do as he wishes."

Denise struggled with her feelings. Had her plan been too transparent? At least Juliette was securely ensnared. For the time being, she must be satisfied with that and when these rumors of war were over, perhaps Marco might reconsider his position. At all cost she must not antagonize him. "I meant well," she said, shrugging in resignation.

The next day she bought a diamond pendant for Sylvana and a gold pocket watch for Michel, both to be kept until they were of age to receive them.

Although Denise could have had every comfort at the Romanelli residence, she chose to stay at the Grand Hôtel des Bains on the Lido, away from the noise of family life. It was also the best place to show off her lace gowns from the latest Landelle collection. Many of her clients had told her that they felt as graceful as swans when wearing these new gowns, and she had the same sensation herself as the delicate lace drifted like a billowing mist and clung lightly to her arms and figure. She wore a cinnamon lace to the christening, gratified to be a godmother and relieved that the other godmother, a Venetian friend of Juliette's, held the baby. Fortuny and Henriette were also present. Denise had been slightly disconcerted at the thought of meeting them, but Juliette had reassured her.

"Fortuny doesn't know how the Delphos robe came into my possession. All I ever said was that I found it."

Relieved of that worry, Denise was curious to visit the Palazzo Orfei and take a close look at all the gowns and fabrics on display there. Henriette, hearing of her wish from Juliette, offered to show her around.

To Denise's disappointment she did not see where the magical pleating was done, although she saw almost everything else. Her jealousy of Fortuny's success flared anew. She thought it unfair that Maison Landalle had to keep finely tuned to every new trend on fashion's horizon, ever fearful of competitors stealing a march, while Fortuny, year after year, kept to his own original prototype. Yet she had reason to believe that despite the interest shown in his gowns and the articles about them in a few select magazines, his output was extremely small in comparison with her own and that of other Parisian couturiers. One thing was certain: he would never become a serious rival to any of them.

Shortly before Denise was due to leave Venice she returned the hospitality she had received at the Palazzo Orfei by inviting Fortuny and Henriette to dinner with Juliette and Marco at the Grand Hôtel des Bains. After a convivial dinner, they sat on the terrace in the warm starry night and drank coffee. Musicians played and the wavelets of the Adriatic lapped the shore only a short distance away. As they sat talking, a Frenchman in his early fifties, who had been smoking a cigar while strolling the lawns, came back up the steps of the terrace. Sighting the group, he paused with a smile of recognition. Henriette saw him first as he approached the table.

"I declare! Look, Mariano! It's Jacques Vernet!" She turned in explanation to the others. "He's an old friend from Paris. We haven't seen him for a long time."

"Then let us invite him to join us," Denise suggested graciously. She had seen the stranger, a tall gray-haired man, not handsome but with a lean figure set off by his faultless evening attire. Such men invariably had wives who chose to dress equally well, and she never lost the slightest chance to further her business.

While the introductions were made, a waiter brought forward another chair and Jacques sat at the place made between Henriette and Denise. Denise learned that he was the head of a large engineering company located in Normandy, but had an office and an apartment in Paris. There was no mention of a wife at the hotel or elsewhere, but he most surely would have a mistress, and Maison Landelle dressed the mistresses of some of the most distinguished men in Paris.

"You are visiting Venice, Madame la Baronne?" he asked.

"Yes, I came for my niece's christening," Denise replied. "It wasn't easy to leave my business, but I couldn't miss such an important family ocasion."

"Indeed not. So you are in business too." He looked interested. "May I inquire as to what that might be?"

It was easy after that. They got on well, and although the conversation soon became general, Jacques seemed very aware of Denise and several times sought her opinion on one topic or another. When Marco suggested that they have a flutter at the gaming tables as the night was still young, Denise managed to walk beside Henriette into the hotel.

"I haven't heard any mention of Monsieur Vernet's wife," she remarked casually.

"Ah, that's because he's divorced. He married an American debutante in New York, when he was on a university vacation, and brought her back to France. The marriage lasted tempestuously for about ten years, and then she went back home and divorced him there. Since then he has lived alone, but not through any lack of amorous liaisons with women who would gladly have married him."

Denise smiled. A string of successive mistresses was even better than one, because once a rich man had opened an account at a particular fashion house, he would always tell the woman in his life to get her clothes there. In many ways men were creatures of habit, especially as they grew older.

The gaming room where Denise and her party settled down to play was dramatically beautiful, for it was one that Fortuny had been commissioned to decorate. The walls were lined with his own rich red silk stenciled with Grecian designs in gold. Denise thought to herself that it was no wonder Fortuny pleased himself by keeping to a prototype for his gowns when so much of his income flowed from such important orders. Even churches had begun ordering large panels of his fabric to set against stone walls and behind high altars. And three of the foremost theaters in Paris had stage curtains designed by him.

It turned out to be a lucky evening at the tables for Denise and Jacques, although the others lost, and this created a kind of bond between them.

"We must have brought each other luck," Jacques joked. "Shall we play the tables again tomorrow evening?"

"Yes!" Denise answered recklessly.

Jacques invited the others to join them, but Fortuny had another engagement, as did Marco, and neither Juliette nor Henriette cared to gamble on their own. Denise realized too late that she should have left her last two evenings free to spend with her sister, but there was no way to change her plans now. Yet there was something she could still do to be with Juliette.

"Bring Michel over on the *vaporetto* tomorrow and we'll spend the day on the sands. I have a tent on the hotel's private beach and we can bathe. I've been in the water every day." Denise turned to Jacques. "Perhaps you'll come too and meet my nephew?"

"That would be a pleasure."

In the event, Jacques did not come down to the beach until the afternoon. By then both sisters had been swimming and had taken a light salad lunch amid tall green plants in the cool of the hotel dining room. Michel was sleeping in the shade of the tent, having tired himself out playing in the soft sand and toddling in and out of the water as he held his mother's hand. A beach assistant placed a deck chair for Jacques next to Juliette and Denise, and he sat down with a contented sigh.

"What a perfect day this is! Not too hot and a cooling breeze. I've spent the morning in the Frari Church and in the glorious Salute. A converting experience in every sense of the word."

"Is this your first visit to Venice?" Denise asked.

"No, I've been several times over the years, but one always has to come back to gaze once again."

"Do you always travel alone?"

He had a pleasing smile. "No, but this time I felt like getting away on my own." Then he saw a waiter from the hotel approaching with drinks on a tray. "I ordered chilled lemonade for us before I came down on the beach."

There was a fourth glass for Michel and Juliette explained he was napping in the tent and said she would save it for when he awakened.

"I know you don't remember," Jacques said, "but we have met before."

"Have we?" Juliette was puzzled. "Where was that?"

"On New Year's Eve three years ago at the Russian embassy ball. You were with Count Karasvin."

Juliette was taken aback. "Yes," she admitted cautiously. "But how is it that I can't recall our meeting?"

"I was in a group when brief introductions took place. There's no reason why you should remember me, since we didn't dance together or talk. But I intend a compliment when I tell you that you're not easily forgotten, Signora Romanelli."

Although Denise had a jealous nature, the interest of men in other women had never caused her the slightest concern. She was never one to harbor romantic notions, but she did dislike sharing Jacque's attention. "Do you know Count Karasvin well?" she asked, knowing it was the one subject her sister would not want pursued.

"No, but I was acquainted with him through knowing his aunt, the second wife of Prince Vadim. She was a Parisienne."

"I met her at the same ball," Denise replied coolly.

"So you were there too, my dear lady." He was apologetic. "Our paths must not have crossed or else I would have remembered, I assure you."

"I forgive you," she said, mollified. "There were at least six hundred people present. Have you seen Count Karasvin since he left Paris?"

"I have indeed. Only a short while ago I happened to meet him in Vienna."

"Was the countess with him?"

"No. From what I heard there, they go their own separate ways."

"Dear me." Denise cast a glance at Juliette out of the corner of her eye and saw that her sister had turned away in distress. With an uncharacteristic rush of remorse she decided to change the subject. "Do you know I think I'm feeling the heat after all," she said, waving her hand in a fan-like gesture. "Would you escort me back to the hotel, Monsieur Vernet?"

"Of course." He rose to his feet immediately and helped her up. Juliette had also risen, but Denise spoke to her reassuringly.

"Stay here, Juliette. Don't disturb Michel. I'll see you both tomorrow."

When Jacques returned to the beach, Juliette and her son had already departed.

When Denise left Venice, Jacques traveled with her all the way to Paris. He liked her astringent mind, her initiative in creating a niche for herself in the cutthroat business world, and her ability to hold her own against fierce competition. Most of all, he liked the fact that she had not shown any of the amorousness he usually encountered in widows her age, and that in itself made him feel at ease in her company. In all he recognized someone as selfish as himself and looked forward to seeing her again. In the meantime, however, he had to visit his own workshops, which had been turned over entirely to the production of armaments for the government. France was preparing quickly for whatever was to come.

Twenty

EVERYTHING was back to normal in the Romanelli household after Denise's departure. Once again Juliette's time was her own. She had many ideas for next year's spring collection, which she had talked over with Denise, but there was no need to set them down on paper as yet. In the meanwhile, she had plenty of time to spend with her baby and Michel. June was proving to be particularly hot and uncomfortable. Friends who had gone on a visit abroad had offered the loan of their villa on the river Brenta and Juliette would have accepted gladly for the children's sake if Marco had not intervened.

"Wait until the beginning of August," he said, "and I'll be able to be with you all the time."

"But you could come now for the weekends," she replied, thinking of how wonderfully cool it would be in the countryside and how beneficial it would be for Michel to play more freely and the baby to breathe sweet air. But Marco was adamant. He did not want to come home to a lonely house and an empty bed. So the sojourn was postponed until August.

It was the twenty-ninth of June when Marco, seated at the breakfast table, picked up the newspaper, which Lena always put ready by his plate, and stared in disbelief at the headline.

"What a catastrophe!"

Juliette set down the coffeepot. "Whatever has happened?" she asked anxiously.

"The Archduke Franz Ferdinand, heir to the Austrio-Hungarian throne, has been killed by a Serbian assassin in the Bosnian capital of Sarajevo. His wife is dead too. Now the fat's in the fire! The Balkans have always been a dangerous source of trouble."

"What do you think will happen?"

"It says here," he said as he continued to scan the columns, "that Austria intends to take severe measures against Serbia, no matter the risk of provoking European complications." Lowering the newspaper, he looked gravely across at her. "If that means using troops, I fear the worst, because Germany is Austria's ally and Russia will never stand by and see the Balkans overrun." He saw her stricken expression and tried to give her some comfort. "Whatever happens, Italy will not be involved. At least we can be sure of that."

But she was not thinking of Italy. If there were war, she did not doubt that Nikolai would fight.

Daily from then onward and throughout July the newspapers reported the deteriorating situation. Soon Serbia had refused Austria's ultimatum and was mobilizing. On the day after Austria declared war on Serbia, Marco was working in his office when his secretary came in. He was extremely busy and glanced up impatiently. "What is it, Signorina Massari?"

"A gentleman wishes to see you, signore."

He continued writing. "I told you I could not see anyone today who had not made an appointment. Inquire his name and ask him to return tomorrow."

"I did, signore, because he was insistent. His name is Count Karasvin."

Abruptly Marco's pen became still in his hand, but he did not immediately raise his head. "What does he want?" he questioned coldly. "Did he say?"

"Only that he wasn't here on business, but he was sure you would see him."

Slowly Marco rested his pen in its tray and sat back in his chair. "Show Count Karasvin in."

As soon as the woman's back was turned, Marco pulled open a drawer and put both his silver-framed photographs of Juliette inside. He had no idea what this interview would bring, and his one thought was to protect his wife from the past. He closed the drawer and stood up just as his unwelcome visitor entered. Nikolai, casually dressed, smiled as he approached the desk.

"How are you, Marco?" he asked, extending a hand. "It's good to see you again."

Reluctantly, Marco responded to the firm handshake. He thought Nikolai unchanged, his good looks heightened by a summer tan, his athletic body still broad at the shoulders and tapering down to narrow hips. Marco was conscious of the extra pounds he himself had put on around the waist in the last couple of years.

"This is a pleasant surprise. Please sit down. But I'm afraid I can only spare you a few minutes." Deliberately Marco snapped open his gold pocket watch and glanced at it as he sat down again in his swivel chair.

"I know. Your secretary told me." Nikolai took the chair that had been indicated. "I won't hold you up for long. You're looking well."

"So are you. Is your wife with you?"

"No, Natasha is at home, spending the summer at her parents' country house." Nikolai did not add that she spent more time with her mother now than she had done before their marriage, constantly seeking a sympathetic ear for her woes, real and imaginary. "I've been on my own for the past three months, first in Budapest and then in Vienna."

"Why were you there? Were you on a diplomatic mission?"

"No. I was just one of many foreign observers keeping our eyes and ears open as we mingled socially at various embassies and at the palace."

"What is the state of Vienna at the moment?"

"Full of the flush of war fever. Soldiers are being cheered everywhere. Patriotic ribbons decorate the chocolate tortes and the playing of waltzes has changed to military music. I saw the old Emperor Franz Josef shortly after the archduke's funeral, and he looked as if he'd aged twenty years."

"The assassination was a terrible outrage. Have you been to Paris at all this year?" Marco was afraid that Nikolai might have heard there of his marriage to Juliette. Whatever happened, he intended to prevent them from seeing each other. He was also determined that Nikolai have no knowledge of Michel's existence lest he draw conclusions that would disrupt all their lives. Although basically an honest man, Marco could lie convincingly in business when the need arose and he had no compunction about using that skill now. "You used to spend most of your time there, didn't you?"

"Yes, but that ended when duty called at home and I married Natasha. I haven't been back to Paris except once to look for Juliette. The Baronne de Landelle refused then to reveal her whereabouts. But what of you?"

Marco shook his head. "A planned visit to Paris fell through. Since then a few business trips to Lyon have been the limit of my excursions into France." He was relieved that Nikolai knew nothing of his marriage to Juliette. There would be no demand to see her, but the danger was not over yet. Already he had decided to send his wife and children off to the villa that very evening. Nikolai would never find them there. "Are you taking a long vacation in Venice?"

Nikolai shrugged. "Nothing like that. I'm probably making the shortest visit to Venice on record. Just twenty-four hours. I have to leave again tomorrow morning."

Marco relaxed and breathed more easily while raising his eyebrows in disappointment. "So soon? Are you here on some kind of official business?"

"Far from it. I made the journey for a personal reason. It's why I came straight to you as soon as I'd checked into my hotel." Nikolai put his hand to the inside pocket of his jacket and brought out the folded page of a magazine, which he spread out on the desk for Marco to see. "Look at this fashion photograph."

Marco had seen it before. It was one that Fortuny had taken of Juliette in her Delphos robe, and it had appeared in several international magazines some time ago. "I believe it's Juliette."

"It is she!"

"The caption is in French. Was the picture taken in Paris?" Marco read it through, although he knew the contents already. It did not give Juliette's name or that of the photographer, only the information that it was a Delphos robe by Fortuny of Venice and including a short write-up about his work as a designer. "No, the caption doesn't say," he added, answering his own question. "Why are you so interested? I remember hearing it was all over between you and Juliette."

Nikolai shook his head. "Not so long as she and I are both living."

Marco was furious at what he saw as Nikolai's arrogant assumption, and thought to himself how easy it would be to dispatch this Russian with any weapon that came to hand. He realized he was playing with a pencil and was on the point of breaking it fiercely in two. Unobtrusively he let it roll away under his fingers. "As I recall, that was not Juliette's opinion. We exchanged a few letters, but it's a long time since I last heard from her. And then it was to tell me she was leaving France to live with elderly friends in New Orleans."

Nikolai's eyes narrowed incredulously. "Do you mean Lucille Garnier and her husband?"

"That's right. Do you have their address?" Marco began to fear that perhaps he should not have given a specific location.

"No. In any case, a correspondence wasn't what I had in mind. I came here to find Juliette. I knew she would be wary of seeing me, but I was sure you'd know where to find her. I didn't expect to hear she was so far away." Nikolai flung himself out of his chair and stood frowning, fists thrust deep in the pockets of his jacket.

"I can see it's a bitter disappointment for you." Marco rose to his feet too, as if in sympathy. "I haven't seen Juliette since I was in London while she was staying with her friend Gabrielle. Whatever made you think you'd find her in Venice?"

"It seemed logical that Fortuny, who is a photographer as well as a painter and designer and everything else, should photograph his own gowns, and where else but at his own fashion house."

"I'm afraid you've had a wasted journey, then. Juliette isn't here."

Nikolai nodded absently. "Wherever she is, I wish her well. All I'd hoped was to see her once more."

There came a tap at the door and the secretary came in. "Signor Torrisi is waiting to see you, signore."

Marco made a quick gesture of acknowledgment. "Count Karasvin is just leaving." He clapped a hand on Nikolai's shoulder while walking with him to the door. "I don't like to hurry you off like this, my friend." Now that all had gone well, Marco felt pity for him; their friendship would have lasted if circumstances had been different. "Let's have dinner together. We'll meet early at the Danieli and have a drink or two before we dine."

"That would suit me well." Nikolai seemed to have collected his thoughts. "I happen to be staying there."

"Good. I forgot to ask you if you'd ever been to Venice before," Marco questioned. They had come to a standstill by the open door into the outer office.

"Once as a schoolboy."

"Then you would have been dragged around to all the sights. Take my advice and spend the next two or three hours in the Accademia. It's quiet there and some of the works of art are among the greatest in the world. Afterward go back to your hotel and by that time I'll be with you."

"That's a good suggestion. I'm in no mood to follow a guidebook around the city. Until later then."

Marco closed his office door as Nikolai departed. The route that the Russian would take to the Accademia and then to the hotel was a safe one, with no chance of his blundering into Juliette, who should be safely home in any case, as she was expecting Doña Cecilia and Maria Luisa.

As Marco returned to his desk he saw that Nikolai had left the magazine page lying there. He crumpled it up fiercely and hurled it into his wastepaper basket. It had been a mistake to let Juliette pose for those fashion photographs in the first place! There was no doubt about it, he had been far too tolerant in the past. More like a lovesick schoolboy than a husband.

He opened the drawer and took out the photographs again. The larger was of Juliette and the two children. His eyes softened. He would still do anything in his power for her except to let her slip again from her rightful domestic niche or allow her a meeting with her former lover. She was his alone now, possessed by him in every way, and he was increasingly aware of murder in his heart when other men paid her too much attention.

Carefully he set both photographs back on his desk again at the angles he liked best. Then he sat down and made a telephone call before he pressed the bell on his desk that would signal his secretary to bring in Signor Torrisi.

Juliette had been playing with Michel under a tree in the walled garden when Arianna brought her the telephone message from Marco. It was unusual for him not to know well ahead when he would be entertaining a business associate, but she supposed that something important had come up unexpectedly. He had said more than once that fine wine and good food could mellow the hardest of bargainers.

Now Arianna had taken Michel upstairs for his nap in the nursery where Sylvana already lay sleeping in her cot. Before changing out of her morning skirt and blouse, Juliette decided to return a book Henriette had lent her. Although it was only a short distance to the Palazzo Orfei, Juliette put on a straw hat, for the July sun was fierce at this hour. Fortuny's would be closed for siesta, but she would go in by the courtyard entrance.

Juliette crossed the sun-baked stones of the Campo San Beneto and went past the grand entrance to the Palazzo Orfei to the narrow *calle* at the side of the vast building. She reached the ancient door set in a Gothic arch and entered the enclosed courtyard where blossoming plants covered the old walls and flanked the lower flight of the great stone staircase. From there she went quickly up to the loggia on the first floor, where she opened the door set with glass that led to the salon-studio.

"Henriette!" she called cheerily, taking off her straw hat and dropping it onto a chair.

Henriette came into sight from behind the lush drapery. "Oh! You're here," she said with some confusion.

"This book was a good read . . ." Juliette's voice trailed away. Coming indoors from the brilliant sunshine, she had not noticed immediately that her friend looked strained and uneasy. Then, with her whole being, she knew the reason. "Nikolai is here!" she breathed, her heart beginning to pound.

"He arrived about ten minutes ago." Henriette spoke in a low voice. "He had been to see Marco, who pretended ignorance of your whereabouts, but Nikolai Karasvin isn't a man to give up easily when he's come so far to find you."

"Did you—?" Juliette could barely voice the question.

"Don't worry. I told him nothing, except that I knew where you lived. When I wouldn't give him your address, he insisted that I telephone you. I was on my way to do that and to ask if you were prepared to see him. You've still time to leave, if you want."

Juliette shook her head, curiously in control of herself. "He knows I'm here," she stated simply. "He didn't need to see me. He's waiting."

Automatically she put the book she held into Henriette's hand and went past her toward the studio end of the long room. Nikolai stood facing her across the distance, his back to the diffused brilliance pouring through the many tiny panes of the great window behind him.

"I've found you, Juliette." He spoke without triumph, but with relief throbbing in his voice.

She remained very still, remembering how once they had rushed into each other's arms.

"You shouldn't have come here," she stated quietly. The closing of a door told her that Henriette had left them on their own.

"I had to see you once more." He did not move other than to raise his hands and drop them again in a gesture of resignation.

"What made you look for me in Venice?" She began to take slow steps toward him, her face expressionless as she kept herself rigidly in check.

"Through the photograph of you in the Delphos robe that I happened to see in a magazine."

"Was that in St. Petersburg?"

"No. In Vienna. It happened by chance. A woman I'd never seen before dropped an armful of magazines she was carrying onto the floor of the French embassy as I was going through the entrance hall. I picked them up for her. One had fallen open at the page with your photograph. When I stood staring at it, saying I knew you, the woman told me to take it. It was my first clue to your whereabouts. I'd say that such a happening shows we were meant to meet again."

She did not answer him. She had slowed down to a standstill, leaving a few feet between them. The sun's glow fell full upon her and the flyaway strands of her hair, which she had disarranged slightly when pulling off her hat, glinted bronze and gold. "Henriette told me you'd spoken to Marco."

"He was determined that you and I not meet. I guessed you had warned him, as you had done Henriette Negrin, that I was not to be told where you were if ever I came looking for you."

"I didn't have to do that. They've both known all along that everything between us ended in Paris."

"Don't say that to *me!*" he erupted with sudden vehemence. "We'll always belong to each other!"

"You seem to have forgotten that you're married to Natasha," she countered coldly.

"The marriage is as empty as I told you it would be!" he exclaimed. "God knows I did what I could to make it work, but even if I hadn't loved you it would have been no better."

"But you made your choice." Juliette heard her own words expressed as harshly as if by a stranger, not out of revenge, but to help them both survive this meeting and carry on with their separate lives. His face was agonized. It was the same expression he'd had running after the speeding motorcar that carried her away. As before, she wondered that her heart didn't stop beating with the pain it was enduring.

"Why did you get rid of our child?" he burst out, his voice rasping. "I'd have looked after you both. You would have wanted for nothing!"

"You'll have other children."

"That chance has gone. There will be no heir for me. The doctors say that Natasha is barren. The child, boy or girl, who would have been yours and mine, would have had everything I could give. I wouldn't have made demands on you if you had wished to go on without me. I would have respected that."

"You say that now!" she cried out. "But you wouldn't have said it then."

"You're right," he admitted. "I've become wiser than I was. Less sure of always getting what I wanted. Now I would have loved you and the child from a distance if only that could be."

She almost broke down. She was thinking of his son, only minutes away, perhaps even now opening those gray Karasvin eyes, an endearing child who always awoke with a smile. Surely she would never do anything more cruel in her life than deny this man knowledge of the son who would have meant so much to him. But she dared not tell him. She had to think of what it would mean. He would want to see Michel at least once, and Marco would never forgive her. It would ruin the stable, contented home life she had wanted for the boy and now for her daughter as well.

"You and I have both had to adjust to new paths. We must continue to follow them without thinking anymore about what might have been." Her throat was dry, her voice tremulous. "All the decisions I made at the time were for the best."

He thought her distress must come from remembering what it had meant to have an abortion. He moved nearer and could have taken hold of her, but still he kept his hands at his sides. Her eyes were closed as she struggled to overcome the wave of love and compassion that threatened to engulf her.

"Look at me," he urged gently.

But she was afraid he might read all her secrets in her eyes. The time had come to use the only defense she had against him. Her lashes glittered with tears as he repeated his request. Finally she did as he asked. "I'm Marco's wife, Nikolai."

He compressed his lips ruefully, showing no surprise. "That's what I began to suspect when I was in his office. Then his clumsy attempt to control my movements in Venice virtually confirmed my suspicions. I'm not attempting to snatch you away from him. As I said, I needed to see you again to say farewell. After all, you gave me no chance to do that in Paris. I had to know that all was well with you."

"Does it mean so much to you?" It disturbed her that he was so calm, so resigned.

"I'd have journeyed anywhere for the chance."

Then she knew why. "You're certain that Russia is going to war!"

He gave a deep nod. "That's why I'm going home at once. I've been recalled. The Tsar has ordered mobilization. I foresee a long struggle ahead."

"But surely any fighting will be settled quickly," she protested. "So many outbreaks of hostility between various nations over the past years have been of short duration."

"Those were little more than skirmishes. Everything will be different this time."

"You speak as if it were inevitable." She tried a lighter note. "Remember I used to tease you about your Russian gloom."

He caught both her hands in his, his eyes searching hers. "I remember everything about you. Your laughter, the hours we spent together, your loving body—"

"Don't!" She snatched her hands away, turning to stand with her back to him, clutching a handful of the drapery. He followed, waiting for her to recover.

"Try not to be angry as you were that last time in Paris," he asked quietly. "Not now. Not today."

She swallowed hard. "We were talking about the possibility of war," she managed to say, wanting their conversation to resume on a level with which she could cope. "But surely Russia has nothing to fear. No nation would attack her."

"Napoleon did," he remarked dryly.

"That was over a hundred years ago!" She swung round to face him.

"Such lessons are never learned. Now it's Germany that Russia has to fear. My concern is that as a nation we have manpower in abundance, but we have not kept pace in the arms race."

"You'll be in the army?"

"I shall enlist as soon as I'm home."

Now everything was clear to her. He had wanted to see her once more in this life because he did not expect to survive the war. Any doubts she might have had about the conflict occurring were banished by his serious words. She realized that both of them, at the back of their minds, had always believed their paths would cross again at some time in the future. And now, when he saw that chance slipping away forever, he had come in search of her.

"I'll pray for your safekeeping, Nikolai." She could not take her eyes from his.

"I'm thankful I need not be anxious about your well-being. You'll be safe here. Even Napoleon never fired his cannons on Venice." A smile touched the corners of his mouth.

Somehow she managed a smile too. For a few moments longer they gazed at each other. Then all the love for him that she had so determinedly suppressed defeated her. When he reached out his arms, she fell into them. Her mouth received his as if in homecoming and they kissed with a wild passion, unable to assuage the long hunger that had tormented him and haunted her.

When Henriette returned to the salon-studio she saw that the glass door stood open, and she went through to the balustrade of the loggia. Looking down into the courtyard, she saw that Nikolai and Juliette were saying good-bye. He was holding her in his embrace, lovingly and protectively, as if nothing could ever come between them. Even as Henriette would have turned away, allowing them their last moments of privacy, they kissed tenderly and drew apart. He opened the door into the *calle,* turned once more to look at Juliette, and then went out. Juliette stayed where she was, listening no doubt to the fading echo of his departing footsteps. Then she flung herself against the door and stood as though held by torturing chains.

Henriette's first inclination was to hasten down to her, but she checked herself in time. There was nothing she could say or do that would ease Juliette's pain. For the moment, the past had been brought hurtling back, and Juliette would have to take her own time to regather her courage and the will to carry on.

Re-entering the salon-studio, Henriette paced slowly up and down as she waited. Eventually Juliette came in again. She was ashen but dry-eyed. Henriette went at once to put a comforting arm about her shoulders.

"Would you like a cup of coffee? Or tea perhaps?" she asked solicitously.

"Nothing, thank you. It's time I went home." Juliette picked up her hat but did not put it on. Instead, she stood turning it by its brim. "Nikolai has gone back to his hotel to check out. He was to have had dinner with Marco, but he'll leave a message that he couldn't stay after all. It's best if Marco never knows that Nikolai found me in spite of all his efforts. It would only worry and distress him."

"I agree."

"Nikolai and I will never see one another again." Juliette looked gratefully at Henriette. "I was so glad he and I were able to meet here, in this beautiful room, especially since it was our shared interest in Fortuny's achievements and my Delphos robe that first brought us together."

"I'm glad for you too." Henriette threaded her arm through Juliette's to lead her downstairs to the main entrance, not wanting her to retrace her steps so soon by way of the courtyard.

Juliette had almost crossed the Campo San Beneto when she stopped, looking toward the *calle* that ran on the opposite side of the Palazzo Orfei. It led to a bridge and then between a row of buildings to a gondola jetty on the Grand Canal. She would be able to see Nikolai from there when he went past on the *vaporetto*. Just one more brief glimpse, one last loving sighting before he was lost to her forever.

She wouldn't go alone! Though Nikolai knew nothing about Michel, that was no reason why her son should not see his father once in his life. Although Michel could not understand and would never remember the occasion, she would know and be thankful she had given him that single moment.

Breaking into a run, she covered the last stretch of ground and rushed into her house. "Michel!" she called out from the hallway. "Where are you?"

She ran upstairs to the nursery. Sylvana was sound asleep in her cot, but Michel was not lying on his bed and the covers had been straightened. Thinking she would find him playing in the walled garden, she raced back down the stairs. Before she had reached the ground level, Arianna came out into the hall and looked up at her.

"Signora—"

"Where's Michel?"

"In the salon, signora. Doña Cecilia has brought him a new toy. They've been waiting for you for almost an hour."

Juliette paused in dismay. "I had forgotten completely that they were coming!" Too late she recalled that she had intended to be no more than ten minutes away from the house when she went to return the book. "Has Lena served them refreshment?"

"Yes, signora."

Realizing that she was still carrying her hat, Juliette threw it aside as she crossed the hall and passed both hands over her hair. Michel came running to her as she entered the room.

"Look, Mama!" He held up a wooden monkey on a stick, laughing as he made it turn somersaults.

She swept him up in her arms. "What a lucky boy you are!" Then she faced her guests. "Please forgive me for not being here to receive you. It was unavoidable."

Doña Cecilia and Maria Luisa sat side by side on one of the brocaded sofas. A silver tray of dainty refreshments lay on the table untouched.

"I'm sure it must have been," Doña Cecilia granted graciously, even though she was considerably put out at being kept waiting. She was also surprised by her hostess's appearance. Juliette's hair was hanging in tendrils, and instead of an afternoon gown suitable for the occasion she wore a striped cotton skirt and a plain blouse.

"Michel has been entertaining us," Maria Luisa said reassuringly. "We waited for you to come before taking any refreshment."

"I'm afraid I have to go out again," Juliette burst out. "Do pardon me once more! I'll try not to be long." She darted out of the room. There was not much time left. Michel had dropped his new toy and uttered a wail. Arianna rushed to pick it up, but she was too late to hand it to him, for his mother had lifted him up and was running with him from the house. Bewildered, Arianna turned to glance back into the salon. Doña Cecilia and her daughter were looking aghast at this further breach of good manners by their hostess.

Juliette sped with the sobbing child out of the square and into the long *calle* by the palazzo. "It's all right, Michel," she exclaimed as she ran. "The little monkey will be waiting for you when we get home again. We're going to watch the boats for a short while."

He liked boats. His sobs eased away and he clung to his mother's neck as they crossed the bridge and rushed onward. When they reached the narrow wooden jetty she sat him on top of the rail and held him protectively while she regained her breath.

She was not too late. The *vaporetto* was still some distance away. Michel, who had his back to it, was watching the gondolas go by. Shading her eyes with one hand, Juliette tried to scan the passengers on board, but the little steamboat was not yet near enough for her to discern Nikolai. If he should be standing amidships on the starboard side the saloon would be between them, but at least she and Michel would be near him for this short time.

Now she could see him. He was on the foredeck, leaning on the starboard rail and looking away from her, which made it safe for her to move farther up the jetty for a closer view. She lifted Michel up and sat him on her hip.

"Big boat!" he cried out, pointing to the *vaporetto*. He liked these vessels with their funnels and smoke better than all the others, and he bounced excitedly.

Then, when the *vaporetto* was almost level, Nikolai turned from where he stood and strolled across to look up at the grand façades of the palazzi soaring behind her. She held her breath, certain that if she made any quick move he would see her. Yet even as she eased a step backward, he gripped the top rail as he stared across at her and the young child she held in her arms. No longer attempting to hold out against what was clearly meant to be, she lifted Michel higher.

"Wave to the man with the black hair like yours, Michel."

Eagerly the boy obeyed her and chuckled happily when there was an immediate response. Nikolai's wave was slow and questioning at first, but became exuberant when Juliette's nod and wave confirmed that this was their son. He cupped both hands around his mouth. "What's his name?"

"Michel!" she called back, knowing he would remember that it was her father's name. "He's two years old in September."

Nikolai threw back his head in exhilaration, rejoicing that Juliette had born his child after all. By now the *vaporetto* was going swiftly past and she saw him break away from the rail to thrust his way through the other passengers to reach the stern. There he stood waving again until they could see each other no longer.

"Good-bye, my love," she whispered, tears flowing down her cheeks.

Michel peered anxiously into her face, his lower lip trembling. "Don't cry, Mama," he begged, almost echoing the very words his father had spoken earlier, and tried clumsily to wipe her cheeks dry with his palms. He had never seen her cry before and he was alarmed.

She hugged him tightly for a few moments and then wiped her eyes with the back of one hand as she conjured a reassuring smile for him. "There! Everything is better now. Did you enjoy waving?"

"Yes." His smile had returned with the cessation of her tears. As she carried him off the jetty he twisted in her arms to wave generally at the water traffic. "Michel come again soon. Mama too."

"We'll do that," she promised. In spite of knowing she still had guests waiting for her, it was impossible to hurry homeward. Somehow she was forced to take her time, sorting through her emotions. She had given Nikolai and his son sight of each other. It was as if the whole event had been inevitable, and she was glad. Surely it was some comfort for any man to face death in battle when he knew he had a son, especially by the woman he loved.

She put Michel down on his feet and he trotted along at her side, talking of the boats. His vocabulary was advanced for his age, but frequently French words were mixed with Italian. She picked him up again as they neared the house, smiling at something he said and kissing his cheek. As they entered, Arianna appeared at the top of the stairs, thankful to see her home again after her extraordinary flight.

"Are you all right, signora?" she asked with concern.

"Yes, of course." Juliette saw that the monkey-on-the-stick was lying on a side table and picked it up to hand to Michel. "Wait for me and then we'll go in to our visitors."

She took a quick look in the mirror. There was no time to comb her hair. She tucked up a few tendrils and then smoothed it with her hands once again. Taking Michel by the hand, she opened the door of the salon and went in. But her guests had gone and the tray had been removed. Behind her the door closed and she turned to see Marco standing by it. Michel ran to him.

"See the monkey, Papa!"

Marco smiled down at him. "That's fun, but go and play with it. I want to talk to Mama." As the child sat down on the floor Marco crossed to Juliette and looked at her with hard eyes. "Where on earth were you all afternoon? I arrived home early after my dinner engagement was canceled and found Doña Cecilia and Maria Luisa just leaving. They were most displeased and offended. I know myself that you invited them today, and then you weren't even here to receive them!"

"I know. It is inexcusable for a hostess to forget she was expecting guests, but that's what happened. I'll call on them tomorrow and apologize." Juliette raised a restless hand and fiddled nervously with a strand of hair.

"But there must be a reason why the visit went out of your head," he persisted.

"I returned a book to Henriette and forgot the time and everything else."

"Doña Cecilia told me that when you did appear you dashed out again, taking Michel with you."

"Yes. I took Michel to see the boats."

"The boats?" Marco exclaimed incredulously. "When guests sat here in this room?"

On the floor Michel looked up happily. "Michel wave to boats. Mama wave. Mama cry."

Marco gave Juliette a long, dark look. Then he went to the child and picked him up. "I want you to go upstairs to Arianna." Opening the door, he put Michel down and watched him cross to the stairs and start climbing. Then he closed the door again and faced Juliette across the room. "Tell me whom you saw at Fortuny's apart from Henriette."

"Nikolai Karasvin." She sat down sideways on a chair, all strength seemingly gone from her legs, and held on to the back of it. "I'll not lie to you as you did to him."

Marco's whole face congested with rage and he clenched his fists as he strode across to stand over her. "How dare you see him again! What I said to Karasvin was to protect you. I didn't want you upset. Or persuaded to leave me!"

"Have you so little faith in my promise to be with you always?"

"But I knew he'd try to take you from me! How could I be sure of anything when he spoke as if you were bound to him forever!"

She leaned her brow wearily on her hand. "The past can't be changed, but the future belongs to you and me. I thought when Sylvana was born that you'd finally trust me, because I believed you knew me well enough to believe that I'd never do anything to cause my children any unhappiness, least of all would I desert them."

"But you could have taken Michel from me at any time!"

Her anger flared and she sprang to her feet. "Never! He has your name! I won't listen anymore to your jealous tirade." She would have swung away, but he grabbed her by the wrists.

"You took Michel from the house today. To see the boats. Or was it for both of you to join Karasvin on the *vaporetto* to the railway station? You meant to go away with him!"

"No!" She screwed her body away from him but could not release herself from his painful grip.

"Why did you weep then? Were you too late? Had he already left Venice? Did you miss your chance?"

"No! No! No!" She struggled in vain to get free. "I thought Michel had a right to see his natural father just once in his life, even though it was from a distance."

"Did Karasvin see him?"

"Yes!"

He hit her then with such force that she reeled back, her eyes wide with pain, and fell, hitting her head on the corner of an inlaid table and sprawling untidily on the floor. Stepping back, his anger unabated, Marco waited for her eyes to open. He was ready to threaten that he would throw her out, toss her to her Russian, never allow her to see the children again, and many other wild and empty utterances that sprang from his own unendurable jealousy.

"Get up!" he roared.

But she did not move. Bending over her, he saw to his horror that there was blood in her hair. Instantly he was on one knee beside her, raising her gently to a sitting position and supporting her neck with his arm.

"My darling! Dear God, what have I done?"

Gathering her up in his arms, he hastened with her to the door. Levering the handle with difficulty, he managed to get it open and rushed with her into the hall. "Lena! Arianna!" he shouted. "Telephone the doctor. Your mistress has had an accident!"

He heard the women scurry as he swept up the stairs and carried Juliette into their room, where he laid her on the bed. Pulling open a drawer, he found a stack of his starched handkerchieves and made a pad for her gashed head. Then he sat on the edge of the bed holding her limp hand. He had never felt more helpless or more ashamed.

Although the doctor lived nearby in the next square, it seemed hours to Marco before he arrived.

Twenty-one

"W ILL MY WIFE recover soon, doctor?" Marco asked agitat-
edly as he and the doctor went downstairs. Juliette had
taken four hours to regain consciousness and a nurse had come to
take care of her.

"Let us go into the salon where we can talk, signore," the doctor replied.

Marco led the way, still in shock from what he had done.
"Would you like a brandy?"

He felt desperately in need of one himself, and to his relief the
doctor, although declining, told him to go ahead. As he poured,
he shot a glance toward the place where Juliette had fallen and was
relieved to see that the blood had been wiped away.

"I never interfere in domestic matters between husband and
wife," the doctor began, "but the swelling on the right side of
Signora Romanelli's face could only have been caused by a hard
blow, and her cheek was cut by a ring. She's going to have a bruise
and probably a swollen eye."

Marco groaned and took a gulp of brandy. "I've never struck
her before. I don't know what possessed me."

"Temper is the most usual cause," the doctor commented pith-
ily. "The speed of her recovery depends on your patience and
understanding. Forget whatever caused the dispute. She must be
kept quiet for a few days and not upset over anything."

When the doctor had gone, Marco telephoned a florist and ordered all the red roses in the shop. When they arrived, he took the blooms up to Juliette, who whispered that they were lovely and closed her eyes again.

By the next day her room had become a bower of flowers as friends heard she'd had an accident. She asked to see the children. The baby was put in her arms for ten minutes, and Michel was intrigued by the bandage around her head. He bawled with rage when Arianna took him away again and escaped from her to come running back, banging for entry on his mother's closed door. The sounds pierced Juliette's aching head and his distress upset her. She feared he would not be let in at all and asked that he be brought to take his nap on the bed beside her the next day. She was allowed no visitors, and apart from the doctor Marco was the next one to see her when he came home from the office. She had been sleeping when he left in the morning, and he had telephoned four times during the day to inquire about her progress.

He sat down in the bedside chair the nurse had vacated, leaving him alone with his wife. It was no more than twenty-four hours since Juliette had been injured, and he was still wretched with remorse and another worry that had been troubling him since that time.

"Are you feeling better?" he asked, taking her hand and enclosing it in his own.

"Yes," she whispered with difficulty, for the swelling on the right side of her face tugged at her mouth. The curtains were closed to spare her the light. In the gloom she could see he looked dejected and anxious, but as yet she did not feel very forgiving. "I'll soon be up and about."

"Yes, indeed," he said with the forced cheerfulness characteristic of bedside visits. Then he shook his head despairingly, engulfed by a rush of emotion. "I might have killed you!"

"I'm not so easily dispatched. I can't regret what I did, but you had no cause to hit me. It must never happen again." Her eyes warned him.

"I lost my reason."

"I know that and I understand, but nothing will be as you suppose. Nikolai will never make any claim on Michel. I'd been going to tell you that in the salon. If Nikolai survives this threatened war, as I pray he will, he'll never come back into our lives."

He narrowed his eyes in disbelief. "But he *saw* Michel! You said that! Didn't he realize?"

"Yes, he did, but he also understands that our lives have taken different paths. He and I said our final good-byes. It's enough for him to know that I am safe and that he has a son."

Marco knew that he should ask no more questions, but there was something else churning and tormenting his mind, and he could no longer resist seeking an answer. "Were you and Karasvin alone at all during the time you were at the palazzo?"

She closed her eyes wearily. Was she going to have to contend with that doubt preying on his mind? "Henriette was there when I arrived, but she went out to give us the chance to talk on our own."

"Where were you?"

"In the salon-studio." She knew he would be thinking of the sheltering drapery and the cushioned couches. "I'd gone in by the loggia door."

"How long were you on your own with Karasvin?" He knew he was firing questions like a prosecuting counsel, but as on the previous day he was being driven by a jealousy he couldn't control.

She opened her eyes again and looked directly at him. "I lost track of the time. That's why I didn't remember I was expecting visitors. Why don't you ask me outright if I was unfaithful?"

He had the grace to look uncomfortable. She was so weak that her whispered query had been almost inaudible. "We'll talk another time when you're stronger."

"No. Let's settle this matter now." She forced herself up into a sitting position, almost fainting from the effort. "What you fear didn't happen. I'm *your* wife. Nothing has changed between you and me. Neither is Michel any less your son."

She collapsed back on her pillows, then, putting a forearm across her eyes as if to shut herself away from further turmoil. Marco sprang up and leaned over her solicitously.

"I believe you. I just wanted your reassurance. Any husband would have demanded the same." He drew her arm down and kissed her closed eyelids. "I must let you rest now."

When he had gone from the room, Juliette opened her eyes sadly. She had told him the truth, but would he ever be able to clear his mind of suspicion? It was like seeing a thread-like crack appear in the framework of her marriage. She would do everything in her power to mend it, for no matter what feelings there were between her and Nikolai, the caring she had for Marco was not changed.

Juliette came downstairs for the first time at mid-morning on the August day when newspaper headlines proclaimed Italy's intention to remain neutral. They also announced that Germany had declared war on imperial Russia and the first exchange of fire had taken place. She thought with compassionate understanding of all the women on both sides, comprehending their feelings through her own farewell to Nikolai.

Her stitches had been removed the previous day, and her face was no longer swollen, although some discoloration remained. A covering of tinted face powder helped to disguise it a little. Henriette was coming to see her later, but earlier in the afternoon she was expecting the formidable lady who had been neglected on her last visit. Juliette was not looking forward to the meeting, but there had been a written request.

When Doña Cecilia arrived, she cut short Juliette's apology. "Say no more about it, Juliette. When I thought about it afterward I remembered that young women who have recently given birth often behave unlike themselves and, after all, Sylvana was only a few weeks old at the time. It's no wonder you ended the day with an accident. You slipped, I was told, and hit your head. That's why I advised Maria Luisa to wait until another day to see you. One visitor at a time is enough at first."

"Perhaps your daughter could come tomorrow?" Juliette did not want Maria Luisa to feel abandoned by her for a second time.

"Very well. That will please her." Doña Cecilia smiled.

The breach was healed. Juliette hoped it was a sign that at least in her daily life everything was getting back to normal. Marco could not have been more at ease in her company since their talk in the sickroom, and she began to wonder if her original misgivings were unfounded after all.

She was still in bed the following morning, about to enjoy the bath that was being run for her, when Marco came into the room looking very serious.

"There are headlines in the morning paper that will be particularly distressing to you," he said gravely. "I want you to be prepared."

She sat forward, fearing the worst. "Is it war?"

He nodded regretfully. "Germany has declared war on France."

"My dear country!" she whispered in distress.

She appreciated his having told her and also the comfort of his embrace.

Inevitably the Kaiser, ignoring Great Britain's warning that it would protect Belgium's neutrality and the French coast, sent his troops thundering onto Belgian soil in the first move toward invading France. Great Britain declared war on Germany, then Austria on Russia and Serbia on Germany. It was as if a terrible madness had been released.

Foreigners had been flocking out of Venice like migrant birds ever since July. Now, any ship that put into Venice was besieged by those wanting to return to their homelands. Hotels emptied of guests, waiters stood idle in restaurants, souvenirs went unsold, and gondoliers saw the greater part of their livelihood fade away. Even those Venetians who had resented the annual flood of overseas visitors would never have wished an exodus to occur for such a cause. The majority of foreigners remaining were those who had transplanted themselves to Venice years ago and had no wish to move under any circumstances. Fortuny was among them. Although he took an immense pride in being a Spaniard and in his Spanish heritage, he was forty-three and above the age for active service even if Spain had not resolved to stay neutral, so there was no call for him to return.

"His devotion to Venice," Henriette remarked to Juliette, "will only end when he draws his last breath here."

When Juliette was well again, she went at the first opportunity to the Church of the Scalzi. By now fighting was taking place on several fronts, and there had been heavy casualties on all sides. Under Tiepolo's glorious frescoes she prayed again for the safety of Nikolai and the young Frenchmen who would undoubtedly be engaged in the fighting. Thinking of the recent German and Austrian threats against Italy for having failed to give them armed support, she prayed also for a swift return to peace and a better understanding between nations.

After sitting for a while in the tranquility of the church, Juliette emerged into the sunshine again. She had arranged to meet three women friends at Quadri's in St. Mark's Square. In normal times it was difficult to get a table in the height of the season, but today her friends had had a choice of tables and there were plenty more to spare.

"What is it to be?" Isabella asked after greetings had been exchanged. "An ice perhaps, or coffee?" She was one of the first friends Juliette had made in Venice, a lively, animated woman, dark-haired and amply curved, who was the wife of a prosperous businessman and the mother of five young children. "Or both?"

"Both!" Juliette declared. "I've time today."

"No designing at the moment?" Angelina queried. She was an artist herself, and always dressed in the flowing styles that suited her best. In her early forties and sharply intelligent, she was older than the others, with a grown-up son at medical school and a husband serving as a captain in the Italian navy. She was a friend of Henriette whom Juliette had met at the Palazzo Orfei.

"No, Maison Landelle had my winter designs long ago, and I've already done most of the redesigning for the spring collection."

"What changes were those?" Isabella had ordered the ices from the waiter, the coffee to be served later.

"It seemed to me that by the spring the war will have affected the pattern of life for all women. The hobble skirt is doomed. I've kept the skirts narrow, but with pleats at the back to give freedom of movement. The whole collection follows simpler lines, except for the evening wear. I know nothing of the effects of battle, but I'm sure that men on leave will want to see their women looking more beautiful and feminine than ever."

"Naturally they will." Elena, who was the same age as Juliette, was a pretty, bird-like young woman, who always dressed in the height of fashion. Childless as yet, with two stepchildren older than herself, she was happily married to a leading Venetian engineer more than twice her age. She had news to tell. "My husband is seeing yours today, Juliette. There's a big conference with representatives of all the museums and art galleries and the churches."

"Marco told me he had a busy day ahead, but he rarely says much when he has his morning newspaper."

Elena knew more. "As Marco is an expert in all sorts of cloth, he's to be asked to supply literally miles of a certain kind of protective covering for all the works of art in the city."

Isabella, about to put a spoonful of strawberry ice into her mouth, lowered it in dismay. "Does that mean what I think?"

Juliette, seeing how upset she looked, tried to reassure her. "It's a sensible precautionary measure, even if those threats by Germany and Austria turn out to be no more than saber-rattling."

"But I read that all Europe expects the war to be over by Christmas."

"I'm sure the Kaiser doesn't," Juliette remarked succinctly, remembering Nikolai's words.

"I agree," Angelina commented crisply. "Although our country is divided between those who think we should side with Germany and save ourselves, and those who are defiant and determined not to be bullied, we shouldn't forget that Austria would like to get its claws on Venice again. This city is vulnerably close to that old enemy."

Isabella flushed an angry red and pushed her ice away. "They needn't think they're going to fly their imperial eagle over Venice again! It's not even fifty years since their hateful occupation ended. My mother remembers curfews and not being allowed in St. Mark's Square when a military band was playing. Such arrogance! My grandmother had terrible tales of the earlier days. Rapes and imprisonments and worse. According to the newspapers, the Germans are behaving no better against the poor Belgians, and they took Brussels yesterday."

Elena regretted having brought up the subject at all. It was spoiling their get-together. "It should be different now the British have landed. How are your children, Isabella? Has Lorenzo recovered from his cold?"

Isabella loved to talk about her children. Her expression changed and she resumed eating her ice. When eventually the little party broke up, it was on a happier note.

Contrary to all hopes, the war did not end by Christmas. The year 1915 dawned with bitter fighting. Already Venice was changing her appearance as the possibility of involvement loomed dangerously near. The four bronze horses of Venice were removed from the facade of the Basilica for the first time since Napoleon had annexed them.

Juliette and Marco were among the silent crowd who stood watching sadly as the horses were lowered by crane from above the great entrance doors. That same morning he had taken her into the Doges' Palace to see how a veil of his fabric had been stretched over priceless ceiling paintings before the laborious and careful work of removing them began.

"What of the Tiepolo frescoes in the Church of the Scalzi?" she asked, hoping to see them once more before they were taken down.

"They're to stay where they are," Marco replied. "Experts have looked at them, but they're on thin plaster and would crack to pieces if any attempt was made to remove them. There are others elsewhere that will have to be left as well."

With the horses gone, workers began to protect the façade of the Basilica itself. Gradually it vanished behind protective cladding and sandbags. To Juliette and many others, it was as if a lamp had been extinguished in the very heart of Venice. Other buildings received similar protection, but not on such an extensive scale. Everywhere the stone lions of St. Mark and and all outdoor statuary disappeared under sandbags. Irreplaceable medieval glass was removed from churches as well as from the Basilica itself.

In a city built on water, with no cellars or vaults, the transport of priceless works of art and church treasures to a place of safety was a seemingly endless task. Dry seaweed was used for much of the packing, and bushels of it were required. Vast canvases were coiled around rollers and slotted into cylinders, smaller paintings packed into flat crates. Some valuable items, too awkward in shape to be transported without the risk of damage, were stored at the Palazzo Orfei in Fortuny's care.

It became a common sight to anyone out after midnight to see the freight wagons mounted on specially-built pontoons being towed along the Grand Canal to the nearest landing stages. From there, the precious cargo would be collected for transport by rail.

Juliette, returning home with Marco from a party at Angelina's, paused on the Accademia bridge to watch one of the wagons pass below. As always, armed soldiers were on board to escort the precious cargo to its secret destination.

Marco, who had continued walking down the steps, stopped when she did not catch up with him and ascended again to where he could see her. She was wearing her Fortuny black and gold gown, the cape thrown back, gilt beads glittering.

"Why have you stopped?" he asked impatiently.

He had not enjoyed the party. Angelina's husband had been there, his ship presently anchored in the Lagoon, and three of his fellow officers had been invited for the evening. All three had flirted with Juliette, and one had paid her what Marco had considered excessive attention, dancing with her at every opportunity. Although Marco could not fault Juliette's behavior, his swift jealousy had refueled the doubt he could not entirely banish from his mind. Often he forgot it for weeks at a time, for Juliette could be a very loving wife, but something about the naval officer's height and profile had reminded him of Nikolai, and he feared she had been responding to that likeness with her smiles and laughter.

Juliette had rejoined him. "I was watching one of the wagons, that's all."

To pacify him she put her hand on his arm as they continued on their way. She thought he had been unreasonable to glare at her as he had whenever she and the officer were dancing. What should have been a delightful party had been spoiled unnecessarily. It was far from the first time. She had done everything she could to make their marriage whole again, and then, just when she thought she had succeeded, he would get upset about nothing.

They walked all the way home without speaking, the silence rising up between them like a wall. Her heart sank despairingly as she preceded him up the stairs, and then something seemed to snap in her. As soon as the door of their bedroom was closed behind them, she rounded on him angrily.

"When are you going to stop punishing me?"

He did not have to ask what she meant. Glowering, he slipped off his evening coat and tossed it across a chair. "So you were remembering him!"

She was bewildered. "What are you talking about?"

"That Russian is never out of your thoughts, is he?"

"It seems he's never out of yours," she retaliated fiercely. "Is the rest of your life and mine to be ruined because you will not put the past away?"

"I did that when I brought you here from Tuscany," he gave back. "It was you who revived the past for both of us. You had a lovers' reunion with the Russian! You took Michel from this house to see him leave!" He turned away, his voice bitter. "Don't speak to me of wiping out the past. It's you who is keeping it alive!"

She moved swiftly and stood between him and the chest of drawers on which he was about to place the pearl studs from his stiff white shirtfront. "I can see you will always hold what happened that afternoon against me."

"And who would blame me." He moved aside and put down the studs in their velvet-lined box.

"I blame you for not accepting the truth! But it makes no difference. I'm staying on here and you'll not get rid of me, whatever you say or do! I will have Michel and Sylvana together with us both and we'll behave in a civilized manner, no matter how much you may come to hate me!"

"What are you saying? I could never hate you!" He was severely taken aback. Her words had instantly conjured up an image of what the house would be like without her. It was like having his heart cut out. "I'd never want you to leave," he roared, taking her by the arms and shaking her until her head fell back. "I love you! If only I could be sure of you!"

The ringing of the telephone, coming at such an hour, took them both by surprise. He released her, taking a step back.

"Don't let it wake the children," she urged with an odd return to normality.

He nodded and hurried down the stairs to answer the commanding ring. She crossed to her dressing table and sat down to remove the emerald necklace and earrings Marco had given her as a wedding gift. She had meant what she said.

By the time she heard his footsteps coming slowly back up the stairs, she had finished undressing. When he entered the room, she could see by his face that he had heard some dreadful news. She guessed the cause even before he told her.

"That was Angelina," he said heavily. "Her husband and his fellow officers have been recalled to their ship. Italy has abandoned neutrality. We are at war with Austria."

She ran forward and threw her arms around him. "It's a courageous step, but I'm so sorry it had to happen."

He held her close. "Perhaps it's as well. At least we'll all know at last where we stand. It's always easier to face the worst than to keep wondering if it will happen."

"You spoke before of bringing me from Tuscany," she said urgently. "Surely the fact that we have come so far along such a difficult path makes what we have now all the more worthwhile? Let us mend the differences between us once and for all. Now more than ever we must be united by love."

It was an impassioned plea. He looked deeply into her eyes, doubt easing away. No one could have hoped more than he that eventually it would disappear altogether.

"Yes, Juliette," he answered huskily. Drawing her to him, he held her in a long and loving kiss. Afterward he made love to her as tenderly as on their first night together.

Twenty-two

AT HIS OFFICE during the next few days Marco began to prepare for his enlistment. The orders for protective coverings
had been a much needed boost to his business, which had dwindled almost to nothing since the German invasion of Belgium.
Those orders were now filled, and most of his male staff had already volunteered for military service. His only option was to close
down until the war was over. He had talked about it to Fortuny,
whose profits had also plunged over recent months, but at least the
designer had plenty of other work to occupy him. The Palazzo
Orfei had become the Spanish consulate for the duration of the
war, and Fortuny himself had been appointed honorary consul for
Spain.

Marco spoke of his enlisting to Juliette. "I'll be given a commis-
sion," he said, "because in my youth I trained in a voluntary ca-
pacity in my spare time. How did you get on today with your offer
to nurse at the hospital?"

She shook her head in disappointment. "I was turned down
because I have no experience and because, as at the other hospitals,
all the nurses are nuns."

"There'll be other voluntary work that you can do." He took
hold of her hands where they sat. "I want you to know that my
finances are all in order and you and the children will always be
well provided for if I should not—"

"Don't say it!" she interrupted quickly. "You're coming back to us when this war is over."

"Of course I am," he declared cheerfully.

The day came when Marco had to leave. He made his farewells to the children first and afterward to Arianna and Lena, both of whom wept. Finally he went to Juliette, who was waiting in the salon. To his relief she showed no sign of tears, although the strain of parting showed in her eyes. She held both her hands out to him and he took them into his own. They smiled, each wanting to cheer the other.

"Finish the war quickly, Marco. I want you home again."

"You may rely on me."

Neither was quite sure afterward what else they said before they finally kissed and embraced, making the most of their last moments together. She went into the hall with him and when he had opened the door he kissed her once again. In the square he turned to wave.

When he had gone, she closed the door and went into the walled garden where the children were playing. Marco was soon to be in the field of war, and she was separated from the two men who meant the most to her, each in his own way.

In the weeks following Marco's departure, Venice suffered air raids, causing bomb damage to several of her beautiful churches. In the Tyrol, Italian and Austrian troops fought relentlessly. The wounded began to be brought in. Again Juliette volunteered to do whatever she could, but again to no avail. Several of her friends were leaving the city with their children, moving to safer places in case there should be more bombing. Isabella was among them, and also Elena, who had discovered she was pregnant.

Juliette organized a group of those who were staying on, and together they rolled bandages and knitted socks, scarves, and sweaters for the troops. They all gathered goods for Red Cross auctions and shook collection boxes in aid of war-linked charities. Juliette also helped the Women's Work Force, whose headquarters was in the grand La Fenice opera house. There she distributed thick gray-green army cloth to women who took it away to make clothing for the soldiers. As this was paid work for the Government, she did not sew herself. There were far too many women, previously employed in hotels, restaurants, and elsewhere, who were desperately in need of the money.

The war news was alarming. Juliette read with dismay that Austro-German troops had overrun Serbia and broken the Russian front in Poland, where they had taken many prisoners. She hoped Nikolai had not been there. London was suffering zeppelin raids, there was ceaseless ground-fighting between the British and Germans in Belgium, and Italy was now also at war with Turkey.

In October there was another air raid on Venice. A bomb fell on the Church of the Scalzi and the glorious Tiepolo frescoes were lost forever. It was some time before Juliette could bring herself to view the damage. Tarpaulins covered the gaping hole in the roof, and the nave was still full of rubble. At least nobody had been killed, although four women were injured.

When an official appeal went out for empty properties to use as hospitals for the wounded, Juliette took it upon herself to offer Marco's business premises. After an inspection, the building was deemed suitable. There had been no time to ask Marco's permission, for mail had been understandably disrupted. She wrote to tell him what she had done, but by the time she received his approval, the building was already in full use, mostly by those already on the road to recovery, who had been transferred from hospital beds more urgently needed for the newly wounded.

Juliette visited, taking books and magazines and often writing letters for those who could not write themselves. Sometimes they were simply illiterate, simple men of peasant stock who had lived in remote villages where virtually nothing had changed for centuries. They did not understand the causes that had brought about this war, and they missed their little vineyards and farms and animals as much as they missed their wives and families.

The year 1916 had arrived with no sign of an end to hostilities. The flood of wounded had increased to such proportions that more nurses were desperately needed. Juliette immediately enrolled in the short training course, as did several of her friends, including Angelina.

All went well. A nun instructed them in bandaging, how to take temperatures, give a bed bath, and all the elementary duties that would have to be done. When all this had been practiced and mastered to the nun's satisfaction, Juliette and the other women, wearing their auxiliary uniforms for the first time, were taken into the wards of a new hospital, formally the Hotel Victoria. Each was put in charge of a nursing nun, who would supervise her until she could be trusted on her own. Juliette's nun was named Sister Ursula.

"You can start, Nurse Romanelli, by changing the dressings on that patient's legs."

Juliette looked in the direction the nun had indicated and her heart contracted with pity. He was young, no more than seventeen, white-faced and hollowed-eyed, wearing a striped nightshirt that was too big for him, with a plaid rug over his knees. She fetched the dressings the nun had told her she would need and put them on a sterile cloth beside him on his bed.

"You're a beginner, aren't you?" he greeted her. "This your first day?"

"That's right," she answered, smiling. "But I was taught how to change dressings, so you needn't be alarmed."

He looked wryly amused. "I'm not scared, but I bet you will be."

She was taking away the plaid rug as he spoke and only just managed to hide her shock. He had no legs below the knees. "Where did this happen?" she asked evenly, kneeling to commence her work.

"In the Tyrol."

The old dressings were stuck with dried blood, and as she tried gently to free them, she saw his hands clench and his knuckles turn white, but he did not cry out. Instead he taunted her.

"You'll faint in a minute!"

"I bet you I won't!"

"The last beginner did. She went flat on the floor."

When his wounds were fully revealed, it would have been easy to follow her predecessor's example, but Juliette carried out her task doggedly, retaining control of herself by continuing their bantering exchange. It helped them both through the ordeal.

It was a heartbreaking day. There were so many shattered men. Their courage humbled her, and tasks that might otherwise have been onerous or distasteful were done willingly, to help them a little in their suffering. Many had the additional agony of frostbite contracted in the bitter cold of the mountains. Some were in too much pain to comprehend what was happening, but the rest were touchingly grateful, some making jokes when their injuries caused them to be clumsy. As the mother of young children, she was expected to spend no more than three days a week at the hospital. She offered to give more time, but the supervisor reminded her sternly that her little ones also needed her care.

Juliette had Michel with her one March morning when she went to the Fortuny shop. She had decided to replace a painting she had never much liked with one of the designer's wall hangings. Michel did not like shopping as a rule, but he was always eager to accompany her to the Palazzo Orfei, where he could play hide-and-seek amid the long curtains and draperies. At three and a half he was tall for his years and sturdy, his angelic looks deceiving to those who did not know how easily he could get into mischief.

"Be good," Juliette admonished as they entered the palazzo shop.

"Yes, Mama."

There were no other customers and only two women assistants, who were bored with nothing to do and happy to play with Michel. All the young men had joined the army and there was only a skeleton staff left in the workroom.

She had almost decided on a cream hanging shaped like an *H* in one of Fortuny's Persian-inspired designs, when she heard the sirens wailing. Another air raid!

"Come, Michel!" she urged quickly, reaching out her hand for his. "We're going home."

Overhead came a clatter of footsteps as the few workers still employed in the ateliers left their tasks to go downstairs where it would be safer. Juliette was soon hurrying with her son across the square. The thud-thud of antiaircraft guns resounded as they fired into the pale March sky. Ahead she saw an army officer, supporting himself on a single crutch, coming from the direction of her home. It was Marco! He had seen her too!

"Juliette!" he yelled jubilantly. "Michel!"

She covered the distance between them far more quickly than he could have done. "What happened to your leg?" she asked anxiously when he had kissed them both.

"Nothing very much," he replied as he hurried with them to the house, "but it's given me sick leave. We can be glad of that."

Indoors Michel, who was wildly excited to have his father home again, broke away as soon as Juliette had removed his outdoor clothes and ran ahead to the shuttered room where Lena and Arianna would be with his sister.

"Papa is home!" he announced, jumping up and down. "Sylvie! Papa's here!"

Arianna and Lena regarded him with amusement, having been the ones who sent Marco out to meet them as soon as he arrived. "Isn't that good," Arianna said, taking Sylvana onto her lap.

Still bounding, Michel returned to the hall where his parents were embracing. At the same time, the vibration of a bomb rattled the windows. Marco turned to take the boy's hand in his.

"Come along, Michel. We'll join the others." To Juliette he added, "Do these raids ever happen at night?"

"Not very often. It's said that the waters of Venice highlight the target areas, but luckily the enemy is never very accurate."

This proved to be true of the current raid. Later in the day they heard that a warehouse had lost its windows, a slipway had been damaged, and the rest of the bombs had vanished into the Lagoon. By then Juliette had learned how Marco had been injured. A bullet had pierced his leg, breaking the bone, but it had been well set.

"The worst of it as far as I was concerned is that it happened the day before I'd been due for leave. So it set back my coming home." He chose not to tell her of the amount of blood he had lost or how close he had come to death, which was why his recovery had taken far longer than she could suspect.

"But where were you nursed?" she asked, dismayed that he had not been brought to Venice.

"I was in a field hospital under canvas at first and then transferred to a hospital converted from an ancient building in a village quite a distance from here. How are you getting on with your nursing these days? You don't write about it in any detail."

"Only because much of the work is harrowing and you experience plenty of those times yourself."

He gave a heavy nod. Like all soldiers briefly home from the horrors of war, he did not wish to speak of anything remotely connected with it. "How about the designing? Any new developments there?"

"Only that mail to and from Paris has become so erratic one never knows when—if ever—it will arrive. But the designing relaxes me, and I snatch whatever spare minutes I have to be in my studio. I'm still making my day clothes practical, the skirts two inches above the ankle."

"It must be difficult for Denise to get certain fabrics."

"I'm sure it is. To judge from my sister's letters," Juliette added with a smile, "one would imagine that the Kaiser had declared war specially to annoy and inconvenience her! Sales, of course, have fallen disastrously. Some of the top couturiers in Paris have enlisted and are serving on the battlefields."

"Dear God! What a contrast for them!" he exclaimed wearily.

Sitting next to him on the sofa, she put her arms around his neck and kissed his mouth to drive away whatever thoughts of war had come into his mind. During the night he woke twice in the grip of nightmares, thrashing his arms and yelling orders, and she held and kissed him again, soothing the horrors away. Once, after making love to her, he wept, his face buried against her breasts, the warm bouquet of her in his nostrils, and did not know how he would ever be able to leave her again.

Yet the time came. By then he had dispensed with his crutch and one of the medical officers stationed in Venice had declared him fit to return to the front. Juliette had made his time at home as happy as she could. She had had her duties at the hospital, but he had been content to be with the children, taking them out with him sometimes for a ride on a *vaporetto*, which both children enjoyed, or to see a battleship anchored in the Lagoon, which meant more to Michel than Sylvana. He set them free in toy shops to choose whatever they wanted, and before taking them home again he never failed to treat them to an ice or a sticky cake or any other sweet that took their fancy. In all, he spoilt them completely, ruined their appetite for meals, and annoyed Arianna far more than he realized.

Sometimes he met Juliette when she came off duty in the evening, and they walked home together. Their only moment of discord occurred during one of these walks. Quite unexpectedly he voiced a question that caught her unawares.

"Have you heard anything from Karasvin?"

She looked at him incredulously. "No. That's over. He wouldn't write to me even in the unlikely possibility of a letter getting through."

"I understand it's possible sometimes through the Red Cross. Karasvin would also have access to diplomatic channels."

"Not if he's in the thick of battle somewhere on the Eastern Front. I've had no letter and neither do I ever expect to receive one."

Outwardly Marco seemed satisfied with her answer, but she realized sadly that it would always be as she feared. He would never truly be free of doubt.

On his last day, Juliette changed her schedule at the hospital to be with him. They spent the time with the children as he wished, taking them to a puppet show. In the evening they dined alone, and at night he made love to her.

When Juliette woke next morning he was gone. An envelope addressed to her was propped on the bedside table. She sat up, pushing back her hair, and read it through. He had written that she was not to be upset, but to say farewell this time would have been almost beyond his powers. He closed by saying he had kissed her and both the children before leaving.

She flung back the bedclothes and hastened to the window just in case he was still in sight, but there was no sign of him.

Twenty-three

WITH NEWS of a new Austrian offensive in the Tyrol, Juliette was consumed with anxiety for Marco. Sometimes, unable to wait for the morning newspaper, she went to St. Mark's Square and joined the crowd that gathered every evening to hear the latest communiqué read out. She joined in with the cheers and tears of relief when it was announced that the Italians had broken through the Austrian lines at Trentino. More Italian victories followed, but the true toll could be found in the lists of casualties published in the daily newspapers.

As the summer advanced, there came further news of minor Italian triumphs. One day, Juliette was resting in the salon, reading the newspaper, when the doorbell rang. Arianna had recently married a sailor, and Lena was out with the children, so she crossed the green marble floor of the hall to answer the door herself. The visitor was a woman dressed entirely in mourning and for a fleeting second Juliette felt a wave of inexplicable fear, as if this stranger might be the bearer of bad news. In the same instant, however, the woman smiled, putting her at ease. There was a gentleness in her time-worn face. She appeared to be in her mid-sixties, gray hair and features as aristocratic as her dignified demeanor.

"Bonjour," she said at once and continued in French. "I believe I have the pleasure of addressing Signora Romanelli. Yes? I am Signora Ottoni, widow of the late Carlo Ottoni of Venice. Doña

Cecilia gave me your name. Forgive me for calling unannounced, but I was most anxious to make your acquaintance.''

"Please come in." Juliette stood aside for her to enter.

"It is many years since I was last in Venice," the widow explained when she and Juliette were seated opposite each other. "That was not through choice, because once we used to spend three months of every year at our palazzo on the Grand Canal. Sadly, my husband's health began to deteriorate and on his doctor's advice we settled in Switzerland, where the mountain air is beneficial to invalids. Although I'd long been prepared, it came as a shattering blow to me when I was recently bereaved."

"Pray accept my sincere condolences."

The widow inclined her head in grateful acknowledgment. In spite of her Italian name, her French bore no trace of accent. Yet Juliette was convinced she was not a fellow countrywoman.

"Carlo was an adventurous traveler," the widow continued. "Whenever possible I would go with him. I used to tell him he must surely be a descendant of Marco Polo." Her little smile showed that it had been a favorite joke between them. "But wherever we were in the world, his heart was always in Venice. It upset him very much when Italy became involved in the war, but he was also proud of her bravery and made generous donations toward the war effort. I've come to Venice to fulfill his last wish, which was that the Palazzo Ottoni be turned into a hospital for the wounded. All equipment, from beds to an operating theater, is to be funded by a special bequest under my jurisdiction."

"That will be a marvelous benefit!" Juliette exclaimed. "And I speak from my own experience, as I nurse three days a week at the Hotel Victoria hospital."

"So Doña Cecilia told me. I went to see her as soon as I arrived in Venice yesterday. Years ago in Rome, my husband and I became acquainted with Doña Cecilia and her late husband, Fortuny y Marsal, who without doubt was one of Spain's greatest artists. Carlo bought a number of his paintings, which he bequeathed to the Prado Museum in Madrid."

"Another munificent gift! So you must surely know Don Mariano and Maria Luisa too."

"Oh yes. Maria Luisa was at the railway station to meet me when I arrived, but I have yet to renew my acquaintanceship with her brother." She linked her gloved fingers on her lap. "But I still haven't explained the purpose of my visit to you this afternoon. Doña Cecilia told me that you had supervised the converting of your absent husband's business premises into a hospital for the duration."

"All I did was offer the place to the medical board and then arrange for the storage of his stock and equipment. After that it was just a question of getting women to wash and scrub."

"That alone tells me that you're practical and would know whom to employ for such work." Signora Ottoni made a little gesture of appeal. "I'll be frank with you. I'm not a young woman, which is only too plain, and I haven't the first idea how I should go about donating this hospital. Naturally, there has to be a legal arrangement, but in the first instance I'd like you to help me. I had counted on Maria Luisa to fulfill that role, but, sadly, she has changed a great deal in the years since I last saw her and it would be out of the question."

"Before I can give a reply I have to point out that a local lawyer could organize everything on your behalf and keep in contact with the medical board at the same time."

"I'm sure of that, and I'm also certain it's what my husband expected me to do, but then the whole venture would be taken out of my hands." The widow spoke emotionally. "It's the last thing I'll ever be able to do for Carlo, and I want to be personally involved."

"I understand."

"So what is your answer?"

Juliette's face bloomed into a wide smile. "It will be a pleasure to help you in any way I can."

Signora Ottoni threw up her hands in relief. "How splendid! That is what I'd hoped to hear. You have my grateful thanks."

"Is the palazzo furnished?"

"Yes, an old caretaker and his wife live there now."

"Are you staying there too?"

"No. I'm Doña Cecilia's guest. She invited me as soon as I wrote to say I would be coming. I haven't been to the palazzo yet. Perhaps you would accompany me in the morning? I'd like us to start as we mean to go on."

"Yes, of course. I shall not be on duty until the following day. I can't begin to tell you how much it will mean for the city to have the benefit of another hospital." Juliette spoke with feeling.

"There are so many wounded. So many poor men are shell-shocked in addition to all else that has happened to them."

"Would you consider nursing at my hospital?"

"I'd like that very much. I'm sure there would be no problem about my transferring."

Signora Ottoni gave a nod of satisfaction. "It will be good to know you're there. You see, Carlo and I never had children. It was a great sorrow to us both. When I knew of the task he had entrusted to me, I thought again how wonderful it would have been to have a daughter to help me. And now you have stepped in."

"I'll do my very best."

Suddenly there came the sound of the two children's voices in the hallway. A few minutes later the door of the salon burst open and Michel came running in, followed by Sylvana. They behaved well and the widow was clearly fond of children, but Lena soon took them away, leaving Juliette and her visitor to become better acquainted. When Juliette had answered her question about where she and Marco had met, Signora Ottoni went on to tell her that she had become engaged to Carlo within days of their first seeing each other.

"It was in Nice. I went there annually with my parents and brothers and sisters to our villa. We were like so many others in court circles who chose to escape the freezing winter blizzards of Russia for the balmy warmth of the Mediterranean."

"So you are Russian, signora!" Juliette exclaimed. "That explains why you speak French so naturally."

"Ah. So you know that French is the language of the educated in Russia and that one only addresses the servants in Russian. I remember questioning the custom when I was a girl, because Russian is such a powerful and descriptive language, but I was told to hush at once. The matter wasn't even to be discussed."

"Do you still have family there?"

The widow nodded. "Those of my generation are depleted in number, but I have plenty of nephews and nieces. Just before the war broke out Carlo and I were visited by the son of my youngest sister. Alexander is one of my favorite nephews and I have quite a few, all of whom are now fighting on the Eastern Front. I haven't seen anyone else from my family since he came, although I have a brother-in-law who is one of the Tsar's ministers and he sends his wife's letters and any from my other sisters through diplomatic channels. At least he did when I was in Switzerland, and I hope that will continue while I'm here."

"Did your nephew stay long?"

"Unfortunately not. He had been in Vienna with a friend who had come to Venice on a short visit. They were meeting again to travel the long journey home together."

Juliette was aware of feeling no surprise at this information or what it was likely to mean. One could not escape destiny. "Were you acquainted with your nephew's friend," she inquired evenly.

"Yes, indeed. Russia has millions of people, but court circles are relatively small and sooner or later one knows everybody, at least by sight. I've been acquainted with Nikolai Karasvin's family for many years. Alexander and Nikolai and several of their friends joined the same regiment when they arrived back. In the last letters I had from one of my sisters before leaving Switzerland, I learned that Nikolai's father had died recently. It's a sad state of affairs when the heir inherits while at war with no son to inherit in his turn should the worst happen." She broke off with a look of concern, having seen Juliette press her fingers over her cheek as if to smooth away her paleness. "Are you not well?"

Juliette dropped her hands into her lap. "A little tired perhaps."

Signora Ottoni was reassured. "That's not surprising when you lead such a busy life. And now I've come to give you still more work."

"I like to be kept busy," Juliette answered quickly. "I welcome the extra tasks more than you can possibly realize."

"The least I can do now is to leave and let you have some rest."

"No, please stay and have some refreshment."

But the widow had already risen to her feet. "There will be plenty of other opportunities."

Arrangements were made for their meeting the following day and then Juliette saw her guest to the door. Returning to the salon, she saw her own pale face reflected in a gilt-framed mirror. If she had known that Signora Ottoni was in any way linked with Nikolai, would she have shouldered this task so willingly? It would have been easy enough for her to find an official to take over, even though that was not what the widow had wanted. But there was no going back now that the commitment was made.

She drove her fingers into her hair, cupping her head in desperation. Was Nikolai's will so strong that she was forever to hear of him when she least expected it? Even Marco had talked angrily of him when he was last at home. Could it be that this was what she had to face for the rest of her life? Any contentment of the heart forever denied her?

The next morning, Juliette went shopping early, as she always did these days. With rationing imposed and many foodstuffs in short supply, much time was spent in lining up, often in vain when supplies ran out before she reached the shop door. The previous evening, knowing she would be busier than ever with the new hospital venture, she had asked Lena if she knew of anyone who could give a helping hand in the house and with the children. Lena had called in Catarina Bellini, a young woman who had been working for a family that had since left Venice for a safer area. When Juliette arrived home with her few purchases, the girl was waiting to see her.

"Would you like to start work at once?" Juliette asked after reading her references and asking some questions.

Catarina, shy, brown-haired, and smiling, had already made friends with Michel and Sylvana. "Yes, please, signora," she replied eagerly.

Juliette, relieved that Lena would have reliable help, left the house again and went to the office of the medical board where, as she had anticipated, she was invited to return with Signora Ottoni at four o'clock. That left plenty of time to look around the Palazzo Ottoni. She called for the city's new benefactress as arranged, and together they went by gondola to their destination.

"How eager the gondolier was to take us," Signora Ottoni whispered to Juliette as they sailed along. "So often in the past it was difficult to get one at all at this time of the day."

"I'm afraid there's little business for them anymore," Juliette replied. She knew that those still left on the canals were virtually destitute and that many were reliant for food on the soup kitchen that had been opened by volunteers.

"I'll tip him well."

"He'll appreciate that."

"We should find the palazzo in good order. I sent the caretaker a note after I arrived in Venice to let him know I would be viewing the property, but that I would not be staying this time."

"Shall you be returning to Switzerland when everything is set-tled?"

"Only until the war ends. I've a yearning to go home to Russia. One of my nieces and her husband now live in the house where I was born, but it is large enough for all of us."

"Russia was a troubled land before the war. What if that unrest should flare up again in peacetime?"

"It won't," Signora Ottoni stated confidently. "Nothing unites people more than a common enemy, and the peasantry have proved themselves the bravest of soldiers." She glanced upward. "Here we are!"

The Palazzo Ottoni loomed above them, its glorious fifteenth-century façade inset with Gothic windows and enhanced by stone balconies delicate as lace. The caretaker had opened the door and, in spite of his age, stepped forward nimbly to hand the two women in.

"An honor to see you again, signora," he said with an old-fashioned bow.

"Are you well, Giovanni?"

"Yes, signora, but I miss my wife."

"Oh, dear. Have you been bereaved?"

"No, not that. She had been unsteady on her legs for some time and not able to do much. Then she fell on the stairs over a year ago and broke her hip. She lives at my daughter's home now and there she'll stay, because she'll never walk again." He did not seem un-duly perturbed. "I've been managing well enough on my own."

His attempts at housekeeping were not, however, as successful as he supposed, and the two women soon spotted a deep green bor-der around the dust sheets covering the furniture in the vast hall.

"What happened here?" Signora Ottoni asked, concerned.

"The Grand Canal flooded last winter."

Signora Ottoni shook her head in dismay as she led the way up the ornate staircase, which was hung with cobwebs, to the great ballroom. Her long black skirt made a swath of dust across the rose-hued tessellated floor as she entered and stood looking nostal-gically around her. Juliette reached her side. The vast room was magnificent, with gilded panels, a turquoise ceiling, and two chan-deliers of Venetian glass, each five feet in diameter, that glittered in spite of a coating of dust. A painted trompe l'oeil of several smiling people, grandly dressed in clothes of an earlier century, looked down over a balustrade amid urns of flowers.

"I'm remembering so many happy times here," Signora Ottoni said wistfully before abruptly straightening her shoulders. "There will be many more of a less frivolous kind when soldiers and sailors recover their health and strength here. How many rows of beds could be accommodated in this ballroom, do you think?"

"Three," Juliette replied. "Two at the sides and one in the middle. There'll be plenty of space between the rows."

It was the start of an all-out effort to change the palazzo into an efficient hospital. The caretaker gave notice, declaring himself too old for such changes, but Juliette had no difficulty finding people to do the work. There were many fine paintings throughout the palazzo, and Signora Ottoni left them in place for the pleasure of patients and staff. Juliette was among those on duty when the first of the patients arrived, and, after a few initial mishaps, the new hospital settled into a routine.

Signora Ottoni had changed her mind about returning to Switzerland as the Palazzo Ottoni hospital became the sole focus of her interest. She took an apartment nearby and went daily as a visitor, talking to the men, reading to them, and writing their letters, as well as giving them sips of water or feeding those unable to do so themselves. It was as if everything she did for a patient was also done for her husband, and, therefore, it was a solace for her.

Among the second batch of wounded to arrive were a number of Russian soldiers. They had been taken prisoner by the Austrians, but in passing from one temporary camp to another they had become caught in the crossfire during an Italian breakthrough of the Austrian lines. Juliette went from one bed to another, looking into the face of each man or reading the names that had been taken from their identification tags. Nikolai was not among them.

Then, as she was leaving again, one of the other nurses told her there was a Russian officer in one of the smaller wards on an upper floor. She ran up the stairs, but even from the ward's doorway she could see it was not Nikolai. She went to the officer's bedside, read his name on the temperature chart, and spoke to him in French.

"How are you feeling, Captain Rostov?"

He had lost an arm and was weak, but was pleased to talk to her. "Much better now that I'm in this bed. Hearing you speak makes me feel I'm back in Paris again."

"You know my city?"

"I was there on my honeymoon."

She smiled. "I can think of no better place."

"Why are you so far from home?"

"I married an Italian. May I ask if you have ever met Count Nikolai Karasvin? I knew him in Paris. He is in the Russian army and I wonder if you know whether he is well."

The officer frowned meditatively and then shook his head. "I'm sorry, but that name isn't personally known to me."

They talked a little longer, and before she left, she promised to visit him again. On the way back downstairs she thought about the fact that this time it was she herself who had chosen to speak of Nikolai, but she couldn't help feeling the power he still had over her.

Signora Ottoni was sometimes called in to act as interpreter, for even Captain Rostov could speak no Italian. Several of the Russians died in spite of all their efforts, and she held their hands during their last moments. Those with minor wounds were thankful to talk to a fellow countrywoman, even though she was of the ruling class. Such differences were lost in the kindness of her words, and some, who were wandering in their minds, even thought she was their mother. She had hoped that the captain might be able to give her some news of her own relatives but, as with Juliette, he was unable to help her. To her surprise, even shock, he spoke openly of his disappointment in the Tsar.

"He put himself personally in charge of the Russian army with disastrous results. We've suffered terrible losses simply because of his incompetence. Hundreds of thousands of our men have been killed already, and the hardships endured by our army defy belief. Admittedly not everything can be laid at the Tsar's door—the failure of ammunition supplies, the lack of food, the boots that leak, and the inadequacy of bayonets in the face of pounding artillery. Did you know that famine prevails in many places at home? It's not only the army that goes hungry."

"What a sad and terrible state of affairs!"

"It will get worse. The old grievances of the peasants haven't been forgotten. There are many rebellious elements in the army. I know of officers whose loyalty to the Tsar is no longer certain. Not even such successes as we have attained against the Austro-German forces and the Turks can nullify growing discontent in the ranks and at home."

Signora Ottoni kept these things to herself and told only Juliette about the hardships the army was enduring. Even then, it upset her to see the young woman's eyes darken with distress.

Juliette continued to write regularly to Marco, often enclosing drawings the children had done specially for him, even though Sylvana's efforts were little more than scrawls with wax crayons. She had no idea when he would be home again.

On the morning two overseas letters were delivered, there was also one from Marco, which she read first. He believed he would be given a new posting very soon, but hoped for leave first. The second letter bore a French stamp and was from Denise. She had written in wild despair. Her last mannequin had left months ago to do war work, as had almost all the seamstresses. Her few remaining clients were wearing their clothes from season to season and new orders had dwindled to almost nothing. She could no longer continue producing the brassieres of Juliette's design, which had sold so well at top prices, because nobody was buying enough expensive lingerie to keep that particular workroom open any longer. Many *haute couture* houses had closed down, and she did not think she would be able to keep Maison Landelle open after next month. She finished her letter with the furious comment that the Germans had ruined everything for her. Amidst these complaints she mentioned that Jacques Vernet spent most of his time at his armaments factories, but that he did get to Paris quite often and always took her to wherever it was still possible to dine and dance in some style.

The third letter was from Gabrielle and written in August, over three months before. It gave her the sad news that Derek had been killed on the Somme and had been posthumously awarded the Military Cross. Gabrielle went on to say that all Derek's family had been wonderfully supportive, she and his mother able to comfort and sustain each other. Her little daughter was her only joy. The last line expressed the heartfelt hope that all was well with Juliette and that it would not be long before the war ended and they could see each other again. Juliette folded the letter and wept for her friend's bereavement.

The war plowed on. It seemed to Juliette and other Venetian housewives that everything was rationed or in short supply. They knew it was the same everywhere and that even in Germany women were facing the same problems.

Many foreigners in Venice had problems greater than the shortage of food, Fortuny and his mother among them. Unable to tap their financial resources overseas, they found themselves desperately short of money. Doña Cecilia parted with some of her antiques, Signora Ottoni moved into an even smaller apartment, and Fortuny himself had to sell one of his most treasured possessions.

"Not the Goya drawings!" Juliette exclaimed in dismay when Henriette spoke of the matter to her. He had shown them to her once, each as powerful and beautiful as the next.

"Yes." Henriette gave a deep sigh, folding her arms as she rested her weight against the edge of a carved table in the salon-studio. "It had to be done. All the workrooms are closed now. The shop is still open, but it's rare that anyone comes, and then I do the serving." She glanced about at the vast room. "Isn't it quiet? Do you remember how this place used to sound like an aviary when Mariano and I held parties here before the war?"

"I do indeed. I also recall how Don Mariano was advised to go to the United States when the war first started and continue his work there. How does he feel about that now?"

Henriette shrugged. "He has no regrets. In spite of everything, he'd still make the same decision to stay in Venice."

"He's a remarkable man in so many ways. Does he still design?"

"Yes, he does." Henriette gave a quiet smile. "He's biding his time. This war will end one day. Wars always do. In my opinion, his Delphos robe will still be admired when the Kaiser has faded from people's memories."

"I'm sure you're right."

Juliette rarely entered her own studio these days. She was busy from morning to night, fitting in her other chores and obligations between her duties at the hospital. She tried to visit Doña Cecilia whenever possible; like Fortuny himself, she and her daughter had decided to remain in Venice for the duration. Although her mother seemed to be bearing up, Maria Luisa had by now retreated completely into a world of her own obsessions.

At night, Juliette fell asleep instantly from sheer physical exhaustion. On New Year's Eve, she slept right through the arrival of 1917, and in the morning she awoke to wonder yearningly if the year would bring peace. The following morning when she went downstairs, there was a letter from Marco letting her know that he would be coming home on leave.

He arrived looking tired and drawn, but after two weeks at home he was much improved. He was passionate and frequent in his lovemaking, starved for her, and it was not long after his departure that she began to wonder if she were pregnant again.

The certainty came on the first day of April, shortly after the Tsar had abdicated and the Bolsheviks had announced their intention of ruling Russia. A dangerous flame had been ignited.

Twenty-four

WHEN, OWING TO HER PREGNANCY, Juliette could no longer continue nursing at the hospital, she reluctantly handed in her uniform and took home the few things that were hers. These included a postcard one of the patients had sent her. It showed a pretty red-haired nurse about to give a male patient a glass of medicine, but being kissed by him instead. It was entitled *Not in the Prescription*. She smiled over it again and put it with her other keepsakes. The sender of the card had been only twenty years old when he was killed during an Italian offensive at Trieste.

Marco's reaction to the news of the new baby was exactly what she had expected. His letter was full of how much a third child would enrich their lives. Apart from his immense pride in fatherhood, it was clear to her that the thought of a new life in the midst of so much death had renewed his hope for the future. For herself, she had not thought of adding to their family until the war was over, but it had happened and she knew she would love the infant when the time came.

The same letter that brought his joyous response to her pregnancy went on to insist that she and the children leave at once for the villa in Tuscany, where she would be well looked after as she had been before. It had worried him far too long that they had stayed on in a city that was being bombed. Juliette would have done as he wished, especially as the official advice had long been for residents to leave for safer zones. Venice, with its great arsenal and sheltered waters, would be a prime target for enemy capture. But she could not leave the city yet. She was still in bed after the worrying threat of a miscarriage.

"You're to stay there until I come again," the doctor had said on his last visit, when she had asked if she might get up. "Then if all is well I'll allow you to leave your bed, but only if you promise to rest with your feet up whenever possible. In my opinion you should have left the hospital earlier but that can't be undone now. We must put matters right as best we can."

When Juliette replied to Marco's letter, she did her utmost to reassure him not only about her condition but also about the occasional bombing. And she promised that after the baby was born she would leave the city if that should prove necessary. When Marco wrote back, he did not question the doctor's advice or her decision. She was aware how much he hoped for a son of his own this time.

To Juliette the main benefit of her pregnancy was the opportunity it gave her to enjoy some leisure time with Michel and Sylvana. She and Marco had always encouraged the children to appreciate books, and now she was able to give her full attention to teaching Michel to read. She also introduced him to simple sums. With her help, Sylvana was able to identify all the letters of the alphabet and those of her name.

Every month of her pregnancy seemed to be marked by dramatic events in the war, including the entry of the United States into the conflict. From August to September, all Venice had been in a state of high tension as fierce battles raged on the defensive Italian lines at San Gabriele and Bainsizza. When the Austrians finally retreated, the Venetians breathed a sigh of relief that once more the city had been spared a land attack by the enemy.

Juliette read with sympathy that the Tsar and Tsarina, with their children, had been sent to Siberia for their safety. Moreover, there was concern among the Allies that the Russians might withdraw from the war to settle their own growing internal troubles, especially since they had suffered a disastrous defeat at the river Riva, which the newspapers blamed on a malaise of discontent in the ranks and mass desertions.

Toward the end of October, she rose awkwardly from her bed to bathe and dress. She paused, listening. An ominous sound was rolling toward Venice from the distance. Hurrying to the window, she threw the shutters wide. It was gunfire! From time to time, when the wind was in the right direction, gunfire could be heard faintly like the rumble of faraway thunder, but this was louder than anything she had heard before. She went to check on the children, but they were still sleeping. As soon as she was dressed, she went downstairs to find Lena and Catarina just coming back indoors. Hastily Catarina bade Juliette good morning and darted past her upstairs to the children.

Juliette remained standing at the bottom of the stairs, alarmed by Lena's serious expression. "What's happening?"

"Nobody quite knows, but according to rumor there's a great battle going on at Caporetto."

"My husband is in that area!" Juliette's face became ashen. "He was posted there only recently."

Lena tut-tutted in sympathy. "Go and sit down at the breakfast table, signora. I'll pour you a cup of coffee. All will be well, I'm sure. Try to eat a little. You have your baby to think about too."

Later in the morning, when Lena went out to St. Mark's Square to see if any communiqués were being issued, it was confirmed that a major battle was indeed in progress at Caporetto. All the city understood that the outcome would be vital, for from there the Austrians could turn their guns on Venice.

"We must pack hand luggage ready for an emergency flight," Juliette said at once, determined to keep her promise to Marco that she and the children would leave for Tuscany as soon as it proved necessary. She had no wish to travel in the final days of her pregnancy, although all seemed to be well with her now. At least there was still enough time to get to the villa before she gave birth.

"I'll pack for you, signora," Lena offered. "Catarina can see to the children's things."

"I'll gather some baby clothes together. We will surely know soon how the tide of battle will turn."

All through the day the bombardment rumbled on, and Juliette's thoughts were constantly with Marco. During the afternoon, she took the children to see Henriette.

"Did you come to see if we've flown?" Henriette joked. She had poured coffee for Juliette and herself and given the children each an apple.

"No, I knew that would never happen. I came to tell you that I'll be taking all my brood off to Tuscany tomorrow."

"I'm relieved to hear it. If the worst happens, Venice won't be taken easily. It will be no place for you and the children."

"I'd like you to keep one of the keys to the house. If Marco should come home while we're still away, he would surely come here at once."

Henriette gave her a reassuring nod as Juliette put the key into her outstretched hand. "I'll keep it gladly."

It was unspoken between them that his arrival would most surely mean a full retreat from Caporetto.

In the evening, Lena went again to hear the latest communiqué and came hastening back.

"All foreigners in the city have been given notice to quit. Only the British consul has refused to leave his post!"

"Don Mariano undoubtedly will also have dug in his heels," Juliette commented, thinking to herself that neither would Henriette ever leave his side.

"There's a special train leaving shortly for the foreigners, only hand luggage to be taken. You're French, signora. You and the children can be on that train. I'll help you get ready."

Juliette made no move except to shake her head. "That's not possible. Remember I'm an Italian by marriage. I no longer have a French passport. We'll all leave together as planned by the first available train for Tuscany in the morning."

"There're bound to be hundreds of others in Venice wanting to leave as well. I'll go to the railway station and get the tickets now. If there's any difficulty, I'll see the stationmaster. He's an old friend."

Juliette fetched her purse and gave Lena the money. "That will be more than enough to cover the fares for all of us. And I'd like you to stop on your way and see if Signora Ottoni would like to accompany us. She is Italian by marriage too, and there would be no place on the foreigners' train for her either."

"I'll do that. May I ask a favor? Could Arianna have the same chance too? She is my niece, and I've kept a maternal eye on her ever since she lost her parents."

Juliette took more money from her purse. "Of course. I should have thought about it myself. Catarina can go now to her apartment and ask her."

"Mind you, I don't know if she'll come. Umberto, her husband, is home at the moment. His ship put in for minor repairs and she may not want to leave until he sails again.''

"She shall be given the address of the villa, and then she can always join us there later. I'm sure her husband would wish her to do that.''

The velvety Venetian night had already descended when Lena went out again, taking Catarina with her. On the narrow ways along the edge of the canals they were alert lest anyone approaching bump into them in the darkness. As had become customary since the blackout began, they gave the gondoliers' cry, *"Scia ohè,"* rarely heard otherwise these days, and the usual reply came back clearly, *"Premi eh!"*

Soon they parted company. Catarina went on to find Arianna, and Lena called on Signora Ottoni, who expressed her appreciation for Juliette's offer but said she was determined to stay with her hospital. At the railway station Lena saw that there were sentries guarding the entrance.

"The station is closed for the night," one of the guards told her when she asked to go in. "Go away now, signora. A hospital train is being unloaded.''

"That's why I'm here," she lied glibly, determined to get through. "The stationmaster sent for me. I'm a nurse.''

She looked convincing: a short, square, full-bosomed woman in neat clothes and a sensible hat. The sentries let her in and she hurried onto the platform only to stop short at the terrible scene in front of her. There was just enough glow from the shrouded lanterns to show vast numbers of stretchers being lifted from the train and conveyed in a stream to the waiting water ambulances and *vaporetti* that would convey the wounded to the landing stage nearest each hospital. There were heartrending groans, some men crying pathetically and so many coughing relentlessly. Nuns moved like pale ghosts among the stretchers, which were manned by soldiers and civilian volunteers, the stationmaster among them. All the wounded were still in their filthy uniforms, caked with mud and blood. Some, who could walk assisted by nuns, had lost their boots; many had their faces and eyes bandaged.

Lena sat down helplessly on a seat. There was nothing she could do amidst this organized chaos, and she was fearful of getting in the way. The scene told her more about the battle at Caporetto than any communiqué could have done. Normally the wounded passed through field hospitals before arriving in Venice, but this time the ghastly wave of casualties had swamped all the facilities near the front line. Venice itself had become a field hospital.

When the last of the casualties was aboard, Lena saw her friend the stationmaster go into his office. She jumped up from her seat and hurried in after him.

She found him slumped into a chair at his desk, head propped in his hands. At the sound of her entry he sat back and looked up, his face haggard.

"Those poor boys," she said in a quavering voice. "That coughing!"

He shook his head at the tragedy of it all. "Didn't you guess the reason, Lena? The enemy is using mustard gas at Caporetto."

She clamped her fingers over her trembling mouth and sat down abruptly in the nearest chair. "I mustn't let Signora Romanelli know. Her husband is there."

"Has she had her baby yet?"

"Not yet. That's why I have to get her out of Venice quickly to the safety of her family's villa near Lucca."

"Don't ask me for advance train tickets," he insisted wearily. "I can't do it. I've had people pestering me all day, here and at home, all wanting priority in getting away."

She pulled her chair nearer and rested her hands flat on his desk. "You and I are old friends, Roberto. Our late mothers, of sweet memory, were friends. We played together as children. Am I not godmother to your married daughter in Naples? Are you still going to refuse me?"

He regarded her with mild exasperation. "I can't do the impossible. When the foreigners' train pulled out earlier, that was the last I could guarantee. Priority is being given to all the hospital trains and, judging from what just arrived, there're going to be plenty of them." He glanced at a clock on the wall. "There'll be another in shortly. What other trains will come and go within the next few days is a matter for speculation."

"You must have some idea," she persisted.

He sighed. "According to the timetable, your train should be departing from here tomorrow evening at eight o'clock, but it will be a matter of luck."

"I'll have six open tickets all the way to Lucca," she declared immediately. "Then, if there are any delays, they'll still be usable."

In triumph she watched him pull open a drawer, take out the book of special tickets, and fill them in.

"Change at Florence," he said automatically as he handed them over. Then, seeing she was opening her purse to pay, he made a dismissive gesture. "I don't even know if there's going to be a train. Pay the railway company after the war if you manage to get on one."

"Thank you, Roberto."

When she arrived back at the Romanelli house, Catarina had already returned. As half-expected, Arianna did not wish to leave Venice until her husband sailed. Lena sent Catarina out again to take her a train ticket, which she could use whenever she was ready.

The next day was spent packing away valuables and preparing the house for their departure. Food and drink were put in a basket for the journey, and the palazzo began to take on an austere tidiness. Still the distant guns kept up their incessant pounding. At midday Austrian planes flew in over the Lagoon, but three Italian aircraft swept in and vanquished them after a short battle that was watched with excitement by everyone below.

In the late afternoon Lena went to see her friend Roberto again to be sure the train would be leaving at eight o'clock. He affirmed that it would. Although hospital trains would still hold priority, it had become vitally important to get people out of Venice too, in whatever time was left.

"Is the latest news so bad?" she asked fearfully.

He nodded, dashing out of his office as another hospital train came in. With a heavy heart she returned home and found that Fortuny and his French lady had called to say good-bye to the family.

Henriette and Juliette hugged each other. "We'll miss you," Henriette declared fervently.

"We hope to be back soon," Juliette replied huskily.

Fortuny kissed her on both cheeks. "I echo that hope. In the meantime, take care!"

There were no other visitors, most of Juliette's friends having already left the city for safer locales. Evening came at last and the little traveling party with hand luggage left the house. Sadly Juliette locked it behind her.

As they stood on the landing stage, waiting for the *vaporetto* to take them to the railway station, Juliette wondered if Nikolai was also on the move. The Bolshevik troops seemed to have found a new leader in a man called Lenin.

"The *vaporetto*'s almost here! Are you sure that piece of hand luggage isn't too heavy for you to lift?" Lena interrupted her train of thought.

"No, it's quite light." Juliette picked it up in readiness. When the steamer stopped, she shepherded her little group on board and was about to follow when abruptly she drew back. Prompted by her thoughts of Nikolai, she realized that she had forgotten to pack her Delphos robe. Suddenly it was impossible for her to consider leaving it behind.

"Hurry, signora!" Lena called anxiously.

Juliette shook her head. "I've forgotten something. Go ahead! There's plenty of time. I'll catch you up at the railway station."

She turned on her heel and hastened back as fast as she could. As a precaution she had asked Lena to hold all the tickets except her own, just in case in her condition she should be slower getting through the crowds to the platform. Why hadn't she thought about the gown before? It must have been because Lena packed the hand luggage for her while she had only dealt with require- ments for the baby.

But her gown could not be left behind! If the Austrians bom- barded Venice the house might be destroyed. And then there was always the chance that, if they took the city, they would loot de- serted properties. Without pause, Juliette hurried on down the long *calle* at the side of the Palazzo Orfei. Only the square left to cross. Yet what a distance it seemed!

She arrived breathlessly at the house and let herself in. The elec- tricity had been switched off somewhere in the kitchen regions, but there were candles and matches in the hall. By the light of the flickering flame, she started up the stairs. Halfway up, she paused to rest. The house was extraordinarily silent. Yet the warm silence was full of almost audible memories. She seemed to hear Michel's running footsteps, Sylvana's newborn cry, the conversation of good friends gathered around the dining table, the clink of wine- glasses, Marco's deep laughter, and the sound made when he once struck her in rage. Even Nikolai was there, haunting her as he had done so vividly for months after her last sight of him, causing her to lie awake when Marco slept after making love to her.

Having caught her breath, she continued her climb. In her bedroom she stood on a low stool to take the Fortuny box from her closet shelf. Stepping down again, she removed the lid and held the robe in her hand for a moment, enjoying the rich, soft feel of the fabric before thrusting it into her hand luggage. Swiftly she tossed the box back onto the shelf and closed the closet door.

She left the bedroom and had reached the head of the stairs when a knife-like pain of such ferocity seared through her that she had to drop her bag and clutch the newel post for support. The candlestick flew from her hand and she was left in total darkness.

Slowly her pain subsided, but another struck before she could move. Somehow she would have to get to the telephone down in the hall! She gripped the banister with both hands, and found the next step carefully with one foot before bringing her other down beside it. The pain subsided only to return in full force, making the sweat run down her face and trickle under her clothes. Would this have happened if she had not hastened back? She had counted on having at least another eight or nine days. Was she ever going to reach the hall? In the inky darkness it was like descending into a bottomless abyss.

Compelled to pause between pains before moving on again, she thought of the children arriving at the railway station, excited by the prospect of the journey ahead. At least they would be safe with Lena. Juliette was certain that when she failed to arrive at the railway station, Lena and Catarina would take the children on to the safety of the villa. Lena would undoubtedly assume Juliette had been planning this all along and would be angry with her. Juliette could see it only too clearly. There was, to begin with, the almost theatrical manner in which she had suddenly drawn back from boarding the *vaporetto*, keeping the baby clothes with her. Her apparently preconceived action would be seen as a way of avoiding a distressing scene with the children, who would not have wanted to leave without her. Lena would expect her to follow with the new baby in her own time and would pacify the children with that promise when they began asking for her.

How quickly would she be able to follow with a newborn child? Would the war even permit it when she was strong enough to travel? Juliette felt mild surprise that her brain should function so clearly between the mind-blanking spasms of torture that she was enduring.

Surely she must be nearing the bottom of the stairs. The midwife who had attended her at Sylvana's birth did not have a telephone, but a call to Henriette would set everything in motion. Fortuny himself would go to fetch the midwife. There was no chance of getting a doctor, for every one of them would be at the hospitals, trying to deal with one influx of wounded before the next arrived.

Her hand met the carved surface of the bottom newel post. She was safely down! With relief she stepped from the last tread, but instead of the marble floor, her foot encountered something soft. In the same instant she realized it was her fallen hand luggage, which had tumbled down the stairs. But already she had stepped down with too much confidence and it slid under her weight, taking her with it. She screamed as she went flying, throwing out her arms instinctively to break her fall. Landing on her side with a heavy thud, shocked through from head to foot, she went crashing against the legs of the hall table.

For several minutes she lay helpless, tears running from under her closed eyelids. A clock on the wall began to chime the hour of eight o'clock. At the railway station the train would be departing. She could picture Lena looking from the window on the chance that she might have changed her mind at the last minute.

Juliette waited for the few precious moments of respite between pains and levered herself slowly up into a half-sitting position. The telephone was on the table by which she had fallen. Tentatively she reached up, searching with her fingers, until she found the instrument and pulled it toward her. She lifted the receiver to her ear and waited for the operator's voice. Nothing happened. She had to wait until another bout of agony had passed before she could bang the receiver's rest several times, but the line was dead.

She sank back onto the floor again, hearing herself shriek out as she was engulfed by a yawning cavern of pain. It would have been easy to escape into oblivion, but somehow she struggled back again. Her baby was being born. It would die if she lost consciousness! Her thoughts tumbled and twisted as if keeping pace with her thrusting and her screams. She did not hear the street door open, but in a final body-tearing effort, her infant slithered with a rush into the world and she heard his lusty wail.

It was morning before Juliette received a full account from Lena of what had happened when she failed to arrive at the railway station. By then she had slept for several hours in her bed, which had been hastily made up to receive her. The night before, Fortuny himself had carried her upstairs to it as effortlessly as if she were a child in his arms.

"Tell me first if there is any fresh news about Caporetto," Juliette asked from her pillows, looking across at the cradle where her son lay.

"I haven't heard anything," Lena lied. This was no time to repeat a neighbor's rumor that Caporetto had fallen and the Italian forces were in full retreat, thousands already taken prisoner by the enemy.

"I've noticed that the guns are quieter. Do you suppose that means the Austrians have retreated?"

"Let's hope so," Lena said quickly. "May I ask what name you're going to give your son?"

"It's my husband's choice. He wanted a son to be named Riccardo after his father."

"I like that. It's a good, strong name."

"I like it too. You know, all I can really remember your saying to me last night is that Arianna had taken charge of Michel and Sylvana."

"You were in quite a panic thinking I'd left them to travel alone with young Catarina." Lena removed a breakfast tray from the bed and deposited it on a table outside the room, talking all the time through the open door. "I would never have done that. The train was packed, but Roberto had secured seats for us. It was just as we were about to leave that Arianna came running along the platform looking for us." Lena came back to the bedside and smoothed the top sheet. "I was still watching out for you, which was how she found us."

"What of her husband?"

"He'd been recalled to his ship sooner than expected and she'd just had time to see him off and get to the train. I told her to take over and that you and I would follow when you were fit to travel after the birth. I never expected when Madame Negrin and I entered the house that we should find the baby had just arrived."

"What made you come back?"

"Suddenly I guessed what had happened. You hadn't left anything behind! That was an excuse, because you had felt your first labor pains and didn't dare to travel. Naturally I thought you would have gone straight to the Palazzo Orfei. But when I called

there Madame Negrin became as anxious about you as I was."
Lena was quite smug in her astuteness at having deduced what she
believed to be the truth. Juliette did not enlighten her.

"I was so relieved to see both of you bending over me in the
lantern light."

"Afterward I've never moved so fast in all my life!" Lena threw
up her hands expressively. "Switching the electricity back on! Finding scissors and twine! I shouted to Madame Negrin to fetch some
linen from the nursery to wrap the baby in and a blanket from the
cupboard for you. She ran about as fast as I did. As soon as you
could be moved, she rushed back to the palazzo and fetched Don
Mariano. They'll be calling in later to see how you are this morning."

When Fortuny and Henriette arrived, Lena warned them before
they went upstairs that she had told Juliette nothing of the disastrous retreat from Caporetto. "To be honest, I hadn't the heart.
Maybe it would be best coming from you, Madame Negrin. But
tomorrow, perhaps? She's exhausted today."

"Yes, you're right," Henriette agreed. "Another full day's rest is
what she needs. I'll look in again this evening, and then tomorrow
morning I'll tell her whatever the latest news may be."

She went ahead up the stairs and Fortuny held up the bottle of
champagne he had brought with him. "Please bring four glasses up
to Signora Romanelli's room. I want you to join us in a toast to the
new baby."

As Lena took the glasses up on a tray, she thought to herself that
even with the Austrian guns only fifteen miles away, perhaps less by
now, Fortuny was his usual immaculate self—from white silk cravat
to patent leather shoes—just as he had been last night when summoned without warning from his fireside. She believed he would
look the same in the midst of the enemy bombardment that was
surely to break upon Venice before long. Not even dust would dare
to settle on the handsome slouch hat he had swept off upon entering the house.

Juliette, in spite of her physical tiredness, enjoyed the time her
visitors spent with her and thanked them for all they had done the
night before.

"It's Lena you should thank," Henriette countered, sitting on
the edge of the bed. "If it wasn't for her I daren't think what the
end result might have been."

"I'm forever in her debt." Juliette smiled gratefully at Lena, who was embarrassed by the praise.

Fortuny proposed toasts to Riccardo, to Marco, and to victory. Such was his charismatic presence and air of supreme confidence that even Lena was half-persuaded things might turn out all right after all.

For the ten days after giving birth, which every woman was expected to spend in bed, Juliette was cocooned in her room. A delayed telegram from Arianna, which arrived on the fifth day, relieved her worry about the children. They were safe and had settled down at the Casa San Giorgio.

Meanwhile the Italian navy was increasing its defenses all around Venice and only soldiers were to be seen on the Grand Canal. The market stood deserted and whole streets presented shuttered shop-fronts. Churches had been turned into temporary shelters for the thousands of refugees pouring in from the war-wasted mainland. The first time Juliette walked to St. Mark's Square after her confinement, she paused in dismay at the pathetic sight. More refugees had landed that morning with their children, their bundles, and some even with pets. Priests and nuns and volunteers were handing out emergency rations.

Gradually they would board various vessels for transport down the coast to safer ground. Juliette, with her baby and Lena, had been allotted passes, and they were making ready to depart from Venice when Signora Ottoni called at the house, obviously in great distress.

"Whatever has happened?" Juliette exclaimed, putting an arm about her and leading her into the salon.

"I've terrible news." Signora Ottoni could scarcely speak. "I felt I had to tell you before you left. My nephew, Alexander, has been killed."

"Oh, my dear friend!" Juliette was overwhelmed by compassion.

"The British consul himself broke the news to me. I don't know by what means it was conveyed to him, except that it had come from a mutual acquaintance in diplomatic circles in Switzerland, who had given him the names."

"Were you told where this tragedy happened?"

"No, only that Alexander and two of his friends, Anatole Suchkin and also Nikolai Karasvin, whom you knew, were shot down by enemy machine-gun fire when trying to rally their men from a retreat . . . Three fine young men cut down like sheaves . . ." She broke into hopeless sobbing.

Juliette sat numbed through by shock, feeling as though her heart had split apart. Then silently she swayed, tipping slowly forward onto the floor in a deep faint.

Twenty-five

JULIETTE HAD BEEN REUNITED with Michel and Sylvana for several weeks at the Casa San Giorgio before she received military confirmation of what had happened to Marco at Caporetto. Candida Bonini came running to her with the telegram.

"This has just been delivered, signora."

She watched anxiously as the younger woman's trembling hands ripped open the envelope. Then she saw Juliette's eyes shut with relief as she crumpled the telegram against her breast.

"My husband is all right, Candida. He's a prisoner of war, but he's safe!"

"I'm so happy for you!"

Candida ran to tell the others the good news. She liked having guests in the villa again, especially the children, for she and Antonio missed their own daughters, who had married and moved away.

By the time summer came, bringing a golden heat haze over the Tuscan hills, it seemed that at last the tide might be turning for the Allied armies. In Russia revolution was raging. The tragic Tsar and his wife and family had been massacred before the White army could save them, and the life or death struggle with the Bolsheviks, renamed the Red army, continued unabated.

Juliette's mourning for Nikolai was private and intense. She had nobody to whom she could talk about it; even Dr. Morosini was away, serving as a medical officer in the army. For the second time in her life, she had to gather all her strength for the future. The war had changed everybody and everything. Reason told her that she and countless other wives on both sides of the conflict would have to build a new and secure existence for homecoming men shattered by the horrors of battle. But women had changed too, the whole mode of their existence changed by coming out of their homes into war work and replacing men in many fields of employment. It would be better for both sexes to be on an equal footing, but it was most likely that the returning men would want everything to be exactly as it had been before they went away. Perhaps even more so.

She had written to Marco through the Red Cross to let him know of Riccardo's birth and a long while afterward she received his joyful reply in the few lines allowed. She was thankful that he would not be returning to find his house damaged by bombs or shell fire, for when everything had seemed at its blackest for Venice the situation had suddenly improved. Sections of the Italian lines had rallied, and British and French troops had arrived to strengthen the offensive. The Italian flying corps, which had done so much to protect Venice from the worst of the bombing, was supported by Allied aviators, and together they had prevailed.

In November, shortly after Riccardo's first birthday, the Armistice was signed and the war was over at last. Juliette was unable to join in the celebrations for she had succumbed to the Spanish flu that had begun sweeping through Europe.

Delirious, she did not hear the church bells ringing in the distance or know that Michel and Sylvana were lying equally ill in a neighboring room. Lena and Candida did most of the nursing with Arianna's help, for Catarina was looking after Riccardo in another part of the house, hoping that they would both escape infection. An elderly doctor had come out of retirement to help fight the epidemic and one night he shook his head gravely.

"I fear Signora Romanelli and young Michel will not survive until the morning."

"That's only his opinion," Lena said grimly as soon as he was gone. "I'll make sure he's wrong."

All through the night she and Candida sponged down their patients, for Arianna had also begun to exhibit symptoms and had been sent to bed. When dawn came, hope revived for the sick child and his mother. By the next day it was certain they would both pull through, and Sylvana was already well on the way to recovery. Before Arianna was on her feet again, Candida collapsed and, although everything possible was done to save her, she died within a week. Antonio was the next victim, and his wife's funeral was over before he recovered. As soon as he was well enough, his daughter Lucietta and her husband came to take him away to live with them in Rome.

It fell to Juliette to lock the door of the villa when she and those in her charge were ready to go home, and to hand over the key to Denise's solicitor in Lucca.

"Does the Baronne de Landelle want me to find another caretaker for her?" he asked.

"I'm sure she will, but I haven't heard from her for several months. Now that everything is getting back to normal, you can no doubt write to her yourself."

The last letter Juliette had received from her sister told of Maison Landelle's final closing, which had left Denise deeply in debt and wallowing in self-pity.

Venice looked pale and ethereal under a layer of snow, the lights gleaming softly in the falling flakes. It was early evening and bitterly cold as Juliette and her little party followed the familiar *calle* by the side of the Palazzo Orfei. She glanced up over her shoulder at the façade of the palazzo as they entered the old square again. Henriette had written that she and Fortuny had married quietly, with only two witnesses. Juliette wondered what had prompted them to take this step after sixteen years together.

The women had all expected to find the house closed and shuttered, a cavern of icy cold, but the windows were warmly aglow.

"Doña Henriette is showing herself to be a good neighbor, and not for the first time!" Juliette exclaimed. "I'd no idea when I let her know the time we were coming home that she would make the house welcoming for us!"

She handed Riccardo over to Catarina and opened the door. She had thought it would be Henriette coming quickly into the lighted hall at the sound of her entry, but it was Marco who rushed from the salon. With a cry she threw herself into his arms.

"Oh, my dear!" she exclaimed, her eyes tight shut in thankfulness as he hugged her to him after they had kissed. "You're home! You're safe! I should have been here for your homecoming!"

"I've been back barely a week, my darling," he answered, smiling, as they drew apart, "and there was no predicting my arrival beforehand." He turned to look down at Michel, who was tugging at his jacket, and lifted him up. "How you've grown, my boy!"

"I've been in the country, Papà!" Michel had wrapped his arms about Marco's neck. "Don't ever go away again!"

"No, I won't." Marco stooped down and scooped up Sylvana with his other arm, holding both children and kissing their cheeks. Juliette took Riccardo from Catarina and waited. She watched as the women greeted him. Marco was directly under the full light of the chandelier, enabling her to see how much weight he had lost and that there was gray in his hair that had never been there before. He was not in uniform and the dark blue suit he wore no longer fit him as perfectly as it had done before the war. His face bore an expression of immense happiness, but when he set Michel and Sylvana down on their feet again and looked toward the baby, an almost ecstatic joy transfigured his features. He held out his arms and took Riccardo from her.

"My son!" he breathed, gazing down into the child's sleeping face.

Michel darted forward angrily. "I'm your son too, Papà!"

"Of course you are!" Marco ruffled the boy's curls, but did not take his eyes from the child in his arms.

Juliette, seeing the sudden misery in Michel's face, ushered him and Sylvana into action.

"Let's go and remove our outdoor things." She took the boy's hand as they went up the stairs, leaving Marco to carry Riccardo into the salon. Sylvana had already rushed ahead, eager to see all her dolls again. "You must try to remember, Michel," Juliette said gently, "that although we've had Riccardo for over a year, this is the first time Papà has seen him."

"He called him his son." Marco hung his head unhappily.

"So he is. Papà calls you his son too."

"But he only called me his boy."

"He meant it in exactly the same way. Papà is going to find things difficult after being away so long in a dreadful camp where he didn't get enough to eat. Did you notice how thin he is? We have to do all we can to make it easy for him to settle down again. Promise me you'll do your best."

"Yes, Mamma." He nodded, but his dejection had not abated.

Upstairs, all the beds had been aired and made up. Henriette had played her part from the moment of Marco's return. He'd had his meals with her and Fortuny, and when Lena went into the warm, bright kitchen there was a pan of pasta and another of sauce ready for serving.

They all sat down together for supper at the large kitchen table. Marco had never eaten there before, but this was an exceptional occasion. He opened some good red wine and served it. By Michel's chair he paused to pour a little into the boy's glass of water.

"You've been the man of the family while I was away and you deserve a taste of wine."

Michel beamed at this special attention and the adults all laughed kindly at his obvious pride. Juliette, regarding him with love, knew well enough that he was thinking it a special treat Riccardo had not shared.

Over supper, Juliette learned that so far both Fortuny and Henriette had escaped the Spanish flu raging through the city, as had Doña Cecilia, although Maria Luisa had been very ill. Marco wanted to know about the time spent at the villa and was saddened to hear that the Boninis' days there were ended. It was not until the elder children were in bed and Riccardo in his cot in the nursery that he and Juliette were able to talk alone in the salon, where a blazing fire had been set. There was some mail for her on the table, and although she would have left it until the morning, Marco pointed out that there was a letter from Denise, which he had read since it was addressed to them both.

"Is she well?" she asked anxiously, taking up the letter.

"Yes, indeed," he replied dryly.

The first sentence informed Juliette that Denise had married Jacques Vernet not long after the closing of Maison Landelle and that he had settled all her debts.

He and I both enjoy the good things in life, Denise wrote, *and he made a fortune in munitions during that hateful war that is over at last. You cannot begin to imagine all the hardships I have endured. Thankfully that is all over now and Jacques is the most generous man. It is a relief to have finished forever with temperamental clients, mannequins screaming at one another in the cabine, crises in*

the ateliers and all the other hassles of running an haute couture
house. In future I shall be the difficult client!

Juliette read through the rest of the letter. Not even the war had
changed her sister in any way. "Denise has finally achieved her
ultimate aim in life. She has money to burn at last!"

Marco was standing in the firelight that accentuated the gaunt
hollows of his face. "There'll be no more orders from Maison
Landelle," he said despondently. "Another buyer that has gone
forever."

She went to him and slipped her hand into the crook of his arm.
"Try not to worry. Conditions are bound to be difficult for a
while, but that will change."

"But when? How soon?" His mood was deep and dark. "I've
spent a couple of days at the office, seeing which contacts I might
be able to pick up again without too much delay. The premises are
empty now, the convalescents and the nursing staff left a while
ago."

"You shouldn't have gone there. You're not well enough yet!"

"I couldn't stay long, I admit. I seemed to lose all strength after
a while."

"That will soon pass too."

"It was disheartening to see how the place had been left. Patients pinned pictures or photographs up on the frescoes. In some
rooms nails have been driven into the walls and temporary shelving
has been left."

"I didn't know. I'm so sorry!"

He put his hand over hers. "Don't blame yourself. You did right
to let the premises be used for the sick. I wouldn't have had it
otherwise. But there's more to tell. The top floor was broken into
and all the stock I had there was stolen. The police think the theft
might well have taken place when shortages were at their worst. So
I'll be starting from scratch again. It's early to speak of it when
you've just come home, but we'll have to watch expenses for a
while. Arianna spoke at supper of returning to her own home tomorrow, and I'm afraid Catarina must go too."

"Oh, no! She has no other home."

"Then she must find employment where she can live in."

"Very well." She knew how upset the girl would be. "But it
must be somewhere she'll be happy. I can't let her go otherwise."

He frowned impatiently. "I've said we must dispense with her services, and that means as soon as possible."

"Are things so bad financially?"

"I simply said we must economize in the present circumstances."

"Yes, of course. You can rely on me. Tomorrow you shall rest and I'll get your premises organized. After that I'll help you at the office. There will be many things I can do. It shouldn't take me long to learn how to type."

He embraced her with one arm as he shook his head. "No, that's my domain. Yours is here under this roof."

With a flash of insight she realized he had come home determined that she would never again step out of the role he had always wanted her to play and that in the future everything would be as he decreed it. The months of misery and idleness in the prison camp had given him plenty of time to mull over his life and the mistakes he believed he had made. She saw now that his determination to let Catarina go was not wholly financial, but to anchor her more securely. She had expected to find him suffering from all he had been through, but not embittered toward her. She understood that the task she had foreseen, of helping him rebuild his life, would be even more difficult than she had anticipated.

When they went up to bed she found that Lena, having unpacked her luggage, had laid the Delphos robe across the bed, not knowing where it was normally kept. Marco snatched it up, the coppery silk shimmering with fire.

"What's this doing here?" he demanded, his eyes blazing.

Juliette became pale, afraid he was going to rip it apart. "I took it with me. Let me put it away." She held out her hands, but his fist clenched even tighter.

"You were only able to take what could be carried on your flight from Venice, and yet you found space for this garment!"

"It weighs so little!"

"But something of more use could have been packed instead!" His face was congested with wrath. "You couldn't leave your precious keepsake behind, could you? You didn't take the Fortuny gowns I gave you!"

"I had a photograph of you!"

"And plenty of Karasvin no doubt!"

"I destroyed those long ago at the villa when I agreed to marry you. I didn't keep even one!"

"You should have rid yourself of this robe as well! I'll burn it myself now!" He started for the door, but her cry stopped him in mid-stride.

"No!" She had flung her arms over her head as she began to sob. "Nikolai is dead! He was killed in action!"

Her grief, hidden and controlled for so long, burst forth then in an ocean of tears she could not stem. Slowly she sank to her knees, as if the weight of it were too much for her to sustain, her body racked by terrible sobs. Marco stood looking down at her without moving, horrified that he had allowed his anxiety and his anger to throw him into such a rage even on their first night together. The war had torn him apart and he was tortured by the age-old shame of the returned warrior—to be still alive when so many friends and comrades had been killed. Memories of death in the stinking mountain trenches tormented him and could not be driven away. Only in the arms of this woman, whom he loved, could he hope for any escape from his mental tortures. Her sobbing was more than he could bear.

He threw aside the gown and reached down to fold her in his arms. Her head sank against his shoulder as she continued to weep. He stroked her hair, murmured to her, and wept himself. When he drew away from her, she continued to stand with her head bent as he undressed her and put her into bed. She fell asleep almost instantly, and he held her close all through the night.

When Juliette awoke it was late morning and she was alone. She guessed that Marco had given instructions not to disturb her. As she sat up, she saw that he had retrieved the Delphos robe and placed it on a chair. His returning it to her was his way of mending their quarrel, but she feared that it would be a long time before his shattered nerves allowed him peace of mind again.

Catarina moved in with Arianna for the time being and found domestic work in a hotel that was being made ready to receive visitors again. Unlike other cities that had been through the war, Venice could count on a swift return to popularity once the Spanish flu scare had subsided. The deadly epidemic was still claiming victims throughout the city, as it was everywhere else in Europe, but there had been plenty of plagues in Venetian history and none had yet defeated the queen of the Adriatic.

With sandbags and cladding taken away, the Lion of St. Mark was to be seen again all over the city, and the worst of the bomb damage was being repaired. Fortuny had reopened his workshops. Orders for his fabrics were again coming in, including some from the grandest of the hotels. Marco also found his business beginning to pick up, but not as swiftly as Fortuny's, for although his Far Eastern suppliers were as eager to sell as he was to import, prices were much higher than before.

At home Juliette found it impossible to make life for Marco as it had been in the past. All her worst fears were realized. She knew he still loved her, and she kept her patience when he was being totally unreasonable, but it was often very hard to do. There were times when he seemed to be regaining his spirits and equilibrium, and then everything would change. He could not control the deep clouds of depression that descended on him without warning, making him angry with everyone around him. Neither could he hide his pride in Riccardo, a favoritism that was not lost on the other two children. It was Riccardo he always went to see first when he came home from the office, the one he tossed in the air, praised, and always addressed as "my son." Sylvana, always placid and amiable, was not so aware of her father's singular devotion to her little brother, but Michel did everything he could to gain Marco's attention. When all else failed, he misbehaved deliberately until Marco's nerves, always close to the breaking point, caused him to explode.

"Try to be more patient with Michel," Juliette begged on one of these occasions, as she had many times before.

"He needs disciplining, that's all," Marco countered sharply. "He was spoiled all that time at the villa surrounded by doting women."

"That's nonsense! The trouble lies with you. You make it so obvious that you favor Riccardo more than Michel and Sylvana."

"I've never been guilty of that!" Marco was outraged. "If I were, Sylvana would be as difficult as Michel is proving to be."

Juliette thought to herself that it was like talking to the proverbial brick wall. She could only conclude that when he had received her letter telling him he had a son, it was like a torch lighting his future, and that the feeling had never left him.

. . . . .

In April, Juliette and Marco took the children to the celebrations on St. Mark's Day when the Basilica once more radiated its golden splendor like a great jewel in the sun. Not all the works of art and other treasures had yet returned from their exile in safe places, and the four bronze horses were still missing from the façade, but before long they would be home again. The square was crowded with rejoicing Venetians, many foreigners among them. With the decline everywhere of the Spanish flu epidemic, visitors had returned and once again honeymoon couples were hiring gondoliers to sing to them as they floated along the Grand Canal.

Bands were playing and there were all sorts of entertainments. Riccardo, who could only toddle, rode on Marco's shoulders to keep him out of harm's way. To Michel's delight, Marco made sure that he and Sylvana secured good views of the jugglers or the acrobats or the clowns and afterward bought him a red clockwork motorcar that he had long wanted. He chose a doll for his sister and a woolly ball for his little brother. They all enjoyed ices at Florian's. Later, Marco let Michel choose where they should eat and, as expected, the boy wanted hot snacks from one of the stalls. Lena took Riccardo home for his nap in the afternoon, leaving the others to more entertainment. As soon as it grew dark there was a spectacular display of fireworks.

"What a wonderful day this has been," Juliette said gratefully as they walked home. Marco was holding Michel's hand and she was thankful that he had finally taken notice of her entreaties to pay the boy more attention.

"We'll do all this again when the bronze horses come back to the Basilica," Marco said. "Did you hear that, Michel?"

"Yes, Papà!" Michel jumped with glee.

When all the children were in bed, Juliette went in search of Marco. She found him looking tired and relaxing on the sofa in the salon, a glass of brandy in his hand. Sitting down on a stool, she folded her hands across her lap and smiled at him.

"The children have all gone to sleep with their new toys on their pillows. They had such a good time."

"I enjoyed it too. Join me in a brandy, Juliette, and give me another."

"Very well." Normally she did not drink any alcohol except wine, but she had the impression that he wanted her to stay with him. She took his glass, stooping to kiss his brow at the same time. With a start, she drew back quickly and put her hand on his forehead. "You're not well! You're burning!"

"Yet I feel quite shivery."

"You have a chill. It's no wonder you look tired! No more brandy. Go to bed and I'll bring you a soothing lemon-and-honey drink instead."

He obeyed her without protest. As she went into the kitchen to prepare the drink, she was gripped by an icy fear. Although there had been no more than two or three new cases of Spanish flu the previous week, Marco was displaying exactly the same symptoms she and the others had experienced.

In the night, she had to telephone for the doctor, who confirmed her worst fears. Marco's fever raged and he grew weaker every day. His time in the trenches and in the prison camp had fatally undermined his normally robust health. He became the last person in Venice to die of Spanish flu. Michel was inconsolable, crying out in protest.

"Why did it have to happen? Papà was just beginning to like me again!"

Juliette thought to herself that she had given Michel a father only for him to lose that relationship too soon. Her own grief was no less deep. Unlike her love for Nikolai, which had been infused with passion from the start, her feelings for Marco were based on gratitude for an enduring and loving friendship, but were no less heartfelt for that.

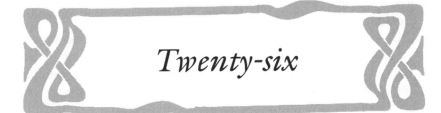

Twenty-six

TOWARD THE END of the year Juliette went back to selling gowns at the Palazzo Orfei. She had no financial need to work, as Marco had left her well provided for, but fashion remained a magnet she could not resist. Michel was at school and Arianna, who had recently had a baby herself, was taking care of Sylvana and Riccardo in her own house. It was an ideal arrangement.

For months after Marco's death Juliette felt as though she were existing in a numbing vacuum, but back at work again she began to regain her stride. Friends were relieved to see her becoming herself once more. She had dispensed early with mourning attire, knowing that Marco would have wanted her to make everything seem as normal as possible for the children and to keep his memory alive in a cheerful, natural way. Yet she would never forget Michel's desperate cry of protest indicating that he saw Marco's death as a further rejection of himself. Once, after she'd been widowed a year, he asked her wistfully if she would soon marry again.

"There are plenty of men about," he stated. "Not all of them have children already. Surely you could find someone who would like a family. Papà wouldn't mind."

She smiled and yet, at the same time, she was touched almost to tears by her son's desperate longing for a father. "I'm sorry, Michel, but I don't want to marry again. As I told you once, I lost both my parents when I was just a little older than you are now, so

I know how you feel. All I can promise you is that I'll always do my best for you and Sylvana and Riccardo."

He nodded solemnly, obviously disappointed. One day when he was grown and could understand, she would tell him who his real father had been. Perhaps he would even remember the day he had waved to the man on the steamboat, for she herself had a particular memory that she knew dated back to when she was two years old. If his looks did not change very much, she would be able to tell him how like he was to Nikolai Karasvin.

In that same year, 1920, Fortuny opened an establishment for his gowns and textiles in Paris, not far from the building that had once been Maison Landelle. Before the war, his sales had never remotely matched those of the Parisian *haute couture* houses, mainly because his gowns appealed only to those who had the confidence to ignore conventional dress. Yet, not long after the Armistice, as if by some invisible signal, women all over the world began to turn their fashion sights toward the Palazzo Orfei.

Whatever the reason, even those who had never seen them began to talk about Fortuny clothes, and the demand increased as never before.

Many women still chose the Delphos robe, but there were new and lovely variations in subtle, melting shades as Fortuny's dyeing skills reached new heights of perfection. Some of the new gowns had long sleeves that clung softly to the shape of the arm, but most were sleeveless and tubular, with a tunic effect achieved with points hanging at hip length on the sides, or with an additional panel front and back. Others had cross straps over the bodice, such as were worn by the women of ancient Greece, which enhanced the shape of the breasts. No woman of taste, it seemed, could resist these garments.

It was fast becoming the mode for actresses of the stage and screen, as well as titled women and others of means, to have their portraits painted in a Fortuny creation. Many young women were choosing to be married in his pleated, silvery-white, often sheath-like, silk gowns, which were enhanced by classically plain veils and simple, yet sophisticated headbands worn straight across the forehead. Fashion editors sent representatives from Paris, London, Milan, and New York to interview Fortuny and get photographs. The magazine that had published the early photographs responsible for

Juliette and Nikolai's reunion reprinted them now, boasting of its early perspicacity. This time it was Juliette's children who gazed in surprise at the printed photograph of her in the Delphos robe, a garment they had never seen her wear.

Toward the end of that same year, the bloody civil war in Russia came to an end with the Red army triumphant, and refugees connected with the defeated aristocracy were fleeing for their lives. Ten million men had lost their lives in what was becoming known as the Great War, and there was no telling how many more had died since the Armistice giving aid to the White Russian army.

For Juliette, the highlight of the following summer was a honeymoon visit from Gabrielle and her new husband, Harry Scott-Moncrieff. Harry was a much older man than Derek would have been, and had an equally distinguished war record. He was very much the English country squire, for generations of his family had lived in the Sussex manor house that was Gabrielle's new home. Juliette was able to see that Harry had the same protective attitude toward Gabrielle that she always seemed to arouse in men, and there was no need to fear for her future happiness. Lucille, unfortunately, could no longer leave Rodolphe, who had become dependent on her in his declining years. As for Denise, the occasional postcard was all that Juliette ever received from her, usually from some fashionable playground of the rich such as Monte Carlo.

One such postcard, sent from London and announcing that Denise and Jacques had been to Ascot races and the Henley regatta, arrived on the morning Juliette went to view the factory Fortuny had opened on the nearby island of Giudecca in what had been a derelict convent. His name in large letters across the front of the building was repeated in an appropriate size on the polished brass doorbell.

Now fifty-one, with gray in his still-thick hair, and a well-trimmed mustache and beard, Fortuny himself was in the hall, talking to one of the men when she entered. He gave her a smiling nod. "When you've looked around, Juliette, meet me here and we'll go back to the city together."

In large airy rooms with views of the Lagoon, his workforce had already started using the machinery Fortuny had invented for putting his textile designs onto an Egyptian cotton, which lent itself particularly well to the effects he wanted to achieve. By using a less-expensive material while maintaining the same standards of design and execution, he hoped to bring his designs within the means of a much broader market.

When she and Fortuny set off again for the city in a *vaporetto,* she congratulated him on another successful new venture. He smiled, well-pleased with the way his plans were working out.

"I saw no reason why simple cotton couldn't be as beautiful as the silks and velvets I'm continuing to supervise personally at the palazzo. I wanted to talk to you because I've something in mind that I'd like you to consider. There's no immediate rush for a decision, but would you consider selling for me in Paris instead of Venice?"

She was completely taken aback. Such a possibility had never occurred to her, but she felt an immediate tingle of excitement at the thought. It was as if, without ever realizing it, she had been waiting for the time when she could go home to France again. "Why do you wish me to do that?" she managed to say.

"You're Parisian, you're an experienced saleswoman, you can be trusted with responsibility, and you probably know more about Fortuny garments than anyone except Henriette and myself. So think it over, please. I would be very grateful."

He did not mention the difference it would make to her financially, because he knew that would not be a consideration to her, no matter how much she would benefit. Her decision would depend on whether Paris still held a greater appeal for her than Venice, and whether she felt able to uproot her children from their schools, their friends, and the only home they had known. For himself, the future was presently unsettled, but only because there were so many new projects he wanted to put into motion, so many new ideas to get down on paper.

It took Juliette a week to reach her decision, but in her heart she had known what the result would be from the moment that Fortuny gave her the chance to go home. She broke the news to Michel and Sylvana. Riccardo was too young at the age of four to understand the concept of going to live in another country.

The house soon found a buyer. Juliette let none of the heirlooms go for sale, shipping to Paris some of the smaller items, including two family portraits that Marco would have wanted his daughter and son to inherit one day. Everything else was shipped to Marco's brothers and their wives in the United States.

There were many farewell parties and promises to meet again. Juliette said good-bye to Maria Luisa and then to Dona Cecilia. Although she would surely see Fortuny and Henriette in Paris, it was still a wrench to be moving away from them. She found it hardest of all to part from Lena, who had been through so much with her, but the woman had firmly refused to uproot herself from her native soil. She went to the railway station on the last day to see Juliette and the children off.

"If ever you should change your mind," Juliette urged from the window when they were aboard, "you have only to let me know and I'll come to fetch you at once."

Lena shook her head. "That won't happen, signora. It breaks my heart to let you go without me, but I wouldn't want to be so far from my family. In any case, it's time I retired."

As the train began to move, Lena hurried alongside, waving to the children until it gathered speed.

In Paris, Juliette and the children stayed in the Vernet mansion, which Jacques and Denise had offered her as a temporary residence since they were on an extended cruise of the Caribbean. In accordance with the terms of Claude's will, Denise had surrendered her home in the Faubourg St. Germain upon her remarriage. But she had an even larger one now, with its own ballroom and double the number of household staff.

Juliette appreciated having some time to find a place of her own, as well as schools for Michel and Sylvana. She also hired a capable nursemaid for the younger ones. An agent lined up properties for her to view and drove her to them in his motorcar. Once they passed the site of Nikolai's studio, which had been replaced by a newly-built library. She finally decided on a spacious apartment with fine rooms dating from the embellishment of Paris by Baron Haussmann that was within easy walking distance of number 67, Rue Pierre Carron.

When she first walked into the prestigiously-sited Maison Fortuny, Juliette might have imagined herself back in the Palazzo Orfei. The wall-coverings and decorative hangings, ceiling draperies, exotic lamps, and certain effects all reminded her of Venice. Some of the gowns, displayed as was his way on mannequins, glowed in tempestuous colors, while others were in delicate pastel shades. Fortuny had created another Arabian Nights spectacular in the very heart of Paris. She was to be in charge of a whole section selling only the silk pleated gowns and their capes and accessories.

The day before Juliette started work, she had her hair cut in the new short style. Since the end of the war, waistlines had been dropping and skirt hems rising to become virtually knee-length. Her legs were a good shape, with slim ankles, and she enjoyed wearing the new length, glad that at last women's clothes were gaining the freedom for which she had always aimed, and which Fortuny had achieved long ago.

Juliette had always enjoyed selling at the Palazzo Orfei, and it was much the same in Paris, except that there were a greater number of *nouveau riche,* whose husbands had been war profiteers. Many of the other customers were women she knew from her Maison Landelle days, and foreigners were plentiful, especially Americans. Only the Russian aristocrats were missing. Paris was among the cities that had become a refuge for countless numbers of White Russians, who had fled their country when their cause was lost. Almost without exception they were impoverished, their land, property, and possessions confiscated by the new regime. They had to take whatever work they could get, and a doorman at any Parisian restaurant might be a grand duke or the head waiter a prince. One singer drawing customers to a Left Bank café was known to be a Romanov and a close relative of the late Tsar.

When Jacques and Denise came home again it was spring, and they gave a grand party. A jazz band played and two hundred guests, Juliette among them, threw themselves exuberantly into all the new dances. Many of Juliette's friends were there too. During the evening she was invited to join a group of them the following weekend at an evening preview of a special exhibition of the works of Rodin, who had died while she was still in Venice.

The preview was a fashionable event, with tickets in great demand. Many people of importance were there, including the President of France himself. All were in evening clothes, with the younger women favoring the shorter skirts. Juliette had chosen to wear one of Fortuny's highly successful cottons, which wafted softly with every movement in a blending of russet, green, and gold.

It was as she was laughing and talking with her friends, a glass of champagne in her hand, that she had the sudden sensation of being watched. The feeling was oddly familiar and yet it made her uneasy. She turned her head casually. Then her heart gave such a lurch that she almost cried out, dropping her glass, which smashed at her feet. Through a gap in the milling throng she saw Nikolai, older and yet the same, standing by a statue of Balzac. He held her startled, anguished eyes with his across the distance between them. Then the crowd shifted and he was lost from her sight.

"Whatever is the matter, Juliette? What's wrong?"

She turned to her friends almost unseeingly. "Nothing! I'm all right." The words seemed to be stumbling on her tongue. "I happened to see somebody I haven't met for a long time. Please excuse me, everybody. I must speak to him."

"I'll come with you," her escort insisted, still concerned, and took hold of her by the elbow.

"No!" she exclaimed again, drawing sharply away from him. "Wait for me here. I'll be back."

He stared after her in consternation as she began to weave her way through the gathering. When she reached the Balzac statue Nikolai was no longer there. Then she saw him waiting in a quiet area away from the crowd. Tall potted palms gave the illusion of a more exotic clime and there were several gilded chairs set in pairs.

They faced each other amid the palm trees, neither one able to believe that they were meeting again. Briefly she stepped forward, and in speechless relief that he was still alive, she laid her cheek lightly against his shoulder, then withdrew again almost at once. They did not kiss. Too much time had elapsed, too much had happened to set them apart. He spoke first.

"You've cut your hair, Juliette." His gaze roamed over its shining neatness before he smiled slowly at her. "It suits you."

"Oh, Nikolai!" Her voice was choked, tears swimming in her eyes. "I was told you were—" She was unable to finish her sentence, but he understood.

"So many people have come back from the dead. When our army collapsed there was total chaos."

"I'm so thankful to see you safe and well!" She struggled to speak calmly. "I can't express—" Again she broke off helplessly, shaking her head.

"It's difficult for me to realize that I'm seeing you too. I thought you were far away in Venice. Are you and Marco visiting Denise?"

"No. Marco came through the war only to fall victim to the Spanish flu."

"I'm truly sorry to hear that. He was a good man and once I was able to count him as a friend." Nikolai hesitated. "Natasha and my sister, Anna, both lost their lives in the revolution." His face had grown strained with the memory of managing to reach his home, hoping to get the two women safely away, only to find the palace ransacked and deserted. His frantic search had ended when he found them both lying raped and murdered next to the bodies of the servants who had fled with them. When he had buried them all, he left the Karasvin estate for the last time.

Juliette, seeing that his thoughts were painful, placed a hand compassionately on his arm. "You have my deepest sympathy," she said fervently, "for the loss of all those near to you and also for losing your own country."

He appreciated her words and took her hand into both of his. "Are you living in Paris?"

"I have been for some time. I work for Maison Fortuny."

"Ah, Fortuny." His tone was a reminder of the memories that the Spaniard's name evoked for both of them. "I often pass his establishment on the Rue Pierre Carron. It never crossed my mind that you would be there."

"How long have you been back in Paris, Nikolai?"

"Five months. Seeing you again, it's as if I'd never been away."

She slid her hand from his clasp, wanting to warn him that nothing could be as it was before. "But we were both away from Paris for a long time."

"Tell me about my son," he requested.

It was the question she had been expecting. Before answering him, she went across to a pair of the gilded chairs and there they sat down together.

"Michel is strong, healthy, intelligent, and sensitive. Sometimes he needs reassurance and at others he's too adventurous for his own safety. He resembles you. His dark hair is curly and grows to a point at the back of his neck in the same way." A smile tilted the corner of her mouth. "He would do much better at school if he were less keen on sports!"

Nikolai gave a quiet laugh. "That was my failing throughout my schooldays."

"My daughter was still a baby when you and I met in Venice, and now I have a younger son too. All three children are with me in Paris."

"Would you let me see Michel?" There was deep appeal in his eyes.

She had known this request would come. "You may, but only on condition that you don't let him know you're his father. I want to tell him when he's old enough to understand."

"I'll do whatever you say. I was anxious for your safety and his when Italy came under attack. I wished all the time there was some way to get news of you."

"As it happened," she commented with a sigh, "it would have been much better if I'd never heard anything of you."

"How did you hear of my presumed death?"

She explained and then asked if the report about his friends had been false too, thinking how much it would mean to Signora Ottini if her nephew should still be alive. But Nikolai shook his head with regret.

"It was correct. I was badly wounded, but they were killed instantly."

She nodded, silently accepting the tragedy. The trauma of their reunion almost overwhelmed her and her voice caught in her throat.

Nikolai leaned toward her. "We can't talk anymore here. Leave with me now."

"I can't," she declared. "I must go back to the people I came with." Her voice still faltered, but she was desperate to learn as much as possible about him. "What happened after your recovery?"

"I eventually returned to the White army and fought under the imperial flag until the last battle. Then I had to flee for my life. After a very complicated journey, I reached French soil and made my way to Paris."

"Are you sculpting again?"

"Yes. I've always had funds in a Paris bank, which enabled me to set myself up in another studio. My work hasn't been forgotten and commissions have been coming in. I'll be holding an exhibition of my own work at the end of the year."

"I'm so glad for you." For a few moments they smiled at each other as something of the old intimacy hovered between them, making the years fade away, but she could not let it last. "I must go, Nikolai."

She rose to her feet, but he blocked her way. "Would you pose for me again?" he asked. "I'd like to replace the bust I did of you that's been lost somewhere in Russia."

"That wouldn't be wise." Her attitude was firm.

"There's nobody else, is there?" He was looking hard at her.

"There never has been as you mean it and there never will be. But everything is different now. It's been over eleven years . . ."

"But later—in Venice—nothing had changed!"

"You're wrong, it had. Even though we knew our feelings for each other were the same, our love already belonged to the past. We didn't speak of it then, but there was no need because we both understood that was how things had to be."

"But neither of us could have foreseen what was to happen! That we should both be free when we met again. I hadn't even expected to get through the war alive!"

"Yet you have, and we're not the same two people we were before. The war changed us as well as everything else. Marco came home a different man. I saw Michel thrust aside for not being his own son. I'd never risk that happening to Sylvana and Riccardo. As I said before, Michel is sensitive and it would distress him to feel that his sister and brother were being left out."

"And you would expect me to do that?" He was incredulous.

She let her hands rise and fall in resignation. "I don't know you now as I did in the past."

At that moment her escort's voice broke sternly in on them. "Juliette! We're all about to leave for supper at Ciro's."

Neither she nor Nikolai had noticed him come to stand just a few yards away, making no move to be introduced.

"I'm coming!" she answered quickly. Nikolai gripped her by the shoulders even as she moved.

"Listen to me!" he urged fiercely. "You and I have been given a second chance, Juliette! It's the rarest of all gifts. Don't throw it away! I would be starting afresh with all three of the children, doing for them all what once I would have done for Michel. They are all yours! How could I not love them equally for being part of you? Because I love you as I've always done. It was your name I repeated constantly when I was wounded and not sure I'd survive. I've always kept the photo of you taken in Montmartre. You will always be everything to me!''

He swept her hard against him and kissed her with passionate violence as if to drive away all her doubts and fears. She responded totally, snatching briefly at the remembered joys and ecstasies of the past. Then, as he withdrew his mouth from hers, she broke away, hurrying to her waiting escort.

Nikolai stood looking after her. "Tomorrow, Juliette! The same time at Larue's!''

She had heard him. He could tell by the last swift glance she threw over her shoulder before her escort clamped a jealous arm about her waist, hastening her away.

Juliette went to Maison Fortuny as usual the following morning, but it was not easy to concentrate on her work. Nikolai's words kept running through her mind as they had done for most of the night. In those last few minutes with him, she had realized that their lives were about to be rejoined. She knew there would be difficulties ahead, problems to overcome, and readjustments in every way, but nothing had ever run smoothly for them in the past and this time they would be facing their problems together.

After work, Juliette told the children a little about Nikolai, whom they were soon to meet. She was about to get ready for the evening when a corsage of orchids, pearly white with green flecks rising from the calyx, was delivered. With a smile, she put the exquisite blooms lightly to her lips.

In her bedroom Juliette took her Delphos robe from its box and slipped it on. Its gold and coppery sheen rippled around her, reclaiming her figure once more. Timeless and beautiful, it transcended all the years between. She pinned on the corsage. Finally, she picked up her Knossos scarf and took it with her.

Looped over her arms, it floated out behind her as she alighted from the taxicab at Larue's. Once she had caused a scandal under this roof by appearing in her Fortuny gown. Now all that was in the past, along with so much else. Nikolai was waiting for her. Full of hope, she went to him, taking that second chance.